THEATRE AND DRAMA IN FRANCOPHONE AFRICA

THEATRE AND DRAMA IN FRANCOPHONE AFRICA

A critical introduction

JOHN CONTEH-MORGAN

The Ohio State University

CAMBRIDGE
UNIVERSITY PRESS

CAMBRIDGE UNIVERSITY PRESS
Cambridge, New York, Melbourne, Madrid, Cape Town, Singapore, São Paulo

Cambridge University Press
The Edinburgh Building, Cambridge CB2 2RU, UK

Published in the United States of America by Cambridge University Press, New York

www.cambridge.org
Information on this title: www.cambridge.org/9780521434539

First published 1994
This digitally printed first paperback version 2006

A catalogue record for this publication is available from the British Library

Library of Congress Cataloguing in Publication data
Conteh-Morgan, John.
Theatre and drama in Francophone Africa: a critical introduction / John Conteh-Morgan.
p.   cm.
Includes bibliographical references and index.
ISBN 0 521 43453 X
1. African drama (French) – History and criticism.   2. Theater – Africa, French-speaking
Equatorial – History.   3. Theater – Africa, French-speaking West – History.   I. Title.
PQ3983.C66   1994
842.009'96–dc20   93-6070   CIP

ISBN-13 978-0-521-43453-9 hardback
ISBN-10 0-521-43453-X hardback

ISBN-13 978-0-521-03471-5 paperback
ISBN-10 0-521-03471-X paperback

To my parents
And to Nyo, Déri and Mei

Contents

Acknowledgements

In writing a book, one incurs many debts and this one is no exception. My single greatest debt of gratitude goes to Professor Martin Banham of the University of Leeds. He gave me encouragement when I first presented the work to him as a research project for a Commonwealth Universities Staff Fellowship award, and was generous with his advice and assistance throughout the book's preparation. As a Visiting Commonwealth Staff Fellow in the Workshop Theatre at Leeds which he directs, I enjoyed the luxury of leisure and the stimulation of the environment. Without that one uninterrupted year of research (1986–7), this study would still have been on the drawing-board. I also wish to thank the Association of Commonwealth Universities for the award and Professor Roger Little of Trinity College, Dublin, for supporting my application for it.

I am very grateful to Professor Abiola Irele of The Ohio State University for comments on an earlier draft of this book, and for sharing with me his vast knowledge of African literature and his splendid library. Professor Clive Wake, formerly of the University of Kent, and the anonymous readers of Cambridge University Press all made suggestions on my manuscript which I found helpful and constructive and for which I thank them. I also want to salute one of my earliest drama teachers, Professor Durosimi Eldred Jones, in whose writings and dedication I have always found inspiration.

This work began in the University of Leeds, was completed at Fourah Bay College, University of Sierra Leone, and revised at The Ohio State University. I am pleased to acknowledge the vastly different but complementary facilities which I enjoyed in all three institutions.

Finally, I extend my gratitude to my parents for their labour, to my dear wife Nyo for accepting even at odd hours to be my interlocutor and sounding-board, and to our loving children Déri and Mei for their supportive affection and for their willingness to deprive themselves often of my company.

The author and the publishers wish to thank the following who have kindly given permission for the use of copywright material: Présence Africaine (Paris) for extracts from *La Tragédie du roi Christophe* by Aimé Césaire, *Béatrice du Congo* and *Iles de Tempête* by Bernard Dadié; Seuil (Paris) for extracts from *Une Saison au Congo* by Aimé Césaire; Nubia Press (Paris) for extracts from *Le Zulu* by Tchicaya U'Tamsi; P. J. Oswald for extracts from *L'Œil* by Zadi Zaourou and *L'Exil d'Albouri* by Cheik Ndao; CEDA (Abidjan) for extracts from *La Puissance d'Um* by Werewere Liking; Haho (Lomé) for extracts from *On joue la comédie* by Senouvo Zinsou and CLE (Yaoundé) for extracts from *Trois prétendants ... un mari* by Guillaume Oyono-Mbia.

Some material in the introduction, chapters 2, 4 and 7, reproduces in modified form articles of mine published in the *Canadian Journal of African Studies* 19, 2 (1985), *African Literature Today* 14 (1984) and 18 (1992), *The French Review* 52, 2 (1983), *Ba Shiru* 11, 2 (1980) and *Comparative Drama* (Special Issue, 1994). I wish to thank the editors of these journals for allowing me to use this material, sometimes in its near-original form.

Freetown and Columbus

Introduction

This book is mainly about African literary drama in French, the dominant but by no means the only form of modern theatrical expression in Francophone Africa. Although I began my research in the late 1980s, the need for an up-to-date book on the subject had fleetingly occurred to me much earlier when I was preparing a list of critical readings for a course I was to teach at Fourah Bay College, University of Sierra Leone. I was then struck by the paucity of recent critical material on the subject, even allowing for the modesty of our library holdings.

There was, of course, Bakary.Traoré's pioneering *Le Théâtre Négro-Africain et ses fonctions sociales* and Robert Cornevin's *Le Théâtre en Afrique noire et à Madagascar*. But by the 1980s the value of these books was clearly limited. Traoré's was published in 1958 when not one major play had been written and it is really a history and sociology of early Francophone school drama – the drama of the Ecole William Ponty, the training college in Senegal, where modern Francophone theatre developed in the early 1930s. Cornevin's, on the other hand, for all its wealth of useful information still only takes the story to 1970 in a descriptive, sometimes compilatory but seldom interpretive manner. A collection of useful conference papers, *Actes du colloque sur le Théâtre Négro-Africain*, was also available. But that was as much as had been devoted in French to Francophone African drama around this time.

In English, helpful historical and critical sections on the subject exist in Martin Banham's and Clive Wake's *African Theatre Today* and Dorothy Blair's *African Literature in French*. A. Graham-White's *The Drama of Black Africa* also contains a few pages on the traditional roots of modern Francophone drama and on the region's early school theatre.

This dearth of critical material contrasted surprisingly with the

vitality of the work that was being done on the other genres of
Francophone literature, notably the novel and especially on Anglophone drama. This was all the more surprising because, as far back
as the early 1970s, Francophone drama had emerged as one of the
fastest-growing areas in African literature, with a significant corpus
of published plays that today stands at more than 300 (Waters 1988).
And this does not include the several hundreds, in countries like
Burkina Faso (Guingané 1990: 67), or literally thousands, in places
like Cameroon (Bjornson 1991 : 430), that exist only in manuscript
form but are regularly staged to live and enthusiastic audiences.

Many of the published plays (by older-generation dramatists) like
Bernard Dadié's *Béatrice du Congo*, Cheik Ndao's *L'Exil d'Albouri*, Jean
Pliya's *Kondo le requin*, Guillaume Oyono-Mbia's *Trois prétendants...
un mari*, Aimé Césaire's *La Tragédie du roi Christophe* and so on are of the
highest standard and are frequently performed in Francophone
Africa. They are widely studied in schools and universities there and
have achieved something of the status of canonical texts, of founding
texts of modern national theatrical cultures.

During the past decade, a younger generation of playwright-
directors and some older ones too have been trying to steer
Francophone drama from Western stage conventions and to create a
new form of drama that is rooted in traditional or modern popular
performance styles. Plays in this vein, like Zadi Zaourou's *L'Œil*,
Tchicaya U'Tamsi's *Le Bal de N'Dinga*, Sony Labou Tansi's *Qui a
mangé Madame d'Avoine Bergotha*, Werewere Liking's *La Puissance d'Um*,
Sénouvo Zinsou's *On joue la comédie*, have not only been very successful
in Africa like their 1960s and 1970s predecessors but, also like them,
in France where some have been performed at the Avignon Festival
and at the Limoges Festival des Francophonies, begun in 1983 to
promote world theatre in the French language.

The Théâtre International de Langue Française, a troupe
founded in 1985 by the French director, Gabriel Garran, has
produced plays by the Congolese playwrights Tchicaya U'Tamsi
and Sony Labou Tansi in theatres in Paris and its districts (Pont-
Hubert 1990: 103–9), while Franoise Kourilsky's Ubu Repertory
Theatre has been promoting Francophone African theatre in New
York since 1987, by organising staged readings and performances of
plays by Zaourou, Zinsou and Maxime Ndébéka, and by translating
some of them into English (Hourantier 1990: 131–9).

Over the past thirty-five years, Francophone Africa has also produced actors of talent like the Paris-based Senegalese Bachir Touré and Douta Seck, the Cameroonian Lydia Ewandé and more recently the Malian Bakary Sangaré. In the 1960s, the first three held roles in productions mostly by Jean-Marie Serreau but also by Roger Blin of plays by Jean Genet, Kateb Yacine, Aimé Césaire, Brecht and Shakespeare (see Cornevin 1970: 94–8), while Sangaré appeared between 1987 and 1990 in plays by the Senegalese Abdou Anta Ka, Césaire and in a production by Peter Brook of the South African play *Woza Albert* and of the dramatised Indian epic the *Mahabharata* (Pont-Hubert 1990: 114–19).

The supporting facilities for theatrical activity have also grown. Since 1980, in addition to national theatre companies like the Kotéba National of Mali, the Théâtre National of Senegal, the Ballets Africains of Guinea, and so on, important experimental and privately sponsored theatre companies like Zaourou's 'Didiga', Labou Tansi's 'Rocado Zulu Theatre', Werewere Liking's 'Ki-Yi' and Souleymane Koly's 'Kotéba Ensemble' have also been founded with a view to promoting new performance styles.

Arts festivals at regional and national levels that provide for the theatre, and school and radio drama competitions are also regular features of the artistic calendar in countries like Burkina Faso, Mali, Guinea and Niger where, probably because of a 'marxisant' orientation of earlier governments, the importance of the theatre as a medium of mass communication of developmental or party political values was very quickly grasped.

All these developments, then, clearly call for more current critical attention. Of course this has not been altogether absent. Some books of African literary criticism written since the mid-eighties contain sections on French-language drama (Chévrier 1984; R. Schérer 1992; Schipper 1984b). Others like Kotchy (1984) and Owusu-Sarpong (1987) concentrate on individual dramatists. Still others are either about specific plays (Antoine 1984; Deberre 1984) or national cultural, political and/or dramatic traditions (Beik 1987; Bjornson 1991; D'Aby 1988).

While all these contributions have enhanced our understanding of Francophone African drama, they remain either too narrow – concentrating on a single play, playwright or country – or too general, contained as they are in books that attempt to study *all* of Francophone literature or, worse still, of modern African drama or literature.

What is needed is a work that focusses on Francophone African drama not just as a genre, a cultural phenomenon with a history and a development, but also (lest this fact be forgotten) as a series of playtexts, from several countries, many of which are memorable both as literature and theatre. This is what this book sets out to do. The book is in two parts. Part I, which is historical and theoretical, has three chapters. The first deals with the traditional roots of Francophone drama in ritual and secular performances. Beyond the usual vague assertion of a relationship between these roots and modern scripted plays, I undertake a consideration of the precise nature of that relationship. In this respect, the often posited ritual/drama continuum comes in for extended examination as it applies to Francophone drama. I establish contrasts with Western and Anglophone African forms of drama to better highlight the issues. The second chapter traces the emergence and development of a literary drama in the Francophone region, and the third deals with its themes. Although my emphasis in chapter 3 is *on* scripted plays, that is *on* Francophone theatre, I also briefly consider other forms of modern theatrical expression *in* Francophone Africa: the modern popular theatre of urban agglomerations and the 'Development Theatre' of rural areas. This first section will perforce be expository and generalising. In Part II, however, I attempt to illustrate some of my general statements in the context of the analyses of specific plays.

The plays I have chosen for study in this section, eleven in all from nine playwrights, quite apart from being to my mind among the more substantial in the corpus, also reflect either individually or between them the main trends, concerns and styles of the African dramatist of French expression. If there is a slight imbalance in favour of history plays, it is only because most of the published plays by French-speaking Africans, even those written today, do in fact belong to that category.

Because the original texts are not easily available and only a handful of them exist in English, I have tried to combine a careful presentation of the material of those I study with an analysis of it. I approach the plays both as literature and theatre. In other words I consider their themes, dramatic techniques, characterisation and so on, but also their performance potential; the non-verbal resources of costume, music and movement which both contribute to their meaning and enhance their status as spectacles conceived for a stage.

My inclusion of Aimé Césaire in a book on African dramatists perhaps also deserves a comment. I have done this for three reasons. First because of his largely common experience and inspiration with African writers, having been, with Senghor, one of the founders of modern French-language African literature. Second because of his important role in the development of African drama in French. The success of his *La Tragédie du roi Christophe* at the Salzburg Festival in 1964 brought the importance of this medium powerfully to Francophone writers. And third because of the type of plays he wrote. *Une Saison au Congo* and *La Tragédie du roi Christophe* do not only deal with issues that are of interest to Africa, as Hale has pointed out: decolonisation, nation-building, ethnicity and so on (Hale 1987: 196). They also refer to or are based on African events and characters when, like *Une Saison au Congo*, they are not actually set in Africa. They also feature prominently elements of traditional theatrical performances, secular as well as religious (Bailey 1987: 239).

The involvement of Césaire's theatre with Africa and his keen awareness in the 1960s of its catalytic role there is further highlighted by his attentiveness to the suggestions of his African actors and the reactions of his public in that continent. Thus he told Rodney Harris that it was on a suggestion of Douta Seck, the Senegalese who played the title role in the 1966 Dakar production of *La Tragédie du roi Christophe* that he attempted to present Christophe as Sango, the Yoruba god of thunder (R. Harris 1973: 112). Similarly the successive faces of Mokutu as inconsequential sergeant in the pay of the Belgians, nationalist politician and brutal tyrant in the 1966, 1967 and 1973 versions of *Une Saison au Congo* were the result not only of his perceptions of the evolution of the real-life character but also of those of his Zairian readers and spectators (Hale 1987: 198–9).

PART I

Theoretical and historical studies

CHAPTER 1

The traditional context of Francophone drama

IN SOCIAL RITUAL

That modern drama and theatre should prove such an attraction to Francophone Africans, as has been observed in the Introduction, and become an important cultural nexus in their region is neither surprising nor fortuitous. Such a potential had always existed for at least two possible reasons. The first of these is linked to the theatricality that attaches to the performance of social roles in these traditional societies. The Francophone region, it should be recalled, encompasses a tapestry of ancient societies with highly stratified and normative social structures stretching back to the period of central-ised state-formation. This began in the Middle Ages, and saw the emergence of the Mali, Macina, Segu-Tukulor, Wolof and Kongolese kingdoms, to take just these examples from West and Central Francophone Africa.

In these societies, the individual is defined essentially in terms of his role, status, age or lineage group – a feature that is the subject of several books on the history and sociology of the region (Balandier 1955; Lombard 1965; N'Diayé 1970). It is also clearly reflected in literary works such as Cheikh Hamidou Kane's *L'Aventure ambiguë*, where the characters are quite simply known as the Master, the Chief, the Most Royal Lady, the *Mbare* (slave) and so on. In these societies, individual conduct and inter-group relations are codified into symbolic movements and actions, stylised gestures and patterned dances, while even speech is formalised into various fixed forms, formulaic expressions and tropes.

The result of this expressivity in behaviour is that relations between individuals assume the character of relations between role-players (social personae) and social life becomes an elaborately choreo-graphed play, characterised by play-acting (as in stage drama)

9

rather than by spontaneous and natural interaction (see Melone 1971: 143–54 on the theatricality of an aspect of traditional African social life).

In the traditional societies of Francophone Africa, as indeed in many others in Africa, even the expression of personal emotions of grief, distress or joy are subject to rules and set formats which transform them from the private to the public realm, from personal experience to public spectacle, complete with chants, laments and dances. Camara Laye (1971) captures this aspect of traditional social reality in *The Dark Child*, where the narrator's father does not savour his gold-smithing success alone in the quiet recesses of his workshop. His joy at an item of jewellery well crafted, the narrator tells us, always finds expression in a piece of exhibited behaviour, the *douga* dance:

At the first notes of the *douga*, my father would arise and emit a cry in which happiness and triumph were equally mingled; and brandishing in his right hand the hammer that was the symbol of his profession and in his left a ram's horn filled with magic substances, he would dance the glorious dance. (*The Dark Child*, p. 39)

Similarly, the smith's female client does not walk up to him prosaically (especially as she is pressed for time) to ask that a trinket be made for her. She hires the services of a *griot* who, in turn, as mediator between client and smith, uses the fixed format of the praise-song to convey her message. Mediation, like the crafting of gold (an activity described by the narrator as a 'festival'), as indeed the expression of joy, become forms of ritualised performance with prescribed rules, steps and operations that must be observed if the right outcome is to be achieved.

It is easy to see, with the above in mind, how Francophone Africans born into cultures possessed of such a pronounced sense of the hieratic, of spectacle and social role-play can be attracted to the theatre as an art form.

Of course, it might be observed at this point that theatricality is not specific to the traditional societies of Francophone Africa or indeed of Africa; that all human social life involves performance, as role-theory sociologists have pointed out (Burns 1972; Duvignaud 1965; Goffman 1959). While this is true in general terms, the fact remains that the stage–drama metaphor is much more appropriate to non-literate and more homogeneous societies such as those in

Francophone Africa. This is largely because of the existence in them of a greater degree of 'ascribed' (by tradition) rather than 'achieved' (through personal initiative) social roles, and of what Morris notes as a 'high ratio of absolute... [as distinct from urban society's] conditional norms' (Morris 1966: 112). The former he describes as norms that are strictly enforced and whose breach is greeted with severe sanctions, while the latter are of 'limited application and sporadic enforcement' (Morris 1966: 112). In traditional societies, in other words (and this includes pockets of such societies in predominantly modern nations) there is, more so than in the highly differentiated societies of the modern world, a more pronounced consciousness of a 'social script' at work (Biddle and Thomas 1966: 4), of a 'grammar of social conventions' (Burns 1972: 33) regulating individual behaviour in the way that a playscript determines the words, movements and gestures of the stage actor.

IN RITUAL PERFORMANCES: SOME EXAMPLES

But there is a second possible reason for the popularity of modern dramatic activities in Francophone Africa. It is the widespread, stubborn survival, in this predominantly Islamic region, of a substratum of pre-Islamic cultural institutions and beliefs, initiation rites and ritual performances. It is therefore not just individual conduct and intergroup relations that are ritualised. Collective life itself in its very rhythms (agrarian and seasonal), social processes (birth, puberty, circumcision, nuptials, enthronement) and responses to life-crises (sickness, death, social conflict, misfortune or natural disaster – all seen as a threatening eruption of disorder) is subject to a never-ending cycle of 'social ceremonial' in which sacred or secular ritual performances are an important component (Kesteloot 1971a: 21–4; Memel-Fote 1971: 25–30; Pairault 1971: 15–20).

Two paradigm cases, one of an initiation rite and the other of a ritual performance, will follow. A documented instance of the first is the *do* of the Bambara people of Mali. Described as 'sacred theatre' by Diawara (1981: 13), the *do* takes place every seven years and marks the end of the initiation ceremony of young Bambara males into the secret society of the same name. It takes a little over three and a half months to perform and is open only to initiates (the *dodem*), a category that excludes casted men, considered indiscreet, women and children. Its performers are masked men and their language is esoteric. During their period of seclusion from routine existence, the young *do* recruits are initiated into the sacred and secular sources of Bambara civilisation: its martial arts mainly, but also its history, its cultural and social values (through the enactment of historical legends and cosmogonic myths), its pharmacopeia, divination techniques and even its theatrical arts.

Theatre is both a medium and an important object of instruction dispensed in the *do*, where four types of complementary performers are trained, with the express mission of organising, on graduation, secular theatrical entertainment in the community. Diawara classifies these performers into the *n'togofa*, a kind of buffoon dressed in old clothes who specialises in comic and female roles and in improvising dramatic sketches on scenes of daily life; the *joburu*, a musician-instrumentalist whose songs emphasise the liberating value of human suffering; the *kanian*, who executes dance-dramas and the *fama-sotigi*, dancer but also conjurer whose tricks and entry on stage on a small wooden horse are always a source of intense theatrical excitement (Diawara 1981: 8–9, 13–17).

Marie-José Hourantier, Werewere Liking and Jacques Schérer (1979) have also provided detailed descriptions of healing ritual performances among the Bassa of Cameroon. One of these, the *djingo*, a written version of which has been provided by Hourantier (Hourantier *et al.* 1979: 21–40) is described by her as a 'solidly structured therapeutic dance' (p. 13). Its opening is preceded by the purification of the acting space and the enactment of a battle between the opposing spirits of Evil, thought to be the cause of the illness, and of Good – with the successful outcome of the ceremony dependent on the victory, not always assured in advance, of the latter.

The performance itself unfolds through a number of stages. First there is the opening or warming-up phase during which, with the help of music and song, the patient's family and entire community congregate around him in an effort to create the right atmosphere of solidarity and psychological preparedness. Once this is achieved and the emotions are sufficiently charged, the healer-officiant enters the acting space, in the second phase of the action, followed by his aides, and executing symbolic dance steps and suggestive body movements. During the third phase, the healer, by now possessed by the *bessima*, the beneficent spirits of water and forest, and apparently only visible to the initiated, proceeds to hand out medicinal plant and magic potions, to perform divination rites and to induce states of trance, all in a charged ecstatic atmosphere of colour, frenzied drum music and dance.

Although it is ostensibly an individual that is ill, the underlying belief that informs a *djingo* performance is that he is only the site of a disease that is in reality collective and social. This explains the dimension of self-examination, confessions and collective stock-taking that is encouraged during the performance. By unleashing the dangerous instincts repressed in the unconscious of the celebrants, by forcing them to plumb the depths of their psyche in order to objectify its contents, the *djingo* liberates the community and renders its members whole again.

Other examples of the many ritual presentations in Francophone Africa that have recently been investigated by students of the theatre include the *kora* exorcism ritual of the Hausa people of Niger and their coronation pageant (Beik 1987: 12–13, 13–15); the *kembe* or, as Diawara translates it, the 'theatre of communion' of the Fufuldé of Mali (Diawara 1990b: 51–8); the *n'depp* healing performance of the Lebou community of Senegal described by Geoffrey Gorer (1949) and Jessica Harris (1981) and Cameroonian Bamiléké royal funerals and enthronements (Doho 1989: 78–82).

RITUAL PERFORMANCE: THEATRE OR DRAMA

What all these performances have in common in spite of differences in structure, function and circumstance of performance is the integrative use they make of the performing arts of music, dance, song, mime, masquerade and sometimes puppetry. This feature, coupled with their recourse to intricate and symbolic body movements, gestures and facial expression and to elaborate costumes that range from body decorations to masks has prompted ritual performance theorists like Turner to describe them in Baudelairean terms as 'a symphony or synaesthetic ensemble of expressive cultural genres' (Turner 1982: 82). To many other critics and theatre practitioners they are straightforward *theatre* (Diawara 1981: 13–17; Diawara 1990b: 51–8; Hourantier *et al.* 1979: 7, 20, 98; J. Leloup 1990: 39; Ndzie 1985b: 60–77). 'Ritual', 'Dionysian', 'Sacred' are some of the epithets used to describe it, but theatre it is and not just performances *with theatrical elements*.

The use by these critics and theatre practitioners of the vocabulary of dramaturgical and modern stage analyses – 'scenic space', 'producer', 'décor', 'actors', 'costumes', 'tragedy' and so on – to describe ritual performances witnesses to their total responsiveness to them as theatre. It is therefore not surprising that a number of them should have adapted some of these rituals for the modern stage in plays like *La Puissance d'Um, La Queue du Diable*, by the Cameroonian Liking; *Pagnes*, by the French duo Hourantier and Jacques Schérer; *Guédio* by a French academic Jacqueline Leloup and *La Termitière* by the Ivorian Zaourou.

But other critics and dramatists have gone even further. Not simply in terms of adapting or recreating traditional rituals into modern plays, but in describing the former not just as theatre (a rather broad category) but more precisely as drama – that sub-species of theatre which since Aristotle's *Poetics* has been characterised by a number of precise elements, namely role-playing, impersonation of human, animal or mythical figures and the mimetic rendition through a sequence of physical actions (sometimes, but not necessarily, backed by verbal language) of an action that is complete.

Now, while many traditional religious presentations do contain story-enacting sequences – like the fight between Evil and Good in the prologue to the *djingo* performance or the dramatised historical and cosmogonic legends that are part of the *do* – it has been, and, to a lesser extent, still is, a matter for legitimate debate in the criticism of African drama, and in dramatic theory in general, whether the sub-class of performances from which they derive (religious ritual) is itself narrowly 'theatre' or, even more narrowly, 'drama' (see *inter alia* Crow 1983: 1–7; Echeruo 1981: 136–48; Graham-White 1970: 339–49; Schechner 1977: 63–98; Turner 1982: 136–48).

All three activities, it is true, have overlapping features. They therefore cannot be treated as discrete entities. Having said this, however, it also remains true that they can all be conceived synonymously only at the risk of surrendering to an 'imprecision in nomenclature' that has been rightly deplored by Andrew Horn (1981: 181–202). For there remain differences between ritual on the one hand and theatre and one of its sub-classes, verbal drama – the others being opera, ballet, etc. – on the other, and these need to be recalled, with examples from the Francophone African region.

The first difference is that although there is a story, or dramatic action, in ritual, it is usually archetypal and implicit. It does not constitute the thrust, the 'soul' of the performance in whose service are then deployed in a *relationship of subordination* the various elements of spectacle, such as song and music. It is the opposite that is true. Elements of spectacle exist on their own terms. And it is the arousal of emotions through their synaesthetic use, rather than their subsumation towards the creation of suspense, suspense born of a crafting of events in a sequence that elicits curiosity, that constitutes one of the distinctions between ritual performance and drama.

This quality of spectacle, indeed of theatre, in (Francophone) African ritual performances and, as has been observed, in (Francophone) African daily life constitutes one of the abiding legacies of the traditional context to many French-language African plays. It is also one of their distinguishing formal features in relation to the predominantly text-based and dramatic plays of the *mainstream* French tradition. A closer study of the former works in Part II will illustrate this observation.

I must emphasise at this point, however, that to say that modern Francophone drama is more theatrical and less dramatic than its mainstream Western counterpart is to describe a dynamic cluster of tendencies for either tradition, and not a static category of essences. It is especially *not* to make a value judgement. The case for theatre as spectacle (such as is found in traditional performances and, to a lesser but still real extent, in many modern French-language plays) has been made by many. Soyinka, for example, wonders, after a discussion of the luxuriance of a variety of traditional festival performances, whether it will not be true to say that 'contemporary drama, as we experience it today, is a contraction' in relation to festival richness (Soyinka 1988: 195).

If as a critic he leaves the question open, as a dramatist there can be no doubt where his sympathies lie, given his efforts (successful it must be said in passing) to appropriate in his plays the 'multi-media and multi-formal experiences' of festival theatre (Soyinka 1988: 194). Césaire, like Bernard Dadié (1979: 26) also insists on the need to integrate in the theatre 'poetry, dance, song, folklore' (in Naville 1970: 261).

But lest the judgement of these men be suspected as deriving from an exercise in nationalist cultural politics, one should turn to Artaud (1958: 33–83). With a rare passion, bordering on the polemical, he dismisses the dominant Western theatre as 'decadent' (p. 42), because of what he sees as its excessive reliance on speech (written or spoken) to the exclusion of a theatrical language 'created for the senses' (p. 38), a language of 'music, dance, plastic art and pantomime' (p. 38). It is, unlike traditional non-European perform-ances, 'a theatre which lives under the exclusive dictatorship of speech' (p. 40), 'a theatre of idiots... grammarians... antipoets... i.e., Occidentals' (p. 41).

Derrida, in a Nietzschean reading of Artaud in *Writing and Difference* (1978: 233–50) similarly denounces what he sees as Western theatre's logocentrism, its 'will to speech' (p. 235) and mimetic impulse (pp. 234–7), its 'passive seated public' (p. 235) and 'enslaved interpreters' – the actors and directors (p. 235). And he classifies it in Comtean evolutionary terms, but with a masterful subversive stroke which stands Auguste Comte on his head (and with him the worldview to which he gave expression) as belonging to the 'theological stage' (p. 235), presumably, of world theatrical development.

What one witnesses in the writings of these and other modern and contemporary avant-garde theorists of 'total theatre' (see Kirby 1969) and in the experimental theatre practices associated with them – Grotowski, Schechner, Blau, Brook (see Heuvel 1991; Innes 1981) and Hourantier, in the specific case of Francophone Africa (see Hourantier 1985; Hourantier *et al.* 1979) – is a revaluation of theatre; a revaluation which now promotes the hitherto 'primitive', undif-ferentiated festival and other performance practices of non-literate peoples to the rank of vital and 'civilised' forms, while those of 'civilised' peoples are devalued as 'primitive'.

The Nietzschean filiation of this revaluation is clear. Where Nietzsche associates the values of the primitive and the vital with Dionysian fertility rituals, Greek cultic and mystery religions, Aeschylean tragedy and, later, with the 'total theatre' of the music drama of Richard Wagner (Nietzsche 1967: 33–76; 119–44), his latter-day epigones see these values of 'healthy-mindedness' (Niet-zsche 1967: 37) as embodied in the rituals of the traditional cultures of Africa and of the non-industrial world. Similarly, decadence, synonymous in Nietzsche with the drama of Euripides – a drama denounced for its alleged un-Dionysian nature and impoverishing dialectic, its 'aesthetic socratism' and rationality (Nietzsche 1967: 76–98), has been generalised by these theorists into a quality of Western theatre.

Of course the current Nietzsche-inspired revaluation of traditional African sensibility and artistic forms is not the first such in twentieth-century avant-garde French discourse on and practice of the arts. Examples of it, as Hawkins has recently reminded us (1992–3), are not lacking – from the celebration and appropriation of the 'fétiches d'Océanie et de Guinée … des Christ d'une autre forme' by Apollinaire and the Cubist poets and artists of his generation (and before them by Rimbaud), to the philosophical irrationalism cultivated by the surrealists and associated in their minds with a pre-industrial African sensibility, especially as it finds expression in the vitalist, négritude poetry of Césaire or Senghor.

The significance of these periodic revaluations as cultural critique, and as they relate to theatrical theory and practice, will be briefly touched upon later. What needs to be pointed out now, however, is that outside the confines of the Western avant-garde, the idea and practice of a modern 'total theatre' of which ritual performance provides a unique model, are at best seen as entertaining exoticism for 'unserious plays' and, if applied in earnest, as a damaging distraction from dramatic action, which is seen as all-important. Susan Smith makes this point in her study of the mask in the context of attempts by writers like Genet, Claudel and Cocteau at a ritualised theatre:

Dance, stylised moment, song and chant are equally important … for they complement the mask and heighten … atmosphere. The great danger of such magnificence, grand scale, decoration and emotionally charged atmosphere is that the total effect is merely spectacular. (1985: 51)

This view is not without its adepts among some Francophone writers – if not in a theory then at least in their dramatic practice. Plays like Moussa Konaté's *L'Or du diable*, *Le Cercle au féminin*, Cheik Ndao's *L'Exil d'Albouri*, Eugène Dervain's *La Reine scélérate*, to give just these examples, are almost exclusively dialogue dramas in the best Western tradition in spite of the gesture, in the last two plays listed, to the *griot* and his harp.

It is perhaps clear now, given the presence of these varied positions within Francophone drama, why we have judged it more relevant to try to determine what the characteristics of this drama really are and their provenance either in ancient traditions or in the colonial legacy and their evolution, rather than what they ought to be. But before we get any further into this, we should return to a second distinction between ritual and drama. This pertains to the status of role-playing. Although there seems to be role-playing in ritual performances, the performers are not, strictly speaking, engaged in any such exercise. If impersonation there is, it is experienced as such only by the outsider (to the culture that is) but not by the performer himself or his fellow celebrants. Thus, although he uses the resources of the stage actor, the healer in a *djingo* performance does not imitate and is not aware of imitating the *bessima* spirits of Good in the second phase of the ceremony (to give a Goffman-type example) any more than, say, an individual who is 'father', 'doctor' and 'husband' does in the execution of his social duties, in the representation of his multiple selves, in real life. He *is* (to himself and the members of his 'therapeutic group', as Hourantier calls it) the *bessima* themselves made flesh.

I do not of course wish to suggest that there is no impersonation at all in ritual performances. There is; especially in those performances such as the Yoruba *egungun* which differentiate into a devotional, non-mimetic phase (the *idan*) and a ludic, representational one (the *efe*) (Götrick 1984: 115–29). Horn also raises the possibility of faked, that is *acted* trances in the Bori-possession ceremonies of the Hausa of Nigeria (Horn 1981: 190–1). What is true, however, is that whereas *all* roles in theatre and drama are impersonated, many in ritual ceremonies are not. The boy who becomes a *dodem* or the man who becomes an ancestor so remain and do not revert, as in drama after the performance, to some 'real' or unfaked status. Perhaps this point can be better appreciated if it is remembered that in rituals which involve a scapegoat or other such sacrificial dimension, the individual who from the outsider's perspective can be harmlessly said to *play* the scapegoat *is* to the insiders *the* scapegoat – a difference in perception which for the person concerned is often no terminological or *playing* matter: be (s)he a non-fictional Emman, Elesin Oba (in Soyinka's *The Strong Breed* and *Death and the King's Horseman* respectively) or Oedipus or Iphigenia of ancient Greece.

But perhaps it is the serious purpose of ritual performance, suggested by the restricted place made in it for the ludic, that is the most basic difference between this form and drama or theatre in general. A *djingo* performance and a modern Francophone play directly descended from it, like Werewere Liking's *La Puissance d'Um*, are not one and the same thing. And this is not so much because the latter's script is the product of an individual talent while the former's proceeds anonymously from tradition, although this is a factor. Neither is it because *La Puissance d'Um* has a better-delineated story which is then enacted through verbal dialogue, movement, song and so on. In reality, as an analysis of the play will show, dramatic action and verbal dialogue (the latter still too incantatory and esoteric, and not sufficiently communicative) are only marginally more developed here. It is mainly because *La Puissance d'Um* like all modern Francophone drama, is, above all, entertainment.

It is not entertainment of the Togolese concert-party type or of the popular boulevard variety beloved of a Daniel Ndo and a Dave Moktoi of the Cameroon and described by Bjornson (1991: 19–34), or indeed of a Souleymane Koly of the Ivory Coast (Hourantier 1984: 19–34). After all, *La Puissance d'Um* aims at provoking the spectator into serious thought and even creating something of the healing ecstasy of the model. But it is entertainment all the same; for the multi-ethnic audience of modern Cameroonians who choose to watch it do so under no social obligation. Furthermore, the actors are not priests, but amateurs or professionals – probably from Liking's pan-African Ki-Yi Mbock troupe – playing roles for which they will be paid. Also, although the play in production allows for some audience participation, modern Cameroonians (to limit oneself to this national audience), go to watch it as spectators and not celebrants or worshippers, as do their real-life rural Bassa, Cameroonian, counterparts. Finally, as cultural outsiders, in all probability, to the latter ethnic community, whose ritual they are now watching in modern dress, members of this audience are unlikely to understand its religious presuppositions. Or even if they did (assuming they are modern Bassa), because of their secular education they would be unlikely to share them. (Those who do share them will, in all probability, stay away in protest against a show that they will see as an aestheticisation, and therefore a trivialisation, of something sacred.)

To these modern spectators therefore, an evening in the theatre watching *La Puissance d'Um* or any other such performance is one of leisure rather than of work or, better still, one of worship; an evening when attention focusses not on the substance of the performance, its semantics, in other words, but on its metaphoric possibilities, sounds, colours, movements and language. It is, in short, an evening mainly of aesthetic experience which, by the same token, is also socially optional.

No such optionality, either in attendance or performance, is possible in the case of a ritual. Without a *do*, *djingo*, *kembe*, *kora* or other such manifestation in times of social crisis or change, the entire community – so its members believe anyway – will be threatened with chaos and possible extinction. Richard Schechner brings out this distinctive nature of the relationship between the audience in theatre on the one hand and in ritual on the other very well when he writes:

Theatre comes into existence when a *separation* occurs between audience and performers. The paradigmatic theatrical situation is a group of performers soliciting an audience who may or may not respond by attending. The audience is free to attend or stay away – and if they stay away, it is the theatre that suffers, not its would-be audience. In ritual, to stay away means rejecting the congregation – or being rejected by it, as in excommunication, ostracism, or exile. (1977: 79)

Ritual performance, in other words, plays a much more fundamental role in the social process of traditional societies (as Turner has demonstrated in his studies of the N'dembu of Zambia) than, say, theatre or drama in modern societies or in the modern sectors of predominantly traditional societies. It is, to use Turner's expression, one of the most important 'modes of redress' available to traditional man – and on a *functional par* with the rational-scientific and technical procedures in modern societies – to understand and control the processes of nature and society through an appeal to a transcendent realm of being that is in need of propitiation (Schechner 1977; Turner 1967; 1982; 1986).

Its function is instrumental: to act on the gods and through them, in the case of healing rituals, on the 'sick' members of the audience. As a symbolic language, ritual performance is, to use the useful modern linguistic distinction between the languages of science and of literature, 'transitive'; that is, action-orientated as distinct from the 'intransitive', aesthetic language of drama.

But, as René Wellek has observed (1956: 22–4), no verbal language is purely communicative or purely aesthetic. There is always a residual aesthetic dimension even in the most referential or factual of verbal enunciations. Similarly the most musical of poetry, short of becoming pure music, still contains what Graff calls a 'propositional' element (1980). In the same way ritual as 'language' also has an intransitive, aesthetic quality. But this is residual and *incidental* to its purpose, in the same way as factual communication (with a spiritual realm) is to theatre and drama.

Indeed, the move from ritual performance on the one hand to theatre on the other is usually signalled when, for reasons including, *but not limited to*, a loss of belief in its underlying theology, a conscious preoccupation on the part of the audience with ritual's symbolic language-units (dance, costume, gestures, music, etc.) *as ends in themselves, as objects of beauty and entertainment* takes precedence over their religious or 'propositional' significance: their original goal-oriented function. This is what happened, for instance, in the traditional *alarinjo* theatre of the Yoruba, to take a well-known example from Anglophone Africa, which evolved from the *egungun* ritual as a result of a political conspiracy gone awry (Adedeji 1981: 221–47). Examples from the Francophone world of such an evolution, albeit for different reasons, include the *hira-gasy* of the Malagasy of Madagascar (de Saivre 1980: 68–71), the *sounougounou* or 'animal ballet' of the Senoufo people in the Odienne province of the Ivory Coast (Prouteaux 1929: 448–75) and the *tyi wara* of the Bambara of Mali (Imperato 1970: 13, 71).

Similarly, theatre, dramatic or otherwise, can evolve back to ritual (whether successful or not is another issue) when its units of symbolic language are perceived by the audience and manipulated by the director in a non-aesthetic, instrumental way. Such manipulation then becomes a means of inducing spiritual or psychological states of mind – trance, possession, ecstasy; of transcending the '*principle of individuation*' or breaking through the '*veil of māyā*' (Nietzsche 1967: 36, 37), in order to establish, as it is believed, contact with cosmic forces; 'to steal', in Nietzsche's poetic phrase, 'a glimpse into the nature of the Dionysian' (Nietzsche 1967: 36).

Such attempts at the ritualisation of drama (as distinct from the dramatisation of ritual recently undertaken by a few Francophone writers), at recapturing for it an *affective* dimension, has been associated in Western theatre with Artaud's Theatre of Cruelty and Grotowski's appropriately named 'para-theatrical experiments'.

Artaud actually conceived of the theatre as a set of technical operations, with a recipe, which he outlines meticulously, for the psychological intoxication and hypnotisation of the spectator. He writes:

I propose to return through the theatre to an idea of the physical knowledge of images and the means of inducing trances as in Chinese medicine which knows, over the entire extent of the human anatomy, at which points to puncture in order to regulate the subtlest functions. (Artaud 1958: 80)

This view of theatre as *weapon* explains his widespread mathematical, geometric imagery in *The Theatre and Its Double* (1958), where he describes a Balinese performance in terms of 'the physics of absolute gesture' (p. 62) and the movements of its actors as a 'kind of detached geometry' (p. 64) by some 'unknown rigorous figure in the ritual of a hermetic formula' (p. 64).

But, of course, Artaud failed in his attempts to ritualise theatre. The fact is that the success of ritual in traditional societies presupposes more than just a set of mechanical operations. It assumes an underlying and *shared* religious belief system which is affirmed and celebrated in performance. If this belief system is dead, as is the case in the modern West, then attempts such as Artaud's or Grotowski's could be dismissed as, or degenerate into, mystifying or esoteric cultic séances of little or no importance to a wider audience, and of potentially damaging consequences to the mental health of its devotees. Turner highlights, in the following quotations from his earlier essays on Grotowski, what, to him, is the socially and psychologically unacceptable nature of this type of theatrical activity in a modern culture:

I relish the separation of an audience from performers and the liberation of scripts from cosmology, ideology and theology. The concept of individuality has been hard-won, and to surrender it to a new totalizing process of reliminization is a dejecting thought. (Turner 1982: 118)

Even as audience people can be 'moved' by plays; they need not be 'carried away' by them...Liminoid theater should limit itself to presenting alternatives: it should not be a brainwashing technique. (Turner 1982: 118)

In present-day Africa, on the other hand, because the religious beliefs connected with ritual are not dead, but are only in various stages of crisis, mostly as a result of the impact of secular modernity and foreign religions – Christianity and Islam – modern African audience reactions to ritual dramas are more complex. Thus, audience reactions, gauged by Hourantier in the Ivory Coast, to the ritual theatre of Werewere Liking have ranged from the purely aesthetic, but dismissive of this theatre's alleged obsurantism (among the most secularised and politically radical members of the audience), to the ambivalent (among those spectators for whom the dramatised rituals might still have some residual efficacy), to the outraged, among those for whom the playwright's theatre is a monumental and, possibly, punishable exercise in profanation (Hourantier 1984: 269–80).

But to dismiss the theatre of Liking as socially unprogressive, as Ivorian critics like Kotchy have done (Kotchy 1984: 239), presumably because it is patterned on a traditional ritual performance is, it seems to me, to misunderstand her radical approach to ritual, and, indeed, to be unclear about the various interesting uses to which this form has been, and can be, put in modern African drama. This is an important issue to which I will return shortly.

RITUAL PERFORMANCE AND FRANCOPHONE DRAMA: ON THE NATURE OF A TRANSACTION

At this point of our discussion, pressing questions suggest themselves. Given the context of ritualised social behaviour, and especially of ritual performances with which the Francophone author grew up, what is the precise nature of the relationship between his or her dramatic work in French and these rituals? Does the former chronologically derive from the latter, as in Europe where drama, especially Greek tragic drama, has been said, again by Turner following a long line of critics, to be 'historically continuous with ritual and [to] possess something of [its] sacred even "rites of passage" structure...' (1982: 41)?

The questions do not admit of easy answers for whereas in the case of ancient Greece the evolution was endogenous, in Francophone Africa, where a similar development was taking place *within* traditional forms (see above p. 21), it was interrupted by the colonial factor. Novel theatrical forms and practices were imposed, with the result that the new drama in French is not always related in any direct and obvious ways to traditional performances, performances which, it must be emphasised, have not been superseded, but continue to thrive and coexist with literary drama. Another problem is that the relationship (between ritual and modern plays), can be viewed from several standpoints: vision, structure, function and performance style and so on.

A useful way to approach the issue would be perhaps to quite simply consider each of the above aspects in turn, starting with the first. How then does the *vision* of Francophone drama relate (if it does at all) to that of its ritual theatrical predecessor in the region? Wole Soyinka's characterisation of the vision of ritual (1976a: 37–60) provides a useful point of entry into the subject.

For Soyinka, the main difference between Western drama and African ritual performance is not one of form, function or structure, but of vision, world-view. Central to the vision of ritual, he submits, is a profound awareness of 'the cosmic human condition' (p. 41), a consciousness of man as engaged in perpetual struggle against external, non-human forces; as caught, to use his dramatic phrase, 'in constant efforts to master the immensity of the universe with his minuscule self' (p. 40). Ritual is shot through and through with a tragic and metaphysical dimension, which explains why its performance space encompasses, appropriately enough, not just some 'purely physical acting areas on a stage' (p. 40) but both earth and cosmos.

More specifically, to Soyinka, the ritual vision interconnects realms of experience – the human, the natural and the spiritual. Like poetic drama, which he considers its legitimate modern heir, it 'expands the immediate meaning and action of the protagonists into a world of natural forces and metaphysical conceptions' (p. 43). He gives the example of the Anglophone Nigerian dramatist John P. Clark-Bekederemo's *Song of a Goat* as a successful modern illustration of this vision. In this play, the sexual impotence of one of the central characters, Zifa, and source of the drama, is not depicted as a mere individual problem, but as one with social, spiritual and moral significance. In Zifa's community where, Soyinka explains, 'The continuity of the species is seen as the highest moral order' (p. 43), the inability to procreate is more than just a personal tragedy. It is a collective tragedy in the way it is bound up with the moral foundations of communal life, threatening it as in this case with disintegration.

A 'cohesive understanding' of the world, a belief in the agency of supernatural deities, now benevolent now malevolent, in the regulation of the processes of nature and of social and individual life – deities with whom man is engaged in a relentless battle for a harmonious relationship – such then are the main ingredients of the tragic vision celebrated in ritual.

It is beyond the scope of this book to address at any length the various aspects of Soyinka's thought that flow from his descriptions of ritual's tragic vision. I have in mind, for example, his postulation of this vision as the *truth* of the human condition; his refusal to conceptualise it as a mode of knowledge that mediates social and power relations in the traditional societies of Africa; his abiding fascination with it; and so on. Several perceptive studies have already been devoted to this area of his thought (Hunt 1985: 64–93; Jeyifo 1985b: 11–35; 1988: viii–xxxii; Wright 1993: 175–86).

What needs to be pointed out briefly, however, is that the tragic vision of ritual he describes is not specific to Africa – any more than the secular vision of what he calls 'realistic drama' is to the West. To postulate, on the one hand, an eternal, poetic, 'African' cast of mind, whose 'cohesive understanding' of life and organic sensibility find expression in ritual; and, on the other, a prosaic, 'Western' mind, whose equally atemporal, 'compartmentalising' and fragmenting qualities are correspondingly expressed in 'realistic drama', is a perfectly understandable exercise in cultural identity-formation and polemics. After all, early Romantic polemics of anti-industrialism were couched in similar terms of an organic (rural-traditional) sensibility and a dissociative (urban-industrial) one. Such a postulate might even give rise to superb and compelling theatre, as in *Death and the King's Horseman* (1975), where these contrasts are dramatically and polemically enacted, but where, at a deeper and perhaps unconscious level, they are also subverted – in the ritual/Elesin Oba/African sequences of the play, on the one hand, and in the latter's drama/Pilkins/Western sequences, on the other. But as a theory, it is unhistorically grounded, and, therefore, is both factually indefensible and, in relation to earlier Soyinka positions, inconsistent.

It is indefensible because 'realistic' drama, as Soyinka defines it – a drama concerned with the exploration of forces no larger than 'the petty infractions of habitual communal norms or patterns of human relationships or expectations' (Soyinka 1976a: 43) – has never been absent from pre-colonial African theatre. Forms like the *alarinjo* or, as we shall see later, the *kotéba* testify to that. Similarly, the poetic and tragic vision of ritual which he appropriates for Africa has been, as is only too well known, a recurring, that is, a historically determined feature of Western culture, from Aeschylus to Samuel Beckett.

Soyinka's theory also puts him in an inconsistent position, in so far as it erects – although with greater subtlety, and a profound empirical knowledge of the particulars and dynamics of African cultures, especially Yoruba culture – an essentialist binary (the 'African' and the 'Western' minds, viewed *sub specie aeternitatis*), of which he has been particularly critical in Senghor's philosophy of culture (Soyinka 1966: 53–64; 1988: 7–14), even if in a more nuanced way in recent years.

Having made these reservations, it is now important to ask whether the vision of ritual so persuasively described by Soyinka is the one that is explored in Francophone drama. In terms of the questions raised earlier in this section, in other words, does Francophone drama proceed from ritual in this specific respect? Does it exhibit a continuity of consciousness with it?

The straightforward answer to this has been in the negative. The *vast* majority of Francophone plays – from Aimé Césaire's *La Tragédie du roi Christophe* and *Une Saison au Congo* to Bernard Dadié's *Monsieur Thogo-Gnini* and *Béatrice du Congo*, through Guillaume Oyono-Mbia's *Trois prétendants ... un mari* and *Notre fille ne se mariera pas*, Sony Labou Tansi's *La Parenthèse de Sang* and *Je, soussigné cardiaque* to Tchicaya U'Tamsi's *Le Maréchal Nnikon Nniku Prince qu'on sort*, to name just these few representative ones – are not concerned with the lofty issue of 'the cosmic human condition' or with allegorising it. Their main concern, as we shall see more clearly in chapter 2, is with (African) man's social and political conditions.

The ravages of colonial conquest and the resistance to it, decolonisation and its dilemmas, the collapse of traditional social structures and values with its ensuing gender and generational tensions, the emergence of ugly post-colonial dictatorships, these are the defining elements of this condition. And this condition, with all the human suffering that sometimes attaches to it, is seen, it must be emphasised, *not* as determined by invisible spiritual forces whose displeasure only happens to take a historical, social or political turn, but by human and only-too-human factors.

The vision of modern Francophone drama then, even when it is one of tragic suffering, is naturalistic and not supernaturalistic; immanentist and not transcendental. The world is viewed in it as an autonomous unit in which events can be explained in their own terms without recourse to transcendence. Even when supernatural characters appear, as they often do in plays like U'Tamsi's *Le Zulu* Dadié's *Les Voix dans le vent*, they are, as shall be shown in the case of the first, more poetic and psychological entities than real forces. In dramas like *Abraha Pokou une grande africaine* by the Ivorian Charles Nokan, an ancient myth is purged of its spiritual content and completely secularised. The episode where Queen Pokou is able to secure safe passage across a river for herself and her people only after sacrificing her child, Agamemnon-like, to a river god – an episode that would have greatly appealed to Soyinka's imagination – is given rationalistic treatment. With Nokan, the sacrificial aspect is left out. Instead of hippopotami (in Dadié's account of the myth (1966)) or baobab trees (in Quénum's of 1946) magically linking up tail to head or root to branch to form a bridge which then disappears once the fleeing party has crossed over, one has energetic men swimming across the river to summon the help of friendly clansmen.

Not even the avant-garde theatre of Werewere Liking, based as it is on the structure of Bassa healing or funeral ritual performances, can be said to project an ancient, metaphysical tragic vision. Her plays use the ritual framework *ironically* and aim at its affective dimension but to contest, even to subvert, its 'cohesive' vision and understanding of life. *La Puissance d'Um*, for example, is a critical exploration of the subaltern position of women in traditional Cameroonian Bassa society. As this theatre's chief theoretician has observed:

This theatre will refuse divine control over human affairs and will reveal to man a different way of dealing with his problems.

If theatre replaces ritual in a society where the latter is in decline, *its inspiration is 'anti-ritualistic'* because it questions the mythical and gives it a new interpretation. It is no longer 'conservative' and 'immobilising' as Girard characterised ritual, but it welcomes change when the need to challenge established forces becomes necessary. (Hourantier 1984: 31; emphasis added)

The upshot of all this is that Francophone drama is a drama of social and political combat, of revolt and not of the lyrical celebration of man's tragic destiny. It believes in the need to awaken the spectator to his condition in an effort to provoke him into action.

Francophone dramatists might differ on the course of action to be advocated. To the older generation and more conservative playwrights like Pliya, Dadié, Ndao, it might be cultural regeneration, while to the more politically radical ones of Fanonian inspiration, like Charles Nokan or Zadi Zaourou, it should be political revolution. They might even differ on the theatrical means, with Zaourou favouring agitprop techniques, at least in *L'Œil*, and Werewere Liking preferring the more psychological and symbolic techniques of ritual to the realistic style of mainstream Francophone plays. However, the one thing on which they are all united is on the need for the theatre to fulfil a transformative role in the realms of society, culture and politics.

Francophone drama can be said in respect of this secular vision and political purpose to be closer to the Anglophone theatre of East Africa as it is represented in plays like Micere Mugo's and Ngugi Wa Thiongo's *The Trial of Dedan Kimathi* on the folk hero of the Mau Mau rebellion, Ebrahim Hussein's *Kinjeketile* on the Maji armed resistance to German colonial rule in Tanzania and Kabwe Kasoma's three *Black Mamba* plays on the rise of Zambian nationalism. It is much closer also to the forceful and flourishing, but still minority tradition in Anglophone West African drama, represented mainly by Nigerian dramatists like Femi Osofisan in plays such as *No More the Wasted Breed* and *The Chattering and the Song* or Bode Sowande in *Farewell to Babylon* or *The Night Before*, than it is to the more internationally recognised and dominant vein of West African playwriting in English illustrated by John P. Clark-Bekederemo, Ola Rotimi and Soyinka. In plays like the latter's *Death and the King's Horseman* and *The Strong Breed*, Clark-Bekederemo's *Ozidi* and *Song of a Goat*, and Rotimi's *The Gods Are Not To Blame*, the ritual *form*, or *elements* of it, are not only dramatised (Osofisan and Liking also do that), its tragic *metaphysics*, unlike in the plays of the latter, is also affirmed (see Jeyifo 1985b: 55–63 for a useful classification of Anglophone drama in terms of vision, and Dunton 1992 on recent Nigerian drama).

But why the predominance of a secular, social and political consciousness in Francophone drama? Several reasons could be given. One is the official cultural influence of the colonising power, France. The latter not only bequeathed her language and technological civilisation to her African subjects, but also her post-1789 aggressively secular and anticlerical hegemonic culture. The Enlightenment belief in man's ability to conquer human suffering through science and its method, later reinforced by the influence of Marxist thought, with its emphasis on the material bases of that condition, in society and its economy, produced in France a deeply humanistic, anti-religious and revolutionary culture that was imposed on Francophone Africa, and held up as a yardstick of the civilised outlook. When this is combined with the French respect, since the days of Voltaire and later of Hugo, for the 'committed' writer, a role given an added boost by the prestige of Sartre and writers of his generation, one can begin to understand why Francophone African élites, schooled and assimilated in such a cultural tradition, should have adopted a similar perspective in and function for their dramatic and other modern creative forms of expression.

However, having said this, it would be wrong to attribute the rise of a secular outlook in Francophone culture entirely to French colonial influence. This would be to imply that such an outlook was unknown in pre-colonial African cultures, and to fall into the simplistic dichotomy of a religion-bound traditional Africa, on the one hand, and a secular-spirited modern Africa on the other. As our discussion of traditional theatre proper (as distinct from ritual performances) will show, the non-religious was also a feature of pre-colonial cultures, and modern Francophone drama can be said, in a real sense, to have built on that tradition. What is true, though, is that the space of this tradition was dramatically expanded as a result of contacts with modern France.

Another possible reason for modern Francophone drama's anti-ritualistic vision could be Islam. While the latter has been unable to suppress ritual, it has, over the 900 years of its continuous presence and social dominance in the region, sufficiently discredited the world-view of nature spirits from which ritual proceeds, to make it rather unfashionable as a publicly held belief and as an idiom for the modern stage. And it is useful to note in this regard that the West African authors (Francophone as well as Anglophone) most interested in ritual and the possibilities of its form and vision for the present come not from the more Islamised Sahelian regions, which happen to be mostly Francophone, but from the coastal and forest regions of Africa that did not endure the full impact of Islam's centuries-old assault against African traditional religions, and where Christianity is a comparatively more recent and unevenly influential religion.

A second aspect of the ritual–Francophone drama transaction that now needs to be considered relates to plot structure. It is our view that Francophone plays derive no more from ritual in terms of their narrative structure than they do in their vision. Many, like *Kondo le requin*, *L'Exil d'Albouri*, *Trois prétendants ... un mari*, and *Equatorium* by the Congolese Maxime Ndébéka incorporate, certainly, within a realistic plot structure, brief ritual sequences of a religious or secular nature: funerals, enthronement, divination rites and so on. But to say this is quite different from saying that either in their surface or core narrative rhythms, these and most Francophone plays are but the embodiment in human terms of ritual archetypal processes or characters. A case can be made, without being reductionist, for a number of plays as scapegoat ritual dramas: for example, Césaire's *Une Saison au Congo* and, to a far lesser extent, his *La Tragédie du roi Christophe* and for Dadié's *Les Voix dans le vent* as the drama of a failed initiation ceremony. But these types of play are few. Besides, they can function perfectly as realistic dramas, which they were meant to be anyway.

The only published dramatic works which from an angle of narrative structure (surface or otherwise) proceed clearly from ritual ceremonies ('ritual intensive' as distinct from just being 'ritual-inclusive', to borrow Derek Wright's very useful classification of Soyinka's plays (Wright 1993: 79)) and which resist any reading in the realist mode are, to my mind, those by Werewere Liking. And, if they can be considered Francophone at all, since their authors are French even if their material is African, plays such as *Pagnes* and *Guédio*. Liking's plays, though few, are crucially innovative and are at the forefront of efforts to renew the form of African literary drama in French. As our study of the paradigmatic *La Puissance d'Um* will show, they all enact the four-part structure of rituals such as the *djingo* or the *mbeng*.

But although Liking's dramas show clear structural affiliation with ritual it should be emphasised that they, like other plays in their mould, were written at least two decades after the first major Francophone plays. This perhaps suggests a conscious *intellectual* and cultural nationalist decision to reconnect with an ancient theatrical form than a case of spontaneous and chronological derivation. This decision also coincided with and so was strengthened by the avant-garde promotion of ritual performance undertaken by the French anthropologist and theatre scholar Marie-José Hourantier in her theoretical writings (1984), Ivory Coast-based theatre and artistic practices, her collaborative efforts with Liking (see chapter 9 below; Bjornson 1991: 360; Hawkins 1991; 1992–3) and her not-unnoticed decision to become an initiate herself under the name Manuna Ma Njock (Hawkins 1992–3: 237).

If there is an area in which Francophone drama carries the unmistakable imprint of ritual, it is, as we mentioned earlier, in performance idiom. But this statement now calls for two important qualifications. The first is that while ritual performance and French-language plays might be both 'multi-generic', the non-linguistic elements are put to very *different functions* in either form. In modern plays (with the exception of Werewere Liking's) they function either as entertaining spectacle or as an illustration of the textual values of the work, a complement to verbal dialogue. Francophone plays, in respect of these functions, are not fundamentally different from plays in the mainstream Western theatre. Of course, where the two sets differ is that while the visual and auditory elements are fewer in French-language plays, in relation to ritual, viewed in terms of a continuum these elements are fewer still in mainstream Western, especially French, drama in relation to Francophone drama and almost negligible (Artaud's complaint) in relation to ritual. Orthodox Western drama gestures only timidly, in a mood of exoticism or spectacle (say in French Romantic drama which in any case, has something of the operatic) to movement, colour, costume, etc. But it is rare to find music, dance or pantomime except in moments of frank entertainment, such as can be found in sequences of plays like Molière's 'comédies-ballets', in melodramas or in the non-canonical genres like musicals, music-hall dramas or vaudeville.

In ritual, on the other hand, these elements are not used in the representational mode, that is, to signify, but instead to create psychological states. These elements are the inevitable elixir, as it were, for the performers' transition into liminal states of trance and religious experience. Sociologically, this flight into non-rational behaviour has been explained by scholars like Turner as an escape, temporary and institutionalised, from the constraints of life in society; a kind of social safety-valve for the acting-out of repressed, alternative but undefined modes of being and behaving, especially in rigid, norm-governed communities (Turner 1982: 28–42). On this account, ritual performance constitutes – to use Bakhtin's description of medieval popular carnivals – 'une brèche joyeuse' ('a gay-loophole'); a space where the established, rigid norms of social life are inverted, subverted but, in the end, upheld (Bakhtin 1970: 450).

Artaud and avant-garde practitioners of ritual drama in the West do not have a fundamentally different explanation of the phenomenon even if they express it in more mystical and philosophical terms. For them, and in a new narrative of the myth of the Fall, the ecstasy and trance often observed in ritual performances are the celebrants' ways of reconnecting with a state of primeval, pre-lapsarian, edenic human wholeness; a 'pre-alphabetic reality' (Kirby 1969: xv) from which man has been tragically severed with the advent of an impoverishing 'logos', self-consciousness and reflexivity. The artistic correlate of this alienated condition is seen, according to these practitioners, in, among other forms, verbal drama (synonymous, to them, with modern Western drama) with its devaluation of the sensory and perceptual in favour of the intellectual and rational; of dance, music and song in favour of speech; of performance in favour of text or, more discriminatingly, of performance as *creation* (sometimes in a mode of genuine or faked altered consciousness) of 'some unknown, fabulous and obscure reality' (Artaud 1958: 61) in favour of performance (when it exists at all) as mere *translation*, mimesis in song, mime, gestures, etc. of a pre-existent *known* social and human reality, of 'determinate meaning' (Heuvel 1991: 4) as this reality and meaning are embodied in the playtext.

An important difference remains, of course, between Turner's explanation and Artaud's: to the former, social constraints, even if in varying degrees of severity, are integral to all human societies, whereas to Artaud they appear to be limited to only modern Western societies. This view makes of Artaud a rather classic latter-day European Romantic intellectual with a primitivist, Rousseauist conception of 'traditional' societies as vital, because close to some 'ur-reality', as Kirby calls it (1969: xiv), and 'modern' ones as decadent because alienated from it. It also explains his fascination, and that of avant-garde Western theatre critics of modernity, with ritual; their desire to see its practices incorporated into any Western drama worthy of its name. With what is seen as its liberating anarchism, its plunge into a deconstructionist type of universe of indeterminacy and flux, this ancient performance tradition, to these critics, constitutes a potent weapon against normative order, structure, fixed meanings and especially scientific rationality – all seen as repressive because mutilating of the 'Whole', and in need therefore of being subverted. Heuvel observes:

For advocates of holy theater [i.e. ritualized drama, or ritual performance *tout court*], the intent to undo the closure of [social] textuality satisfies a social and *utopian* thrust, a yearning for the breakdown of rational structures of thought and feeling and for the revelation of new worlds and transcendent signs based on holistic relationships discovered in the act of performance itself, where a true, 'total' act takes place in the body. (Heuvel 1991: 83, emphasis mine)

Nietzsche, writing over a century earlier in the era of triumphant modernity, expressed a similar view even more graphically, and it is worth quoting in full:

Under the charm of the Dionysian [i.e. of ritual performance] not only is the union between man and man reaffirmed, but nature which has been alienated, hostile or subjugated, celebrates once more her reconciliation with her lost son, man... Now the slave is a free man; now all the rigid, hostile barriers that necessity, caprice, or 'impudent convention' have fixed between man and man are broken. Now, with the gospel of universal harmony, each one feels, himself not only united, reconciled, and fused with his neighbor, but as one with him, as if the veil of *māyā* had been torn aside and were now merely fluttering in tatters before the mysterious primordial unity. (Nietzsche 1967: 37)

The hedonist project of an untrammelled liberation of the individual, his instincts and especially his body from '"impudent convention"'; the religious quest for some mystical totality (Artaud's 'fabulous and obscure reality') – where the contradictions of man's social and natural existence are transcended in a kind of nirvana – might be worthy and necessary goals in a postmodern West, seen by its critics as alienated and alienating, and in search of a lost spirituality. But as formulated above, these goals constitute a luxury, indeed a 'utopian thrust' that Francophone, indeed, African dramatists cannot afford to put on their agenda. For it is not enough to undo the 'closure of [social] textuality' in a grand gesture of refusal of its 'authoritarian' meanings without substituting alternative 'liberating' but *necessarily* determinate meanings. This would be too anarchistic. And yet the alternative vision sometimes suggested (when one is suggested at all) – the resacralisation of existence – appears vastly inadequate. For, after all, the crisis of spirituality experienced in certain segments of the Western intellectual world is *not* everybody's crisis. On the contrary, the Francophone region suffers from the concrete, material problems attendant on a *surfeit of* '*spirituality*' or a deficit of modern, rational procedures of thought and organisation.

The problem in this region, like that in the rest of Africa, is, in other words, not so much the existence of a constraining, normative order, or of fixed meanings, which therefore need to be subverted, but on the contrary, one of the instability or, in some cases, of the total absence of any such meaning; of the growing ascendency of the unformed, of the 'in-between and in-betwixt', (to adapt Turner's expression in another context), consequent on the colonial enterprise. The latter destroyed the integrity of old structures of thought, feeling and doing, without adequately replacing them with new ones. It thus created twilight or liminal zones between worlds. So whereas Western avant-garde theatre practitioners can celebrate, or, indeed, spiritualise liminality and, through the medium of a ritualised drama, even call for its rebirth in their societies, (to liberate them from the tyranny of '"impudent convention"'), in modern Africa the liminal, which is a fact and experience of daily life, is perceived not as a liberating, spiritual experience, in the manner of Artaud or of Nietzsche, but as a form of social, moral and political chaos; a morass from which deliverance is sought.

It is therefore not surprising that to most African dramatists, especially those from Francophone Africa, the somewhat less mystical task of contributing to the creation of determinate meaning, in this case rational and humane structures of society, politics and thought in their region remains, and rightly so, the issue of importance. This is why, perhaps, these dramatists have carefully chosen elements of performance from ritual, and on occasion dramatised an entire ritual, while rejecting (in a move that highlights the secular and social nature of their works, and incidentally their similarity in this respect to those of canonical Western drama) not only the uses to which these elements are put in their source form, but also the latter's vision.

The second qualification that needs to be entered relates to the scope of the performance dimension *within* Francophone drama. Although non-verbal elements are a characteristic of this form, as several references have suggested, the mix of these elements varies significantly between plays (sometimes even by the same author) and periods – a situation which makes any generalisation more than a little hazardous. Thus it will be discovered, for example, that plays of an earlier generation by authors like Eugène Dervain in *La Reine scélérate*, Césaire in *Une Saison au Congo*, Ndam Njoya in *Dairou IV*, Dadié in *Béatrice du Congo*, Ndao in *L'Exil d'Albouri*, Séydou Badian in *La Mort de Chaka*, Jean Pliya in *Kondo le requin* and Charles Nokan in *Abraha Pokou une grande africaine* are literary, oriented towards text rather than performance. Their emphasis is on plot, form and character depiction, the exploration of ideas as well as on the construction (reflecting in this regard a French Classical drama influence) of rousing speeches in the style of Corneille, persuasive and built on rhetorical devices. The aim of these plays is rational intellectual communication.

But rational communication in French speech, and a highly

literary one at that, automatically excludes the mass of the public in Francophone Africa for which all these dramatists claim they wrote, but for which, deriving from their oral cultures, theatre is above all performance, process, creation and not product. The result is one of those paradoxes of literary drama in Africa: that of being popular in intent, but élitist in form and preoccupation. It is partly to circumvent this problem, to give Francophone drama a status equivalent to that enjoyed by performances in traditional societies – a privileged mode of communication with a mass audience – that since the late 1970s and early 1980s, there have been attempts by new-generation playwrights, sometimes by some old-generation ones too, to create a drama which, while still in French and written, textualises more systematically the performance modes of traditional theatre. Their idea is to overcome the obstacle of the dialogues in French by the integration of the non-verbal languages of song, music, dance and so on.

Among the principal (published) practitioners of this performance-oriented theatre are Senouvo Zinsou of Togo in plays like *On joue la comédie*, *La Tortue qui chante*, Alexandre Kuma Ndumbe III of Cameroon in *Lisa, la putaine de*, Sony Labou Tansi in *Qui a mangé Madame D'Avoine Bergotha*, Werewere Liking in all her plays and Bernard Zaourou in *L'Œil*. Many other plays in this category like Zaourou's *La Termitière*, Jean-Marie Tuèche's *La Succession de Wabo Defo*, and the many works collectively created by theatre companies like the 'Rocado Zulu Theatre' of Congo, the 'Groupe Nyogolon' of Mali, the 'Ensemble Koteba' and the 'Ki-Yi Mbock' of Ivory Coast are (still) unpublished. They exist, rather like the ritual, or other secular performance idioms which they wish to appropriate, only in performance. But even if they are later published, the authors would prefer to see their texts more as signposts for directors and actors than fixed and closed forms to which they should rigidly adhere.

The rough distinction we have sought to establish between a pre-1980s text-oriented and a post-1980s performance-oriented drama (but both firmly within the literate, university tradition of Francophone theatre) might suggest that plays in the former category are intellectual, unstagey and only good to be read, while those in the latter hold no appeal for the intellect. This would of course be incorrect. The later development has never been absent from the earlier plays. One need only read with a director's eyes 1960s or early 1970s plays like Guillaume Oyono-Mbia's *Trois prétendants ... un mari*,

Mba Evina's *Politicos*, Alexandre Kuma Ndumbe III's *Lisa, la putaine de* to realise what a lively theatrical event they would make, with their scenic composition and their expansion of dramatic space to encompass both the stage and the auditorium. And in spite of the preponderance of rhetoric in them, 1960s works like *L'Exil d'Albouri, Kondo le requin, La Tragédie du roi Christophe* remain visually impressive in their depiction of valor and battle scenes, their manipulation of space, especially in *L'Exil d'Albouri*, and their recourse to colourful funeral and enthronement ceremonies.

Conversely, the 'New Drama' plays, if we can call them that, however exciting as stage performances, explore issues that continue to appeal to the intellect long after production. A closer study in Part II of plays from both categories will better illustrate this point.

THE TRADITIONAL BACKGROUND IN SECULAR PERFORMANCES: SOME EXAMPLES

If ritual has been a factor in the shaping of Francophone drama, it is by no means the only performance genre to have done so. There are, throughout Francophone Africa, side by side with it but sometimes deriving from it, forms of *secular* performances whose quality as theatre and sometimes even as dramatic theatre has never failed to strike the observer. For example, this is how the French administrator Delafosse describes in 1916 what he saw in the Ivory Coast:

> I heard *griots* recite stories in which their heroes were made to speak; stories which in their hands came alive in theatrical scenes with several characters played by a single narrator. (Delafosse 1916: 353)

Since Delafosse, much research has been carried out into the region's diverse secular theatre forms by scholars like Diawara (1990: 28–30), Meillassoux (1964: 28–61), Brink (1977: 36, 61–5; 1978: 382–94), Arnoldi (1977) and many more. Their structure, functions and themes have received attention. Given this chapter's attempt to situate modern French-language African drama in a context of pre-existing theatre traditions, we will consider here at least three of these forms. Their intrinsic value and relevance to modern practices are the deciding factors in the choice.

One of the most popular forms of traditional theatre proper in Francophone Africa, and possibly the one referred to above by

Delafosse, is the oral narrative performance. Folktales depicting animal or human characters are an integral part of the cultural heritage of these societies and an example of such narratives. The physical and behavioural characteristics of animals like Bouki-the-Hyena, Leuk-the-Hare, Golo-the-Monkey in Birago Diop's appellation of them (1958) are a source of permanent delight to the audiences of young and old in these communities. Through their many adventures, told with economy and a sense of drama and excitement, are celebrated the traditional values of the group.

Another popular form of oral narrative is the epic. The 'African epic belt' which John Johnson (1986: 30) observes as stretching from the Sene-Gambia area of West Africa through the countries of the Sahel to Gabon, Zaire and Ruwanda-Burundi in Central Africa in fact coincides almost exactly with the Francophone region. In elaborately composed texts that sometimes run into thousands of lines, the societies of this region chronicle their long and colourful histories and the memories of their cultural heroes. Among the best known of these texts are the Soundjata epic of the Mandé people of Mali (Niane 1960), the Mwindo epic of the Nyanga of Zaire (Biebuyck 1971), the Da Monzon epic of the Bambara (Kesteloot *et al.* 1972) and the Silamaka and Poullori epic of the Peul of Macina (Séydou 1972).

But if these narratives are about fictional animal figures or, in the case of epics, about historical events, they are also works of art, conceived to please. A principal source of their pleasure lies in the handling of language by the *griot* or the oral narrative performer. His or her ability to evoke mental pictures of the scenes described (particularly important in epics with their numerous battles, marriages, enthronements and so on), to choose and pattern images that have the proper affective appeal, to achieve the right diction and voice modulations are all qualities expected of the *griot*.

No less important is his talent to use language to generate theatrical excitement. One example of such language use, in Tamsir Niane's *Soundjata ou l'épopée mandingue*, is the verbal battle that the narrator, attempting stichomythia, makes the young challenger and would-be emperor of the Mandinka engage in with the battle-experienced Soumaoro:

SOUMAORO Arrête, jeune homme. Je suis désormais roi du Mandigue; si
    tu veux la paix, retourne d'où tu viens...
SOUNDJATA Je reviens, Soumaoro, pour reprendre mon royaume. Si tu

veux la paix, tu dédommageras mes alliés et tu retourneras à Sosso où
tu es roi
SOUMAORO   Apprends donc que je suis l'igname sauvage des rochers, rien
ne me fera sortir du Mandigue
SOUNDJATA   Sache aussi que j'ai dans mon camp sept maîtres forgerons
qui feront éclater des rochers, alors igname je te mangerai
SOUMAORO   Je suis le champignon vénéneux qui fait vomir l'intrépide
SOUNDJATA   Moi je suis un coq affamé le poison ne me fait rien. (Niane
1960: 111–12)

But in conveying an exchange such as this, the *griot* does not simply
rely on words, however charged. He also seeks to create visual effect.
This he achieves by moving out of his role as narrator, banal
declaimer of speeches (especially in epics) to actually imitate the
characters he is depicting. He dramatises their actions through
gesture, facial expression, mime, movement and, sometimes, like his
religious counterpart in ritual, also through music and dance.

It is this combination in oral narrative performances of the arts of
oratory and acting that gives them, even if in a less elaborate way
than in ritual, their dimension of theatre. Less elaborate because
what the audience is treated to is not a case of several performers
interacting in an acting space, as Finnegan has observed (1970:
501–2), but of one man or woman acting several roles using a format
that is part drama, part narrative.

For a more developed traditional form of secular theatre in
Francophone Africa, one would need to turn to a type of comic
theatre complete with several actors (incidentally trained in the *do*),
a chorus, costumes and props practised by the Bambara people of
southern Mali. Labouret and Travélé, the first scholars to describe it,
characterise its productions as

real plays that are perfectly organised, and which use human actors to
dramatise vigorously-composed plots. (Labouret and Travélé 1924: 74)

Variously described in the literature as *kote-tlon*, *kote komo manyaga*
or *kote nyogolon*, this theatre is part of a larger spectacle of music, dance
and drama – the *kotéba* – which takes place during festive occasions
in the months following the harvest season (Arnoldi 1977; Brink
1978: 382–94; Ligier 1990: 149–53). A *kotéba* performance divides
into three distinct sequences: an opening ballet, a prologue and a
succession of short plays, the *kote-tlon* proper that can last from a few
seconds to fifteen minutes.

The opening ballet sequence consists of a circular dance, the *kote bamuku*, supported by rhythmic handclapping, song and drum music, in which a group of four drummers in a middle circle is surrounded by inner and outer circles of male and female dancers respectively. It is the visual aspect of this dance formation, representing in its rotating concentric circles the shape of a huge snail, that gives its name to the *kotéba*, a word derived from *kote* (snail) and *ba* (giant).

The second phase of a *kotéba* spectacle, the prologue, consists of a song-dance, the *kaga* and a few short mimed sketches such as the 'Blacksmith Dance' or the 'Dance of the Buffoon' performed by young uninitiated boys (Brink 1978: 387). In a convention reminiscent of the warning issued by many a fiction writer that all events and characters in books are imaginary and that any resemblance to real events and persons is fortuitous, the performers reassure their adult spectators (the real target of the satire to follow) of the playful and fictional nature of the forthcoming representations. This reassurance is provided by their constant reference to their social status as non-initiates, with its connotations of immaturity, and the buffoonery in which they engage through the imitation of culturally defined clowns like the *koredugaw*. Their licentious gestures and songs complete the reassurance while at the same time prefiguring the comic and satiric modes in which the plays that follow are keyed.

The performance proper of these plays, collectively called the *kote-tlon*, constitutes the third and final phase of the *kotéba*. As many as twenty of these plays can be represented in one evening. The characters are all social or physical stereotypes: the boastful hunter, the Tartuffe-like *marabout*, the bow-legged man. More recent character types, representing modern society, are the tax-collector and the European.

Social criticism is the dominant theme. *Kote-tlon* drama is conservative and patriarchal in its social vision and preaches a rigid adherence to normative behaviour patterns and values, especially for women, who are forever depicted as fickle, adulterous and therefore potentially disruptive of the social order. But this conservatism is asserted, in the end, only after enough transgressive free rein has been given to the bawdy, the licentious and the irreverent of constituted order and values.

Like all theatre, the *kote-tlon*, as Brink's studies have shown, is regulated by fixed conventions (Brink 1978: 391). Characters, for example, are identified through costume, movement and song. Thus the 'European' carries a watch which he is made to consult at ridiculously short intervals. The adulterous woman (a role played by a man) dresses ostentatiously with pearls in her hair and numerous bracelets (Labouret 1928: 79). Convention also governs the enactment of activities such as hunting, cooking or farming. These are rendered either through elaborate stylised movements, or sound effects mimetically represented. Thus a man playing a musical instrument can render sounds associated with these instruments rather than actually play it on stage. In the absence of scenery, the identification of scenic space and theatrical time is also subject to precise conventions that presuppose a knowledge of the culture.

Despite its standardised nature with regard to themes, characters and plot outline, *kote-tlon* drama does make room for individual inventiveness. Individual performers are judged by their ability to create new dialogue, add unexpected twists to the action and to display skill in miming, dancing or singing.

A unique theatrical form in Francophone Africa worth mentioning as a final example of secular performance is the 'ballet of animals' or *sougounougou* in the Odienné province of the Upper Ivory Coast, described by Prouteaux (1929). The performers of this 'ballet' (actually not strictly speaking a ballet in so far as it contains speech) consist of a chorus of seven or eight hunters and a distinct group of actors comprised of the stock character Nanzégé, his beautiful wife Niofolityé, a hunter, a spirit figure and various animal characters, from lions to porcupines.

A distinguishing feature of this theatre is its very detailed costuming, with the chorus members conventionally wearing old hats and carrying hunting implements; Nanzégé dressed in a pair of knee-length shorts and holding a walking-stick and his wife (a role also played by a young male) tying her head with a scarf, her waist with a piece of cloth and wearing a coral necklace. The various animal roles are played by young men of different ages who wear stylised animal-skin masks and make-up and either stoop as they walk, go on all fours using sticks to lengthen their arms or, as in the case of antelopes, maintain an upright posture.

A *sougounougou* performance is divided into two parts – an opening sequence during which the chorus sings its way up to the acting arena and engages in farcical knockabouts and gags that delight the arriving audience, while giving it time to settle down, and a play session proper. This consists of the dramatisation of the many misadventures of Nanzégé and, as is to be expected in an 'animal ballet', of hunting expedition scenes.

An irreverent, boastful and happy-go-lucky young man, Nanzégé is always quick to criticise in others weaknesses of which he himself is guilty. If it is not the hunters who are cowardly, it is the village head who is irresponsible. Sometimes religion, both traditional and Islamic, provides the butt of his ridicule. An example of such satire is contained in a sketch described by Prouteaux, in which the hero is shown holding his slate of Koranic verses upside down and interspersing his chanting with the most salacious jokes and irreverent remarks (Prouteaux 1929: 464). Such conduct gets him into difficulties. Additionally, he has to contend with men who constantly seduce his wife in his presence and, on occasion, actually abduct her. It is his reactions to these problems that is the source of delight for the audience. And Nanzégé's reactions range from threats of suicide that are never carried out, once he is confronted with the reality of death, to tearful wailing, fights and other stratagems that come to naught.

In the end, however, he always manages to triumph. Not through his efforts, but through the devotion of his wife who uses her magical powers to escape from her abductors, and to solve whatever problems he might have encountered in her absence.

Although Nanzégé's adventures constitute an important part of the performance, they are only part of the entertainment. Most of this is generated by the skills of the performers as dancers and mimes. And there is plenty of opportunity to demonstrate such talent, especially the latter, in the dramatised hunting scenes. Here, the ability both to mime with realism the movements of the hunter as he stalks his prey, crouches, crawls and takes aim and to convey his states of mind; as well as the ability to portray the behaviour of the animal sensing danger, cocking its ears and breaking into a gallop, are the benchmarks of a successful performance.

TRADITIONAL SECULAR THEATRE AND FRANCOPHONE DRAMA

If the secular tradition of theatre in Francophone Africa has been described in some detail, it is because of the major influence it exerts on the region's modern drama. Oral narratives, for example, have been adapted for the stage in a variety of plays like *La Tortue qui chante, Les Aventures de Yévi aux pays des monstres* by Senouvo Zinsou and *L'Os de Mor Lam* by Birago Diop, which are all based on folk-tales. Eugène Dervain's *La Reine scélérate, La Langue et le scorpion*, Charles Nokan's *Abraha Pokou*, Sory Konaké's *Le Grand destin de Soundjata* are based on epics. But when it is not the narrative itself that is put in dramatic form, it is its content that provides the subject-matter, as is the case with the scores of history plays that constitute the bulk of the dramatic production of Francophone Africa.

These history plays have not only borrowed format and subject from the epic form, they have also appropriated some of its formal. features, conventions and procedures. One such feature character-istic of the epic is its tendency to move from the world of observable historical facts to which it is moored and of which it purports to be an account into that of fantasy and magic; to crystallise all the action around a central figure, the hero, whose deeds are then magnified, embellished and swamped in an atmosphere of the supernatural, to confer mythical status on him. Thus Soundjata in Niane's version of the narrative is born to a mother who is half-buffalo and half-woman. Soundjata miraculously gains the power of his limbs after a seven-year period of congenital paralysis and uproots an enormous baobab tree in a show of supernatural strength.

This mythical and fantastic imagination of the oral narrator/performer is one that is discernible in the Francophone playwright, especially the historical playwright. His central character, when the play starts, be he, for example, a Patrice Lumumba in *Une Saison au Congo*, an Albouri or a Gbéhanzin in *Kondo le requin*, is usually an ordinary human being, grappling with problems which however intractable are very human: the cultural, economic and political reconstruction of a disunited and hitherto colonised society in the case of Lumumba; the defence of sovereignty against the vastly superior might of the French in the case of Albouri and Gbéhanzin. By the time the play ends, however, these very human and social forces in conflict have been endowed, as in the epic, with non-human qualities, with the heroes invariably achieving near-mythical stature and embodying in defeat (they are usually defeated) that which is noblest in their societies.

Thus Lumumba becomes 'an invincible idea', 'pollen dust', 'a tree', while Albouri, the symbol of Djoloff independence, becomes 'a star broken free from the heavens' and, with his people, 'eternal spirit wanderers galloping across oceans at full bridle and haunting the dreams of the brave' (Ndao 1967: 90). The defeat of the hero, in other words, is transcended by a drive towards mythical immortality. His physical death is transmuted into moral triumph.

This epic quality of the Francophone history play is forcefully brought out by Oyie Ndzie when he observes:

Francophone drama practice becomes *ipso facto* mythological; that is, a 'utopian reconstruction of the real'. The heroes and situations depicted are held up as sublime examples, ultimate references and Olympian values. They crystallise all the quintessential qualities of perfection of the society to which they are held up. (1985a: 30)

Another formal feature of the oral (historical) narrative in the Francophone African play is the episodic nature of the action. The organisation of events in plays like *Kondo le requin*, *L'Exil d'Albouri*, *La Mort de Chaka* or, especially, *Abraha Pokou*, takes its interest mainly from what it gradually reveals of the hero's character, rather than from a sequential plot construction that depicts development and change. It is principally concerned with exhibiting, in a series of representative episodes, idealised qualities of character in the heroes that are supposed to exemplify certain permanent truths or move audiences to emulate them.

But Francophone drama has not only used the format, subjects and some of the formal procedures of the oral narrative. Even the performer of this form, the *griot*, has become an important dramatic character in modern plays. As Djeli Madi in *Le Grand destin de Soundjata*, Latsoukabé in Amadou Cissé's *Les Derniers jours de lat Dior*, Maliba in Ndao's *Le Fils de l'Almamy*, Le Revenant Provocateur in Maxime Ndébéka's *Equatorium*, the Public Entertainer in Sylvain Bemba's *L'Homme qui tua le crocodile*, the *griot* functions as a kind of presenter of the play, commentator on its action and hidden meanings and link between the stage and the auditorium. But in plays like Eugène Dervain's *La Reine scélérate* or Ndao's *L'Exil d'Albouri*, he is integrated as a character. In fact, in the former play he is a key actor as it is his defection to the Court of the King of Koré that sparks off the murderous conflict between the kingdoms of Ségou and Koré. The *griot*'s technique of acting several characters in the course of the same performance is also widely used in a play like *On joue la comédie*, in which the Presenter Xuma acts the hero Chaka in a playlet within the play, *Equatorium*, where the roles of the Spectator-Comedian and Minister of Culture, Native Affairs and Human Duties are also played by one actor.

But Francophone theatre has done more than just integrate the *griot* as a dramatic character. It has also sought inspiration from his improvisational style of acting. Unlike the modern performer of a scripted play, who is constrained by the written text, literally effacing himself behind the role as it has been conceived by the playwright, respectful of the set speeches and submitting to the pace of events as determined by the producer, the performer of an oral narrative is, to a much larger extent, his own master.

Because the text of his performance (epic, folktale, *kote-tlon* or *sougounougou* play and so on) exists only in his memory and even then only as what a critic describes 'as an outline of a verbal structure... suggestive signposts... of a discourse that is still in the future' (Irele 1990: 258), he is at liberty within the plot outline to invent dialogue, speeches and expressions and to display gestures and movements that carry the badge of his inventiveness.

In the traditional oral theatre, in other words, what counts is not so much the communication of meaning or the outcome of a plot action. These are in any case well known. It is what Biodun Jeyifo has called in connection with the Nigerian Travelling Theatre performances 'the sheer power and expressiveness of the [performers'] stage presence and acts' (Jeyifo 1984: 22). It is an *actor's* theatre *par excellence*; the one dreamed of by Artaud watching Balinese performances, where meaning is not prosaically represented in words alone but finds 'objective materialisation' (Artaud 1958: 61) in movement, gesture, song and so on. A theatre, put differently, where non-verbal language, like a Flaubertian sentence, aspires to become the thing represented, in its materiality and sensuousness almost, and not its medium of representation.

It is this improvisational acting style, massively appropriated by modern popular theatrical forms all over Africa – the kantata and concert party of Togo, the Yoruba Travelling Theatre studied by Jeyifo, the theatre of Daniel Ndo and Deiv Moktoi of Cameroon – that has recently been systematised by performance-oriented Francophone literary dramatists, and especially, theatre practitioners. This acting style is implied in many earlier Francophone plays, for example *Trois prétendants... un mari* and *Lisa, la putaine de*, but it is in more recent ones like *On joue la comédie* that it has been fully explored. And as Hourantier (1984: 35–58) and Kotchy (1984: 232–53) have shown, it is at the centre of the endeavours of various theatre companies that emerged in the Ivory Coast in the late 1970s. Earliest among these was Griotique, founded by the Abidjan University lecturer Niangoran Porquet. This is how the latter describes his technique, *griotisation*:

The totality of artistico-scenic devices which, by integrating poetry, music, choreography and theatre, and by using mime and appropriate gestures, seek to highlight the literary, historical and social values of Africans. (in Hourantier 1984: 44–5)

This troupe produced no plays. What it mounted instead were sessions of poetry, legend and folktale recitals, like the performances of the *griot* which it sought to apply to modern circumstances. And, like these, its performances were real theatrical events during which vocal, bodily and facial resources were combined in recital to make memorable visual and auditory events of purely narrated texts.

Another important troupe to emerge during this period is the Kotéba Ensemble by the Guinean-born Ivorian Souleymane Koly. Its emphasis is on collective creation. Once a theme, suggested by the director, is agreed upon by the cast, roles are chosen by the actors on the basis of their competence. Dialogue is then improvised within the broad framework of the story-line, as are movements. The role of director in the Kotéba Ensemble is reduced to that of coordinator of the various activities of the performers themselves into a harmonious whole. As with the Griotique, the Kotéba Ensemble productions are mostly dance-dramas, where spoken parts alternate, as in a traditional oral performance, with sung or danced parts.

The third and perhaps most substantial company of this period was that of Sidiki Bakaba, a theatre arts professional, former student of the French director Jean-Marie Serreau and devotee, Kotchy tells us, of the Ivorian television folktale perfomer Okro. An evening's performance by Bakaba's troupe consists not of a single play but, like a *kote-tlon* performance, of several sketches, loosely strung together and illustrating the same theme. His theatre also prides itself in being non-illusionistic. Scene, costume and role-changes are all effected in full view of the audience with a director who sometimes suddenly moves from his seat among the spectators to act a role on stage; a stage expanded to include the wings and conceived on two levels: a larger level where the action takes place and a smaller one where it is narrated (Kotchy 1984: 248).

Sidiki Bakaba came to prominence in the Ivory Coast with a popular play, *C'est quoi même*, on the fate of the urban poor whose pidginised French gives the play its title, and a notable production of Zaourou's *L'Œil* that will be discussed in Part II, chapter 11.

One final feature of Francophone drama borrowed from traditional theatre is worth mentioning. It is the transactional relationship with the audience that is encouraged and sometimes provided for in plays like *Guédio, On joue la comédie, Monsieur Thogo-Gnini* and (in their opening scenes) *La Tragédie du roi Christophe* and *Une Saison au Congo*. This relationship which, as has been observed, is catered for often by the expansion of scenic space to include the auditorium, takes the form of choral singing, dancing and sometimes verbal exchanges between pit and stage. It also accounts for the quality of festiveness that surrounds many of these plays.

If, as we have observed, there has been a more systematic cultivation of performance values in recent Francophone theatre, the reasons for this development, it needs to be pointed out, vary between theatre practitioners. One such reason, already noted, is the desire to make the contents of serious drama more accessible to a wider audience of ordinary people. Therefore, integrating more assiduously in plays, as has been done lately, the people's performance mode is a means of achieving such accessibility. But for some of the more activist playwrights like Zaourou, Liking and Zinsou, the option for a performance orientation to their drama is more than a mere gesture to rural/traditional or urban popular forms, or an exercise in experimentation. Their relationship to these forms is not only artistic, in other words, it conveys a political statement.

To bring these forms to the centre of the modern, dramatic stage – a stage on which they had been relatively marginalised, or sometimes reduced to folkloristic status – is, as Wa Thiongo has argued in relation to the use of African languages in modern literature (Ngugi 1986), to promote these forms socially and culturally and, by extension, to rehabilitate the people whose performance idioms they are. It is, in other words, to bring people and forms to centre-stage in a metaphorical, political and not just literal, sense.

But two points need raising immediately in relation to this option. The first point is that while the use of African performance media is a positive step (from a cultural/nationalist point of view), it is clearly an insufficient one. For the ability to communicate theatrically, which the use of these media facilitate, does not in itself guarantee the communication of *interesting* views or, for that matter, of *any* views at all. At the very worst, the deployment of these forms could become an end in itself. And this is a powerful temptation, considering the large, popular and tourist market that exists for the display of such forms, and the handsome commercial returns that could be reaped from exploiting it. Souleymane Koly and his Kotéba Ensemble seem to have recognised this in the Ivory Coast.

But even when views are communicated, the fact that such communication is done in an African theatrical language does not mean that the message will be necessarily wholesome or challenging. On the contrary, such views as the dramatist may wish to transmit can sometimes be unprogressive: either confirming the spectators' ancient and worst prejudices, or, as has been observed by Hourantier in connection with some of Souleymane Koly's productions, indulging their escapist fantasies (Hourantier 1984: 50).

The second point worth raising relates to the fact that even if the playwright's message is critical and stimulating, its accessibiliity is not necessarily guaranteed by the use of African theatrical forms. Some of these forms, especially the ritual performances, were, and remain, élite idioms even within traditional societies, understood only by a small and privileged minority of initiates and elders. To use them, therefore, on the modern Francophone stage, as Werewere Liking does, for example, and to assume that because they are African, they will be automatically understood by all Africans, is clearly to subscribe to a unanimist view of African societies as a seamless whole, undifferentiated by ethnicity, gender and class.

Such a view makes sense, however, if it is remembered, in the case of Liking, that she is working within a problematic of cultural nationalism whose task has been, since the days of Senghor, for Francophone Africa, to define a monolithic 'African' cultural identity, considered popular, which is then held up in contrast to an equally monolithic 'Western' identity, deemed élitist. But that African spectators should be among the most vocal in condemning Werewere Liking's plays as recondite, avant-garde and élitist should put critics on guard against her facile assumptions, and be a reminder that while these constructs and assumptions are ideologically useful in anti-colonial cultural wars, they remain sociologically naive and inaccurate.

Of course, not all recent Francophone dramatists are using their performance-oriented dramas as strategic acts to prosecute such cultural-nationalist wars. Some, like Senouvo Zinsou, are using them to prosecute intra-African battles. What interests Zinsou is not so much an African theatrical culture that must be defined and forged against an imposed Western theatrical culture, but an African *popular* theatrical culture that must be defined against an equally African, but *élite*, theatrical culture. To Zinsou, in other words, the word 'popular' does not refer indiscriminately to any and every performance idiom in the traditional sector. He reserves its use for those forms that are associated with the non-privileged majority in both the traditional and modern sectors of African societies. This is why he uses neither rituals nor very Westernised theatrical forms in his plays. He taps, instead, on the popular forms in both spheres: the traditional story-telling and *kotéba*-type performances of the rural areas, and the popular, concert party forms to which they have given rise in the urban setting.

So the shift to a performance dimension, while an important feature of recent Francophone theatre, is clearly not a panacea for the problems with which this theatre is grappling. Just as the use of French speech and theatre forms does not automatically signify unprogressive theatre, so the use of an African theatrical language and, occasionally, even speech does not guarantee progressive theatre. The challenge facing performance-oriented Francophone dramatists would be both to communicate and to stimulate. How playwrights like Zaourou, Werewere Liking and Zinsou have met this challenge will be examined when I discuss their plays in Part II.

But before we get to that, it will be necessary to look at the process of transition through which modern drama emerged in Francophone Africa from the traditional theatre forms that have been discussed above.

CHAPTER 2

From oral performances to modern drama: on the growth and development of a genre

African drama in the French language emerged only·in the inter-war years, but modern dramatic activities in Francophone Africa have been traced by historians of theatre in this region to the turn of the twentieth century. The centres for these activities were Roman Catholic schools where religious plays and scenes from the Bible – the nativity, the passion, the crucifixion and so on – were performed by pupils as part of their new religious education and in observance of various feasts of the Christian and school calendars. Robert Cornevin singles out Senegal, Benin and the Cameroon – where a modern theatre in the local languages was encouraged by the then colonising Germans – as among the countries where a religious school theatre was particularly active (1970: 44–50).

In the public schools in the region, theatre was also encouraged. But here the plays performed were mostly the farces and comedies of Molière – *Maître Pathelin* and *Le Malade imaginaire* seem to have been favourites – plays by Courteline, Labiche and Racine's comedy *Les Plaideurs*, which is reported by Amon D'Aby to have been performed by students of the Ecole Primaire Supérieure de Bingerville in the Ivory Coast (D'Aby 1988: 19). The Ivory Coast also experienced a special form of modern theatre in the 1920s. This came from the then neighbouring Gold Coast from where secondary school pupils constituted themselves into itinerant acting groups which toured the border regions of both countries during the vacation, performing, in the common languages, scenes of daily life (D'Aby 1988: 16). In Senegal, the administrative, economic and intellectual capital of the then French West African Federation, modern theatre also came by way of the performances of visiting French troupes en route to South America.

But if modern theatrical activities had existed in colonial French-speaking Africa from the earliest days of France's involvement in the continent, it was not until 1933 that the first African play in French was written. This was *La Dernière Entrevue de Béhanzin et de Bayol*, a dramatic sketch by the Dahomean students at the Ecole William Ponty on the historic encounter between the proud and independent nineteenth-century monarch of Dahomey, Béhanzin, and an expansionist Frenchman determined to conquer his territory. Although the piece has not survived, a contemporary review of it gives a fair idea of its content:

The dances and songs which opened and closed the play, the proud and haughty attitude of the brutal despot... all that was rendered with vigour and conviction in a manner that clearly impressed the audience. The discussion, rather long winded, between the Frenchman who defends his rights and the chief who feels his power threatened yielded moments of real tension. (Cornevin 1970: 56–57)

The composition of this play in 1933 and its performance that year in school celebrations to mark the new academic year were not, however, fortuitous acts. They were not sudden bursts of creative inspiration in the ways of modern drama on the part of students who have been nurtured on oral theatrical forms, and whose only exposure to Western drama had been in the form of school readings and performances of Molière. They were the result of a process that was inscribed in the pedagogical activities of the Ecole William Ponty – that 'laboratory' as it has been called – of Francophone African drama (Condé 1978: 29–35; Jukpor 1982: 47–64; Mouralis 1986: 130–40; Traoré 1971: 37–48).

Founded in 1903 in Saint Louis in Senegal and transferred in 1913 to the island of Gorée in the same country, the Ecole William Ponty had as its principal vocation the training of what William Ponty, the governor-general after whom it was named, described as 'reliable auxiliaries of [France's] civilising mission' (in Gary Warner 1976: 105). Its students were recruited throughout the colonies of the French West African Federation by competitive examination and, on graduation, they proceeded to occupy teaching, paramedical and junior administrative positions in the colonial administrations of their countries.

An important component of the school's syllabus was the so-called 'devoirs de vacances' (Traoré 1958: 48–50). These holiday assignments, given to students proceeding to their third and final year of study, involved elementary research during the long vacation into aspects of the folklore, traditional customs and practices of their respective peoples. The investigation took the form of interviews with village elders, oral historians, as well as observation. On their return to college after the holidays, the students would be asked to write up their findings into extended essays.

Three basic motives informed the 'holiday assignment' idea. The first was to improve the French-language writing and compositional skills of the students. Another was to give them an intellectual rootedness into their traditional cultures at a time when they ran the risk of total alienation from them as a result of their new French education. But a third motive, discerned by Warner, was not so disinterested. He has argued that it corresponded to the need, increasingly felt by the colonial authorities in the late 1920s and 1930s, to better understand, for the purposes of efficient control, what a French Inspector of Education at the time, M. Charton, called 'la mentalité indigène' (Gary Warner 1976: 106). Quoting the 1931 speech by the governor-general,

We expect the educated natives to reveal to us some of the secrets of their peoples' soul, to guide our action, to help us achieve through intelligent and sympathetic understanding this rapprochement of the races which is one of the levers of our mission (Warner 1976: 106)

Warner has shown persuasively that the 'holiday assignment' idea, with what it revealed to the French educators at William Ponty of 'the native mind', was an expression of this new policy orientation.

But whatever the reasons ultimately for their institution, these assignments provided the subjects and framework for the earliest African plays in French. Students were asked to adapt the best of them for stage performance – which is how *La Dernière Entrevue de Béhanzin et de Bayol* came to be produced.

From 1933, a steady stream of dramas flowed from the students' pens. After the Béhanzin play came, in 1934, *Le Mariage de Sika* and in 1935 *L'Election d'un roi au Dahomey*, both by the Dahomean students at Ponty, with the second play performed before an audience of more than a thousand spectators. The 1935/36 academic year saw the triumph of the Ivorian students, with Bernard Dadié's play on the ritual of electing and crowning a chief among the Sanwi people of the Ivory Coast, *Assémien Déhylé*. The year 1937 saw the composition of many more sketches: a historical piece, along the lines of the Dahomean 1933 play, by Guinean students entitled *L'Entrevue de Samory et du Capitaine Péroz*; *La Ruse de Diegué* by the Malians on the twelfth-century Mandinka king Sunjata, a social satire by Ivorians on traditional marriage customs, *Les Prétendants rivaux* and *Sokamé* by Dahomeans on the theme of ritual sacrifice (Cornevin 1970: 54–60). The best of these early dramatic compositions, like Dadié's *Assémien Déhylé*, were taken on tour to the capitals of the other West African colonies in the Federation and then to Paris in 1937 for the Colonial Exhibition, where they were enthusiastically received; they were later published in one of the cultural organs of French West Africa, *L'Education Africaine.*

If the plays of this early period were the product of the students, the latter cannot be said to have been totally in control of their production. Their French teachers saw to it that the theatre remained within the role prescribed for it in the school: a source of entertainment, a release from the tedium of academic work and *not* a medium for the criticism of the colonial order. This means they did more than just contract the length of plays or correct grammatical errors, contrary to Charles Béart's assertion in connection with Dadié's play:

I cut out a good many portions ... corrected errors of syntax; but not a single line is mine. (quoted in D'Aby 1988: 28)

They might not have added lines, but they carefully oriented the choice of subject – in a move Traoré equates with censorship – to the non-political area of traditional beliefs, social customs and practices. This policy, combined with the students' awareness of their French audience's thirst for the exotic, accounts for the preponderance of sketches such as have been listed above on marriage customs, royal election and coronation rituals, sacrificial rites and so on *and* their folkloristic mode of presentation.

History was not a proscribed area for dramatic works; but when a historical topic was chosen, like *La Dernière entrevue de Béhanzin et de Bayol* or *L'Entrevue de Samory et du Capitaine Péroz*, the African historical past was often presented in a deprecatory manner consistent with official colonial history. Thus in the Samory-Péroz play, the Mandinka monarch, Warner explains (1976: 109), is depicted as a 'brigand', a 'terrorist', an impediment to the civilising mission of France that Péroz was prosecuting. This depiction earned the approval of the colonial authorities, who described it as 'an accurate and fine piece of historical reconstruction' (in Cornevin 1970: 59). Similarly, the official review referred to earlier of the Béhanzin/Bayol encounter talks satisfyingly of 'the proud and haughty attitude of the brutal despot' (in Cornevin 1970: 56).

Such was the officially-encouraged negative presentation of Africa, her past and her customs, reflected in early Francophone drama that honest Frenchmen like M. Maupoil, worried by its implications, raised an alarm:

We would especially not want Africans to echo some of the current nefarious legends on their ancestors. By depicting some of the most representative characters of their past – kings, priests ... from the angle of tyranny ... they run the risk of providing ammunition to those Europeans ... who still claim that no civilisation has ever touched Africa. In the event in which [Africans] decide to depict Béhanzin or King Gléglé, we would like to see them respect history and surround themselves with *disinterested* advice. (in Traoré 1958: 101 emphasis mine).

But whatever the shortcomings of the Ponty School theatre tradition, it remained the decisive factor in the emergence of Francophone literary drama. Important theatrical careers like those of the Guinean Fodéba Keita, founder in Paris in 1949 of the first professional African troupe, Theatre Africain; of Dadié, the first major Francophone dramatist; of Amon D'Aby and Coffi Gadeau, significant Ivorian playwrights, were subsequently built on it. And even for those later dramatists who did not attend the school, the convention of theatre which it established, with its predilection for social and historical themes, loose plot structures, singing and dancing interludes, remained influential.

The next important factor in the development of Francophone theatre after William Ponty was the setting up throughout the Federation of cultural centres with library, public lecture, cinema and, of course, theatre facilities. A few of those centres already existed but it was not until 1953, with the transfer of Bernard Cornut-Gentil from French Equatorial Africa to the post of Governor-General in West Africa, that the idea became generalised. Within two years of his appointment he had had 117 more centres constructed in virtually all the district capitals and major regions of the Federation (Cornevin 1970: 109). He saw these centres as the necessary successors to William Ponty (where incidentally all theatrical activity had ceased by 1949 when it concentrated exclusively on academic work) in stimulating theatrical creativity among Francophones. And he enjoined their directors not to allow them to be transformed into 'sanctuaries' for a Westernised élite contemptuous of its traditional culture, but to promote them as meeting-places for the cross-fertilisation of ideas and the production, similar to William Ponty, of theatrical styles that derived from traditional and modern sources (Cornevin 1970: 109).

The cultural centres did fulfil the role envisioned for them. Although they left no major plays, they created a favourable climate of opinion for and increased popular interest in the modern theatre. Most centres reported at least an annual performance and some, like those in Rufisque and Saint-Louis in Senegal, put on monthly performances of locally composed plays in French or African languages. These activities became sufficiently significant to warrant regular columns in the cultural pages of *Traits d'Union*.

Drama competitions, promoted by the centre directors, provided an additional impetus to the growth of early Francophone drama. A system of elimination within and between colonies got the best centres to compete against one another in quarter- and semi-final championships, until a federal winner (whose play was then broadcast on Radio-Dakar for the entire Federation) emerged. The performances had to be in French except for the songs, and were limited to one and a half hours and twenty-five participants.

These inter-centre drama competitions lasted only three years (1955–7) and collapsed with the demise in 1958 of the French West African Federation. But, like the William Ponty School before them, they had advanced the cause of modern theatre in Francophone Africa. New troupes had been established in the various colonies for the competitions – participation or success in which became a question of territorial honour – and old ones came into federal prominence. It is interesting to note that the idea of drama competitions established by the centres and the format of their rules survived into the post-colonial era in states like contemporary Niger (Beik 1987) and the socialist Guinea of Sékou Touré – 1958–82 (Touré 1987: 86–96), Mali (Richard and Mazauric 1990: 38–43) and Burkina Faso (Guingané 1990: 67–72).

The immediate pre- and post-Independence period saw the institution of several practical measures by the French government to support the theatre in Francophone Africa. Among these were the construction of the modest Théâtre du Palais in Dakar, later replaced by the independent government with the grand Theatre Daniel Sorano, complete with a Conservatory of the Dramatic Arts, an African Ballet troupe, a theatre company proper and a traditional ensemble of *griots* (Senghor 1985: 5–34); the establishment of theatre arts institutes like the Ecole des Beaux Arts of Dakar, the Ecole Normale d'Art Dramatique in the Ivory Coast and the Institut National des Arts both in Abidjan and Bamako; and the creation of a scholarship fund for the training in Paris of Francophones in the theatre arts.

France also financed tours by very many French troupes to Francophone Africa (fourteen between 1963 and 1968), including one by Jean Vilar which visited sixteen towns and cities in 1966. And this assistance does not include the visits by theatre academics like Jacques Schérer or practitioners like Henri Cordreaux, Raymond Hermantier and George Toussaint who organised workshops and seminars for the budding dramatists of Francophone Africa (Cornevin 1970: 165–9; Edebiri 1984b: 168–79).

A third factor (after Ponty and the cultural centres), and perhaps the single most important factor in the growth of Francophone drama, was the establishment in 1966 by the French Office de la Coopération Radiophonique of an Inter-African Radio Drama Competition. The only requirement for participation was to be sub-Saharan African and to submit a play in French which was hitherto unpublished or unbroadcast. The subject and length were left entirely to the discretion of the author. Two prizes could be won: the first was a Listeners' Prize. The second was judged by a panel selected from theatre critics, radio representatives from the twenty participating countries, four officials of the African Cultural Institute and a representative of the French Ministry of Cooperation. This prize consists of a scholarship for the winner to pursue theatre studies in France and a subvention for his play to be taken on tour to other Francophone countries (Cornevin 1970: 157–62; Edebiri 1984b: 168–79; Ligier 1982: 30–44).

In 1967, when the first playscripts were invited, 130 were received in under six months. Nine were selected and broadcast on the radio networks of all the participating countries. By 1969, the competition had become an annual event. It became so popular that within twelve years of its institution, by 1978 that is, it had attracted more than 4,000 plays. Cameroon topped the list with 845 plays, then came the Congo with 531 plays and then Zaire with 513, Benin with 310 and Senegal with 289 (Ligier 1982: 37).

But the drama competition's organising body, the Office de la Coopération Radiophonique, did more than just award monetary prizes or broadcast the winning plays. The best of these were also published in the Répertoire Théâtral Africain series of French Radio (the ORTF), an initiative which made this organisation, like P. J. Oswald of France, the Protestant Centre du Livre Evangélique editions in Cameroon, Présence Africaine and Les Nouvelles Editions Africaines – jointly owned by Francophone African government and French private publishing interests – one of the major publishers of Francophone drama.

Scores of playwrights have launched out on successful dramatic careers thanks to this competition, whose international audience and publication possibilities have provided them with the necessary stimulation. Among these playwrights are Sylvain Bemba, Sony Labou Tansi, Senouvo Zinsou, Jean Pliya, Abdou Anta Ka, Gaoussou Diawarra, Guillaume Oyono-Mbia, Amadou Koné, Werewere Liking and Kossi Efoui. Ligier's study carried out in 1978 showed that more than 80 per cent of all Francophone plays then were competition entries (Ligier 1982: 35). The availability of such a wide range of playtexts led additionally to the growth of troupes.

The competition celebrated its twenty-third anniversary in 1993. In 1992, it changed its name to Radio France International-Théâtre, and offered participation to all Francophones, from Vietnam to Québec, and not just to sub-Saharan French-language African dramatists.

Equally important to the development of the theatre in the Francophone region have been the World Festivals of Negro Arts; these have devoted a large part to drama. The first festival took place in Dakar in 1966 and was important in that it brought to French-speaking Africa for the first time Aimé Césaire's *La Tragédie du roi Christophe*, a play which revealed to Francophones the rich possibilities of the theatre for a serious meditation on issues of history, politics and society within the format of combined Western and traditional African theatrical styles. The 1966 festival also consecrated the reputation of Senegal (then under the leadership of the poet-president Léopold Senghor) as an important sub-Saharan capital of the modern arts and, with its visiting troupes and their productions, acted as a stimulus to the creative activity of its men and women of the theatre.

The second festival was held in Algiers in 1969. It saw not only the participation of many Francophone countries but also the triumph of Cheik Ndao's *L'Exil d'Albouri* and Bernard Dadié's *Monsieur Thogo-*

Gnini, which won first and second prize respectively. This was followed in 1977 by the Festival of Negro and African Arts and Culture which took place in Lagos, again with strong Francophone participation symbolised by the enthusiastic reception of Zinsou's *On joue la comédie*.

Francophone theatre continued to benefit in the 1980s from various supporting measures. However, not many of these came from the national governments. At best, governments have remained indifferent and at worst suspicious of, or even hostile to, an artistic activity which was becoming increasingly critical of the post-colonial order, and which they were and are therefore anxious to show up as élitist and non-developmental. Where there have been active national efforts to promote the theatre – beyond the early creation of national companies with their inevitable dance troupe components – like in Sékou Touré's Guinea, Mali, Niger, Burkina Faso, the result, as has been observed, has tended to be a theatre of social or political propaganda.

No proper theatre buildings exist in most Francophone countries. Apart from the Daniel Sorano in Dakar, most theatres are either a part of sports complexes as in Mali or, in a telling statement on governmental designs on theatre activity, of National or Peoples' Parliaments in countries like Togo, Cameroon, Burkina Faso, Guinea and the Congo.

In the absence, then, of any serious and sustained national government assistance, Francophone theatre has continued to rely on outside help and the French, combining a traditional love of the arts with a keen recognition of the importance of those of Africa to the spread of their language, have not failed to give it. The nature of their help has not changed much from the days of Governor Cornut-Gentile. Now, however, they are not constructing cultural centres as such – although they occasionally renovate dilapidated ones – but rather are making theirs available to local companies for a small fee.

In the Congo, for example, where French help to theatrical activity has been very significant – forming part of a bilateral Cooperation Agreement with that country – the French Cultural Centre of Brazzaville decided in 1984 to professionalise and promote one of that country's private troupes: Labou Tansi's Rocado Zulu Theatre. As part of the agreement with this company, a French director has been sponsored each year from 1984 to co-produce a play with a local counterpart. Thus, in 1984 Guy Lenoir produced *La Peau cassee* with Labou Tansi. In 1985, it was Pierre Vial who, working with his Congolese counterpart Pascal Nzonzi, staged *La Rue des Mouches*. In 1986 Daniel Mesguish, director of the Théâtre Gerard Philippe, produced *Antoine m'a vendu son destin*. Other French directors who have participated in the programme include Michel Rostain in 1986 and the late Jean-Pierre Klein in 1987. Assistance to the theatre in the Congo has also included the secondment to the National Theatre Company of the theatre academic and practitioner Jacqueline Leloup, the renovation of the Bacongo Cultural Centre and the Centre de Formation et de Recherche en Arts Dramatiques and the expansion of France's own centres in Brazzaville and in Pointe-Noire (Baños-Robles 1990: 134–9).

On the regional level, France's recent contribution to Francophone theatre has taken the form of the sponsorship of African companies to the various international theatre festivals held in France: in Avignon, Nancy, Bordeaux and Limoges. The Limoges Festival International des Francophonies especially has been closely involved with African theatre. Founded in 1983 by Pierre Debauche and Monique Blin with the help of the French Ministry of Culture, its aim is to promote world theatre in the French language. The festival lasts a fortnight and takes place in the first half of October each year in Limoges and its districts. Apart from the performances proper, workshops and colloquia bring together actors, stage designers, producers and critics from different parts of the French-speaking world. Among the regular participants from Africa are Souleymane Koly and his Ensemble Koteba, Zadi Zaourou and his Didiga Theatre, the Rocado Zulu Theatre and Werewere Liking and her Ki-Yi Mbock.

The Festival also has a three-month writers-in-residence programme which has benefited such playwrights as the Congolese Sylvain Bemba, the Malian Moussa Konaté, the Zairian Yoka Mudaba and the Gabonese Laurent Owondo. Further, some of the best Limoges productions have attracted the attention of publishers who have issued their works in print, and they have found a wider listening audience in Africa thanks to Radio France Internationale.

A not insignificant element in the promotion of interest in Francophone theatre are the conferences held either by academics, theatre practitioners or cultural development agencies. In 1988, for example, a conference was organised at the Ecole Normale Supérieure in Bamako, Mali. Its useful proceedings were published in 1990 under the title *Théâtres Africains*. In 1989 the Franco-Forum Theatre conference was held in Burkina Faso under the auspices of the International Commission of Francophone Theatre, the French Ministry of Development and Cooperation and its Burkinabé counterpart. This conference brought together companies that derive some of their performance practices from Augusto Boal's Forum Theatre Techniques. Among the participants were Boal himself, the Atelier Theatre Burkinabé, the Brocoli Company of Belgium, Théâtre and Co. of France, Théâtre sans Détour of Québec and Mali's Nyogolon theatre (Deffontaines 1990: 90–5).

In 1990, the French Ministry of Cooperation organised a conference in the Théâtre National de Chaillot in Paris on the theme 'Artistic Creation, Dialogue of Cultures and Development'. The conference was significantly devoted to the theatre and its papers have also been published by the Ministry of Cooperation under the title *Afrique en Créations*. Two other conferences worth mentioning are the 1970 symposium on African theatre held in the University of Abidjan, whose proceedings *Actes du Colloque sur le Théâtre Négro-Africain* constitute the earliest academic examination of the subject, and the 1978 conference held at the same venue under the auspices of the African Cultural Institute, whose proceedings have also been published as *Quel Théâtre pour le développement en Afrique?*

Francophone African theatre, it is clear from the foregoing, was not only created by France more than half a century ago but has continued to depend heavily and, to my mind, unhealthily on that country for its survival. An immediate conclusion that could be drawn from this situation is that such vital assistance as is provided by France cannot proceed without some interference on her part in the form and content of modern Francophone drama. While such a conclusion is reasonable, it has not been borne out by the facts, at least not since the days of William Ponty when, as we saw, students were encouraged to eulogise, in their dramatic compositions, France's colonial mission in Africa and to write plays 'au plus proche du goût européen' (closest to European tastes). As Ligier reminds us (1982: 33), the fact that some notable anti-French plays like Pliya's *Kondo le requin* and Pierre Dabiré's *Sansoa*, against French forced labour, have been prize-winners of the Inter-African Radio Drama Competition attests to the freedom of the playwrights in their choice of theme. Concerning the form, there has been no evidence either to suggest that Western stage conventions are being promoted at the expense of African performance modes. In fact the opposite seems to be the case.

For example, advice to participants in the radio competition always focusses on the need for them to draw on their traditional theatrical forms in writing their plays rather than on French plays they might have read (Ligier 1982: 34). Also, if Francophone drama's French sponsors were hostile to African performance styles, Labou Tansi's theatre would never have been promoted, rooted as it is (as he himself reminds us in the preface of *La Rue des mouches*) in the traditional *kingizila* theatre of the Congo, and in the gestural language of the Bakongo.

Where the French have been totally uncompromising, however, is in the language. Form and content may be discretionary, but the language of Francophone drama has to be French if it is to be sponsored at all. And this is precisely this theatre's Achilles heel. For drama written in a language that can be understood by only 20 per cent of the population cannot possibly hope to have a national resonance or significant social impact beyond the confines of the Westernised élite. For such a resonance, one would need to turn to the various forms of popular theatre in the Francophone region. But before we do that, it would be necesary first to discuss the principle themes of Africa's French-language literary theatre.

CHAPTER 3

Francophone drama: the thematic dimension

THE DRAMATIST AS HISTORIAN

Central to the thematic preoccupations of Francophone literary drama is the presentation of events and figures drawn from Africa's historical past (see Dailly 1970; Granderson 1978; Malanda 1980; Spronk 1982; Warner 1975; 1984). This view, it will be remembered, was already significant in the 1930s school productions at William Ponty. But it was not until the immediate post-independence period in the 1960s and after that it actually flourished: in the Sudano-Sahelian countries of Senegal, Mali, Guinea, Niger accounting for more than half of the national dramatic output (Huguet and Diawara 1984; Ndiaye 1985; Zell 1983).

A preliminary classification of French-language African history plays will reveal two categories of works: first, those which are set in clearly identifiable time-schemes and deal with acknowledged historical figures and events in spite of the romance and magic in which they are swamped, and second those which are set outside historical time and recount the careers of heroes or heroines whose factual existence – assuming they even existed – has been totally obscured by time and the myth-making imagination. To this second category belong plays such as Charles Nokan's *Abraha Pokou*, Eugène Dervain's 1969 one-act play, *Abra Pokou*, both on the alleged founder of the Baoulé people of the Ivory Coast, Queen Pokou, and Ola Balogun's *Shango*, also on a presumed one-time ruler of the Yoruba empire of Oyo in Nigeria. The plays in the first category can be further subdivided into those set in the mid- to late nineteenth century – and they are in the vast majority. To take some examples: Jean Pliya's *Kondo le requin*, Cheik Ndao's *L'Exil d'Albouri*, Djibril Niane's *Sikasso ou la dernière citadelle* all deal with the African resistance to European colonial conquests; and those like Eugène Dervain's

Saran ou la reine scélérate or Sory Konaké's *Le Grand destin de Soundjata*,
which, respectively, describe events that occurred in the near and
distant pre-colonial, but firmly historical, past: the early nineteenth
century in the case of the first and the thirteenth century in the
second.

But whether they are derived from undisputed and verifiable
historical facts occurring in specific time-schemes or from tales of
uncertain factual validity set outside historical time, the great
majority of French-language African history plays have one thing in
common: a *celebratory* and *commemorative* nature. They are like
canticles intoned to the memory of illustrious ancestors. In exalting
terms, they depict the careers of various African warrior-kings. Lat
Dior (1842–86), the damel or king of Cayor and Baol in the territory
covered by present-day Senegal who chose suicide rather than
submit to the French troops of Faiderherbe; El-Hadj Omar
(1747–1864), founder of the Tukulor empire, which at its height
extended for more than 1,000 kilometres, and intrepid fighter against
the French; Gbéhanzin (1842–1906) of ancient Dahomey, self-styled
the 'shark' in affirmation of his will to protect his country from
foreign invasion; Chaka (1787–1828), empire-builder and king of the
Zulus, are among the many rulers of the African past whose names
have provided the titles of many historical plays. In noble and poetic
accents, their patriotism, real or imagined, is sung and their courage
extolled. Through a dramatic recreation of their heroic struggles to
defend or sometimes to expand their territories, and of the elaborate
court splendour and ceremonial that attended their lives, is conveyed
a living sense of pre-colonial African societies at their most glorious.
And in their defeat, a tragic sense of lost heritage.

But lest it be thought that the heroism celebrated in this drama is
limited to male characters, it should be pointed out that female
historical figures are also part of the gallery of portraits depicted
(Tidjani-Serpos 1974: 455–81). Doña Béatrice (1682–1706), prophetess and founder of a syncretic form of Christianity in seventeenth-
century Kongo and active campaigner against Portuguese colonialism is the subject of the play *Béatrice du Congo* by Bernard Dadié, as
is Nokan's piece *Abraha Pokou*. And in Massa M. Diabaté's *Une si belle
leçon de patience*, Ba Mousso Sano, King Tiéba's wife, incensed by what
she judges to be the weakness of her husband's successor Ba Bemba
towards their hereditary enemy Samory, declares war herself in these
terms:

Arise, oh ye women, and heed my call; the call of your queen, Ba Mousso Sano! Rise up and join me with your guns, sabres, bows and arrows, with your empty hands. Oh, join me, women of Sikasso, to avoid having to pound millet for the women of Ouassoulou ... (*Une si belle leçon de patience*, p. 98)

Similarly, Yangouman, the queen of Abron in Atta Koffi's play *Le Trône d'or*, literally takes over the affairs of the country from her weak and pleasure-seeking brother, Adinngra, and stands up to the threats of her powerful neighbour, the Ashanti. In the defence of her people's honour, she goes to war with them, is defeated and commits suicide. But even when the female characters portrayed are not historical, like Aminata or Siré in Niane's *Sikasso ou la dernière citadelle*, the image given of them is often positive, heroic.

This preoccupation with historical topics in Francophone drama contrasts sharply with the situation in the English-language theatre. The latter, especially in the works of playwrights like Ngugi Wa Thiongo, Ebrahim Hussein, Femi Osofisan and Kole Omotoso, is mostly concerned with contemporary social and political issues and – among the earlier writers, Soyinka, J. P. Clark-Bekederemo, Ola Rotimi – with the use of myth and ritual, African as well as European, to thematicise certain problems of the human condition (Banham and Wake 1976: 1–60; Etherton 1979: 57–85; 1982). Anglophone drama contains far fewer history plays and even those that exist do not indulge in an indiscriminate extolling of African history. In these plays, in other words, the past does not emerge as a kind of 'golden age' when all and everything exuded honour and dedication, but also as a period of strife and senseless warfare and of leaders beset with human weaknesses and tragic failings.

This aspect of Anglophone African drama is clearly brought out in a history-based play like Soyinka's *Death and the King's Horseman*, where the Elesin Oba, the chief on whose ritual suicide the salvation of his community depends, fails to live up to his responsibilities. At the crucial moment when he is to show himself worthy of the high office he carries, by that ultimate act of self-sacrifice which most Francophone dramatists tell us is of the essence of traditional kingship, he falters. He displays an unheroic attachment to the carnal which deafens him, with tragic consequences, to the call of duty.

Mata Kharibu, the monarch in the same author's imaginary thirteenth-century African empire in Part 2 of *A Dance of the Forest*, is even worse. There is nothing elevating about him. The Elesin Oba can at least evoke, and not without some justification, extenuating circumstances: the interference of Pilkings, the English colonial officer. But all we feel for Mata Kharibu is contempt. He is tyrannical and ignoble, and his court is full of shady and unsavoury characters like the Slave Dealer, or intellectuals like the Physician who are either spineless or, like the Court-Historian, traitors to their vocation and intellect. But the King is not just ignoble, he is a lustful pleasure-seeker determined to plunge his country into war for no other reason than to recover his wife's trousseau. And which wife? One that he stole from another ruler.

At least Chaka's military opponents in Séydou Badian's *La Mort de Chaka* – to take a totally contrasting example of a history play in French – admit that no matter what his faults, to him: 'The grandeur and power of the Zulu people, the people of the sky, is of primordial importance' (1962: 192). Mata Kharibu's chief warrior, on the other hand, has only this to say about him:

I took up soldiering to defend my country, but those to whom I gave the power to command my life abuse my trust in them. I am suddenly weary of this soldiering where men must find new squabbles for their cruelty. Must I tell the widowed that their men died for another's trousseau? (Soyinka 1973: 50)

A similarly ironic view of the past is contained in Ola Rotimi's *Kurunmi*. Here again, what the reader is presented with is a vision of an African society – the nineteenth-century Yoruba kingdom of Oyo – torn by fratricidal wars. And these are not caused by lofty reasons of state, but by old warriors and leaders – Kurunmi and Ogunmola – inflexibly wedded to traditions which they do not themselves respect, and whose personal antipathies to each other engulf their communities in wars of mass destruction (Johnson 1983: 39–54).

But even when the past is presented positively, as is the case in Micere Mugo's and Ngugi Wa Thiongo's *The Trial of Dedan Kimathi* or, to an extent, in *Death and the King's Horseman* (after all this play is also a dithyramb to Yoruba cultural beliefs and language), the Anglophone dramatist tends not to be interested in it for its own sake, but rather for the framework it provides for him, or the necessary distance it lends to a philosophical, social or political meditation on issues of contemporary relevance: the responsibilities of leadership, societal redemption through the exercise of the individual will, the interaction between the cosmic and the human realms, in the case of the Soyinka play, or the neo-colonial nature of the state in Kenya in the play on Kimathi. A *critical* and *metaphorical* as opposed to a wildly celebratory use of the past is, then, what distinguishes the Anglophone dramatist from his Francophone counterpart.

The view expressed by Soyinka that the 'past clarifies the present and explains the future but [that] it is not a fleshpot for escapist indulgence' (Soyinka 1968: 19) is one that seems implicit in the work of most English-language African dramatists, including the otherwise diametrically opposed Ngugi Wa Thiongo, who warns:

the past has a romantic glamour: gazing at it ... is often a means of escaping the present. It is only in a socialist context that a look at yesterday can be meaningful in illuminating today and tomorrow (Ngugi 1972: 46)

The question that arises, of course, is why the obsession with history, especially of the heroic and celebratory type, in Francophone drama?

Several reasons can be adduced for this. The first, which is often overlooked, is artistic: the sheer dramatic and theatrical potential of the material which *in itself* exhibits a model of stage action that is Aristotelian in its completeness, magnitude and structure. There are periods of disruption, as Domenach, following Duvignaud, points out in connection with the French Revolution (violent military and political conflicts for example) when history becomes more dramatic than literary drama itself; when the struggles of larger-than-life characters against huge and fateful forces and events, when the fiery rhetoric, the sense of excitement, of exaltation or of tragic inevitability all move from the stage in the playhouse, with which they are usually associated, to the larger stage of life: the streets or the battlefields (Domenach 1967: 75–97; Duvignaud 1965; 1973).

One such moment of crisis and social drama in African history is the period of colonial confrontation with Europe in the mid-nineteenth century. With its fiercely independent African monarchs and its no less determined and expansionist Europeans, its tales of epic battles between conflicting forces, of treaties signed and repudiated; with its climate of ambition, conspiracy and shifting alliances (see Crowder 1978), the history of this period contains all the ingredients for literary historical drama in the grand manner. It is therefore understandable that it should have caught the imagination of the dramatist.

But perhaps a more significant reason for the appeal is cultural: the influence of the oral tradition. As is now widely recognised, the traditional societies of tropical Africa do not 'lie beyond the days of self-conscious history ... enveloped in the dark mantle of the night' (Hegel, quoted in Ngugi 1972: 41). In spite of their non-literacy, they display a high degree of *historical consciousness*. Interest in history, expecially of the genealogical kind, is deeply embedded in their oral traditions and constitutes a vital aspect of their outlook. In many such societies, individuals are able to recite the names of their ancestors and rulers; eulogise their high deeds and qualities, recount the founding of the clan, dynasty or tribe and detail the significant events of its life: wars, migrations and so on. Such knowledge is not merely a matter of theoretical interest, but one of immediate practical utility. For it is through it that the community maintains its identity, gives itself inspiration and a sense of destiny; through it that it regulates inheritance, territorial and other disputes; through it, finally, that its most cherished moral and social values are upheld (see *inter alia* Bâ 1981: 166–203; Hama and Ki-Zerbo 1981: 43–52; Vansina 1971: 442–68).

A sense of history is particularly strong in the highly centralised states – the Mali, Benin, Segu Tukulor, Dahomey Kingdoms of West Africa, to limit oneself to just this region. Here, in addition to recording a distinguished past which sometimes stretches back centuries, it provides by its accounts of how power came to be conquered by the present rulers, what Ruth Finnegan has described as 'a mythical charter for the existing distribution of political power' (Finnegan 1970: 372). Indeed, such is its importance that its custody and dissemination are the preserve of a caste of professionally trained oral historians. One of them, Mamadou Kouyaté, made famous by Tamsir Niane in his *Soundjata ou l'épopée mandingue*, explains their task thus:

We griots know the history of kings and their kingdoms; this is why we make the best royal advisers. Every great king needs a griot to perpetuate his memory, for it is our duty to preserve the memory of kings. (Niane 1960: 78)

What emerges from all this, then, is that the widespread use of heroic history as a theme in modern French drama is the expression of a sensibility that is deeply rooted in tradition. And it is interesting to note in this regard that the playwrights most interested in it – Cheikh Ndao of Senegal, Djibril Niane of Guinea, Séydou Badian, Sory Konaké and Massa Makan Diabaté of Mali, Jean Pliya of Benin, ex-Dahomey – are all descended from highly centralised former empires with strong *griot* and, by extension, heroic historical traditions. By extolling in their plays the valour, fortitude and sacrifices of a Gbéhanzin, an Alboury, a Soundjata or a Samory, these writers merely continue an ancestral practice characterised, as Niane's *griot* tells us above, by the celebration of royalty. The emphasis, now as then, is on the same things: military exploits, heroic deeds, noble ancestry and so on. The only thing that has changed, apart from the language obviously, is the medium through which the old theme is conveyed – European-style drama produced on the Italian stage, rather than legend narrated in the village square.

At this point of this discussion, two questions need to be asked. The first is why should it be only Francophone dramatists who are particularly inspired by the oral tradition when this tradition is so widespread in Africa? The second is related to the celebratory *function* which their plays share with their oral counterparts, especially the epic narrative. If, as Ruth Finnegan has shown in her discussion of the social significance of the latter (Finnegan 1970: 141–6) it reflects, in its emphasis on courage, self-sacrifice, physical action and so on, the military and aristocratic ethos of traditional societies, with their penchant for the values of competition and the heroic and the need to enshrine them in song, poem or narrative, then why should it continue to be a viable form, even in modern, French dramatic dress, when the conditions of its emergence and development have disappeared?

The answer to both these questions is political. It lies in what Ernest Gellner has described as the tendency 'for emergent nations to revive or invent a national history' (Gellner 1961: 81); to resurrect, that is, events and heroes of the past as unifying myths and sources of a national consciousness. The nationalist phase of North African history has been shown, for example, to coincide with the rediscovery and celebration of the heroic virtues of cultural, religious and political figures like the early Caliphs, the successors of the prophet Muhammad; Averroes and Avicenna, the famous medieval Arab philosophers and scientists; Ibn Khaldun and Ibn Battuta the historians; the Emir Abdelkader who fought against the French in Algeria from 1832 to 1847, and even Jugurtha and Massinisa, in whose resistance against the Romans almost 2,000 years earlier twentieth-century Tunisians sought inspiration in their struggle against the French (Gordon 1971: 71–3, 133–73).

But this tendency, though widespread throughout the recently colonised Third World, is universal. It has always been present among peoples the world over who are reacting to a feeling of cultural dispossession. In Europe, the example of eighteenth-century Germany is often cited. Prussia's defeat at the hands of Napoleon and the feeling of national dishonour and humiliation that ensued gave rise among Germans to a wave of national resistance to the conqueror (Lukács 1962:18–29). This found expression in the reawakening, aided by historians and men of culture in general, to a sense of past greatness and to an interest in old German culture and especially history. Thus the contemporary German historian Stein wrote about his work:

I have wished to quicken the taste for German history and facilitate its study, and thereby to contribute to a preservation of the love of the common fatherland and of our great ancestors. (in Gooch 1928: 65)

Böhmer, for his part, wanted his historical writings widely circulated and used in schools; for, he declared:

To know what has been and is no more, to see how much of what is rooted in the past still stands – that seems... the beginning and condition of all higher culture. It is of special importance for a people who wants to raise itself, not by continuing the last few centuries of decadence, but by linking itself on to earlier times of power and greatness. (in Gooch 1928: 70).

This linking of the group 'to earlier times of power and greatness', recommended by Böhmer to his eighteenth-century compatriots, became a deeply felt need among French-speaking African intellectuals who, ironically, were also fighting two centuries later against the same French rule. And that their fight should have taken a marked cultural, history-oriented dimension was due to their intensely negative cultural experience under French colonial rule.

More than any other colonial power, as has often been pointed out, France pursued, in addition to political and economic domination, a coherently articulated policy of cultural control (Fanon 1970; Memmi 1957). Convinced of the special value of its civilisation and of the need to bring it to its benighted subjects (who, it believed, in the best tradition of the Enlightenment, shared a universal human nature, but nonetheless occupied the bottom rung of the human evolutionary ladder), France proceeded to devalue and destroy their culture and replace it (in theory at least) with its own (Leclerc 1971).

An aspect of that culture that came in for special attack was its history. When it was not distorted as a simple tale of predatory raids by petty and bloodthirsty tyrants (Semidei 1966: 56–86; Wilks 1971: 7–17) it was quite simply denied. And such interpretations were not always the work of 'crude denigrators', as Gellner is a little too anxious to believe (1961: 80) or of official ideologues. They were present in the findings of even the most distinguished scholars. Thus Henri Brunschwig, in a disturbing conflation of history as modern academic discipline concerned with *reconstructing* a people's past, and history as that past itself, was able to write in 1962:

Africans have never been dispossessed of their history because they have never had or felt the need for one. (1962: 875)

While a judgement such as the above could be seen as deriving from the limitations of a narrow conception of history (one equated with literacy, written documents and a linear view of time), not all such judgements were errors. Many were the result of a deliberate choice to distort or falsify. An example of such deliberateness, and its openly political motives, is provided by George Hardy, colonial education administrator and prolific historian of Africa.

The history syllabus in African schools, he directed, should aim specifically at discrediting the historical accounts of the *griots*, which he reduced to 'foolish and perfidious lies' and at propagating the view that:

We came to a poor country ravaged by tyrants and depopulated by slavers; we imposed peace on all, put an end to slave raids and the slave trade, extended agriculture and built hospitals. (in Mouralis 1981: 115)

Not to spread this gospel, he argued against his colleagues who saw history as irrelevant and wanted it abolished from the curriculum, was to leave the field open to the 'custodians of indigenous history' (in Mouralis 1981: 114) as he called them, and to run the corresponding risk at a time of Franco-German rivalry of seeing them swing entire French colonies into the arms of 'some Kaiser or other, protector of Islam' (in Mouralis 1981: 115). It also meant depriving the French colonial enterprise of a powerful legitimisation tool, for, he asks, 'Are the advantages to French power of being able to prove and justify itself in this way not clear?' (in Mouralis 1981: 115). The status of a lot of French, indeed European, historical writing on

Africa during the colonial period as 'invention' or, in the idiom of post-structuralists, as 'discourse' or 'narrative' – with all the connotations of fiction-making as distinct from fact-revelation implied in these terms – this status then could not have been more clearly acknowledged and its *power* affirmed (Miller 1987; Mudimbe 1988).

One can now better understand why, when Francophones later revolted against French rule, history either as a discipline or just as a theme in literature, especially in drama, should have become so attractive a weapon. Francophones had seen it used by their masters, and not unsuccessfully, for colonial political purposes; they now saw no better tool with which to further *their* anti-colonial political ends. They came to the conclusion that as a condition for political and psychological freedom, they had to take part in, at the very least, if not take over, the *production* of their own self-image; to create a counter-hegemonic historical discourse that would break the intellectual dependency which made them the mere consumers of a collective identity, a historical discourse fashioned elsewhere, often distorted for political reasons and imposed on them as *the* truth.

The predilection for historical themes in the work of the dramatists among them is a reflection of the awareness of this need, and an attempt to meet it. By putting on stage the politico-military achievements of, say, a Chaka (one of their favourite heroes), achievements which include the forging, from a mosaic of ethnic peoples of a well-organised and prosperous kingdom of more than 100,000 square miles and the creation of a large, ferociously efficient army, the dramatists were doing several things. They were repudiating the myth of a history-less and insignificant past on which (French) colonialism based its claims; restoring theirs and their people's injured pride; rousing in the people a sense of patriotism and finally creating, as we mentioned earlier, myths and symbols for national self-consciousness and unity (Kuper 1975; Neale 1985).

But the recourse to history in drama did not have only anti-colonial functions. That this theme continues to be prominent long after the 1960s is indicative of its importance also in the post-colonial era. Just as dramatists used this subject to provide people with ideal images, *exemplars* with which to meet the challenges of the struggle for independence, with models of heroic virtue and behaviour, so now they are doing it to help their African spectators confront the problems of nation-building. Its function in uniting the fissiparous groups within the community, important then, is even more so today when the external enemy has gone, and the dangers of disintegration through the reassertion of ethnic loyalties have never been more real.

Another way in which it is used is to exorcise that quality of illegitimacy that stubbornly attaches to many new African governments, to confer prestige on them and justify their policy options. It is worth remembering in this respect that a good many African dramatists of French expression – Badian, Pliya, Senghor, Césaire, Dadié – were or still are practising politicians. David Apter describes the process as 'traditionalisation' and defines it as the 'validation of current behaviour stemming from immemorial prescriptive norms' (Apter 1968: 115). It is the attempt to mediate innovation, what he calls 'extra-systemic action', by charging it to antecedent values or prestigious ancestors.

A good example of this is provided by Séydou Badian's *La Mort de Chaka*. Two aspects of the Zulu hero's policy goals are highlighted in this play: his desire to unite hitherto warring ethnic groups into a strong and centralised state, and his determination, symbolised by his own selflessness, to put the interests of the state above those of the individual. Thus the author has Chaka say to his people after their last victory:

We won it because we knew how to obey, because we knew what we wanted, because we were able to forget ourselves, for the sake of unity we believed greater than the individual. (Badian 1962: 150)

That it should be these qualities of the man that are celebrated is no coincidence. At the time that Badian wrote the play, he was Mali's Minister of Economic Planning in a one-party 'socialist' state (Modibo Kéita's) which demanded absolute loyalty of its subjects. In its foreign policy, that state was also active, with Nkrumah's Ghana and Sékou Touré's Guinea, in the pan-African movement for continental unity – a kind of 'Chakaesque' union of the ethnic groups within a greater whole. Now, by emphasising Chaka's ideals of unity and development through an all-powerful state, Badian is in fact suggesting or perhaps even manipulating a parallel between them and those of Modibo Kéita's Mali. This parallel works to the advantage of the latter, in so far as it establishes it as heir to a political philosophy, African socialism, which pre-dates the colonial era and finds its origins in a renowned predecessor. Through the Chaka story Badian, to use David Apter's words from another context, transformed Mali's socialism into 'a living and continuous feature of the African past...'traditionalised" [it] and made [it] comfortable' (Apter 1968: 114).

But the preoccupation with and practice of a celebratory historical drama has not been without its critics (Fanon 1970: 95–139; Kane 1971: 227–8; Soyinka 1968: 14–21; Ngugi 1972: 39–46).

While its corrective psychological and political functions are fully recognised, this type of drama also carried with it, these critics have argued, certain dangers: those of being an escapist retreat from the present, of degenerating into folklore and blind idolatry of the past, of becoming a disabling and reactionary political ideology.

This, it appears, is what has been happening for some time now. At a time when Africa's encounter with modernity imposes on both writer and intellectual a duty of critical exploration of the past to see which aspects of it ought to be preserved, reformed, or quite simply discarded, many a Francophone dramatist, decades after the heroic nationalist struggles of yesteryear, keeps concentrating on resuscitating the splendors of the past, on prospecting, in Soyinka's words, 'archaic fields for forgotten gems' (Soyinka 1968: 17). In so doing, the playwright abdicates his chief responsibility, which is to provide 'a voice of vision' to his troubled post-colonial society, with its many dislocations and homespun injustices.

But to critics like Fanon, the problem is more than just one of abdication or escapism. It is one of an ideological cover-up, so to speak. He sees, in the efforts to keep alight the myth of an exclusively glorious past, a deliberate ideological attempt, a rhetorical strategy, to obscure from the 'people' the reality of their contemporary misery. In an observation on the use of history by Africa's post-colonial leaders which holds equally true for its dramatists, Fanon writes:

Years after independence, incapable of working out a future for the people, the leader can be seen harking back to the days of the struggle for independence. Because he refuses to break the national bourgeoisie, he asks his people to flow back to the past, to get drunk on the epic struggle for independence. (Fanon 1970: 111)

An even more radical, class-oriented criticism levelled at this drama concerns what is seen as its élitist historical perspective, its preoccupation with what Orlando Patterson calls the 'three p's': princes, pyramids and pageantry (Patterson 1971). This preoccupation, ironically, derives from a certain pre-Marxist European model of history and also from the dynastic nature of African traditional history as it is embodied in the heroic songs of the *griot*.

Plays like *L'Exil d'Albouri*, *La Mort de Chaka*, and *Kondo le requin* ignore, it is justifiably pointed out, the lives, actions and historical experiences of the common people. They see history uniquely from the top: as the product, that is, of the actions of kings and queens. Such a perspective, it is pointed out, does not only distort the true picture – which as Ngugi Wa Thiongo tries to show in *The Trial of Dedan Kimathi* is often one of ordinary people and their leaders fighting valiantly against foreign domination and making their history – but reveals the 'bourgeois', 'élitist' or feudal orientation of the dramatists. An orientation which sees the masses as uncreative and inert, and the great decisions and actions affecting them as not their affair, but as that of a ruling class of exceptional individuals.

Biodun Jeyifo sees this type of drama, which he describes as '"bourgeois" historical tragedy' (Jeyifo 1985a: 107), and under which he specifically includes Soyinka's *Death and the King's Horseman* and, in footnote, Séydou Badian's *La Mort de Chaka*, as an instance of African literature in the service of an élite and not of the people:

the protagonist hero in these plays are [*sic*] scions of bourgeois individualism and solipsism: lone tragic heroes, proposed either as great historical personages or cultural heroes and avatars dominate the action; their connection to us is never dialectical; it is symbolic. (Jeyifo 1985a: 107)

In reply to these objections two remarks are worth making. The first is that while as political criticisms they are clearly valid, they do not always enlighten the reader as to whether the plays criticised are, within *their* chosen ideological perspectives (however misguided), *artistic* successes. In other words one senses in the remarks of a Fanon, a Jeyifo or a Ngugi Wa Thiongo the danger that has always haunted the criticism of African literature: that of predicating artistic success on ideological 'integrity'. The second point worth stressing is that not all African history plays in French indulge in self-complacent narcissism. There are authors like the Dadié of *Béatrice du Congo* and *Iles de Tempête*, the Césaire of *La Tragédie du roi Christophe*, the U'Tamsi of *Le Zulu* or *Le Bal de Ndinga*, the Ndébéka of *Equatorium* and the Senouvo Zinsou of *On joue la comédie* who, like some of their English-speaking counterparts, and as a study of their plays will reveal, adopt a critical, satirical or metaphorical approach to history. Their repertory of heroes includes the selfless and the patriotic as well as the ambitious or the just plainly misguided. Admittedly, their kind of plays are relatively few. They constitute so far very much a minority tradition. But to the extent to which they are often also more exciting from the point of view of drama, they are a powerful minority.

THE DRAMATIST AS SOCIAL CRITIC

If serious plays derived from historical and legendary sources still constitute the bulk of the published dramatic production of Francophone Africans, comedies which aim at social and moral criticism and are based on an observation of society and its customs are not absent either. As a matter of fact these go back, like the history plays, to the very origins of Francophone literary drama in William Ponty in compositions like *Les Prétendants rivaux* by Ivorian students, which was a forerunner of Oyono Mbia's *Trois prétendants ... un mari* and *Sokamé*. In the 1950s social dramas continued to develop with minor pieces like *Nos femmes* by Germain Coffi Gadeau of the Ivory Coast, which satirises women who throw all moral restraints overboard in the conduct of their lives because of materialism, and Dadié's *Min Adjao*, which dramatises the problems of succession in matrilineal societies. But it was only after Independence that dramatists became more interested in the customs, practices and injustices of their societies, and sensitive to the comic and dramatic potential in some of the changes wrought upon them by modernity. And just as the serious, historical plays have their roots partly in a certain type of oral narrative, so the modern comedies also have antecedents in the oral satirical theatrical tradition of which the *kotéba* and the *sougounougou*, as described in chapter 1, are examples.

Unlike the history plays which address their energies to extolling the past and denouncing colonial rule, the dramas of social criticism focus on exposing, through satire and comedy and in a realistic mode, the inadequacies of past and present-day society. Their central characters are not the models of virtue and integrity of the serious play, but rogues, corrupt civil servants, hypocrites and charlatans. In one of the important texts of this theatre, *Monsieur Thogo-Gnini*, Dadié depicts a grotesque upstart who uses money he has acquired illegally from shady dealings with European businessmen to further dominate his people. Similarly, Sony Labou Tansi in *Je soussigné cardiaque* exposes injustice and corruption in the story of a conscientious teacher, Mallot, who runs foul of a powerful and well-connected notable, Pérono, and ends up by being imprisoned and later shot.

The immorality and corruption of the new administrative élite are also the themes of Pliya's *La Secrétaire particulière*, Zadi Zaourou's *L'Œil* and Patrice Ndédi-Penda's *Le Fusil*, while Oyono-Mbia in *Trois prétendants ... un mari*, *Jusqu'à nouvel avis* and Moussa Konaté in *L'Or du diable* hold up the image of a rural community that is ensnared in the self-calculations of greedy old men, stifling and exploitative marriage customs and religious obscurantism.

Diviners and their practices are the object of ridicule in Guy Menga's *L'Oracle* and *La Marmite de Koka Mbala*, where they are deflated and exposed as charlatans, vile manipulators of the unsuspecting and purveyors of obscurantist beliefs.

The exploration of social problems like the position of women in traditional societies, gerontocracy, the collapse of traditional values in the face of modernity and the sense of alienation to which such modernity gives rise are also at the heart of the theatre of Werewere Liking in plays like *Rougeole Arc-en-ciel*, *Du sommeil d'Injuste* and *La Puissance d'Um*. But, unlike the social dramas of an Oyono-Mbia or a Labou Tansi, she does not use satire as a means of changing human conduct, nor does she see the solution to these problems in social or political change, violent or gradual. Social change to her is not a question of reforming collective structures through legislation, but of the moral and psychological transformation of individuals – which is why she resorts to the symbolic and non-realistic mode of ritual to achieve her ends.

A significant difference between social comedy and historical plays in the Francophone repertory is what Wake has rightly described as the former's 'superior dramatic quality' (Banham and Wake 1976: 63). While in general the history plays are more interested in conveying a sense of nobility and pageantry, with their procession of armies, notables and choruses, the comedies work on suspense. The dramatic situations the comedies create are interesting in themselves. They build up tension in the spectator and arouse expectations of the development of further situations. Also, their dialogue is less ponderous and literary. The language of history plays can be enjoyed for itself, for its lyricism and formal qualities, but not for what it contributes to the action. The language of the comedies on the other hand is more dramatic – presenting and enacting situations and not just describing them.

THE DRAMATIST AS POLITICAL CRITIC

A third significant source of inspiration for Francophone dramatists is politics. The political corruption and ugly tyrannies that have sprung up in post-colonial African countries have attracted fierce criticism. U'Tamsi in *Le Maréchal Nnikon Nniku Prince qu'on sort* (1979), Maxime Ndébéka in *Le Président* and *Equatorium*, and Labou Tansi in *Qui a mangé Madame d'Avoine Bergotha*, for example, dramatise the abuse of power by African Corporals-turned-Marshals-turned-Presidents, with their delusions of grandeur and contempt for human life, while Césaire in *Une Saison au Congo* and Alexandre Kum'a Ndumbe III in *Kafra Biatanga* explore the relationship between political instability in Africa and foreign interference. But this theatre does not limit itself to the issues of political power or, for that matter, of African politics. In Ndao's *La Décision*, Zinsou's *On joue la comédie*, Naindouba's *L'Etudiant de Soweto* and Lisembé Elébé's *Le Sang des noirs pour un sou* – an adaptation of Peter Abraham's *Mine Boy* – the issue of racial segregation is considered: in America in the Elébé play, and in South Africa in the others.

Political plays share with social comedies a superior theatrical quality over historical drama. Indeed, social comedies and political plays both constitute most of the performance-oriented works in the Francophone dramatic repertory. Unlike historical drama, which is mostly concerned with elaborating a national cultural identity, the former are committed to advancing the cause of social and political change through revolution or reform. The aim is to make the theatre fulfil the mass pedagogical function long claimed for it by Francophone dramatists from Césaire to Ndao, but in practice never quite fulfilled for reasons of language and European stage conventions.

Such, then, in broad outline are the dominant themes in Francophone African drama. Issues of dramaturgy, characterisation, language and so on will be examined in the study of specific plays. But before we move on, it should be borne in mind that the classification of plays in this introduction is not meant to be taken rigidly. While in terms of their setting, characters, language and inspiration plays can indeed be described as belonging to a historical, social or political theatre, the fact remains that these preoccupations more often coexist in various degrees within the same work.

POPULAR THEATRE

Side by side with the literate theatre of the intelligensia, there exist in the informal cultural sector of many Francophone countries genuinely popular forms of modern theatrical expression that are not the product of the school system, or of radical playwrights in the formal cultural sector. Urban, as opposed to the also popular rural theatre of oral narrative performances, consistently comic and satirical in tone, the preserve of no special caste of performers (*griots*, the initiated or ritual priests), but rather belonging to the general mass of the emerging working class, these forms combine elements of rural traditions of performance and of the popular culture of urban agglomerations (see Barber 1987: 1–78 for an excellent discussion of the notion of popular art in general).

A common thread runs through urban popular theatre. It is not based on scripted texts, and plots and dialogue are improvised on the basis of a broad outline. Plays are collectively elaborated by members of the troupe guided by its lead actor-manager and are not the product of an 'author'; finally, the subjects are topical and of immediate practical and moral concern to the socially and economically deprived who constitute their audience, characters and performers. Other characteristics of popular theatre include heavy didacticism (a carry-over from the oral tradition) and the use of language that is either completely African, as is the case with Niger's popular *Hausa* theatre, or, for the multi-ethnic urban audiences, a pot-pourri of pidgin French and local languages. Audience participation is also a salient feature of this type of drama, as is the technique of conducting the action essentially through song, dance and mime.

A good example of this species of theatre activity is the Togolese concert party. This has been estimated by one of its early investigators, Alain Ricard, to attract as many as 3,000 spectators a week (Ricard 1975: 80). Among its leading practitioners in the 1970s and 1980s were Pascal d'Almeida and his 'Happy Star' group and Adenyon Kodzo, popularly known as Kokuvito, and his 'Kokuvito Concert Band'.

Of Nigerian and Ghanian origin and probably arriving in Togo in the 1920s, the 'concert party' is an evening of musical and theatrical entertainment sometimes lasting for six hours. Performed in schoolrooms, town halls or improvised stages out of doors, say in a courtyard, the concert party divides into three parts: an opening session, mostly of highlife music, song and dance, a prologue of skits and story-telling whose beginning is signalled by the entry on stage of pierrot-like characters performing practical jokes and engaging in knockabouts and finally a theatrical representation.

Although the sketches Ricard summarises dramatise a variety of situations – the neglected and maltreated orphan in *Agbenoxevi* (also a favourite folktale topic), conjugal infidelity in *Les Amants de Georgina*, corruption in *Bob Cole* and so on – they are all set within the framework of a moral code that enables the audience to judge the types of conduct depicted. It is this moral-guidance dimension in the concert party that partly accounts for its enormous success with its spectators; spectators whose relatively recent migration from country to city, as Ricard has pointed out (1975: 78), confronts them with the problem of competing values, traditional and modern, and therefore of the need for such guidance.

Performed in a mixture of languages (Ewe or Mina, Togo's lingua franca and pidgin French) and tones (comic, burlesque, satirical) and interspersed with dance interludes and vibrant electric guitar music, the concert party puts on stage stock characters like the Idiot, the Houseboy, the Charlatan, the Prostitute and so on. They are easily recognisable from their conventional costumes, disguises or make-up. Thus the Prostitute – a role acted by a man in this entirely male theatre – always wears bright-red lipstick, sunglasses and an 'afro' hairstyle, while the Houseboy, locally known as the 'massa boy', a Togolese Scapin, powders his face black with charcoal dust and carves out extra full lips with white chalk. Also, like the Idiot in his tailcoat, he wears a pair of worn-out shorts over his well-tailored trousers. Another popular character is the sleek city lad, like Francis in *Francis le Parisien* who, with briefcase, cigar and glasses, lords it over his rustic brothers and mistresses, talks about his (fictitious) trips to London and Paris and sprinkles his Mina with French and English words.

A characteristic feature of concert party performances is their improvised nature and style of acting. With no written text, similar to the late 1960s America theatrical genre the 'happening', no rehearsal sessions and with only the sketch of the storyline, the performers – usually illiterate and untrained actors – have to invent everything in the course of the actual performance. For this, they rely on their imagination, fine sense of repartee and their talent to mime, dance and sing.

Giving direction to the action within the format of the storyline, imposing a rhythm on it and controlling its tempo is the job of the lead actor, the 'meneur de jeu'. A kind of actor-producer (a relic from the officiating priest in ritual), he is the play's moving spirit. He chooses the play to be acted, distributes roles before or during performance and contrives dramatic situations that will bring out the talents of his individual actors. Finally, he prompts his fellow actors, regulates the relationship between them and the audience, and elicits the latter's remarks, suggestions and participation.

Although the concert party is not patronised by educated Togolese, its value to the creation of a popular literary drama has been recognised and utilised, as shall be shown, by Zinsou in his theatre, notably in *On joue la comédie*.

An earlier form of popular theatre in Togo that has now gone into decline but is still worth mentioning is the Kantata. Of missionary origin, this genre, which also spread from Ghana, dramatises Bible stories and moralities, for example as in *La Vie de Daniel* and *Le Mariage d'Isaac et de Rebecca*. Danced and sung in its entirety to Christian piano music, especially in the hands of its first Togolese practitioner Morehouse Apedo-Amah, it later evolved to include dialogue. But some Kantatas were lay, and improvised on Togolese or oriental lore. An example of the latter is *Mille et une nuits* and the hugely popular *Ali Baba et les quarante voleurs*, which ran from 1947 to 1953 (Ricard 1975: 62). The lay Kantata, unlike its religious counterpart, is sung and danced to traditional music and instruments. It also has a greater degree of fantasy, which Ricard attributes to its oriental subject-matter as well as to the influence of popular Indian films, aspects of whose scenography and choreography it reproduces (Ricard 1975: 63).

Another Francophone country with a crowd-pulling popular theatre that flourished especially in the 1970s is Cameroon. Bjornson, who has devoted an interesting study to it (1990: 28–33), gives its three principal practitioners as Daniel Ndo, Dieudonné Afana and Deiv Moktoi. Seeds of this type of theatre were, however, already contained in the plays of their compatriot and predecessor Guillaume Oyono-Mbia. And it is the latter's *Notre fille ne se mariera pas* in particular which seemed to have sparked off in Ndo, who acted the part of Mbarga in a 1970 production of the play, the idea of an independent career in popular theatre.

Like Oyono-Mbia and his Mbarga, Ndo conceived and created a

character whom he named Uncle Otsama – old, rustic, uncompro-
misingly traditional – whose picaresque adventures in the city
constitute the substance of the performance. Of course, the focus of
his performance is not on the action – there is very little – but on the
stage presence, the physical language of Uncle Otsama, his reactions
in strange and unfamiliar situations, his dress, idiom and mannerisms.

In spite of its concentration on the character and his act, the
theatre of Ndo – and for that matter of Dieudonné Afana who also
created the stereotypical Jean-Miché Kankan – is not indifferent to
social issues. Bjornson summarises three typical Uncle Otsama
adventures. The first is with a bank 'sous-directeur' whom he
innocently but maliciously understands to be a 'directeur plein de
sous'. The second is at the police station, and the last is with his
citified daughter. And it is clear that Ndo uses these adventures as a
pretext, rather like Oyono-Mbia does with those of his villagers, to
raise, in the comic mode, the issues of public-servant venality, police
injustice and the extended family (Bjornson 1990: 30). Cameroon's
popular theatre, like Togo's concert party, is a medley of performances: dramatic sketches as well as sessions of poetry readings and
storytelling, of jazz, singing and dancing, and it depends for its effects
on slapstick, puns, costume and, sometimes, licentious jokes.

A third country with a popular theatre tradition is Niger, and
Janet Beik's *Hausa Theatre in Niger* (1987) is almost entirely devoted
to it. She distinguishes three types of troupe as its main promoters:
the *samariyas*, traditional youth associations, the national radio and
television service and students. Some of these troupes specialise in
either or both of two kinds of performance: well-choreographed
dance-dramas popularly known as 'ballets' and involving dancers,
singers and musicians, and dramatic pieces that emphasise spoken
dialogue (Beik 1987: 35–7). While the dance-dramas enact traditional subjects – ritual ceremonies or historical episodes from pre-
colonial history – the plays, like the other popular traditions seen
above, deal with the urgent social issues of Niger. And Beik
summarises these as 'juvenile delinquency, the changing status of
marriage, traditional caste divisions [and the] ... embezzlement of
public funds' (Beik 1987: 44).

A striking feature of Niger's popular theatre troupes is their female
membership (Beik 1987: 60). Though women are few, numbering no
more than ten in the most liberal of troupes, whose membership
hardly exceeds forty, and recruited only from the ranks of prostitutes,

divorcees or single girls, their very presence not just as members but also as actresses is a departure from the practices of a genre which in Togo, for example, is an all-male endeavour. Niger's popular theatre also differs in a significant way from the others described above. It has, over the years, fallen under government influence. Consequently, it has found itself having to walk a tightrope between eulogising government – a duty particularly demanded of it with the advent of the military government of Seyni Kountche in 1974 – and continuing in its generic function of being the people's truculent and irreverent voice of criticism.

COMMUNITY DEVELOPMENT THEATRE

A third and final form of modern popular theatrical activity in Francophone Africa is the Community Development Theatre or, as it is described by one of its leading practitioners, Prosper Kampaoré of Burkina Faso, the 'Theatre of Social Intervention' (see Deffontaines 1990: 90–5; Guingané 1990: 131–42; Kampaoré 1990: 147–56; Morrison 1991: 29–40). Born in the late 1970s in the wake of the spectacular failure of many development projects, and the realisation that one possible reason for this could be the lack of understanding by and involvement in these projects of the target communities, various popular communicative strategies were elaborated to reach them. The Community Development Theatre was one of them. Its underlying philosophy, as Morrison points out, is that

external forces and resources, people and their traditional culture should be creative participants in the development process and not manipulated clients of it. (Morrison 1991: 33)

Widely practised in Mali by troupes like the Nyogolon, in Niger by the Samariya theatre associations (see Beik 1987: 131–63) and in Burkina Faso by Kampaoré's Atelier Théâtre Burkinabé and Jean-Pierre Guingané's Théâtre de la Fraternité, the Community Development Theatre is used in education, health and agricultural campaigns. Its objectives are to impart specific information, to criticise and discourage behaviour patterns deemed incompatible with desired social values and objectives and to elicit popular participation in the realisation of the latter. Among the diverse subjects treated are issues of family planning, vaccination, child abuse, farming methods and – especially by the troupes in Niger – political and administrative corruption.

The Community Development Theatre shares several features with the urban popular theatre: a rootedness in traditional performance styles, a participatory quality, the use of African languages and open spaces for performance, didacticism, simple plot structures and so on. But fundamental differences also remain. And these are not connected with the commercialism of the urban popular theatre or with the fact that the latter is addressed to an urban illiterate as opposed to Community Development Theatre's rural illiterate public. It has to do with the fact that the Community Development Theatre is not really a people's theatre in the sense in which, for example, the Togolese concert party is. In other words, it is created, organised and promoted not by the ordinary people as such but by non-governmental organisations, international donor agencies like UNICEF which work closely with the Atelier Theatre Burkinabé, cultural officers of the local ministries of culture and university-educated theatre activists. It is a theatre *for* the people by progressive members of the formal cultural sector and not *by* them. So that even when critical comments from the public are encouraged and participation sought, as it very often is, in the choice of subject, actors and elaboration of scenario, it is done with the overall aim ultimately of integrating the public more readily and harmoniously into a system of social or political organisation whose parameters are not up for discussion.

PART II

The plays

CHAPTER 4

Aimé Césaire: 'La Tragédie du roi Christophe'; 'Une Saison au Congo'

La Tragédie du roi Christophe, one of the classics of the theatre of decolonisation and the first play by a black Francophone writer to win international acclaim, was first performed on 4 August 1964. Not in France, as one might have expected (French backing, according to Pierre Naville (1970: 239–96), had shied away from it because of high production costs, a large cast and an unusual subject), nor in Africa, for whose audiences Césaire claims he wrote it, but in Austria, at the Salzburg Festival. After a successful première there, in a production by Jean-Marie Serreau, the play toured various European capitals: Berlin, where it was performed at the Hebbel-Theater, Belgium where it ran at the Theatre National and Italy, where it was staged at the Venice Theatre during the Venice Biennale. In September 1965, two years after its publication and with several European productions behind it, the play finally reached the French stage.

It ran to packed audiences at the Odéon for a fortnight; was staged in Caën and Amiens in March 1966; and in April 1966, it received its first professional production in Africa at the Festival of Negro Arts in Dakar, Senegal. This was followed a year later, May 1967, by a performance in Montreal at the World Exhibition. Its most recent performance was at the Comédie-Française in Paris in 1991 in a production by the Burkina Faso film director Idrissa Ouédraogo.

The opening run in Paris of *La Tragédie du roi Christophe* was a major theatrical event in France, indeed 'one of the most beautiful moments of the spring of 1965' in the words of André Alter (in R. Harris 1973: 77). It marked the advent on the French stage of the Third World, both in its post-1960 political preoccupations, which constitute the subject of the play, and in its cultural forms. It also brought to the attention of French theatre audiences the existence in their country of black actors of talent: notably the Senegalese, Douta Seck, who

played the title role with 'elegance', 'humanity' and 'sincerity'
(Naville 1970: 262), but also his compatriot James Campbell and the
Haitian, Yvan Labejof. Finally, it revealed to them a poetic drama
such as had rarely been written in France since the days of Claudel.

Jacques Lemarchand, writing in *Le Figaro Littéraire*, described the
play as 'a dramatic revelation', a perfectly structured tragedy 'shot
through with violent, cruel and delightful poetry' (in R. Harris 1973:
76), while André Alter saw it as 'one of the most important plays of
the contemporary French-language theatre' (in R. Harris 1973: 77).
To Serge Sautreau and André Velter, writing in *Les Temps Modernes*,
it constituted, together with Césaire's other works, a welcome
'antidote of the greatest potency to a [French] civilisation which
under the pretext of sobriety [was] bordering on literary sterility'
(1965: 370).

La Tragédie du roi Christophe cannot be easily classified. Its tones
range from the harrowingly tragic through the intensely satirical and
comic to the grotesque. The play combines, especially in the hero, a
concern with politics and history as well as with myth; aspects of
popular Afro-Caribbean culture coexist with European theatrical
traditions. In short, it provides actors and producers with a variety of
elements that can be fused into a new and exciting theatrical whole.

For the actors, there are several interesting parts. The role of
Christophe himself, with his intense love for his people, the contempt
and cruelty with which he paradoxically treats them, his sudden
outbursts of rage at their indolence, his obsession with bequeathing
them a citadel, his fits of self-pity, his sudden switches from king to
buffoon, his language, now loftily poetic, now irredeemably vulgar,
offers a great challenge to the actor. Another obvious stage role is that
of Hugonin: court-jester, king's confidante and messenger of death.
Pétion's part, with the hypocrisy, machinations and hollow rhetoric
that it involves, also has its attractions. Each one of the other
speaking parts, however episodic – like the disillusioned Métellus
who prefers to die rather than continue to see his country destroyed
by Christophe and Pétion, or Madame Christophe whose realism is
in stark contrast with her husband's dreams – emerges as a distinctive
character, a presence. The language of the play, too, is as varied as its
characters. It ranges from the oratorical and poetic through the
earthy and sometimes downright crude. Haitian French, a mix of
Creole and Spanish words, expressions and rhythms, is also liberally
used by the characters.

Set in nineteenth-century Haiti, the play covers a fourteen-year period in the island's history – from Henri Christophe's accession to power in 1806, through the civil war to his death by suicide in 1820. (On Haiti's history, see Nicholls 1979.) The play opens with a short prologue describing a popular Haitian sport: cock-fighting. This otherwise unpromising scene, a performance within a larger performance, complete with its audience, assumes importance in the light of the metaphorical meaning with which it is invested. The fight to the death between two cocks, significantly called Pétion and Christophe, to the ecstatic cheers of their respective supporters, prefigures the political fight in the play between the two leading Haitian politicians of the period after whom the cocks are named, and who are the principal characters in the drama.

An interesting feature of the prologue worth noting, because of its extensive and multidimensional use (not only to describe events as here, but also situations and characters) is its mode of presentation: parody. From the moment the curtain rises, Césaire sets about undermining, through parody, the heroic content of his play. He deflates the seriousness of the forthcoming struggle between Pétion and Christophe by reducing it to one between characters who are no more than winged combatants in a pit.

That he should have adopted such an attitude to the history of an island where, in his proud words, 'negritude stood up for the first time and proclaimed its faith in its humanity' (1956: 44) is itself not gratuitous. But Césaire's reason for adopting this attitude is not, as might be thought, to entertain. Neither is it to express his disillusionment with or contempt for the Christophian era in Haitian politics.

While Césaire is clearly critical of the methods used by Christophe and may have used parody to indicate this, he also remains a great admirer of the man and his ideals:

It is obvious that I care for him, although I disapprove of his Stalinist-type dictatorial policies. (quoted in Mbom 1979: 65)

Bernard Mouralis, it seems to me, is correct when he argues that the parodic mode in the play is used to problematise the independence of Haiti, to raise its fundamentally ambivalent nature rather than just to celebrate or condemn it (Mouralis 1974: 504–535). But, more than this, Césaire uses parody in a Brechtian perspective: to estrange the spectator from the characters and their fates and to encourage in him

or her a non-identificatory and critical attitude. He also uses it as a
weapon to preserve his own detachment from a subject in which he
is deeply involved.

The action proper of the play starts in Act I. It is here, in a series
of rapidly changing scenes between the mulatto-controlled South
and the black-controlled North, that the major events are sketched
in. The events include the Senate's offer of an emasculated office of
president to Christophe and his indignant rejection of it; Christophe's
retreat to the North which he proclaims a separate state, indeed a
monarchy; his coronation as king, the ensuing hostilities with Pétion's
republic and Christophe's decision not to press his military advantage
against the South in the interests of future unity. The act ends with
a grandiose statement of his dreams for his people.

The dominant tone of Act I is a mixture of high seriousness and
formality on the one hand and of gay abandon and even vulgarity on
the other. But neither of these sets of qualities is restricted to any one
event or character. The most serious events have a comic or
sometimes grotesque touch to them, like the coronation ceremony,
while a seemingly unserious character like Hugonin embodies a
wisdom and foresight that Christophe would have done well to heed.

If the first act represents the conquest of power and the policy-
making stages of Christophe's career, Act II represents the im-
plementation stage. Freed from the immediate pressures of civil war
and of external (French) threats, Christophe sets out in this act to
translate his dreams into reality. The result, however, is not a nation
of free and proud men as he had thought, but a savage tyranny. This
naturally provokes the resistance of his people. At first muted and
polite, the resistance becomes more open in Act III where it culminates
in open rebellion. Deserted by his friends and most loyal soldiers who
defect to the army of the republican South (now led by Boyer),
demoralised by the paralysis caused by a stroke and with his dreams
in tatters, Christophe commits suicide.

Unlike the previous two acts, where scenes of buffoonery and
comedy enliven the action, the third is one of unrelieved tragedy as
Christophe, completely possessed by his political passion, raves and
rants, hallucinates and staggers helplessly to his death.

But although the material dramatised in *La Tragédie du roi Christophe*
is historical, Césaire's purpose in writing his play was political. It
was, like Edouard Glissant's purpose in *Monsieur Toussaint* (1961), to
provide 'a prophetic vision of the [Haitian] past' (Glissant 1961: 7);

to quarry from it, that is, useful meaning for the present and the future.

This need on Césaire's part to extract lessons from Haitian history for the present was made all the more urgent by certain developments during the period of elaboration of the play. Between 1959 and 1963 when he was working at it, many states in the Third World, especially in Africa and the Caribbean, were either poised for or, as with Ghana, Algeria, Mali, Guinea, Cuba, had only recently gained their independence. It was a period of high expectations, of euphoria even, in Africa and in progressive circles the world over as these states, finally free from centuries of colonial rule, and sometimes only after bloody wars of liberation, took their place in the concert of nations and set about rebuilding their shattered identities.

To Césaire who, taking upon himself the lot of a suffering mankind, had earlier described himself as 'a kaffir-man / a hindu-man-from-Calcutta / a man-from-Harlem-who-doesn't-vote' (1956: 36), and who had spent more than thirty years of his life fighting for the recognition of the humanity of the colonised and their right to self-determination, it was a moment of great pride which he recorded thus in *Ferrements*:

> I can see nations sprouting everywhere
> Green and red flags, gorges of ancient winds
> I salute you all, Mali, Guinea, Ghana
> Listen:
> > from my distant island
> > from my watchful island
> I say hurrah. (1960: 83)

But Independence was also a period of great fear and anxiety. For Césaire knew, from the 1960s, thanks to the example of the world's first black independent nation, Haiti, that 'the apotheosis of independence could also become the curse of independence' as Fanon put it (1970: 55): that freedom from colonial rule could be dreadful freedom.

Haiti's independence did not bring about the hoped-for freedoms and prosperity for which a revolution had been waged and a bitter war against France fought. On the contrary, it unleashed a military dictatorship in every way as repressive as anything the country had known during the worst days of French rule. It exacerbated the rivalries between classes, races and political leaders. Socio-economic inequalities deepened; the population, miseducated in false values or not educated at all, remained deeply opposed to all change; the former colonial power also attempted to undermine the young nation's sovereignty. In the end, civil war and chaos descended upon the country (see Nicholls 1979: 33–60).

How then did the dreams and hopes generated by Haitian independence degenerate into such a nightmare? Such is the tragic paradox that Césaire sought to explore in *La Tragédie du roi Christophe*. He also hoped that the problems raised by the Haitian experience, and dramatised in his play, would be pondered over by the newly independent and would-be independent states of Africa (Hawkins 1986: 144–53; Kesteloot 1964: 131–45).

The central theme of *La Tragédie du roi Christophe* can be summed up in the reply given to Vastey by the Deuxième Dame in Act II, scene 2: 'What a charming paradox! King Christophe would in short further the cause of liberty by using the methods of slavery' (1970: 80). The action of the play is conceived in terms of this antithesis. The latter's most immediate application is in the hiatus between the hero's generous intentions and his achievements. Of course, generosity is not the first impression that Christophe creates upon the reader. Rather, he strikes one as self-centred and ambitious. He interprets the changes made to the presidency, for example, as an affront to his person:

The amendment made to the Constitution by the Senate is an act of defiance against me and my person; an insult to my dignity and I'll have nothing to do with it. (p. 20).

But very quickly this impression changes as Christophe emerges as a leader for whom power is not an end, but only a means to be put in the service of others. He is impelled by a noble ideal – that of giving his people their lost sense of identity, a distinct cultural personality which he sees as a prerequisite for any act of authentic decolonisation and development.

Using an uncharacteristic image borrowed from nature, he compares his project with that of a farmer whose task it is to nurture carefully a plant which has been forcibly uprooted from its natural environment and transplanted elsewhere. What Haitians need, he tells Pétion, is not just formal liberty, but

something thanks to which this nation of transplanted people will sink roots, put out buds, blossom out and send on the face of the world the perfumes and fruits of their luscious beauty ... something which forces them to self-regenerate. (p.23)

The use of the expression 'to self-regenerate' here is important. Christophe does not see independence simply in terms of an improvement of the existing political structures. It is the total destruction of the inherited structures of a particular society and the creation of new ones. It is, in a word, a re-birth.

It is precisely in the context of the symbolic re-birth that is independence that Christophe's decision to change the French names of his subjects and to replace them by African ones must be understood:

Come on!
With glorious names, I wish to cover your slave names, with names of pride, your names of shame ... It is about a rebirth that we're talking! (p. 37)

By renaming them, Christophe – to borrow Benston's words on the 'topos of (un) naming in Afro-American literature' – 'unnamed the immediate past' to symbolise 'the long unacknowledged nascent selfhood that had survived and transcended slavery' (Benston 1984: 153).

But the hero of *La Tragédie du roi Christophe* is also keenly aware of the fact that authentic freedom is not created by a mere change of name. While such a change is perhaps a positive indication of a new sense of identity and awareness, he realises that it has to be strongly backed, if it is to be meaningful at all, by self-discipline and hard work:

Haiti has less to fear from the French than from herself! The enemy of this people is her indolence ... her hatred of discipline. (p. 29)

Unlike Pétion, his rival, who thinks of freedom as a gift or an entrenched article in a constitution, Christophe thinks of it as a conquest which can only become real and lasting through action and concrete achievement. It is, indeed, in the light of this burning conviction that he mobilises his people into the task of building an enormous citadel that should stand as a living testimony to their spirit of endeavour and greatness:

this people must obtain, aim at and achieve something impossible! Carried by our wounded hands, the mad challenge ... I mean the citadel, the liberty of an entire people. (p. 62)

Through the experience of the manual labour involved in constructing this monument, the Haitians will be transformed, so Christophe thinks, into regenerated citizens. They will discover the exacting realm of responsibility; be drawn from their passivity and inaction to participate, as they have never done before, as actors and not just as spectators in the making of their destiny.

Christophe's role as *creator*, as founder of a people, can be seen not only from his intentions, but also from the texture of his language, his imagery. Although on occasion he borrows images, as we saw, from the field of farming or from education such as when he compares himself to a teacher brandishing the cane over the heads of unwilling pupils (p. 86), the majority of comparisons made either by him or about him are taken from the world of inanimate objects or from that of the creative professions, especially architecture (see Benamou 1975: 165–7; Naville 1970: 244). Thus in Act I, scene 3, Vastey describes him as having a sense of formal beauty and expresses admiration for his 'powerful potter's hands kneading the Haitian clay' (p. 32). In scene 6 of the same act, Christophe himself likens Haiti to a vast terrain that is full of dust and that lacks the solidity of rock or concrete:

> dust everywhere, no stone,
> I'm looking for stone, for cement.
> All this debris,
> Oh! putting all that upright,
> Upright and in the face of the world,
> solidly. (p. 45)

He explains his plans for Haiti to his loyal supporter, Vastey, in terms reminiscent of those of a worker in the steel industry: 'Vastey, the human material itself needs to be resmelted. We'll try in our small workshop' (p. 50). In Act II, scene 6, he explains to his Council of State that before his accession to the throne, Haiti was an 'enormous foundry, an endless stretch of mud' (p. 98) as opposed to a concrete structure. And he uses a neologism, 'raque' (p. 98), to describe the sludge that was the country.

These images, coupled with the frequent use of verbs connected with building or creating – 'to do', 'to build', 'to construct' (*La Tragédie*, pp. 38, 62, 98 etc.) – show that Christophe sees himself and, indeed, the revolutionary leader first and foremost as a kind of craftsman or technician, whose task it is to construct a state, as one would an edifice. Indeed, Christophe describes himself as a 'constructor' in the 1963 edition of the play: 'Oh, what a beautiful job; how I'd like to be the *maker* of these people' (p. 64). To him, then, Haiti is a building-site in need of an engineer.

Like a Sartrean hero in the throes of existential anguish, Christophe is nauseated by the viscous and the sludgy, which he associates with underdevelopment, and fascinated by the concrete and metallic, which he attributes to development. It is this fascination that explains his obsession with constructing a citadel – 'a heavy stone shield' (p. 63). For him, independence or development is the ability to impose lasting socio-political and physical forms on chaos; the capacity to forge a distinct cultural identity. It is the ability to create.

This conception of development is clearly highlighted in Christophe's burst of enthusiastic fervour over Besse's suggestion that a citadel be built. The latter has hardly spoken when Christophe already visualises the monument coming to life:

Look at this distended chest of the earth, the earth which was concentrated but is now stretching out, rising from its sleep, taking its first step out of *chaos*, its first step towards the heavens. (p. 62, emphasis mine)

The construction of the citadel, like the development of a nation, is considered by Christophe as a victory of order over chaos, of man over nature, of human will over fate. He insists on the role of the will to his wife:

If we want to move upwards, visualise the effort demanded of us; our taut feet, the tension in our muscles, our clenched teeth. (p.59)

Elsewhere, he tells his Council of State:

Gentlemen, the real question facing us is that we are poor and it depends on us to be rich, that we are hungry and there is land in abundance awaiting only our arms, our *will*. (p. 98, emphasis mine)

This determination to establish a new order of experience through human endeavour (both physical and moral) firmly characterises Christophe as an embodiment of 'Negritude' (see Irele 1973: 22–43). Not only does he revolt against cultural mimeticism and extol the previously decried values of his peoples, he moves out of his purely subjective attitude to attempt to create by fiat a new psychological and political reality. Christophe is not only a poet-politician, but is also, as Bénamou has acutely observed, a demiurge (1975: 165–7).

To better understand his voluntaristic notion of development, it will be useful to contrast it with that of his friend Wilberforce. Unlike him who sees development essentially as creation, Wilberforce conceives it as growth. Christophe puts a premium on the will, Wilberforce on the role of time. In his letter to Christophe, he writes:

A tree isn't created. It is planted! Fruits aren't extracted from it, they are left to ripen. A nation isn't an act of creation, but a process of growth. (p. 57)

This processual notion of development, this idea of the leader as farmer, as a man, who in Wilberforce's words, sows 'the seeds of civilisation' (p. 57) and guides and watches them grow into maturity also characterises the vision of Madame Christophe. Like Wilberforce, she warns her husband, in one of her few appearances, of the dangers attendant on an unbridled faith in the human will. Like him, too, she borrows her imagery predominantly from nature, comparing the leader not to an engineer, craftsman or creator, but to the 'round and thick foliage of the huge mombin tree under which a shade-thirsty cattle seek refuge from the scorching heat of the sun' (p. 60). Wilberforce and Madame Christophe think, unlike Christophe, that rather than seek, suicidally, to transform or dominate nature, man must be attuned to her, be subject to her beneficent rhythms.

'Creation' or 'growth'? Such then are the alternative political strategies explored in *La Tragédie du roi Christophe*; strategies which not only faced the Haiti of the early 1800s, but have also been at the centre of the on-going Third World debate, particularly intense in the late 1950s and the 1960s, between rival ideologies of decolonisation and development advanced by proponents of revolutionary and evolutionary change.

Of course, Césaire himself does not endorse either option – his aim is to show the limitations of each, to pose the problems associated with them. The one thing that is obvious, however, is that by consistently choosing stone and cement as opposed to wood, by likening the political leader of a developing country to an engineer as opposed to a farmer (Wilberforce's choice), Césaire's revolutionary hero also evinces a preference, unconsciously perhaps, for a certain type of society: the industrial as opposed to the agricultural. Or more precisely, he would seem to be equating development with industrialisation. But if, indeed, such is his choice (and the evidence from the imagery is overwhelming) is it not sharply at variance with the entire ethic of Negritude that he otherwise embodies, with its exaltation of the values of agrarian, non-industrial cultures? (On the theme of Negritude in the play, see Wolitz 1969: 195–208.)

Indeed, it is one of the many ironies and contradictions in this play that contrary to one of the central planks of the doctrine of Negritude, Wilberforce, a white man, should count among those who urge patience and advocate a relationship of harmony with nature. Given the insistence with which Césaire posits, in *Cahier d'un retour au pays natal* (1956: 68, 71, 72), scientific rationalism and intuition as the distinctive traits of the white and black minds respectively one would not have expected his hero to be so attracted to the science, language and philosophy of social or civil engineering. Rather, he should have been wedded, by virtue of his race, to a mode of existence which Césaire describes thus:

> Ma négritude n'est ni une tour ni une cathédral
> elle plonge dans la chair rouge du sol
> elle plonge dans la chair ardente du ciel
> elle troue l'accablement opaque de sa droite patience. (1956:
> 117)

In *La Tragédie du roi Christophe*, Césaire the dramatist shows the limitations and, perhaps, the ultimate falsehood (from a truth-value as opposed to an ideological point of view) of the doctrinal tenet of Césaire the poet.

But whatever the conclusions that can be drawn from his imagery on the type of society that he has in mind, it is clear that Christophe's metaphor of nation-building as creation also holds the key to his tragic failure. By premissing his politics on the notion of man's infinite plasticity, by considering his subjects as bits of metal that can be moulded at will, by devaluing the role of time in the formation of nations, he only succeeds in unleashing a reign of terror in his country and in transforming it into a 'mighty slaveship' (p. 118).

It is not the least of tragic ironies in a play full of ironies that a man who is so obsessed with building a state, with moulding the personality of a people, should choose destruction as his favourite weapon.

Christophe is all the more tragic because his fate, if inevitable, is undeserved. He is destructive and yet commands the sympathy of the reader. This is because at the bottom he is not an evil man. His hubris is not reprehensible personal ambition but, as has been shown, an intense love for his people.

His error lies in his relentless and uncompromising pursuit of this ideal without due consideration for the only-too-human fallibility of his subjects, the inertia of nature and the inescapable realities of a 300-year history of slavery and colonisation. Like most revolutionaries, Christophe forgets the actual individuals whom he set out to defend. He removes his political means from the sphere of moral judgement, arguing that only the ends they are meant to serve should be used to justify them. He sneers at compromise and rejects persuasion. To his wife, who suggests caution and warns of the dangers of his ideal begetting the fatal rock on which it will run aground ('Sometimes I wonder whether in attempting to do everything, you're not more like the mighty fig tree which hugs all the surrounding vegetation and stifles it to death', p. 60), he replies contemptuously: 'who can offer me something other than the prudent sayings of a woman?' (p. 61). And to Wilberforce, who insists that development is an evolutionary process, he retorts defiantly:

We've got no time to wait... What a strange idea to have to rely, for the destiny of a people, on the sun, the rains, the seasons. (p. 58)

It is precisely this Romantic all-or-nothing view of action in time, this all-consuming passion for the absolute, this voluntaristic conception of development as creation and not growth that leads to Christophe's downfall and death. His statement to Hugonin: 'Each of your words is littered with debris of my dreams' (p. 39) is a tragic recognition, an anagnorisis, of the distance separating his dreams from reality.

But Christophe's death does not mark the end of his career. On the contrary, it heralds a new life for him. It is a period of transition during which he is transformed or, more appropriately perhaps, elevated from the ranks of man to that of god.

This idea of an elevation, of a consecration, is suggested in three ways: theatrically by the passage from secular theatre to ritual performance; visually by the choice of a mountaintop as burial place and symbolically by the name of the place itself: Ife (see Antoine 1984: 73–8 on the play's imagery and symbolism of heights). Holy city and spiritual home to the Yoruba people of Nigeria, Ife, to Christophe's voodoo subjects is, as Régis Antoine explains, a mythical region 'under water... the equivalent of the Apostle John's celestial Jerusalem' (Antoine 1984: 96; on the play's voodoo dimension, see Case 1975b).

By ascending to Ife in a ritual ceremony which though simple is nothing short of a second enthronement or a canonisation, Christophe ceases to be a mere figure of history, mortal, misunderstood and reviled by his people, as his wife notes in her graveside tribute to him; he becomes a powerful figure of myth, an indestructible idea. Like the brightly coloured phoenix which Vastey recommends as his emblem or the immortal Memnon, Christophe dies only to rise again from his ashes, to gain eternal life.

But the exact mythical figure which Césaire's hero represents is a problem (see M. Bailey 1987: 239–50; 1992: 151–87; Moreau 1987: 269–87; Pageaux 1987: 251–6, on the play's mythical dimension). Many figures have been used to describe him, but none seem to fit perfectly his contradictory qualities. To some critics, and to Césaire himself to whom the analogy was suggested, according to Harris, by his African actors (R. Harris 1973: 112) Christophe is the Yoruba mythical god of thunder, Sango. Others, and this again includes Césaire, have described him as representing the Promethean ideal (Bradby 1984: 148) while others still, more recently, see him as the embodiment of a 'post-Nietzschean tragic myth figure' (Arnold 1986: 135): that of a 'surhomme nègre' (Arnold 1986: 140).

While a case can indeed be made for these different analogies, they all remain at best partial. Christophe may share Sango's self-will, cruelty and tyranny (Idowu 1966: 89–95 on Sango). He may indeed, like him, and as one of the legends on the latter has it (Idowu 1966: 90), have resorted to suicide to escape the wrath of his long-tyrannised and now-rebellious subjects. But he also displays a passionate commitment to justice which seems to be signally lacking in the Yoruba god.

Conversely, in the case of the Prometheus parallel, Christophe has, in common with the Greek god, a love of oppressed humanity. Against the Zeuses of his age – history, nature and a hostile former colonial power – who seek to destroy and keep his people down, he rises up in resolute defence. As a culture hero, a master-artisan himself, he seeks to instil in them a desire for perfection and, as we have seen from his imagery, a thirst for craftsmanship that will make them the creators of new worlds, of their destiny. In this respect, he is like Prometheus. But unlike him too, and this is where the analogy breaks down, he is also a tyrant, a destroyer of men.

This problem of imperfect analogy also faces the Nietzschean reading of Césaire's play that has been recently proposed. The idea that *La Tragédie du roi Christophe* is a Passion play in the Nietzschean sense; one in which the hero (Christophe-Dionysius) endures ritual suffering and sacrifice (Arnold 1986: 140) so that a new world may come into being for his people; one in which the plenitude of myth and lyrical aspirations are no longer at variance with historical reality, is an attractive and persuasive one. It also has the merit of elucidating Césaire's expressed acknowledgement of a Nietzschean influence on his idea of tragedy (in Leiner 1993: 138–9). But this reading is not without its defects. As in the Prometheus parallel, it fails to take into account the dual nature of the hero, who is both sacrificed but also, and very significantly so, sacrificer.

The mythical or archetypal hero that Christophe comes closest to, it seems to me, is the blacksmith king, the creator-of-civilisation hero of many traditional African societies as he finds expression, for example, in historico-legendary figures like Chaka of the Zulus, Sunjata of the Mandigoes or Ntinu Wene of the Bakongo (see Balandier 1968: 27–41; 1970: 101–17 on the theory of the Black-smith-King). And this parallel is not only limited to his attributes, but extends also to the unconscious narrative structure of his career. A characteristic of these archetypal heroes is that they are what in modern terms would be called 'self-made'. They suffer from an infirmity, social or physical, which in normal circumstances would have put power beyond their grasp. Chaka, for example, was an illegitimate child who, for this reason, was expelled, together with his mother, from his father's home and literally disinherited. Sunjata was paralysed for seven years and like Chaka had to flee home with his mother to escape possible death at the hands of Sassouma Bérété, one of his late father's senior wives. Christophe was a recently freed slave, ill-educated, black and a cook in a society where power and privilege were racialised (see Césaire 1962: 31 on the hierarchy of race in Haiti then). Ntinu Wene, Balandier tells us, was a '"youngster" thought to have no hope of acquiring authority and privileges, although he proves to be impatient to "command", to prove himself as a "strong and fearless warrior"' (1968: 35)

But in spite of their disadvantages or perhaps because of them, these men are fired by a passion to rule, to dominate men. This leads them, in a second phase, to conquer power after breaking with the existing social and political order and to establish a new society that is *subject only to their law*. Thus Chaka and Sunjata both return after long periods of wandering and valiant service in foreign armies to defeat their rivals and seize power. Christophe rejects the position offered him by the Senate, retreats to the north and establishes a monarchy, proclaiming:

I'm king neither by the grace of God, nor by that of the people, but by the will and grace of my fists. (p. 129)

As king he exhibits, like our examples above, two faces: one murderous and tyrannical and the other intelligent and justice-loving. In other words, he is both a powerful warrior and murderer and a bearer of civilisation and Blacksmith-King. In his latter capacity he seeks, to use his appropriately creationist metaphor, to shape the pieces of metal that are his people into durable forms. It is this duality in the man, characteristic of primordial sovereign power in many traditional African societies, and also of modern revolution-aries, that is highlighted by his page at his graveside:

> Father, we install you in Ife on the hill
> with three palms...
> In the beginning
> Bi-faced
> Here patience and impatience
> defeat and victory
> Force of night and tide of the day. (p. 52)

Christophe's sovereignty, to use Balandier's words describing the civilising hero of the Bakongo, Ntinu Wene, 'is full of contradictions, his power is ambivalent: although violent... it is at the same time based upon the wisdom and knowledge of the man who loves justice. It destroys one social order to create another. It is sacred violence' (Balandier 1968: 57).

But Christophe is not just a great figure of history, tragedy or myth; a man who elicits our and the dramatist's unreserved admiration. He is also a comic character, the butt of satire. In a comment on this aspect of his character, Césaire writes:

He combines in his character features of Prometheus, Peter the Great and the 'bourgeois gentilhomme'. (quoted in Harris 1973: 76)

An aspect of him that comes in for ridicule is his decision to proclaim himself king and to create a European-style court, complete with nobility. True, this decision, like most taken by Christophe, is well-intentioned. It cannot be lightly dismissed as a case of mindless

imitation of foreign models or of self-aggrandisement, such as we
have been accustomed to by many a recent African leader. It is born
of the belief – profoundly mistaken, of course – that only a monarch
can give a young state enough dignity, and earn it the respect of
European nations; in this case especially France, for which Christophe is so eager.

Furthermore, with the high sense of formality and ceremony which
it imposes, royalty to Christophe is a metaphor of his political project.
He sees the master of ceremony, whom he brings from France for his
coronation, as performing in his sphere the same function as
Christophe performs in his: one of giving form and discipline to a
clumsy and unshapely mass of courtiers.

But whatever his intentions, Christophe's decision here as elsewhere results in shambles. Only that this time, it is in comic shambles.
In place of the high seriousness and pomp normally associated with
a coronation, we have grotesqueness and unrelieved comedy. The
comic derives from the contrast between the aristocratic, Monsieur
Jourdain-like pretensions of Christophe and his vulgarity, both in
language and behaviour. In an extraordinary display of poor taste he
slaps the behinds of his female courtiers, holds one of his dukes by the
scruff of the neck and swears: 'Mon Dieu! Qu'est-ce qui m'a foutu
des cocos pareils!' (p. 36). The courtiers themselves are as ridiculous
in their borrowed robes as they are in their newly created titles: for
example, the Duke of Limonade, the Duke of Marmelade, or the
Court of the Band of the North.

But perhaps the most comic of all is the highly effective theatrical
spectacle of these men and women trying to cultivate, under the
direction of the master of ceremonies, rigid and formal movements
that are completely out of tune with their portly bodies and foreign
to their more exuberant and spontaneous ways.

Christophe is not the only victim of Césaire's powers of parody and
caricature. His political rival, Pétion, is another. A mulatto and
leader of the republic, he appears, on the surface at least, as
Christophe's opposite in every respect. Unlike the latter who, during
their very first meeting, is concerned only with his power and his
person, Pétion emphasises principles: 'I've spoken *principles* and you
insist on referring to your person' (p. 20) he rebukes Christophe.
Pétion is a stout defender of liberal democracy, or so it seems, and a
believer in its principles – an opposition, a free press and the
sovereignty of the people.

But Césaire is no more seduced by the man and his ideological position than he is by Christophe. So he subverts Pétion's profession of faith in democracy in the very act of its proclamation. The area Césaire concentrates on to achieve this subversion is Pétion's language. Here is an extract of a speech by him to parliament:

If the opposition, and it is our glory here to tolerate an opposition, if the opposition then, as I was saying, had been less guided by a spirit of haste and perverse distrust than by those qualities of measure, prudence and probity which should always inspire the legislators of a free republic, then, Gentlemen, no one ought to have given our enemies pleasure by troubling this hour of national unanimity with such a useless quarrel. (p. 48)

With its combination of rhetorical clichés, pluperfect subjunctives, orotund phrases and its appeal to abstract moral categories, this speech reveals in Pétion a cheap orator, a man who, like most of his colleagues in the Senate, is more interested in the formal aspects of parliamentary democracy than in its substance. And it is indeed a measure of his weak commitment and that of his colleagues to democracy that at the slightest threat from Christophe, they should cry out for the return of France – 'Louis XVIII rather than Christophe' – a country whose rule in Haiti was no more democratic than Christophe's, but which at least had the advantage, from the point of view of Pétion and his colleagues, of guaranteeing their property rights, now threatened by the revolutionary Christophe.

In Pétion and Christophe, Césaire shows the limitation of two of the ideological alternatives open to developing countries and the betrayal of the ideals of independence to which they could lead. But one character in whom these ideals remain pure is Métellus. In a moving scene in which he lies wounded by Christophe's troops and asks to be killed, he condemns with raging disgust the

> trivial pantin piteux
> Christophe! Pétion!
> ... la double tyrannie
> celle de la brute
> celle du scéptique hautain. (p. 43)

He restates for posterity those values for which the Haitian War of Independence was fought, which for a moment united all Haitians, and for which he would now rather fight again and die, than continue to see betrayed:

We were going to found a country
   all to ourselves
Not just this piece of island!
One open to all islands!
To all Blacks! Blacks of the entire world! (p. 43)

But although admirable, Métellus' position in Césaire's eyes is not without its shortcomings. And the main one is that it is a vision without an adequate politics to give it concrete expression. The dilemma which is posed by *La Tragédie du roi Christophe* and which Métellus' death again reveals is the irreconcilable rivalry between moral idealism and effective politics.

Among the other significant characters in the play are Hugonin and the group of peasants. Described by Césaire as 'something of a parasite, a buffoon and a political agent', Hugonin has been compared by several critics, and very rightly so, to the Fool in *King Lear* (Deberre 1984: 29; Naville 1970: 248; Oddon 1973: 92). But another figure to whom he could be compared with equal validity, and who is perhaps not unknown to popular Haitian culture, is that of the Village Jester or Fool in many traditional African communities (Duvignaud 1965: 20–5).

Usually a kind of dimwit or harmless idiot, and living at the edge of social life, in that blurred space between social normality and abnormality, this character, whom anthropologists would call a 'liminal' figure, is greatly valued for his jokes and songs but also for his wise sayings, which are couched in riddles and proverbs. Of uncertain mental health, but also thought, like most not-very-normal people in these communities, to possess special powers (of prescience for example), his welfare is largely the affair of the community. He is provided for not only by the villagers in whose homes and company he is always accommodated, but also significantly by the ruler in whose court he is a frequent visitor. Because of his large web of contacts, the Village Fool is of especial interest to a ruler. He both entertains and roisters with the ruler while at the same time he provides him with valuable information on the affairs of the community, and acts as a barometer of public opinion. But more than just amuse, he uses his freedom from the social obligations that are binding on the more 'normal' members of society to criticise and to reveal, in mock-joking fashion, sometimes unpalatable truths. Because of this dual function as clown and critic, the Village Fool is a figure at once patronised and feared.

Such, it seems to me, is precisely Hugonin's position in Césaire's play. Now he is with the ordinary people, in the market-place for example (Act I, scene 2), now with the king and his courtiers in the palace. In both instances, he amuses his audience with salacious jokes, puns and witty sayings. Here is an example of an exchange he has with a lady noisily advertising her wares in the market:

MARCHANDE: Rapadou! Rapadou! Par ici tout ce qu'on homme peut désirer.
(*s'adressant à Hugonin*)
Du rapadou, Papa? ou du tassau?
HUGONIN: Dis donc la belle, ce n'est pas du rapadou que je veux, c'est toi, doudou! (p. 24)

Some of Hugonin's interventions with song and dance are at moments of high drama or formality, such as during the coronation or the siege of Port-au-Prince, and they are meant to ease the tension. But, as with the Village Fool, his interventions are never innocent, pure entertainment. They always contain a sting in the tail. Thus his song in Act I, scene 7, during the anniversary feast of Christophe's coronation, is a criticism of the way the rulers offer themselves sumptuous meals while the people are left, in the words of his song, 'to lick the plates' (p. 52). Similarly his song about 'a male louse and a female louse fighting on a stool' (Act I, scene 7) is a parody, a deflation of the conflict between Pétion and Christophe.

Elsewhere Hugonin comments on the significance of events to the people at large. In Act I, scene 2, for example, he explains to them the implications of the French ship sailing around their coast. He expresses Christophe's hidden desires as when he greets him with 'Long live King Christophe' (p. 29) before the idea becomes official. He ferrets out information for him, as when he breaks the news of Pétion's death and succession by Boyer (p. 117), or of the defection of his once faithful general, Magny, to the enemy (p. 135). In a reference that is presumably lost on the king, he even reveals his future fate to him (p. 95). Finally, after Christophe has been deserted by all towards the end of the play, Hugonin comforts him and, in a role that seems purely Haitian, appears just before his death as Le Baron Samedi, the voodoo god of death.

But these functions apart, Hugonin also lends a popular and highly comic vein to the play. To reinforce this aspect further and to develop the work's theatrical resources, Césaire vividly depicts rambunctious and picturesque scenes of the market-place and the pit. He also brings on stage popular characters like the peasants and raftsmen, and integrates in the play various elements of traditional mass Haitian culture such as songs, dances, religious beliefs and rites.

Let us analyse each of these elements, starting with the peasants and raftsmen. The latter do not appear as individualised characters, but as representatives of the rural masses; of the majority, that is, of Christophe's subjects. They appear twice – first in the interlude preceding Act II, and in the first scene of that act, and again in the interlude before Act III. Their interventions constitute oases of stillness in the otherwise frenzied and turbulent atmosphere of the play. As a group, the peasants and raftsmen represent an attachment to nature that is anathema to Christophe, as well as a popular wisdom, made up of a mixture of fatalism and realism and expressed in proverbs and homely images, that is in stark contrast to his culture-hero ambitions.

But the appearance on stage of these rural characters does not only add fullness and local colour to the play, it also underlines the gulf separating the regime and its citizens and the inevitable failure to which the former is condemned. The peasant figures also comment on the action: either openly, such as when they express bitterness over the savage repression that prevents them from observing even their elementary religious rites (p. 75), or over Christophe's decision to distribute lands only to the military (p. 110), or obliquely. The best example of an oblique comment is in the first interlude, where the presenter implies that the difficulties of Christophe's task are like those of a man steering a 10-ton, 50-metre-wide raft down the violent Artibonite river, with neither rudder nor sails (p. 66).

The songs in *La Tragédie du roi Christophe* are, as has been briefly mentioned in connection with Hugonin, an important theatrical device. Césaire deploys a large body of them, sung by individuals (Hugonin, of course, but also Christophe himself, pp. 104, 120, 142; Madame Christophe, pp. 141, 142–3; the Foreman of Works, p. 102; the Apprentice Raftsman, p. 67; Isabelle, p. 87) or by groups of characters (the Peasants, p. 77; the Chorus, pp. 40, 130, the Workers, p. 103). And they vary from the simple work-songs of the citadel labourers through to the satirical lines of Hugonin or the chants of the voodoo cult intoned by Christophe.

But whatever their nature, they are not just decorative. They are either an important accompaniment to or comment on crucial moments in the drama, or are complementary to setting and theme.

The examples of three sets of songs will be given to illustrate this point. The praise-song to Christophe 'the valiant warrior' in Act I, scene 4 is not only appropriate to the mood of the occasion, his coronation, but through its sudden transformation into a hymn to Sango, the song comments, prophetically, on the hero's own future deification. Madame Christophe, with her touching and poignant song in Haitian Creole about her illness and call from God, announces her imminent position as widow:

> Moin malade m-couche m-pa sa lève
> M-pral nan no-e, mpa moun icit-o
> Bondié rèle-m, m-pralé. (p. 141)

Freely rendered from the French to which it has been put by Régis Antoine (1984: 87), this song reads:

> I'm ill and bed-ridden,
> I'll go northwards; I don't belong
> to this place
> God is calling me, I'll go.

Finally, Césaire uses the ballad of Ourika, sung by the Première Dame's daughter, Isabelle, to the clavecin, as an appropriate indication of this family's middle-class background but also as an ironic denunciation of its philistinism. For the content of the song on Ourika, the black girl from West Africa whose illusions about France are sadly shattered by her bitter racial experiences, seems to be completely lost on the family. Ironically, it undermines the Première Dame's previous arguments against Christophe who, as Vastey reminds her, is fighting precisely so that young girls like Ourika will no longer 'find in their colour an obstacle to the accomplishment of their hearts' desires' (p. 82). Isabelle and her family are interested in the song for the status it confers on them as a cultured family in the eyes of Vastey. But the demonstration misfires.

A central feature of *La Tragédie du roi Christophe* is its linguistic resources. These include not only different varieties of French ranging from the standard to the popular, but also Haitian Creole, or sometimes a mixture of the two. Césaire uses language not only to differentiate character, but also to underline theme and setting and to create atmosphere. On this last aspect especially, he explains:

I've tried to recreate the Haitian atmosphere: first in the language itself which mixes French with Creole words and expressions. (quoted in Mbom 1979: 66)

Examples of such words and expressions abound in the text. A few examples will suffice. Among the most notable are 'père-savane' (p. 55) for a not-so-well-qualified rural priest in Haiti; 'maldioque' (p. 95) for evil fate, 'chemin malouc' (p. 96) for a dangerous path, 'clairin' (p. 24), 'tafia' (p. 24), 'branbancourt' (p. 53), for different types of locally brewed drinks; 'cocomaque' (p. 74) for a baton, and 'récade' for the staff of office. Haitian Creole proper is used mostly in the songs by the chorus (p. 40), Hugonin (pp. 132, 148), Christophe himself (p. 142) and, as we have seen, by his wife (pp. 141, 142–3).

A category of characters clearly differentiated by their language are the peasants and raftsmen. Their basilectal French, like that of Maupassant's peasants, is mostly characterised, to borrow Deberre's headings (1984: 63–5) by (a) coinages and colloquialisms: 'un sacré beau pays' (p. 75), 'mauvaiseté' (p. 74), 'ça c'est recta' (p. 73), 'un petit coup de clairin pour vous défatiguer le corps' (p. 73); (b) syntactic changes: 'N'y a rien tant que' (p. 73) in which the French impersonal pronoun 'il' has been dropped, or 'Y a des choses à pas dire' (p. 74) where the negative particle 'ne' has also been elided in addition to the impersonal 'il'; (c) pronounciation defects: 'quèque chose' for 'quelque chose' (p. 110), 'pt'et' for 'peut-être' (p. 111); and (d) a liberal use of interjections and onomatopoeias: 'Plakata, plakata, plakata', for example, to denote the sound of the military police descending on idle workers.

At the other end of the linguistic spectrum stands Christophe. His heightened awareness of the situation of his people surfaces in the charged and highly poetic nature of his language. Thus, in one of his evocations of their slave past, he exclaims:

> Ilôt pierreux, milliers de nègres demi-nus
> que la vague a vomis un soir
> d'où venus! dans leur fumet de bête de chasse à
> courre. (p. 38)

> (Stony islet, thousands of half-naked blacks
> vomited one evening by the waves!
> port of origin unknown, exhaling their smell of hunted
> animals.)

What these lines convey poignantly is, first and foremost, the sense of thousands of black men being tossed around helplessly by the waves and finally thrown up on some sterile, stony island. In addition, the mood of frustration here proceeds from Christophe's heightened awareness of the predicament of a people who were not only at the mercy of nature, but also of men.

This same bitterness can be seen in the dehumanising process depicted in these lines from another speech by the hero:

> Jadis on nous vola nos noms!
> Notre fierté
> Notre noblesse ...
> Pierre, Paul ... Toussaint! Voilà
> les estampilles humiliantes dont on
> oblitéra nos noms de vérité. (p. 37)

Christophe does not refer here to the institution of slavery in abstract terms. He gives it, by the use of a single image 'estampilles' (brand-marks) a concrete presentation that powerfully suggests the owner-ship and right to property which slave-holders exercised over their human cattle.

But Christophe, as we saw, does not only use poetic language to evoke the past. He also uses it to conjure into existence a future of grandeur and freedom. His explanation to Martial Besse of the significance of the citadel is in this regard instructive. It is delivered in such emotional terms that his prose takes on a surrealistic, almost hallucinatory texture. The citadel emerges from the text not just as a colossal monument in granite, a testimony to human endeavour, but also a living force whose coming of age (as it were) will signal the death of the slave trader.

> Regardez ... Mais regardez! Il vit
> Il corne dans le brouillard. Il s'allume
> dans la nuit. Annulation du négrier!
> La formidable chevauchée! Mes amis, d'âcre
> sel bu et le vin noir du sable, moi, nous,
> les culbutés de la grosse houle, j'ai vu
> l'énigmatique étrave, écume et sang aux
> naseaux défoncer la vague de la honte. (p. 63)

Christophe is, like Lumumba in *Une Saison au Congo*, both a politician and a poet. The lyricism of his language and the dominant images he uses are a reflection of his basically idealistic, Promethean and conquering cast of mind while the language of, say, the peasants, with its time-honoured sayings, reveals an attachment to tradition that puts them on a collision course with Christophe. It is a measure of Césaire's greatness as a dramatic poet that the different themes and conceptions of political development he explores in his play are not just stated flatly and discursively, but that they are enacted through characters who are sufficiently individualised by their language.

Césaire's second play, *Une Saison au Congo* was first performed in March 1967 in Brussels by the Théâtre Vivant. In September of the same year, it was produced at the Venice Biennale. Its first French performance, in a Jean-Marie Serreau production, was at the Théâtre de l'Est Parisien on 4 October 1967, and its most recent was in September 1989, in the Théâtre de la Colline in Paris.

Like *La Tragédie*, this play also borrows its subject straight from history. This time, however, not from the distant, late-nineteenth-century history of a Caribbean island, but from the cauldron of 1960s African decolonisation politics. It presents a moment, 'a season', in the political history of an African country: the former Belgian Congo, present-day Zaire. It dramatises the turbulent career of one of that country's most controversial politicians: Patrice Lumumba (1925–61) – skilful orator, militant pan-Africanist, prime minister and, to his supporters and admirers, martyred hero (Legum 1962: vii–xxix; Lierde 1975; Lumumba 1962; Sartre 1964a: 194–253).

But although the events of the play are closely woven around him and it is he who confers unity on an otherwise loosely structured work, Césaire is only marginally interested in Lumumba as an individual. What is of greater concern to him, here as in the case of Christophe, is the character's representativeness, the exemplary nature of his career. He states:

It's no accident that I didn't entitle the play *Patrice Lumumba* but rather *A Season in the Congo*. It's a slice of life in the history of a country. (quoted in Naville 1970: 249)

What makes the Congolese leader an interesting figure of drama for Césaire is the fact that the Christophe-like problems he experiences – a state bitterly divided along ethnic and ideological lines, an alienated or uneducated population, a massively interfering former colonial power – are characteristic of emergent nations. Through him, he can once again address the wider public in these nations.

Like its central character, who is described by one of his political rivals Kala as 'a constantly leaping flame' (p. 69) and like the period itself it recreates, *Une Saison au Congo* is dramatic in the extreme. Not only does it accumulate a considerable number of events in the short span of time that it covers (thirteen months in all, November 1959 to February 1961), but its action is continuously shifting. When it is not in a prison in Africa or around the negotiating table in Brussels, it is in a brothel, a bar, the cabinet office, the public square or, more unusually for a play, in a plane or radio station. It also contains some tense moments, such as when, during Independence-day celebrations (Act I, scene 5), Lumumba, unmindful of all decorum and diplomatic niceties, fiercely denounces Belgian colonial rule in the presence of that country's king, or when, shortly after Independence, he faces a near-mutiny in the army. 'Coups de théâtre' are not absent from it either. A notable example occurs in Act II, scene 8, where Kala Lubu, President of the newly independent Congo, abruptly dismisses his Prime Minister Lumumba over the radio, accusing him of arbitrary rule.

The surface structure of *Une Saison* is very similar to that of *La Tragédie du roi Christophe*. The first of the play's three acts opens with a tout haranguing a curious crowd gathered around him in a popular district of Leopoldville. Like the Presenter in *La Tragédie du roi Christophe* who introduces the play's main theme by way of a commentary on a fight between two cocks, (in a kind of performance within a performance), the tout informs the reader of the political situation in the Congo by way of references to various brands of beer. Just as there are different and rival ethnic groups in Belgium, so there are in the Congo, he explains, different and competing types of beer, the best of which, however, is Polar.

> I've come here to talk about the
> best of beers, the very best of all the
> beers in the world:
> Polar!
> – Polar, the freshness of the poles
> in the tropics!
> Polar, the beer of the Congolese!
> Liberty!
> Polar, the beer of Congolese friendship
> and brotherhood. (pp. 11–12)

This reference to Polar beer, which, with its pun on the 'freshness of the poles in the tropics', sounds more like an inspired radio advertisement than anything else, turns out to be politically significant. Its full meaning is revealed in a comment to his younger colleagues by one of the Belgian policemen keeping a watchful eye on the crowd: 'behind Polar stands the minister ... Yes indeed ... the minister of the Congo' (p. 13).

From a dramatic point of view, this vague but awed reference to the 'minister', complete with its eloquent silences, arouses the spectator's curiosity. But the latter has hardly had time to register the minister's name than it is revealed that he is 'under [Belgian] police surveillance' (p. 13). So, at once popular with his people, indeed a symbol of their unity as we have been told, and yet under constant surveillance, Lumumba emerges from the outset as a controversial figure. What scene 1 manages to convey through this information, with humour and light-heartedness, is an unmistakable sense of impending crisis.

And this indeed breaks out in the second scene where we learn of Lumumba's arrest and imprisonment and the restlessness among his supporters provoked by this action. But here again, close on the heels of this information comes that of his release so that he may participate in a Round Table Independence conference in Brussels and, moments later, that of the successful outcome of the negotiations. The various reactions to this news in Belgian and Congolese circles and the Independence celebrations constitute the high point of the act. The rest of Act 1 is devoted to the Belgian military intervention in the Congo – ostensibly to protect Belgian lives against the mutinous Force Publique, but in reality to reconquer it – the secession of Katanga and Lumumba's appeal for help from the United Nations.

Act 1 then, which historically covers a period of nine months (from November 1959 to July 1960) can be said to be concerned with Lumumba's struggle for Independence, its attainment and immediate aftermath. From the point of view of theatre, this act like the rest of the play is notable for its resolute non-naturalistic approach. An example of this approach can be seen in four short scenes (scenes 2–6) totalling no more than sixteen pages of text, where the action changes location four times between and within countries, covers a 6-month period and, with barely any explanation at all, shows Lumumba passing from folk-hero to reviled prisoner to worthy negotiator and then to Prime Minister. In fact, some of the events are not represented at all. One learns of them through the reactions of the parties concerned (the Independence negotiations being an example) or through stage effects.

An illustration of the latter is in Act 1, scene 9. Here the violence unleashed on Belgian citizens in the Congo and their government's intervention are suggested (in the case of the first event) through the device of a group of white refugees walking across a dimly lit stage carrying what they can of their possessions and (in the second) through the use of talking war-drums to signify foreign aggression. Even the way scene changes are suggested in Act I – in full view of the spectators and with the use of placards to indicate the new setting – contributes to maintaining the critical distance between audience and action.

Sketchy characterisation is another technique Césaire uses extensively. With the exception of characters like Lumumba and Mokutu who already in Act I achieve some individuality, the rest are no more than pasteboard figures representing various interests or positions, a fact underlined by his reference to them quite simply as, for example, First or Second Banker, A Woman, A Citizen, The Tribalist Mukongo and so on.

One last example we can give of Césaire's Brechtian approach to the theatre is the technique of interruption through song and dance. While it is true, as we saw in *La Tragédie*, that the songs are often a commentary on the action, and are therefore not foreign to it, because of their allusiveness (especially the Sanza Player's) they require an effort of reflection which is incompatible with the realist illusion.

A final comment on Act I concerns its diversity of tone. Popular when the play starts and each time the Sanza Player intervenes, the tone becomes fiercely satirical in the portrayal of the Belgian bankers in their top hats, clutching fat cigars and declaiming second-rate verses, and intensely poetic in some of Lumumba's speeches. A hint of the tragic is not altogether absent in Act I either. This is contained not only in the ominous sayings of the Sanza Player, who announces in scene 2 a period of blood and suffering for the Congo, but in the increasing solitude of the hero. At variance with his cabinet colleagues, under pressure from the army and with the threat of succession from Katanga, Lumumba sees his dreams crumbling barely a month after Independence.

This process of crisis and disintegration is accelerated in Act II. The main events of the act, which cover a 2-month period, are the outbreak of civil war in the Congo, Lumumba's dismissal as Prime Minister by Kala-Lubu and the *coup d'état* by Colonel Mokutu which finally puts an end to the squabbles between the two leaders.

Act II, with its eleven scenes, describes a symmetrical structure. The first five scenes are devoted to bringing out Lumumba's personality. This is done through a series of dialogues between him and the other main characters. First there is Mokutu, who is shown disagreeing with him on the issue of whether politicians should, on assuming high office, continue to visit places like popular bars. This dialogue brings to the fore the populist and élitist tendencies of Lumumba and Mokutu respectively. Then there is the Lumumba–Dag Hammarskjöld discussion where the latter refuses, contrary to the wishes of the former, to send in UN troops against the Katanga secessionists. The final dialogue is with Kala Lubu, during which Lumumba on the one hand deplores the massacre of the Balubas by government forces, while justifying it on the other in terms of the need to preserve the unity of the state.

After a transitional scene (Act II, scene 6) where Lumumba, dancing with the evocatively named Hélène Bijou, prophetically announces his own death:

Bijou, when I'll no longer be; when I shall have destroyed myself like a blind, blinding meteorite in the nocturnal sky ... continue to be beautiful ... (p. 68)

the last five scenes show him in open conflict with all three men in reverse order. First there is Kala, who sacks him, then Dag Hammarskjöld's UN forces which, in the person of Ghana, refuse him access to the radio station and finally Mokutu, who arrests him.

Unlike Act I which displays a variety of tones, the dominant tone in Act II is that of tragic irony. Here the net is fast closing on Lumumba. From the second scene, where he promotes Mokutu Chief of Staff against Mpolo's warning ('treason prowls all around you, but you don't see it!', p. 57), through his discussions with Hammarskjöld, which end with words more applicable to himself than to the Scandinavian statesman ('whatever happens, I hope you don't one day pay too costly a price for your illusions' p. 64), to his premonitory dreams ('I was a man attacked on all sides by birds of prey', p. 86), the spectator sees a Lumumba who at once lays the bases for and prophesies his own demise.

And the demise does occur in the last act. Although, strictly speaking, this act covers a period of five and a half years (from mid-September 1960 to 1966) the bulk of the action which ends in scene 6 lasts only six months. Three main episodes are dramatised in it: the arrest and imprisonment in Thysville of Lumumba and his friends Mpolo and Okito, their unauthorised release by their guards and their rearrest and murder. The last two scenes (additions to the 1967 edition of the play) depict Lumumba's rehabilitation by Mokutu.

If tragic irony is the dominant mood in Act II, Act III according to critics like Rodney Harris, is pure tragedy (Harris 1973: 146). For it is here, he argues, that one sees the hero moving inexorably to his end. Lumumba does indeed emerge in Act III as the plaything of superior forces. Of course, these forces do not wear the religious face of a divinity in *Un Saison au Congo*, but rather the secular one of politics. They take the form of a web of international and domestic economic and political interests and intrigue from which the innocent Lumumba cannot escape. His wife warns him:

Patrice, I fear for you... My God! I can see the threads of their dirty plots tightening up around you. (p. 72)

Representing the international component of these interests are the Belgian bankers. It is easy to see in the generalised treatment given to these men a problem that bedevils modern Third World states. While Lumumba thinks of repossessing his country, the bankers continue to see it, even after Independence, as little more than a rich reservoir of strategic minerals, and his militant nationalism, which they interpret as communism, as a threat to their interests that should be corrupted or destroyed. The Quatrième Banquier works out a strategy to neutralise the nationalism of Congolese leaders. He asks:

What do they want? Positions, titles as President, Member of Parliament... cars... villas... Let us stuff them with these. The result? They will soften up and their disposition will become pleasant. (p. 22)

Unable to achieve the former objective with Lumumba, however, they resort to destroying him, colluding with the domestic political forces of a largely uneducated population for whom Independence is a product that arrives by plane (p. 23) and, more dangerously, with those of ethnicity. Symbolising the latter are men like Mukongo, for whom Independence is the appropriate time to expel the Bengalas to their villages (p. 24); Kala Lubu who, in spite of his title as president, considers himself as no more than the chief of a powerful ethnic group, the Bakongo ('a president is the chief, the king', p. 70); and

Tzumbi, for whom it is either secession, which he eventually resorts to, or control of the state by his ethnic group.

But Lumumba is not just victim of a fate external to him. He contributes to his fall through a defect in character. An important aspect of this defect is his impatience and impetuousness. Like Christophe he is a man in a hurry. To Kala, who implores him, 'All I ask of you is a bit of patience, for it's only with time that a banana ripens' (p. 99) he angrily replies, 'I hate time, I detest your gradualism' (p. 99). Also, when angry soldiers ask for an Africanisation of the officer corps and the massive promotion of all to higher ranks, he instantly yields to their demands (p. 36). Even the final choice of general and colonel is not really his. For under further pressure, he abandons his own candidates – Lundula and M'polo – and appoints instead Mokutu, who is imposed on him by the military. Closely linked to Lumumba's rashness is his intransigence. At the end of a fruitless argument in which Kala and Mokutu try to convince him to reach a compromise, he is warned:

MOKUTU: Too bad for you, Mr Lumumba. It is your rain, you've asked for
    it and you'll be soaked in it to the bones! (p. 101)

An equally important flaw in Lumumba's character is his exasperating lack of realism, of a sense of the politically possible at any given time. Denouncing Belgian colonialism and deciding to take on that country head-on a day after Independence is in itself an act of great personal courage which merits respect. But as Mokutu warns with a traditional saying, 'only attack a beast when you're sure of killing it' (p. 31), such a position, while heroic, can easily lead to severe national and personal difficulties for a newly independent country whose army and economy, nevertheless, are still dependent on Belgium, in this case, and which is torn asunder by personal and ethnic rivalries. And this is precisely the situation faced by Lumumba. But even when the prospect of difficulties, indeed, disaster, stares him in the face (sometimes he even predicts it) he remains uncompromising.

Finally, there is Lumumba's uncritical trust in people. Evidence of this is provided in his very first discussion with Pauline. A better judge of character and more realistic, Pauline warns her husband insistently of impending treachery (p. 72). She specifically puts him on his guard against his so-called friends ('some of them will sell you off for a plate of lentil peas' p. 72); denounces Mokutu, in particular, as a former Belgian informant and Kala as a 'copper god' whose only interest is in keeping his sceptre. Lumumba, however, remains unconvinced. If anything, he accuses his wife of being unnecessarily alarmist and, characteristically, rushes to his friends' defence: justifying Mokutu's behaviour in terms of his predicament – 'to die of hunger... or play the informant' (p. 73) – and reasserting his trust in Kala (p. 73). As Césaire himself explains about his hero:

[He] was too much in advance of his time, too much out of tune with reality to succeed... He lacked realism. (quoted in Harris 1973: 149)

But if Lumumba's defects in character are fatal to his career as a politician, they are precisely the qualities that lend a dimension of nobility and myth to his enterprise. Compared to him, the wily, realistic and, in the short-term, politically successful, Kala and Mokutu shrink in stature and significance. They are more eager to survive than to achieve. Their struggle is presented as personal. Lumumba's, on the other hand, is collective, concerned not merely with the fate of the Westernised few – a subordinate and yet relatively privileged group in the colonial dispensation – but also, perhaps especially, with the 'dispossessed' as he calls them: 'the mutilated', 'the house-boys' (p. 28), in short, the casualties of colonial rule.

Unlike Mokutu and Kala, he has an integrationist outlook to national politics. While Kala talks of reinforcing ethnic particularisms within the new state ('I want you to know that... Independence, a friend of ethnic groups, hasn't come to abolish law or custom' p. 28), Lumumba insists on the need to revise and modernise 'one after the other all the laws and customs... [to rebuild] one after the other all the parts of the old edifice' (p. 29). And it is not accidental in this regard that he rejects the traditional symbol of power – the leopard skin – offered him by the Sanza Player (p. 93). For he refuses to be a tribal chief in prime ministerial clothing.

The dominant image of Lumumba that emerges in *Une Saison au Congo* is not so much that of a politician as of a *moral force* that transcends social and racial boundaries. In an outline of the vision of the stakes being played out in the Congo he explains to Mpolo:

Here, take a look at the two letters I've just received... One is from Van Laert, the other from Luis. Don't you find that wonderful! Luis is Spanish! What has he got to do with the Congo, and Van Laert is Belgian... A blood friendship across the seas ('Une amitié d'outre-sang!') Yes, they are one of us! For they realise that what is at stake here isn't just Africa's fate, but that of man, of man himself. (p. 88)

It is his willingness, indeed his determination to pursue this vision, even at the expense of his life, that transforms him from tragic hero to martyr; from failed politician to god. As a figure of myth, he serves, in Césaire's definition of the latter, as 'a catalyst for the aspirations of a people, a prophet of their future; as the site where reason and emotion both fuse and are exalted' (in Leiner 1993: 90) – a role which indeed Lumumba played in the heady days of radical African and Black nationalism.

But the hero of *Une Saison au Congo* is not just an inspirer of grand action. He is also an archetypal figure of ritual – the scapegoat or sacrificial lamb whose destruction is supposed to regenerate and redeem the community (on this figure in European drama, see Dahl 1987: 1–32). The ritual figure to whom Lumumba is most easily compared and to whom he is likened in the text (and frequently by critics [Bailey 1992; Moreau 1987] and the dramatist himself [in Leiner 1993: 140]) is, of course, Christ. Reacting angrily at the discovery that his assistant Cordelier was an accomplice in the Congolese leader's murder, Dag Hammarskjöld, suggesting the analogy, asks:

Tell me, Cordelier, what do you think of Jesus Christ? ... On whose side would you, Matthew Cordelier, have been 1,961 years ago when one of your contemporaries, a certain Jesus, was arrested and put to death in Judea, then under Roman occupation? Now leave my office, you assassin of Christ! (p. 107)

Lumumba emerges in the play as a visionary and a prophet. He takes upon himself the suffering of his people. He experiences temptations (from Kala and Mokutu) and solitude. He is misunderstood (by all but his wife and a couple of very close friends), betrayed (by Mokutu), tortured (by M'siri and his men) and finally put to death; a death which is given a redemptive quality.

If there is a tragic figure in *Une Saison au Congo* at all, it is Dag Hammarskjöld. For it is he who, unlike Lumumba, is truly a victim, it is he who is manipulated by superior political forces; indeed it is he who, unwittingly, serves as the instrument of these forces' designs. And yet when Hammarskjöld first appears on stage, he leaves the spectator in no doubt that he is sincere, impartial and in full control of his Organisation. His, he explains, is not a banal peace-keeping mission:

We're working for the future of the world [no less, he tells his adviser] ... Let's therefore give the most of our minds towards the work of creative evolution in which we are privileged to participate. (p. 45)

What he does not realise, however, is that at almost the same time as he is enunciating high-minded UN ideals, the West – a major force in his Organisation – is threatening, in the person of its collective ambassador, to undermine the young 'Congolese state, seen as communist' (p. 47). But even more ironical is the fact that his deputy, Cordelier, does not share his ideals. Indeed, the latter confesses later to not particularly liking Lumumba (p. 105), an antipathy which leads him, as the man in the same field, to use the UN's principle of neutrality to stand idly by while the Congo is being dismembered by secessionist troops using Belgian arms.

Dag Hammarskjöld refuses to commit UN troops against Katanga because he sincerely wants to give negotiations a chance. Cordelier, on the other hand, more wily, lends support to this policy because he wants to see Lumumba's 'Communist' government defeated. By the time the ingenuous Hammarskjöld realises this, that in fact the UN 'was holding [Lumumba's] hands while others were beating him' (p. 106), it is already too late. He has been used. Lumumba has been handed over to his enemies to face certain death. Hammarskjöld's anguished cry, 'My God! Why was I chosen to preside over this devilish intrigue?' (p. 112) is a tragic recognition of this fact.

Up until now, we have concentrated on the political themes and socio-cultural concerns of *Une Saison au Congo*. But however important these might be, a more complete evaluation of the play requires a fuller discussion of its theatrical and linguistic resources. A striking feature of this latter aspect of the play is its imagery.

If the predominant images in *La Tragédie du roi Christophe* relate to the world of architecture and engineering, those in *Une Saison au Congo* are essentially zoomorphic (d'Alméida 1976). Thus the turbulent political situation in the Congo is compared to a 'herd of elephants charging through a bamboo forest' (p. 40) while Independence, in the way it has ruined the country, is compared to an 'invasion of crickets' (p. 88).

To better evoke Lumumba's qualities of pugnacity, Kala describes him as a 'fighter of a bird' (p. 69) and himself as 'a tortoise' (p. 70).

Animal images and stories are also used to illustrate and comment on
the situation of various characters. Thus, when immediately after
Mokutu's appointment by Lumumba as head of the army the Sanza
Player intones the sad little tale of the bird which, absorbed in frantic
activity, forgets there is a trap nearby and falls into it, the spectator
realises he is referring to Lumumba's imminent fate.

> Pollen de feu
> ivre temps de sémailles
> petit oiseau qui va et vient
> oublieux petit oiseau
> de la glu comme de la sarbacane
> quelle cervelle d'oiseau, dit le piège,
> l'oiseau a oublié le piège
> le piège se souvient de l'oiseau. (p. 38)

Sometimes, the constant references to animals by men like Kala,
Mokutu and the Sanza Player, and the recourse to traditional animal
stories and proverbs, indicate a rootedness in tribal culture and
traditions that is conspicuously absent in the more urbane Lumumba.
In fact, Lumumba shows no sympathy for this stylistic feature of
traditional African discourse, as he makes clear to Mokutu. The
latter has hardly proposed to illustrate a political point (Lumumba's
mistaken strategy in attacking the Belgians head-on) by means of a
hunter's tale than he is dismissed abruptly by Lumumba: 'I hate
parables' (p. 30).

But over and above these functions, animal imagery in *Une Saison
au Congo* is used to develop the play's theme. Expressed in general
terms, this is the conflict between the anti-imperialist forces of
freedom and human dignity on the one hand and those of colonial
oppression and of mindless traditionalism on the other; between
those of soaring idealism and of crass selfishness. This conflict is
realised in a cluster of antithetical animal images; for example,
between those animals that creep and crawl on the one hand and
those that fly, indeed that soar majestically in space; between those
that live in crevices and holes as if to hide their cowardice and
treachery and those that live in the open; between the predatory and
the non-predatory. In short it is a conflict, on the metaphorical level,
between noble verticality and contemptible horizontality.

In the category of the verticals belong Lumumba especially but
also his most faithful associates Okito and Mpolo. Not only is
Lumumba described as a bird by various characters – 'a crowned

crane' in the words of the Sanza Player (p. 78) – he also aspires to be one. In his Independence Day speech, for example, he explains:

I'd like to be a toucan, the beautiful bird, the announcer across skies and races that to us a king, the Kongo, is born! (p. 29)

Elsewhere he explains to his followers that his 'wild soul', which he claims to have once met in the forest, has the shape of a bird, and he exhorts them to use 'the bronze-feathered ibis' as his emblem (p. 93). It is also to a surreal bird, 'the great rainbow bird', that he likens himself in a famous encounter with Mokutu:

Mokutu, do you realise what you're about to do? You're about to destroy with a great stroke of your baton that big rainbow bird which is visiting the ceiling of 150 million men, holding out a promise of life and hope to them. (p. 82)

The bird is also the creature to which he compares memorable events and great people. Thus, African Independence, which first became a reality in Ghana, is compared to a bird that rises up fearlessly into the sky, despite the wings clipped by centuries of colonialism (p. 76). In one last example, he advises Hélène Bijou not to be broken down by his imminent death, but to withstand the political storm blowing over the Congo with the dignity of a humming-bird emerging from a storm (p. 69).

In contrast to the verticals are the horizontals, the creepy-crawlies – connotatively, the trucklers, the shady. To this category belong all the forces and characters that are opposed to Lumumba and his vision. Chief among these are the Belgians, but also all colonial powers. The Belgians are variously described as wounded 'buffaloes' (pp. 14, 17, 86, 87), the 'beasts' that must be tracked down (pp. 31, 91), 'monsters' whose nostrils must be ripped apart (p. 44) or 'wolves'.

Lumumba's African enemies fare no better. When they are not likened to 'voracious and insatiable dogs' (p. 90), they are 'tortoises' (p. 70), 'snails' (p. 34) or, as in Pauline's dream, 'termites, frogs, spiders, all ugly animals in the service of envy' (p. 72).

But Lumumba's enemies are not just brutal, slimy or creeping horizontals. They are also sometimes birds. Not the graceful variety that are the hero and his friends, however, but birds of prey. The type whose beaks, dripping with blood, tear into Africa's flesh:

I see Africa assailed from all sides by rapacious birds. She has scarcely escaped from one than the other is on her, its beak dripping in blood. (p. 93)

When alive Lumumba is compared to a bird; dying he becomes 'an invincible idea', 'pollen dust' (p. 109) and finally a tree (p. 111). With its dual character of being at once firmly rooted in the earth and yet like a bird reaching out defiantly into the skies, the tree is the symbol of permanent verticality.

Une Saison au Congo is, however, not only distinguished for its imagery, but also for the rich variety of its language. First there is the language of the Belgians. When it is not formal and paternalistic, like King Basilio's, which describes the Congolese as 'children in orphanage' who have been entrusted into the kind care of a god-fearing Belgian nation (p. 25), it is ridiculous in its literary pretensions with the bankers or colloquial, when not vulgar, in the mouths of the prison warders.

Then there is Kala Lubu's. As befits the occasion, his French, during Independence Day celebrations, is appropriately elevated, even if of the servile variety. The following is an extract from his speech which in its hollowness reminds one of Pétion's:

Sir, Your August Majesty's presence on this memorable day is yet another proof of your solicitude for the entire population of this country which you've loved and protected. (p. 27)

But Kala, like Mokutu, is also capable of using a standard French interspersed with Africanisms. He says about himself:

I'm described as a tortoise full of mischief. It would be better to say full of common sense! I move slowly... Koukoutou Bouem! Koukoutou Bouem. (p. 70)

The language that retains our attention most, however, is that of Lumumba. 'A master wordsmith' (quoted in Naville 1970: 246) as Césaire describes him, the hero states his main function as that of arousing his people from their slumber through the power of his words:

I see myself as neither a messiah nor a mahdi. My weapon is the power of my speech. I speak and I awaken people. I speak and I restore Africa to herself ...! I speak and, attacking oppression and slavery at their roots, I make brotherhood a possibility, a real possibility for the first time. (p. 94)

And speak is precisely what he does during the Independence celebrations. Unlike the diplomatic prose of Basilio and Kala, Lumumba's language that day is densely poetic: an eruption of intense anger at his people's slave past,

Moi, sire, je pense aux oubliés. Nous sommes ceux que l'on déposséda, que l'on frappa, que l'on mutila; ceux que l'on tutoyait, ceux à qui l'on crachait au visage. (p. 28)

of profound joy on their achievement of Independence,

> et voici: nous avons vaincu
> Notre pays est désormais entre
> les mains de ses enfants.
> Nôtre, ce ciel, ce fleuve, ces
> terres nôtre, le lac et la fôret
> nôtre, Karissimbi, Nyiragongo
> Niamuragiza... (p. 28)

and hope in a reconstructed future:

Camarades, tout est à faire, oui tout à refaire, mais nous le ferons, nous le referons. Pour Kongo! (p. 29)

What the first part of this speech vividly conveys is an image of human misery that is economic, physical and psychological. In contrast to it is Lumumba's exultation in the second part. With its repetition of the possessive adjectives and pronouns (notre/nôtre, followed each time by what is possessed (lakes, forests and especially thunderous-sounding volcanic mountains) this section of speech is an act of reappropriation, of reassertion of a lost unity with one's physical environment.

But speech is not the only medium through which meaning is conveyed in *Une Saison au Congo*. As in *La Tragédie du roi Christophe*, Césaire makes use of songs, especially the Sanza Player's, as an instrument of theatre. Their themes are appropriate to the situation and setting. Some are threatening and portend trouble:

> A period of red blood,
> Such is the period I
> foresee. (p. 18)

Others, as we saw, warn of impending treachery. Others still, like the mercenary's (p. 108), give an insight into motivation.

Another element of traditional culture that Césaire draws upon to great theatrical effect is the premonitory dream, described by the hero himself as expressing 'a truth quickly forgotten in wakefulness' (p. 86). An instance of this can be seen in Act II, scene 8. Kala has just decided to dismiss Lumumba as Prime Minister. Although only the spectator is aware of this explosive decision, Pauline, with great prescience, warns her husband against Kala, but to no avail. Shortly after their discussion, Lumumba falls asleep. He has a dream in which Kala, Mokutu and the Bishop conspire against him. When he is woken by Pauline to listen to the daily news bulletin on the radio, his dream and her worst fears are brutally confirmed. Through the dream technique then, the hero is woken up literally and metaphorically to his errors, to reality. The rest of the play is the story of how he awakens to other errors (his confidence in the impartiality of the UN troops, in African unity) and his hopeless fight to combat them. In a sense Lumumba can be said to be in touch with reality only when he literally dreams (pp. 74, 85, 86) and to dream metaphorically when he is awake.

Lumumba might not be a messiah, as he says, but his creator, Césaire, is certainly possessed of a messianic, eschatological vision of politics. Both *Une Saison au Congo* and *La Tragédie du roi Christophe* are shot through with the idea of a community in a state of (political) bondage and degeneracy, and which can be *saved* from it only through the redemptive suffering and epic actions of heroic individuals.

While the belief in the possibility of a kingdom of political grace, a political parousia implicit in this vision, is a powerful and often necessary catalyst to political action, it remains equally true that single-minded attempts at achieving it in the real world often prove to be problematic or downright dangerous. When they do not degenerate into dictatorship, as in the case of Christophe, they remain as in Lumumba's grand but futile gestures; psychologically inspiring but of doubtful practical relevance.

CHAPTER 5

Bernard Dadié: 'Béatrice du Congo';
'Iles de Tempête'

Born in 1916 in the Ivory Coast, Bernard Dadié was educated at the local Catholic school in Grand Bassam and later in Senegal at the Ecole William Ponty, where he was deeply involved in the nascent but dynamic dramatic activities of the college. On graduation, he worked for eleven years (1936–47) in the French Research Institute for African Studies in Dakar, which later became l'Institut Fondamental d'Afrique Noire, and in 1986 was renamed L'Institut Cheikh Anta Diop. Here he developed a life-long interest in traditional African cultures. On his return to the Ivory Coast, he commenced a distinguished public career: first in teaching, then in the civil service, where he became successively Director of Research and of the Arts and Inspector-General of Cultural Affairs, and then, finally, in politics where he was, for a long time, Minister of Culture and Information (Bonneau 1972: 20–1; Magnier 1976: 49–62; Vinciléoni 1986: 7–27; Zell et al., 1983: 370–2).

But it is, of course, as a writer that Dadié is best known. In this capacity, he has been described variously as the '[Paul] Eluard of the black world' (Quillateau 1967: 140) and more recently, as a result, no doubt, of the sheer volume and diversity of his work, and also of his fiercely satirical cast of mind, as the 'Wole Soyinka of Francophone Africa' (Adé-Ajo 1983: 76). The author of travel chronicles, folktales, short stories, novels and poems, Dadié has also written several short plays and six full-length dramas. Indeed, it is on his achievements as a dramatist that his reputation as one of Francophone Africa's most eminent writers rests. To Chévrier, he is 'a first-rate dramatist' (1984: 158), while to Clive Wake he deserves to be placed in a category by himself because:

he recognises and uses the theatre imaginatively as a total medium in its own right. He writes plays to be acted and to be enjoyed by an audience, not just to be read ... He is the only playwright to have written historical plays which

123

are thoroughly meaningful to a modern, post-independence audience. (quoted in Banham and Wake 1976: 63)

One of these plays is *Béatrice du Congo*. Performed first in 1971 at the Festival d'Avignon, then in October 1975 in the Palais des Congrès de Cocody in the Ivory Coast, and again in 1977 at the second World Festival of Negro Arts in Lagos, *Béatrice du Congo* is a richly satirical analysis of European colonisation. Set partly in the ancient kingdom of the Kongo and partly in the imaginary European state of Bitanda (a thinly veiled reference to Portugal), it dramatises a well-known theme in African literature, that of the European who, under the guise of spreading Christianity and enlightenment to a benighted African people, erodes and finally destroys their sovereignty.

Béatrice du Congo is, in the essentials of its plot, historical and specific. Its action spans more than two centuries and unfolds on two continents. It describes events ranging from Prince Henry's defeat of the Moors at Ceuta, through the discovery in 1482 of the kingdom of the Kongo, the establishment of trade relations with it, to its final decline after the death at the stake in 1706 of the mystic and the proto-nationalist Doña Béatrice.

The enactment of this pattern of historical events along purely documentary lines is, however, not Dadié's prime objective. If it were, he would have had to bolster his plot with large chunks of factual socio-historical information. To take just one example, he would have had to present – in the interest of a minimum of historical truth – not just one nameless king as the chief actor on the African side, in a drama spanning more than two centuries, but the twenty-odd monarchs from Nzinga a Knuwu (baptised as Joao I) to Pedro IV, who reigned during this period. He would also have had to weave in information on their political strategies and on how their ambivalent policies towards the Portuguese, now welcomed and now spurned in favour of other powers, turned the Kongo into a theatre of European rivalries and contributed to its collapse (Balandier 1968; Hilton 1985).

Such information, however, is kept to an absolute minimum, with the little that is included being highly stylised. Dadié's method in this play is clear. He has compressed more than 200 years of historical time into a few years of dramatic time. In the process, he has excised all historical material that would obscure the crucial symbolic and critical value he wants to give to the work, that would destroy its dramatic unity, and that would detract attention from its main theme.

In fact, to achieve his aim more effectively, Dadié not only leaves out material which he deems irrelevant to his artistic purpose, but also invents certain key episodes. Thus, to bring out their greed and abject inhumanity, he has the Bitandese, contrary to historical fact, murder the Kongolese king (the Mani Congo) when he attempts, in a moment of nationalist awareness, to re-assert his declining authority over the uncertain fortunes of his kingdom.

Similarly, with a total disrespect for the actual chronology of events, Doña Béatrice is made to outlive the Kongolese monarchy. In reality, she was burned at the stake for heresy in 1706 during the reign of the Kongolese Pedro IV (see Balandier 1968: 257–63). By creating the impression, however, that she was actually put to death by the Bitandese after the fall of the Kongo and its occupation by them, Dadié succeeds in transforming her from her significant but limited historical role of prophetess and priestess of a highly syncretic Christian sect (rather reminiscent of Simon Kimbangui's sect in twentieth-century Congo) to that of a straightforward African nationalist fighting for independence. The message of the historical Doña Béatrice was essentially religious, though it had important political implications, whereas that of the dramatic Doña Béatrice is essentially political (see Smith 1982: 818–23 on the historical and dramatic Doña Béatrice).

Finally, in a riotously humorous scene inspired probably more by Molière's *Le Bourgeois Gentilhomme* than by historical fact and calculated to show the cultural arrogance of the Bitandese and the lifeless formality of their civilisation, the Mani Congo, in preparation for a visit to Bitanda, is forced to take lessons in Western table etiquette, which is presented to him as superior.

These inventions and modifications indicate that *Béatrice du Congo* is not and makes no claim to be a historical document in dramatic form. Dadié is interested in the Kongolese experience only in so far as it symbolises that of most pre-colonial African kingdoms and offers him the opportunity to explore in dramatic form the mechanics of colonisation. His concern is to lay bare the gap between the latter's theory and practice in order to deflate what he sees as its pompous humanitarian rhetoric.

Dadié's historical realism in this play is critical and not, as it were, photographic (see Etherton 1982 ch. 4; Lindenberger 1975; Lukács

1962 for a discussion of the theme of history in dramatic literature). He distorts history in order to present a more truthful picture of it. In other words, his infidelity to the specifics of the Portuguese colonial enterprise in the Kongo enables him to explore the deeper meanings and processes at work in all colonisation. With the satiric verve and acid humour of a Ferdinand Oyono, Dadié shows that economic self-interest and not philanthropy is the prime motive behind Bitandese and, by extension, European colonial expansion overseas as a whole.

Much of the satire of *Béatrice du Congo* derives from the discrepancy between the audience's knowledge of what the Bitandese are and want by their unwitting admission and the idealistic rhetoric with which they delude themselves. For example, they call their ships reassuringly *Le Notre Dame de la Miséricorde* and *Le Jésus de la Paix*, yet use them to transport slaves. They describe their mission as 'a test imposed on us by God' (p. 15), yet their vocabulary and aims are secular and mercantile: 'an alliance with Prester John will not only enrich paradise with new souls but will secure us a pre-eminent place ' in the courts of Christendom' (p. 15). Finally, they condemn and confiscate the Kongolese masks and statuettes seen as the materialisation of pagan beliefs, yet they are quick to sense their commercial value as *objets d'art* well before the early twentieth-century primitivist vogue in European art. It is the exposure of contradictions such as these that unmasks the Bitandese and sustains the action of the play.

This process of unmasking is described in the dramatic movement of *Béatrice du Congo*. After exposing their intentions in generous terms in Act I and describing their initial contacts with the people of the Kongo, Dadié shows the Bitandese in Act II systematically pursuing policies that are the opposite of their stated objectives. They emerge as arrogant and intolerant of cultural differences, and prepared to resort to guile to further their material interests. They are quick to see in the extreme generosity of the Kongolese a weakness to be exploited and in the conversion of the Mani Congo to Christianity not a great spiritual event but an opportunity to isolate him from the traditions of his subjects and, subsequently, to undermine his authority. By the time we get to Act III, the Bitandese have been completely stripped of their mask. The elaborate fiction of a civilising and Christianising mission with which they justified their expansion overseas in Act I has been demolished. In the place of this fiction stands the reality of self-interest, furthered through conquest and murder.

To the three dramatic movements of the play – arrival, feigned cooperation and brutal conquest – correspond three basic tones. Comedy and satire dominate in the first two acts, and outright tragedy in the third. The Mani Congo painfully realises in Act III that he has been nothing but a victim: 'I've been caught in a trap' (p. 123). His last and longest speech is a moving soliloquy in which he comes to the full realisation of his predicament and seeks a desperate but futile reconciliation with his physical environment and ancestral traditions.

Great cross for the crucifixion of my people and you medals jingling on my chest, I've been nothing but your masters' servant. I now return to my traditional Africa; to my Africa which had no rope around its neck. (p. 133)

Dadié does not present the Mani Congo as an altogether hapless incompetent, entirely acted upon by a wicked group of Bitandese. Rather, the king's extreme generosity and uncritical attitude towards the Bitandese are presented as contributing partly to his demise. In a remark that can be reasonably interpreted as reflective of Dadié's critical views on the Mani Congo's character, he has the Bitanda-educated Kongolese, Joao Texeira, warn the king: 'too much confidence, your Majesty, this is still our sin, the black man's sin' (p. 123). An example of this excessive confidence can clearly be seen in the Mani Congo's remarks to Doña Béatrice about King Don Joao of Bitanda, whom he has never met but about whom he feels free to declare: 'My beloved brother of old Christian stock cannot possibly dupe me. I have trust in him; total, Christian trust' (p. 87).

Also convinced that the Bitandese are the envoys of the gods, the Mani Congo lavishes generosity on them, offers them the island of Sahotoga, invites them to settle in the mainland, and has his priest bless them for their forthcoming battle against (ostensibly) the many wives they have been forced to accept: 'Sustain them in this new battle... strengthen their hearts and backs' (p. 40).

What the king and his subjects do not realise is that their words carry a meaning totally different from that which they intended. Ironically, it is with their blessing that the Bitandese engage not in a metaphorical contest with women, but in a real battle with their Kongolese hosts – one from which the latter will emerge subjugated and dispossessed of both land and sovereignty.

But the Mani Congo does not only inadvertently bring suffering upon himself and his people. Because his alliance with the Bitandese is also motivated in part by the possibility of personal political and material gain, he can also be said to carry some measure of moral responsibility for his predicament.

The component of self-interest in his behaviour, as opposed to the simple-mindedness denounced by Texeira, comes out in the first tableau of Act II. The Bitandese have just returned to the Kongo and are making various offers of poisoned gifts to the Kongolese. These include a patron saint, a national flag with the ominous symbol of the shark, and a reorganised administration along Bitandese lines. The king remains silent and indifferent. Suddenly, a gift that flatters his vanity and holds promise of great personal advantage is offered. It is his portrait. This item, the Bitandese argue, will not only bring him money and publicity when printed on mirrors, scarves and dress-making material, but will also constitute an invaluable source of intelligence. Their concluding argument is a model of defective logic:

Those who like the king will buy his portrait and display it prominently. Those who do not like it will not buy it...By having your portrait prominently displayed on walls, you'll clearly become the brain, the centre, in short, the father of the nation. (p. 72)

The possibility hinted at in this last sentence of his becoming a rich and absolute monarch is what finally puts the Mani Congo firmly on the side of an alliance with the Bitandese. He sees himself emerging as his country's strongman, a kind of Louis XIV *avant la lettre* without whom the Kongo will plunge into chaos and decline. He repeats mechanically after Diogo: 'After me, chaos, the deluge, without me Zaire will no longer be Zaire' (p. 72).

The Mani Congo's subsequent repudiation of his traditional religion, like his espousal of monogamy, is all part of a strategy to enhance his own position through the adoption of the externalities of Western civilisation. Though his innate intelligence often advises against such a move, his urge for power (when it is not for wealth) is always quick to overcome his doubts. Thus, he expounds intelligently on the political advantages of polygamy, 'each one of my wives symbolises a pact with the tribes that constitute my kingdom' (p. 77), only to renounce it when given some money. The expression 'as powerful as him' (i.e., his Bitandese counterpart), is one that recurs constantly in his language. Indeed, with it on his lips, he succumbs in a comic scene to the sacrament of baptism after some initial reticence and doubt as to the character of Satan (p. 80).

It is clear at this point that although describing events of more than 200 years ago, *Béatrice du Congo* is infused with great contemporary relevance. References in it to practices current in today's Africa – the printing of the portraits of national leaders on mirrors, scarves and dressmaking material (p. 71); the stationing of foreign troops on African soil (p. 77); the offer to the continent's leaders of luxury villas abroad (p. 80), and so on – are enough to alert the audience to the author's wider intentions. The period might have changed. Africa might indeed have gained her independence. But her leaders, Dadié seems to be saying, still allow themselves, like the Mani Congos of ancient times, to be manoeuvered for personal benefit into signing away their nations' sovereignty. Viewed in this light, *Béatrice du Congo* is not only a dramatic reconstruction of a past epoch but also a commentary on present-day Africa, a fierce political satire (Mudimbe-Boyi 1976: 9–26; Ojo-Adé 1974: 67–75).

But if the Mani Congo does not emerge unscathed from this play, the author reserves the burden of his criticism and the butt of his satire for the Bitandese. First to be attacked are their double standards. When the play opens, they are jubilantly celebrating their victory over the Moors, a victory which will put an end to that period in their history characterised by arbitrary arrests, imprisonment and insecurity.

Up to this point, the audience sympathises and rejoices with the Bitandese. But this fund of sympathy very quickly disappears when they embark, with a total disregard for consistency and the universal implications of their victory, on a policy the ultimate result of which will be to reduce other people to servitude: 'Our duty now after this wonderful God-sent victory is to spread the true religion, to spread it throughout the world' (p. 12).

The irony of this situation is reflected in the somewhat symmetrical structure displayed by the first and last tableaux of the play. Both deal with a revolt against a foreign oppressive regime. The Bitandese are ranged against the Moors in the first tableau of Act I, the Kongolese against the Bitandese in the fourth tableau of Act III. Thus, in each of the revolts, the Bitandese are involved – as victim in the first and, ironically, as victimiser in the second. Doña Béatrice's moving invocation in the final tableau of the play, 'I pray that my country cease to be a mere reservoir, a granary, a quarry, an appendage ... for others while it remains hell for us' (p. 146), is a poignant echo of the words of Henri recalling the misery of the

Bitandese in the hands of the Moors several years earlier: 'We had become appendages, a subject people, producers of revenue, of taxes, of wealth for others' (p. 11).

Unaware of the total implications of their reference to themselves as the new angel with the flaming sword (p. 13), the Bitandese, like the Archangel Michael of Revelations 12, were indeed to drive the Kongolese out of 'heaven'. The difference, of course, is that Michael drove out Evil in the person of Lucifer whereas the Bitandese drive out a virtuous people.

How in any case could the Kongolese be anything else but virtuous when their country is described by the Bitandese themselves as 'un paradis terrestre' (p. 5)? Diogo and his friends are not only struck by the country but also by the people: the sense of community that pervades their society; their generosity (p. 55); their organic relationship with nature, 'all humanity is at one with the water, plants, animals, and with everything' (p. 56); their profound taste for life in all its vibrant fullness, 'It's the grain which bursts open at full noon to give life to other plants' (p. 52).

Diogo is indeed so captivated by the quality of life of these noble savages whose peals of laughter ricochet against the wooded banks of rivers that he comes to a deeper and renewed understanding of what it means to be a Christian and by extension to be civilised. He tells the king: 'Seeing them, I wondered; I asked myself: is a society in which all are happy not a Christian society?' (p. 56).

By making Diogo, a representative Bitandese, undermine the avowed *raison d'être* of his country's Kongolese project so thoroughly, Dadié heightens the audience's interest by giving an unexpected dramatic twist of uncertainty to the action. Will the Kongo be colonised or not? The possible alternatives he leaves open to the Bitandese are all distasteful and calculated to ridicule them. They can abandon their project now that they know the Kongolese are civilised in a profound, philosophical sense of the word. They can pursue it, admit to economic motives and be accused of selfishness. Or they can cling tenaciously to the idea of a civilising mission and risk deadly ridicule by having to redefine civilisation in a manner totally incompatible with what Diogo has seen in the Kongo but wholly repugnant to universal common sense.

They choose this third possibility. Unprepared to forgo the Kongo's vast natural resources yet anxious to maintain the mask of altruism, they justify their overseas adventure, after Diogo's soul-searching, in terms of the need to bring to the Kongolese the 'noble' and 'civilised' practice of rape and abduction. They insist on the urgency of throwing

these hordes into the fortifying torrents of civilisation ... of forcing them at last to ask themselves questions ... to carry life on their backs as one would a burden ... to grind time ... to live for the future ... to live in anguish. (pp. 58–9)

The satire here issues from the ironic presentation of the negative aspects of industrial culture as the hallmark of civilisation.

Another Bitandese trait that receives a severe lashing is religious hypocrisy. Throughout the first tableau of Act I, the Bitandese labour under the illusion of a divinely ordained mission and advance purely religious explanations for their actions. Thus, in a speech to his people on the occasion of their victory over the Moors, Henri insists on the need to go 'wherever darkness is king and to show forth the white light of love, the passionate love of the faith' (p. 18). To this exhortation, Diogo replies on behalf of the Bitandese sailors: 'All the Bitandese are ready to die for the greater glory of God' (p. 13).

With such religious fervour, one would expect the Bitandese to venture, without any prompting, across hostile seas into the most inhospitable of countries in search of souls to convert. But what happens? When the prospect of leaving ceases to be a mere theoretical possibility, they balk. Hitherto prolix about their willingness to risk their lives in the service of God, personal considerations now become uppermost in their minds. They evoke in vivid terms all sorts of threats to their safety, ranging from 'the tropical furnace ... to the violent anger of savage nature' (p. 16). The Bitandese are finally persuaded to go only when their stated spiritual objectives have been completely discarded, and material advantages are brandished before them:

Go forth, go forth: it's the Lord's wish. What do these Gardens of Delight conceal? Fabulous riches await you there, not to talk of glory, im-mor-tality ... We have to snatch from them the monopoly in the cinnamon trade, the ginger trade, the trade in cloves ... There is Gold, Diogo, Gold, I tell you, Gold. (p. 18)

The presentation of the Bitandese at this point is fiercely caricatural and comical, with the mere mention of gold and diamonds bringing out in them the most mechanical and Pavlovian of reactions.

But Dadié not only satirises double standards and religious hypocrisy in the Bitandese but also holds up their civilisation to ridicule. Its representatives, seconded to the court of the Mani Congo as technical advisers, carry names that are both comic and significant: Bonnechère (Mr Goodliving) for the man in charge of food; Lapoudre (Mr Gunpowder) for the adviser on war affairs and, most ominously, Laboursepleine (Mr Fullpurse) for the adviser on the Mani Congo's finances.

In an extremely humorous scene, referred to above, the Bitandese attempt to teach the Mani Congo an aspect of their civilisation, table etiquette. Here again, the presentation is caricatural. In contrast to the Kongolese, the Bitandese are made to appear still and lifeless in the extreme. They creak under the weight of artificiality and formality. In a statement that could be applied to other aspects of their civilisation, Bonnechère tells the king: 'Your Majesty, please be informed ... that at table, the way of eating is a thousand times more important than what is eaten' (p. 105).

He exemplifies this maxim by the elaborate appetite-killlng instructions he gives to the king on matters such as the angle at which his fork should be held and the position of his chin in relation to his dish:

Let's start with the pâté ... You use a fork to cut it but never a knife. You then bring it to your mouth, Your Majesty, with a fork ... Now let's start. Step one, you cut it, step two, you stick your fork into it ... step three, you lift the fork to your mouth ... Turn it, turn it towards your mouth ... with your fingers two-thirds up the fork's handle ... Mind your chin's position over the dish. (p. 106)

But Dadié presents this elaborate sophistication as only skin deep. Despite Lopez's advice to the Kongolese that 'reason must prevail over sentiment' (p. 107), the Bitandese still subscribe to irrational beliefs. To the Mani Congo, who mistakenly spills his table salt, Bonnechère insists: 'Let's exorcise bad luck. Quickly, three pinches of salt over your shoulders' (p. 107). This episode degenerates into farce when, in an effort to heed Bonnechère's advice, the Mani Congo mistakenly throws salt into the former's eyes.

But the technical advisers serve another function. Through them, Dadié exposes what he sees as the true nature of foreign aid. Such 'aid' is often based on the calculation of the advantages – economic or political – that will accrue to the donor country rather than on the real developmental needs of the recipient. In the case of the Kongolese, their 'needs' are decided upon in their absence, and without their participation, in faraway Bitanda – a situation which provokes one of them into outraged sarcasm: 'May God bless the Bitandese for opening our eyes onto our real problems, etc. ... etc. ... etc. ... ' (p. 70). But that these 'needs' have very little to do with the Kongolese, but everything to do with their 'helpers' becomes obvious very rapidly when the latter justify the suggestion of a change of flag for the Kongolese thus:

DIOGO: We have them in huge quantities, and our factories are producing
   more to satisfy your needs. (p. 70)

This suggestion is quickly followed by others for palatial summer and winter homes for the king, dukedoms for his close collaborators, a huge cathedral and other prestige projects for the newly renamed city, the net effect of which is not the progress of the recipients, but the destruction of their political unity and their permanent dependence on the Bitandese.

From a purely artistic point of view, *Béatrice du Congo* is a very lively play. It might not be original in theme and structure, but it is competently organised. Amusing incidents are strung together and knotted at the end into a tragic climax. Despite frequent changes of scene in the first act, singing and dancing by various crowds and the innumerable characters brought into play (most of them no more than pasteboard figures) the action moves unfettered by digressions to its ineluctable end. There are some important dramatic moments, such as when, in the second tableau of Act II after a long period of blindness caused essentially by his greed, the Mani Congo at last begins to see through his 'benefactors'. But these 'benefactors' are not going to allow themselves to be found out so easily and so they invent an array of excuses and explanations designed to continue to fool him.

First, they dismiss his legitimate fears that they are supporting rebellious local governors as nothing but the jealous propaganda of England and Holland, countries which, they add to frighten the king that he is, and discourage him from having any dealings with them, have committed regicides. Then they explain the Mani Congo's problems as the work of his local enemies, notably Doña Béatrice, whose nationalism they now increasingly see as detrimental to their purpose, and who, they advise, should be silenced (p. 100).

When the king ignores this advice and other diversionary tactics, and presses on with his growing suspicions by using the example of the Bitandese Gourg caught inciting the Kongolese against him, the Bitandese counter with an explanation that reveals the low esteem in which they hold his intelligence: 'Your Majesty is wrong. M. Gourg is an English citizen with French nationality' (p. 102). From a dramatic point of view, this is an extremely tense moment, as it leaves the spectator wondering whether the king will continue to be fooled or, if not, how the inevitable conflict that will ensue from his shattering discovery will be resolved. In the end, seeing that all the old ploys have failed (and these include a hurriedly announced state visit to Bitanda) they unsheath their claws and let fall their masks. To the Mani Congo who, in a last-ditch attempt to reassert his authority, tries to abolish slavery in what he insists is his kingdom, they ask mockingly: 'Is his Majesty not deluded to talk of his kingdom?' (p. 129). At this point the play's tempo moves very fast as the king realises what has happened to him and tries desperately to counter it by returning to his people – a move which ends with his brutal murder.

Béatrice du Congo also displays a skilful handling of structural correspondences between certain scenes. Apart from the parallel already referred to between the first tableau of Act I and the last of Act III, there is another beautifully exploited correspondence between tableau 3 of Act I and tableau 1 of Act II. In the former as in the latter, a king is consulting a diviner. In the former, the Bitandese diviner has only good news for his king: 'Trade in human beings and in talents; entire races of human beings will be your subjects' (p. 46). But in the latter, the Kongolese court oracle, the Nganga, unfolds tales of woe and misery to his king:

> Friends divided ...
> Families divided ...
> Blacks armed, Bitandese armed
> under the astonished gaze of birds of prey
> dying of indigestion. (p. 67)

In the stage directions for Act I, tableau 3, we are told about the Bitandese king: 'The king has his future foretold by a diviner' (p. 45). But to show how much the Christianity of the Bitandese coexists with superstitious practices that they otehwise denounce in the Kongolese, Dadié adds maliciously: 'Crucifix on the wall' (p. 45).

Another notable feature of *Béatrice du Congo* is the briskness of its dialogue. As Wake has observed, Dadié is among the few Francophone dramatists with the

ability to write a dialogue ... suited to the dramatic situation, a dialogue which can be spoken and heard without ever jarring, which gives dramatic life to the ideas, and which contains within it the potential language of gesture so important in the theatre. (quoted in Banham and Wake 1976: 76)

An example of this is provided in the encounter between Doña Béatrice and the king in which the latter is warned against his policies towards the Bitandese and denounced, to his surprise, as a non-Christian and a prisoner of foreign interests:

DOÑA BÉATRICE: Prisoner of the Bitandese!
THE KING: I, the king, prisoner? Whose prisoner?
DOÑA BÉATRICE: Of money, of the Bitandese, of your appetite...
THE KING: I'm a Christian...
DOÑA BÉATRICE: No! You're still not one...
THE KING: What, you mean me?
DOÑA BÉATRICE: Yes!
THE KING: I who have had four cathedrals built and tens of churches; I who boast a son bishop... (he brings out a purse which he caresses slowly).
DOÑA BÉATRICE: Yes!... We all know who you are...
THE KING: Me...
DOÑA BÉATRICE: Yes, you're a coloured Bitandese... a Bitandese agent, and your days are numbered...
THE KING: You don't understand me... (stroking his purse... There is a knock on the door. He dashes off to hide the bags of money). (pp. 89–91)

Here the king's unconscious stroking of his moneybag, a visual image of his cupidity, and his rather undignified dash to hide it when he hears footsteps are part of the total dialogue, and confirm in an unexpected and comic way some of Doña Béatrice's accusations, which he otherwise denies so vigorously.

But if the themes explored in *Béatrice du Congo* can be grasped essentially from a reading of the written text, the play's full impact – by virtue of its scenic composition or production possibilities – can be fully felt only in the theatre. One such production possibility is the physical appearance of the Bitandese. Although Dadié indicates in a stage direction that they wear 'clothes marked with the initials of their regiments' (p. 9), Michel Raffaëli designed something more striking for them for the 1971 Jean-Marie Serreau production of the play at Avignon: a corset (Auclaire 1986: 133).

The corset, to Raffaëli and Serreau, not only gave the Bitandese an air of fantasy which they thought appropriate to their status as men of the Portugal of the Spanish Inquisition, but was also a metaphor for their colonial enterprise, which they saw as that of keeping the Kongolese firmly in position, as does a corset to a female body.

This choice of costume and its supposed meanings seemed to have created confusion in the minds of the Avignon spectators (see Sandier 1970). A simple but equally effective element of costume that can be used is, to my mind, a mask. Arriving on Kongolese soil for the first time, the Bitandese could be portrayed as wearing masks, the features of which symbolise their stated goals. As the play unfolds, however, and their real motives become apparent, the masks could be made to slip until the final sequences where they are completely shed to reveal Dracula-like characters. This approach has the advantage of being not only an effective visual symbol of the theme and the structure of the play, but of conveying that sense of horror experienced by the Mani Congo on discovering the truth about his 'guests': their rapine nature which he is alone in not spotting on time; taken in, as he was, by the masks.

If the dramatic potential of the costume of the Bitandese is left as a mere possibility to be exploited by a director, that of the Mani Congo is carefully indicated by the playwright himself. The very first encounter between the Bitandese and the Mani Congo is marked by an exchange of gifts which include, from the former to the latter, a 'parasol, clothes and [a symbol of their indifference to the usefulness of their gifts] a winter coat' (p. 40). As the Mani Congo gets more entrapped, so he is given more clothes and bedecked with various insignia, decorations and crosses whose weight on him symbolises his enslavement. And it is precisely these objects, viewed in his moment of nationalist awakening as alienating and artificial, that he decides to rid himself of in order to return to an original state of near-nudity, now synonymous with cultural authenticity and naturalness. The donning of (Bitandese) clothes in the first part of the play, like their removal in the end, becomes a visual expression of the trajectory of the Mani Congo from enslavement to freedom.

In addition to the effects derived from costume, Dadié also makes use of those derived from lighting. A particularly good example of this is in the first tableau of Act II where the stage device of the spotlight to isolate a character or group of characters in the surrounding obscurity is extensively used. The rapid shift of the spotlight, from Diogo and the Mani Congo to the Duke of Ovando, the Baron of Mbata and Diogo's associate, to other Kongolese notables and so on (pp. 81–2), conveys a visual sense of a society now fragmented into rival groups, of conspiracy and (on the part of the Bitandese) of wily machinations. For at the same time as they are egging on the Mani Congo into constructing a luxury mansion for himself, they are prodding his subordinates into rebellion.

But of all the theatrical resources used by Dadié, auditory stage devices are the most abundant. As Nicole Vincileoni has observed, 'There is a real dramaturgy of the ear in *Béatrice du Congo*, a use of acoustic space that needs emphasising' (1986: 261). Entire situations are aurally represented. For example, the war between the Bitandese and the Arabs with which the play opens. This is not evoked in words, but by the conflicting sounds of Western and Arabic music: 'Western music drowning Arab music. Calls of the muezzin punctuated at intervals by weak sounds of church bells' (p. 9). The war's outcome is also announced in sounds, with the amplification of Western music which swells into a tocsin, symbolically signifying victory over the Arabs whose music is completely drowned: 'Arab music becomes weaker while Western music becomes louder '(p. 9). The combination of these sounds and of the bodies of dead soldiers on the stage when the curtain rises is one of the most effective theatrical moments in *Béatrice du Congo*.

But it is not just in the opening scene that music is used. It fulfils several other theatrical functions throughout the play. It is used, for example, in the first tableau of Act I to characterise the Bitandese. The discordant jangle of sounds in their country – church bells, the Te Deum, the Angelus, the blaring of ships and the music of military trumpets – is a vivid, composite aural image of a civilisation steeped in contradictions: at once pretending to be religious and at the same time deeply mercantilist and militaristic.

Music – that of drums – is also used as a form of speech. It does not simply characterise people or evoke events, as we have seen. It actually takes part in the action *by saying the lines*. Thus in the second tableau of Act I the first arrival of the Bitandese in the Kongo is economically communicated to the court of the Mani Congo through the language of drum music. This is then decoded and translated into verbal language (p. 31).

A final example of the use of auditory elements in *Béatrice du Congo* is in the third tableau of Act II. Here it is used to indicate a character's state of mind. Diogo's love of the Kongo which, it will be recalled, he earlier described as 'an earthly paradise' is signalled by the music of drums which he alone 'hears' in faraway Bitanda and at the precise moment that he is arguing with his king against the latter's determination to colonise the Congo.

DIOGO: Your Majesty, I certainly bring you a kingdom, but is it absolutely necessary to trouble the peace of the people? (p. 55)

At this point the stage direction takes the spectator into Diogo's thoughts –

(*Distant choruses, drums*
Zaire emerges in Diogo)

– thoughts which he finally externalises in words:

Drums, Your Majesty, drums! Which remind all of the true meaning of existence which is joy, unity. (p. 55)

It is Dadié's ability in scenes like the above to associate textual and scenic writing that marks him out as one of Francophone Africa's distinguished playwrights.

ILES DE TEMPÊTE

With *Iles de Tempête*, Dadié's 1973 play, we move from the ancient kingdom of the Kongo to the Caribbean island of Haiti. But not to the Haiti of Césaire's Christophe – independent but bedevilled with the problems of nation-building – but to the pre-1803 slave colony, then known as Saint Domingue. *Béatrice du Congo* dealt with the vicissitudes of an African monarch whose greed and naivety, among other factors, led to the destruction of his kingdom, his death and the subsequent enslavement of his people. *Iles de Tempête*, on the other hand, is about the arrival of those people in the Caribbean as slaves, their epic and legendary struggle for freedom under their leader, Toussaint Louverture, and the latter's defeat and capture by the French armies of Napoleon Bonaparte. In spite of the differences in setting and subject-matter, however, *Iles de Tempête* displays certain similarities to *Béatrice du Congo*. Like the latter, not only are its events and most of its characters firmly rooted in history, but the action, which is a mixture of scenes of high drama and social observation, spans many centuries and takes place in several continents. Also, *Iles de Tempête* emphasises the big, significant moments in the destiny of a people (it is a kind of anthology of exemplary historical episodes) and evokes the complex set of factors, domestic and international, that went into the shaping of that destiny. Of course, certain key historical figures emerge as the focus of action and attention: Toussaint, Moyse, Dessalines, Grand'Ville and so on, but, like the characters in *Béatrice du Congo*, their real significance lies in their role as symbols of certain attitudes or political positions, rather than in themselves. But perhaps the strongest link between the two works lies in their treatment of history.

Iles de Tempête, like *Béatrice du Congo*, does not aim to be a piece of history wrapped up in dramatic form. Dramatised historical events to Dadié, as we have seen, are useful only for the parallels that can be established between them and contemporary Africa and because of the lessons they hold for it. Thus, to him, the recreation of the history of Saint Domingue is not an act of commemoration of a celebrated assertion of freedom (significantly the event itself is consigned to a mere stage direction at the end of the third tableau). It is one of reflection on a past that in some senses is still very present. Like Corneille's *Cinna* which, in the words of Balzac, 'nous [fait] voir Rome tout ce qu'elle peut être à Paris' (Morawski 1962: 8), Dadié's *Iles de Tempête* depicts an eighteenth- and early nineteenth-century Saint Domingue that cannot be more like contemporary Africa. Commenting on this approach to history by the Ivorian dramatist, Kotchy observes:

he re-organises his universe to correspond with the concerns of the moment. Thus he looks for characters and situations in history that are somewhat similar to those of our time. (Kotchy-Nguéssan 1984: 146)

In the specific case of Toussaint Louverture, Kotchy notes that, what interests Dadié are 'the errors of his government' (1984: 144) and that is why, he continues,

drawing inspiration from the example of events narrated by [C. L. R.] James, he puts greater emphasis on those areas that are more likely to move his African audience. (1984: 144)

But before examining those areas of similar concerns referred to by Kotchy, it will be useful first to take a closer look at the play's organisation and at the way it handles its historical material (see James 1938 (rpt 1984) on the history of revolutionary Haiti).

Divided into seven tableaux, *Iles de Tempête* stretches over a period of 170 years and takes place in three continents. Its action constantly shifts between and within tableaux from Europe, to Africa, the Americas and back. This constant movement, coupled with the many scenes of brutality and insurrection, of political debate, war and revolution, confer on the play an atmosphere of stormy movement and turbulence that is implied in its title. By evoking so many arenas of action, sometimes simultaneously (in Tableau II, scene 3, for example, the debates in and resolutions of the French revolutionary Assemblies are relayed to the Assembly of Colonists in Saint Domingue through the voice of an absent Mirabeau or Robespierre), Dadié reminds his audience that Saint Domingue was not just a remote island of little consequence, but a territory which was inextricably linked to the vital international political and economic interests of the period. In theatrical terms, this simultaneity recommended by Dadié for the six scenes of Tableau I (three of which take place in France, two in the Caribbean and one in Africa) can be achieved by dividing the stage into sections and then training the spotlight on them in rapid succession.

Unlike Edouard Glissant's *Monsieur Toussaint*, which also treats of the same subject but where the past is seen through the eyes of the hero, Toussaint, who relives it in captivity, *Iles de Tempête* starts from the beginning and progresses in linear fashion to the end. But although organised in chronological order and within specific tableaux, there is hardly any connecting thread between the various events evoked. What gives them unity is the slave population, whose fate constitutes the main subject of the play. When *Iles de Tempête* begins, we are in France. The date is roughly 1642, the year when, historically, Louis XIII endorsed his country's participation in the slave trade. This first tableau, which is partly set in France and partly in the Caribbean and Africa, sketches three important events: the efforts by the French to encourage the emigration of their citizens to populate Saint Domingue; the African slave markets and the transactions made therein; and finally the outrageous brutality of the slave-owners, for whom 'the golden rule of all civilisation is to make profits from everything' (p. 1).

By the time we get to the second tableau, a period of thirty-four years has elapsed. Thomas Jefferson's agitation in Tableau II, scene 1 tells us that we are in 1776. This second tableau can be said to unfold under the banner of liberty, for it depicts successively the American

War of Independence and the French Revolution. But more than this perhaps, it dramatises the confusion into which the latter events threw the colony. Unwilling to bow to the pressures for reform unleashed on it by the events in France, the Colonial Assembly is portrayed as responding with an ever-increasing ferociousness towards its mulatto and slave populations. This policy culminates in a successful slave revolt at the end of the third tableau. From now on, the action is no longer played out between warring factions, but around the figure of a single individual: Toussaint. From slavery through revolution to freedom in the first three tableaux, the play focusses from the fourth tableau onwards on the exercise of that freedom by Toussaint. It deals successively with his domestic policies and the increasing disaffection to which they give rise among the ex-slaves and two of his most trusted lieutenants, Moyse and Dessalines; with his War of Independence against Napoleon's France, his defeat and death in France paralleled with Napoleon's in the hands of the English.

Iles de Tempête takes several liberties with history and it would be tedious to cite them all; two examples will suffice. The most glaring example occurs towards the end of the play when Toussaint's defeat by the armies of Napoleon and his exile to France are made to coincide with events that took place some twelve years later in 1814: Napoleon's abdication and exile to Saint Helena, and his subsequent death in 1821. This ironic coincidence in the fortunes of the two men – France's most celebrated eighteenth-century military leaders and both self-styled consuls – is underlined by the constant change of setting in Tableau 1 from one prison to the other, and the almost identical reactions of the prisoners to their common predicament. A deep sense of injustice and outrage at trust betrayed and greatness humiliated is the substance of this reaction. To Toussaint's complaint about the treacherous circumstances of his arrest:

A crime has been committed for I was going, in good faith, to hand myself over to General Brunet when I was arrested. (p. 127)

rises, thousands of miles away, as if in echo, Napoleon's

No! Never. It's an injustice ... an act of felony. I won't go to St Helena. I appeal to all Europe. It's treason. (p. 125)

Like Napoleon, who finds it ironic that the wages of patriotism should be suffering and death – 'I've loved my country and who can be blamed for loving his?' (p. 129) – Toussaint asks his gaoler:

Who can be blamed for loving his country? And besides, is it a crime to break loose from one's chains? (p. 126)

Finally, clutching onto their titles as the only objects of value left to them in a degraded existence, Toussaint and Napoleon solemnly remind their gaolers –

TOUSSAINT: I am a French general and I'd like to be treated respectfully. (p. 125)
NAPOLEON: I am Napoleon, Emperor Napoleon I. (p. 128)

– a reminder which brings out the same laconic response from each of the gaolers: 'All I have here is a prisoner' (p. 128).

While Toussaint never gets to know of Napoleon's fate the latter, chastened by his bitter experience of injustice in Saint Helena, where he rails against everything, including the hot tropical climate, comes to appreciate what his prisoner must be going through in his fortress-prison in the snow-capped mountains of Eastern France. By the time he authorises his release, however, (which in any case he had no more power to do, having been deposed himself) it is too late. Toussaint has died.

It will be tempting to see in the parallel between these two careers (which theatrically could be suggested by a rapid alternation of the scenes) an attempt on the part of the dramatist to satisfy a sense of poetic justice or an artist's love of parallels. But there is clearly more to it. When taken together with other parallels, such as those in *Béatrice du Congo*, for example, where, as we saw, a scarcely decolonised Bitandese rush headlong to subjugate another people, and where Doña Béatrice denounces their domination in terms identical to those they used against the Moors, or the parallels in *Iles de Tempête* itself, where Toussaint the victim of yesterday becomes the victimiser of today, or where the conquering Napoleon is himself defeated, it would seem to reveal a pessimistic view of history. This view would deny that suffering leads to moral growth and sees human societies as condemned to an unending and futile game of role-changing between conquered and conqueror (Koudou 1981: 187–93; Pageaux 1984: 16–20; Vinciléoni 1986: 264–8).

But the Toussaint–Napoleon episode is not the only example of licence that the dramatist takes with his historical material. In the third scene of Tableau II, he radically modifies the historical chronology of events and brings together into a new dramatic whole events which happened in different places and at different times. Scene 3 is made to take place in the Colonial Assembly of Saint Domingue after the fall of the Bastille, and therefore presumably in 1789, and contains and presents as contemporaneous debates and events that took place in an earlier period. The elections with which it opens took place historically in 1788 (and not, as suggested, after 1789), when the colonists were trying to secure representation on the then freshly summoned Estates-General in Paris. In fact, it was also at a meeting of that body that Mirabeau's famous speech about slaves, mules and horses was made; a speech which in the play (p. 30) is echoed in a stormy session of the Saint Domingue Assembly, thereby giving the impression of simultaneity between the two meetings.

What these modifications confirm is Dadié's method. Here, as in *Béatrice du Congo*, he seeks to give his play a minimum of unity by bringing together into a new whole a series of disparate episodes. But while he can be faulted on points of historical detail, the organisation of his historical material is done in a manner which in its broad outlines leaves it both factually correct and (his constant pre-occupation) understandable by his African audiences and applicable to their situation.

In *Iles de Tempête*, the material is organised along the axis of colonisation and enslavement in Tableau I, revolt and freedom in Tableaux II and III and freedom and its aftermath in Tableaux IV to VII. One need only substitute the word 'Independence' for 'freedom' to see in the experience of Saint Domingue a precursor to that of modern African countries.

But what, more specifically, are the common points that are highlighted between the two situations and how are they presented? The most important is that of a post-colonial ruling élite that is either corrupt, or well-intentioned but a prisoner of methods or a mentality that prevent it from effecting the structural changes necessary for meaningful independence. In either case, the result is a country where, in spite of the change of personnel, the old problems remain. This is precisely the situation of Saint Domingue in *Iles de Tempête*. The slaves have replaced the slave-owners but slavery remains. This situation is brought out in Tableau IV where Toussaint has hardly assumed power as the island's governor than his close associates are already buying up white plantations. The property that once belonged to the Marquis of Rocher de la Casse, we are told in the stage directions of scene 1, now belongs to General Coutou. But the idea that the change that has taken place is one of form rather than substance is suggested by the methods used by General Coutou, the new knight of the shire, as it were. Informed that the labourers on his plantation come late to work, he orders, like the recently overthrown white slave-owners of Tableau 1, scene 6, that five of them be shot, adding proudly 'slavery has been abolished, but the system stays' (p. 60).

But more than just their property, the new leaders have also taken over the life-style of their erstwhile masters and oppressors. Thus Mercure, described as a 'top personality in the new regime' (p. 60) insists that the servant whom he has inherited from M. du Rocher serve him with his customary elegant manners and deference. In only two scenes, then, Dadié has embodied in two characters – Mercure and General Coutou – some of the ills of the new nation-states.

But Dadié does not so much use his powers of satire and ridicule against them as against Toussaint himself. There are, of course, clear differences between the latter and his men. Toussaint's aims are noble and national. Those of the men are personal and selfish. He wants to control the unbridled appetites that have been unleashed by the advent of self-government: 'How can I control all these appetites?' (p. 61); 'to give pride to his once enslaved people' (p. 61); 'to unite the different social and racial groups' in his country (p. 63); to liberate the peasants. In short, he wants to transform a society disorganised by years of war, slavery and licence into a community of free and responsible citizens. The men, on the other hand, think solely in terms of exploiting for themselves the new opportunities created by the revolution, of 'catching up on lost time', as Mercure puts it (p. 61).

But if Toussaint's objectives are praiseworthy, he adopts an approach which makes it impossible for him to fulfil them. Firmly convinced that the only way to avoid economic chaos is by satisfying the settler population, which he believes will see it is in its own interest to cooperate with his government, he invites it to return to the country from exile and restores the lands, complete with black labourers; a policy which he justifies in terms of its inevitability:

I'm blamed for having brought back the settlers, for having given them back their lands and for putting blacks to work on them. Was there any alternative? (p. 65)

But more than just land, he also gives all the top positions in the state: 'Aren't they the experts in trade, manufacture and administration?' (p. 65). To Dessalines, who warns him of the total folly of a policy whose stated objectives are to unite the races and classes and yet whose practice favours only one group, he asks:

Which important posts can I offer free blacks who have neither expertise nor capital to develop the country? (p. 65)

Toussaint's conciliatory policy need not itself be dismissed out of hand in a country such as his, faced with the problems he has outlined so well. But for the policy to be meaningful, it should be part of a general strategy, the ultimate aim of which would be to make such expertise available to wider society. His error is to have made it an end in itself. The result, from making concession after concession to his former masters, is a position where he recreates in free Saint Domingue the *status quo ante*. The only difference is that from slaves the ethnic Haitians have become labourers, while their erstwhile slave-owners have become capitalists.

What on the face of it had looked like a sound pragmatic policy degenerates, shortly after Toussaint's accession to power, into a totally misconceived one. This becomes obvious when, in addition to the unilateral concessions, Toussaint proscribes indigenous religious organisations, like the voodoo cult which constituted the basis of his power as a slave leader (p. 67).

From noble in thought and language when he first appears, the Haitian leader rapidly becomes ridiculous half way through his career. Dadié now satirises him as caught in a frenzy of proscription which makes him ban mechanically anything that anyone cares to mention:

TOUSSAINT: I ban all meetings not held in the Hôtel de la République. I forbid civil servants to live under the same roof with their wife and mistress. I forbid interventions. (p. 67)

Furthermore, and as if he were not sufficiently going in the wrong direction, Toussaint now displays a besotted attitude towards, and naive confidence in, France that ultimately proves fatal. On the eve of the Napoleonic invasion of his country, Toussaint talks pompously of his 'trust in France's wisdom and objectivity' (p. 105); when the English envoy, pressing a Declaration of Independence on him, addresses him as Toussaint Louverture, he replies: 'No, add French General' (p. 69).

And yet, like the Mani Congo in *Béatrice du Congo*, Toussaint's untutored genius displays remarkable flashes of intelligence, such as when he says of the French authorities of his day, 'they always see themselves as either gendarmes or tutors' (p. 68); or when he tells his French technical advisers – a category also satirised in *La Tragédie du roi Christophe* and *Béatrice du Congo* – that undertaking their suggested architectural extravaganzas (palaces of marble, Turkish gardens, musical fountains) will lead to a waste of scarce development funds and detract him from his objectives (p. 72). But these advisers only need reply that what they suggest is what is done in France, and by Bonaparte for that matter, for Toussaint to cave in immediately. In a dialogue calculated to ridicule him, Toussaint is made to parrot out, in the manner of a well-learnt lesson, the rest of an answer from an adviser to his own question:

SECOND TECHNICIAN: ... you need a Turkish garden.
TOUSSAINT LOUVERTURE: Why Turkish?
PREMIER TECHNICIAN: Because right now, General Bonaparte is having one constructed near the Sublime Door.
SECOND TECHNICIAN: It's also important that the garden with the capital's finest flowers ... face the East.
TOUSSAINT LOUVERTURE: And why the East?
THE TECHNICIANS: Because ...
TOUSSAINT LOUVERTURE: ... General Bonaparte's gardens all face East.
THE TECHNICIANS: You've made the right guess, Your Excellency. (p. 73)

But it is in his relationship with his French personal assistant, Grand'Ville, that Toussaint is most heavily criticised. It is sufficiently dangerous for him to have employed in this position the citizen of a country that has never quite made a secret of its colonialist designs on his. But it is even worse when the Frenchman's advice is then taken without the necessary circumspection. With the settlers, Toussaint gave everything and got nothing in return. 'What are all those settlers whom I've invited back into the country doing to help me?' is his anguished cry when they betray him. Now the same blind trust, denounced by Joao de Texiera in the Mani Congo, is at work again in Toussaint.

Even when all the signs point to an impending invasion by Napoleon's France to scotch his experiment with liberty, Toussaint shows total confidence in Grand'Ville's pompous but empty declarations of principle on behalf of his country: 'France will never take back that which she has freely given' (p. 106). The relationship achieves a farcical climax in the invasion scene, where Grand'Ville manages to convince Toussaint that the invading troops, though European and French-speaking, could not be French. And this, in spite of the evidence to the contrary provided by a messenger:

FIRST MESSENGER: All France has come to wreak vengeance and massacre on the Haitians.
TOUSSAINT LOUVERTURE: France?
GRAND'VILLE: Certainly not France!
FIRST MESSENGER: But the navy is spread out in the Bay of Samana. We've counted as many as forty-seven ships...
TOUSSAINT LOUVERTURE: You mean close to fifty thousand men, Grand'Ville, to turn back the wheel of history?
GRAND'VILLE: France will never repudiate her agreements...
TOUSSAINT LOUVERTURE: Indeed, who says these boats are French?
FIRST MESSENGER: But the men speak French.
TOUSSAINT LOUVERTURE: But then we speak French too, but aren't we black?
FIRST MESSENGER: But they are white.
TOUSSAINT LOUVERTURE: Are all white men French? (pp. 105-6)

In the end, when he accepts the reality of the invasion, it is not so much the fear of a return to slavery that bothers him as the reminder that he is not French and that he will not sing the Marseillaise as part of the French nation: 'That's what we've always wanted: to sing the *Marseillaise* together!... Oh! if only Napoleon hadn't made this impossible!' (p. 112).

With this attitude, it is hardly surprising that Toussaint should have been captured with so much ease by General Leclerc. For even when he is warned by Mme Debelleville of the plot to seize him, Toussaint, true to himself, dismisses this on the grounds that the French General has taken an oath before God and man to defend the freedom of the island (p. 119).

Although, in the main, the image of Toussaint contained in this play is derived from C. L. R. James, Dadié has modified it in certain ways to make it look like that of some contemporary (Francophone) African leaders. True, the historical Toussaint was loyal to France, but, as Eric Williams writes, he 'never wavered or compromised the abolition of slavery in Saint Domingue' (Williams 1970: 251). Furthermore, his loyalty was part of a general strategy designed not to provoke France unnecessarily into intervening in the island's affairs – for, after all, Saint Domingue was still part of France, though self-governing.

This is not the perspective that comes out in *Iles de Tempête*. Here, Toussaint's loyalty is presented as blind and uncritical. The mightily intelligent hero of James' narrative, the man who never trusted the French or for that matter any European nation with the destiny of his country (James 1984: 283–5) is presented here as a complete sell-out.

James approves Toussaint's policies towards the French. His only fault, according to James, is that he took his followers for granted and failed to explain his policies to them. Dadié, on the other hand, disapproves of these policies so, unlike James who sees Toussaint's defeat as resulting from an error of judgement, he presents it as almost deserved. The historian's case of calamitous misjudgement, in other words, becomes with the dramatist one of obsequiousness and stupidity. To drive this image home, Dadié's Toussaint does not even fight when his island is invaded (which is historically incorrect); he moans, wails and complains.

Totally opposed to Toussaint's position, however, in *Iles de Tempête* are Dessalines and Moyse. Like Doña Béatrice, who kept warning the Mani Congo of the perfidy of the Bitandese and of the dangers of relying on them at the expense of his people, Dessalines warns Toussaint against a facile belief in the willingness of the settlers to make the necessary sacrifices. At the height of the French invasion, he suggests to Toussaint a Declaration of Independence, explaining that real freedom is not granted, as he is wont to believe, but conquered through struggle and suffering.

But Moyse is an even sharper critic of Toussaint. He denounces the latter's refusal to make landowners of the peasants, the harshness of the new labour laws and above all Toussaint's disastrous obsession with France:

General Toussaint Louverture, when shall we ever stop living with our eyes permanently fixed on Europe? We're constantly in search of a favourable place in her opinion or of our *raisons d'être* in her judgement. We must give the land to those who cultivate it. (p. 80)

In this vibrant denunciation of the asphyxiating presence of France in the affairs of Saint Domingue, one senses the voice of the Ivorian dramatist whose country more than most strives, as Toussaint's did, to maintain 'the French connection as necessary in its long and difficult climb to civilisation' (James 1984: 283; on the Ivory Coast/Saint Domingue parallels, see Vinciléoni 1986: 219–20). Moyse's forthright demands for a society that seeks original solutions to its problems earns him the popularity of the ordinary man and the intense displeasure of Toussaint. In the end, he is killed by Toussaint as Doña Béatrice was by the Mani Congo. But his death also sets the seal on Toussaint's regime, for from that point on he is increasingly estranged from his people, deserted by his most trusted supporters and the prisoner of powerful local and metropolitan economic interests that finally engineer his downfall.

Iles de Tempête can be interpreted ultimately as a play about a revolution betrayed. But it would be an error to see Toussaint as the sole traitor. It is true that the dramatist reserves the weight of his criticism for him. But Napoleon also stands indicted. He is shown as ridiculing the self-styled generals of Saint Domingue when he, like them, is a self-proclaimed Consul and Emperor. To the liberating ideals of the French Revolution, he substitutes expansionist concerns: 'it is of the utmost importance and of vital necessity that France rule the world' (p. 92). He also emerges as racist in his determination to restore Saint Domingue to her former status and to re-establish slavery: 'The Republic isn't a game for children let alone for niggers' (p. 96). Napoleon's reasoning is nothing more than a farrago of pride, prejudice and self-delusion. That the black Consul of Saint Domingue and the First Consul of France should die in similar circumstances is Dadié's way of visiting retribution on men who in his view betrayed their countries.

Iles de Tempête, even more than *Béatrice du Congo*, uses a variety of scenic effects. In the first three Tableaux especially, stage designs communicate not only information (which would otherwise need reams of dialogue), but also depict situations and events, convey not only emotions but the urgency and movement implied in the play's title.

Plantation slavery and its toll on human life is visually suggested in Tableau I scene 6, by a group of slaves held in chains and dripping with blood. They stagger on to the stage one after the other at regular intervals, only to be shot by ruthless guards with tell-tale names like Durrocher and Laflamme, 'armed with guns, pistols, daggers and whips' (p. 14), who accuse them of laziness or rebelliousness.

The cruelty of Louis XIII's regime, his insensitivity to human suffering and his expansionist ambitions are all visually portrayed in the setting of Tableau I scene 2, even before he utters his first words. The stage directions show him gazing fixedly at a globe, surrounded by wife and courtiers and serenaded by a minstrel while an executioner is merrily chopping off heads near by.

The complexity of Caribbean society, with its entangled and antagonistic social groups of white colonists and plantation owners, of mulattos, of freed slaves, black slaves and so on is also conveyed in the opening stage direction of Tableau II scene 1:

a public square with passers-by. Some exchange greetings, others don't. Whites don't respond to the greetings of mulattos, the latter don't respond to those of the blacks...lines of Europeans are followed by their black servants. (p. 24)

Iles de Tempête makes use of gestural language. Entire scenes, like those representing executions in the court of King Louis XIII or depicting plantation slave labour (Tableaux I scene 6, p. 21) or the very first arrival of slavers on the African coast and their transactions (Tableau VII, scene 5, p. 13), call for actors with training in the art of mime. But, as with *Béatrice du Congo*, it is perhaps the additional auditory elements that are its defining theatrical feature. The play's action unfolds against a permanent background of sounds: the sounds of death instruments, guns, pistols, whips; the sounds of music, negro spirituals (p. 26), work songs (p. 20), military marches (p. 42) and drum music. Over and above its entertainment, atmosphere-creating or morale-boosting functions, the music in the play often appears as a central dramatic character.

This is particularly clear in the first part of the play (Tableaux I–III), which unfolds against the background of slave unrest, which, however, is never seen on stage. Rather it is suggested by the rumbling of drums calling on the slaves to revolt. Thus, towards the end of Tableau I scene 6, we hear the voice of L'Abbé Raynal asking (in France) 'Where is this great man who will raise the sacred banner of Li-ber-ty?' (p. 22) and immediately, as if in echo and joyous approval, we hear 'the distant sounds of tom-toms' (p. 22). And the meaning of these sounds is not lost on Durrocher and Laflamme, who remark:

more incitement to burn workshops and to desert; to rebel ... they have to be mad to destroy with such rage. (p. 22)

As the play's action unfolds and the rebellion gathers momentum, so the drumbeats become more intense and less distant – interrupting white conversations as if part of them, albeit an uninvited part, drowning them and, towards the end of the third tableau, actually dominating the stage (pp. 44–58). The successful progression of the slave revolt under Toussaint, in other words, is never physically shown on stage. It is suggested instead by the skilful use of musical instruments.

CHAPTER 6

Cheik Ndao: 'L'Exil d'Albouri'

Born in Senegal where he currently teaches English, partly educated there but also in France at the University of Grenoble and in Swansea, Wales, Cheik Ndao is one of his country's best-known writers. The author of a volume of poetry, short stories and a novel, he has also written six plays including one of the earliest history plays by a Francophone African which won the first prize in the 1969 Algiers Arts Festival: *L'Exil d'Albouri*.

Although, like most works in its category, it derives the fundamentals of its plot from history – in this case the late nineteenth-century history of the Woloff empire of north-east Senegal (Monteil 1966: 615–30) – *L'Exil d'Albouri* stands apart from most of the rest in so far as it is more dramatic than theatrical. It presents a unified plot with a solid core of moral dilemmas. Its action is not created and maintained through public exploits as in, for example, *Kondo le requin*, but through political conflicts between a king and his officials, and private dramas between himself and his wife. Very little by way of overt action takes place and yet, for the most part, the play leaves the reader with a profound sense of drama.

To achieve this, Ndao invents within the identifiable historical context of his play – the 1890 French invasion of the Woloff Kingdom of Senegal – the highly charged dramatic situation of a king whose decision to flee, in order to avoid the destruction of his people and his humiliating capture, is bitterly opposed, at least initially, by his mother and sister (a serious problem in a matri-lineal society) and, throughout, by his brother and the strongman of the regime, Prince Laobé Penda. This invented conflict not only helps the playwright to create credible dialogue which then est-ablishes the reality of his main characters, it serves as the mainspring of the action. But to make the situation even more intense, he has the first outbreak of conflict between king and brother preceded by scenes of a public display of confidence and harmony between the two men.

When the play opens, preparations are under way for an important meeting of the entire community, convened by the king. Samba, the *griot*, is busy imploring his Sun-God for divine inspiration as he prepares to recount yet again at a meeting the exploits of his king.

Oh Sun, Breath of the Buffalo in the savannah!...Dispenser of wisdom! Grant that my words be as cutting as your rays. (p. 17)

Although at this point the audience is not quite sure of the purpose of the meeting, remarks by one of the first arrivals at the House of Assembly, Le Premier Homme du Peuple, about disquieting news from the neighbouring kingdom of Cayor, and the *griot*'s angry reaction at these 'rumours', suggest that a grave situation is at hand. The suspense created by the rumours and, even more, by the fact that two thrones, instead of the usual one, are being put into position, quickly subsides when it turns out that the meeting has been called to honour Laobé Penda for his distinguished services to the kingdom. But the audience's interest has hardly died down when it is again abruptly awakened by news that neighbouring Cayor has been overrun, the *Damel* (king) killed and the invading French troops from the sea, armed with 'fire-spitting machines', are advancing. This news puts an end to the festivities, brings the freshly celebrated unity between king and brother under strain and sets the stage for a bitter confrontation between them.

In this expository first tableau, Ndao not only presents the basic dramatic situation and the main characters, he establishes in a visually spectacular way the play's cultural setting. He skilfully introduces elements of performance, from the traditional oral culture, in the person of Samba, the *griot*. Samba functions as an integral part of the drama, revealing, in his opening incantations to the sun, the presence, in the predominantly Islamic culture of the Woloff, of an animistic substratum; providing in his praise songs, conceived on the mode of a call from the singer and a response from his audience, background information on the main characters, their ancestry and exploits (pp. 21–4). Samba also comments on events, cautions the warring parties with words of wisdom and, finally, acts as counsellor and confidante to the king, and intermediary between him and his subjects.

If the first tableau ends on a note of disagreement between king and brother, it is in Tableaux II and III that these differences actually erupt into major confrontation. Ndao, however, does not hasten the climax but maintains the spectator's interest without giving him or her clues into the nature of the climactic confrontation. This he does in the second Tableau by having his hero convene a meeting of his military governors, *diarafs*, and various dignitaries to work out a response to the French threat. But the meeting does not go Albouri's way. Instead of a more reasoned response, which would have been in agreement with his as-yet-undivulged plans to flee to Ségou, the governors all argue vehemently, counting mistakenly on Albouri's past record of bravery, for a headlong clash with the French:

DIARAF OF THE SLAVES: Oh Ndiaye! With a king like you at the helm, nothing is impossible. Speak and we shall act.
DIARAF OF THINGUE: We from Thingue are ready.
ARDO: I, Ardo, won't be remiss in my duty. We're listening. (p. 27)

From a dramatic point of view, this meeting creates a dilemma for the hero: either he confronts his *diarafs* with his diametrically opposed response and puts his throne at stake, or he aligns himself with them and opens his country, as he has been arguing, to total destruction. Unable to solve this problem, he suspends the meeting while he tries privately to woo his brother to his side. But he not only fails to secure his brother's support, he finds his mother and sister, La Linguère, also totally opposed to him. While these political conflicts rumble on behind closed doors, a parallel conflict between the women – Albouri's mother and sister on the one hand and his wife, Queen Seb, on the other – is taking place.

By the time we get to Tableau III, Albouri has at last decided to have the courage of his convictions and to announce them in a reconvened session of the defence council. This is the climax of the play. As was to be expected, his plans cause consternation among his military chiefs and the dignitaries whose disbelief is pressed in two words: 'Exile? Exodus!' (p. 44). They also touch off the long-expected clash with Penda who, anticipating that his uncompromising stance at the meeting might tempt his brother to have him arrested, secretly stations, as a precautionary measure, 500 loyal troops around the palace. Their chance discovery by Samba after the breakdown of the talks and at the point of departure of the various parties; the panic this causes because of fears that they could in fact be the French already in the capital, and Penda's admission that it was all his doing, bring him and the king to the brink of physical conflict. But this situation is quickly defused by Samba.

The possibilities for even more dramatic action which arise later from the murder of an Albouri spy on the orders of Penda, the latter's departure for war and his surprising turnabout which leads him to open negotiations with the French governor, remain totally un-exploited. Instead of having the king try to recover his lost authority, thereby forcing a resolution to the confict, Ndao sets him off on the long road of exile to Ségou. But this decision, coming so soon after news of Penda's treaty with the French and his imminent ap-pointment as king, looks more like a resigned acceptance of defeat than a heroic gesture of refusal to compromise. Ndao's attempt to infuse life into the last tableau with the sudden discovery, again by Samba, that Queen Seb is in the exile party, contrary to her husband's instructions, ends in failure because of her totally unconvincing profession of an ethic of self-renunciation when confronted by him.

But whatever its weaknesses toward the close, *L'Exil d'Albouri* still contains much that is of dramatic interest. It shows a refreshing concern with plot structure, a desire to craft an absorbing story that is often absent in French African history plays. This is not to say, however, that Ndao neglects the celebratory role of the African past that has come to be expected of this type of play. He not only shows a keen awareness of this past by the inclusion of a *griot*, he clearly sets it out in his prefatory note as being at the centre of his concerns: 'My aim is to contribute to the creation of myths that galvanise people and carry them forward' (p. 15).

The myth which he creates of a Woloff people fiercely jealous of their independence and prepared to face the hardship of exile rather than submit to the comforts of French rule is embodied by the hero Albouri. In a series of memorable pronouncements – 'Exile rather than slavery' (p. 78), 'When one's honour is safe, one has everything' (p. 45) – he rejects the calls for compromise with the French made by some of his people.

Ndao underlines Albouri's selflessness by contrasting his attitude with that of men like Ardo or the *Diaraf* of Thingue, whose sole preoccupation is with saving their class privileges. They make no effort to conceal this either from Albouri or from Penda during separate and secret meetings with each of them:

ARDO: Oh King! Think of all that we'd be leaving behind and would not be sure of finding in Ségou. (p. 44)

DIARAF OF THINGUE: I'm much too accustomed to my privilege not to see that Albouri is really demanding nothing short of our total ruin. (p. 55)

Against this profession of faith in the material interests of the self, Albouri is presented as defending the fundamental values of the kingdom. In a passionate plea to his followers he exhorts them to forgo all the gold of the legendary mines of Bouré and Bambouk in the defence of their country:

Whatever the fate of our army, may our hearts be fortified against cowardice. May dignity be our only weapon. We've lost a kingdom for the greater glory of eternity. (p. 89)

But, more than just honour, Albouri also has those qualities of reflectiveness and caution that are the mark of the mature leader. To an impulsive brother whose first reaction to the news of a French attack is 'Oh Albouri, Bourba, grant me the honour of leading the army into battle' (p. 25), he proposes caution: 'Think first, my brother, think!' (p. 25). Another trait of Albouri's character is pragmatism. Although his country's motto, as Penda reminds him, is: 'Advance no matter what' (p. 32), he realises that changed circumstances, notably the infinitely superior power of the new enemy, France, dictate a new and more realistic approach. The traditional motto, he explains:

was valid for the period when our ancestors fought against enemies who used the same weapons as theirs. (p. 32)

Not to recognise this fact, he argues, is a sign of irresponsibility, not courage.

But Albouri is not all unalloyed heroism. His characterisation is much more complex. Unlike Gbéhanzin, Christophe, Séydou Bad-ian's Chaka who are superhuman in their devotion to duty, Albouri displays human weaknesses. He experiences a range of emotions from fear through self-doubt to guilt. Aware of the controversial nature of his plans he hesitates to reveal them to anyone, including his mother, and suspends meeting after meeting with his officials while he tries to drum up support for them in private. He suffers from being misunderstood when, after Penda's total rejection of his explanations, his most trusted allies, his mother and sister, fail to accept his explanations for choosing to flee:

THE QUEEN MOTHER MAM YAY: You call it exile? It's more like fleeing. Exile to where? No, my son! Die in your capital among your people.
THE KING: Wasn't I correct? You, my mother, you're accusing me without even listening to me, without understanding me.
LINGUÈRE MADJIGUÈNE: Exile must be a last resort. Let's first put up resistance against the onslaught. (pp. 35–6)

It is the implication in these statements that his decision can be called anything but honourable, the suggestion that it could in fact be concealing rather selfish motives (because honour plainly commands that he fight and die in his capital) that cause him the greatest distress.

But then, and here is his complex nature, he does nothing to dispel this impression. If anything, his constantly changing reasons for wishing to go to Ségou seem to suggest that he is as little convinced of the disinterestedness of his motives as the critical audience. Now this reason is military (the need to join forces with Amadou at Ségou and to defeat the French before they invade Woloff territory); at times the reason is humanitarian (the need to save his people from unnecessary destruction by a vastly superior French force); at other times his motive derives from heroic politics (the preservation of the honour of the Woloff by avoiding humiliating capture). The inconsistency displayed here raises suspicions about the possible existence of other motives. For if, as Albouri argues (p. 52), Woloff country had long ceased to be his – presumably from the moment the neighbouring kingdoms of Cayor and Baol had fallen – then the argument about protecting its sovereignty by going to Ségou seems a little feeble. Furthermore, Albouri does not leave only with soldiers and court officials, which would have been in keeping with the idea of a government in exile, he actually encourages an exodus of his people, which points to a simple flight.

The possibility of unheroic emotions having coloured his decision, cowardice perhaps, or personal pride, is confirmed by Albouri himself when he confesses to his wife:

For the past three days, I've been wondering about and even questioning the wisdom of my situation. Was I right to do it? Haven't I yielded to haste? *Haven't I hidden behind my people to advance personal goals? Wouldn't it, by any chance, be pride that is egging me on?* (p. 83, my emphasis)

It is questions such as these that make Albouri the most human, and one might say Racinian, of heroes in Francophone history plays. For he is not just pure Corneillian nobility or rationality in thought and action. There also exist in him obscure and not always rational zones of self-interest and passion. Nowhere is this better manifested than in his relationship with his wife Seb.

Of course, the image of Albouri as lover is not one that will readily strike the audience. On the face of it, he seems to be just another Chaka concerned only with war and politics, and dismissive of love as a passion for the weak. For has he not, in preferring service to his people to devotion to his queen, subordinated, in pure Corneillian terms, love to political duty? A closer analysis of some of his statements soon reveals, however, that this is not quite the case. Albouri is not Badian's Chaka who sacrifices his love for Noliwé to the greatness of the Zulu. He is more like Senghor's hero, for whom politics is the evil necessity that prevents him from fulfilling himself.

This comes out clearly in the sixth Tableau where, after several failed attempts, his wife finally succeeds in speaking to him. What we see then, after his veneer of high seriousness has cracked, is a man who not only relives with pleasure the days of courtship with his wife, but one who confesses to the scourge that is politics:

Often, during the most serious business ... my thoughts stray towards you! I get lost in dreams which some attribute to depth of reflection ... Oh! to govern and yet to be human. What a prison! People don't suspect that I'm just like the most humble of my subjects. (p. 71)

The Racinian tonality of this play, first created by a simple plot structure that depends for its movement on the interplay of passions and interests, and now strengthened by the character of Albouri, becomes even more obvious when one listens to Seb, one of Ndao's most individualised creations.

Twenty years old, and a princess from the royal family of Cayor, Seb, like Racine's Bérénice, is possessed of a fiery passion that is in the service of a cause no higher than that of the self. All she wants and cares for is her husband:

To be left alone with Albouri is my only joy, as with any wife. (p. 38)

Je ne demande qu'à me consacrer. (p. 39)

But, like Bérénice who is frustrated of her love for Titus by political factors (Rome is opposed to monarchs and she is a queen), Seb is also cheated of her husband's care by a critical political situation that takes all his time, and a matrilineal system that makes her subordinate, in her marital home, to her husband's sister. She revolts against this situation and expresses her frustration in near erotic terms:

I'm no more than a shadow in this palace. I live on the memory of my dead dreams. Oh! look at my breasts and how they're blooming! Each night, I toss alone on my bed, my eyes wide open. (p. 37)

In a complaint that is supposed to shed light on royal Woloff marriage customs and specifically on the role and position of the wife, she tells her sister-in-law, Linguère:

You stand between me and your brother. Always having to take recourse to you; to confide all in you, so that you can convey my problems to your brother; always having to receive advice from you … even when I'm in total disagreement with what you're saying. (p. 40)

But Ndao is no Guillaume Oyono-Mbia, always ready to lend support to his young, emancipated and rebellious heroines against what they consider to be oppressive and anti-feminist marriage customs. He stands solidly behind these traditions through his hero, who calmly states the matrilineal case to his irate wife: 'That's the tradition! It's her sons that should inherit the throne if we stick to the ancient rules' (p. 67), but above all through Linguère, the play's 'anti-Seb' and embodiment of traditional Woloff womanhood.

Unlike Seb who talks rights – the right to enjoy with her husband the emotional and physical pleasures of a love unfettered by interfering in-laws and politics – Linguère talks duties. The duty to be submissive to one's husband and to be constantly at the service of his community:

The role of a wife is to obey, to wait for her knight to deign to knock on her door. (p. 38)

Elsewhere, she explains to Seb: 'It's in the gift of oneself that one finds the greatest joy … I've learnt to put country before all else' (p. 40). But Linguère is more than just meek submissiveness and self-sacrifice. She is also capable of heroic sentiments. Informed of her brother's decision to exclude her and other women from the exile party on the grounds of weakness, she exclaims:

What! My brother knows me. I can climb on horseback and shoot a gun like any warrior. (p. 62)

Clearly then, Linguère is portrayed as the female replica of Albouri and a model of good conduct to African women. In her contest with the 'misguided' Seb, the lady who dares challenge the all-powerful role of a husband's mother and sister in her society; who puts passion before duty, in other words private sentimental interests before public political interests; who fights for the recognition of her rights as a wife and who, finally, defends the values of love and life against the life-denying feudal ethic of self-renunciation and abstract honour of her society, she emerges triumphant. The young, non-conformist queen in the end confesses to having strayed from the path of 'righteousness' and asks to be forgiven and reintegrated into the fold. She explains to her husband repentantly,

My youth has sometimes made me capricious. (p. 82)

I'll now cease to be the spoilt princess of Cayor; I'll become an example of devotion to other wives... (p. 83)

But with this sudden maturity on Seb's part, one senses the disastrously interfering hand (at least from the point of view of characterisation) of the playwright. Unable, for ideological reasons, to leave Seb alone as rebel (it would have looked like endorsing a socially subversive position), he artificially breaks her up. While this solution might leave the playwright's values protected and even earn him the applause of the traditionalists in his audience, it reduces *L'Exil d'Albouri*, like so many other plays in its category, and despite some other successful features, into a didactic work.

Just as Seb, before her sudden and radical conversion, stands in a relationship of opposition to Linguère Madjiguène, so Laobé Penda does to Albouri. Apart from the former's impulsiveness, which we have noted, his ultimate objective is (at least so it seems) different from Albouri's. The latter is concerned with the defence of the interests of *all* his subjects:

Albouri Ndiaye isn't only interested in our House. Without the people, Ndiadiane would be nothing. What would we have become without the labour of our peasants and craftsmen? (p. 51)

Laobé Penda, on the other hand, is more narrowly preoccupied with safeguarding the royal interests of the House of Ndiaye; with seeing to it that its throne does not fall: 'Let's secure the throne for the House of Ndiaye, whatever happens' (p. 45).

With a position such as his, it is fairly clear – although he did not seem to realise it at the time – that if adequate safeguards were provided for his interests by the French, he would have to reach a compromise with them. And this is exactly what happens. He sets out to fight only to be informed, on his arrival in the battlefield, that the French governor has agreed to 'leave the throne with the Ndiaye' (p. 73). Thinking that he has in fact managed to save what matters most, he signs a peace treaty. In Laobé Penda, Hasan el-Nouty has observed, the Senegalese dramatist has depicted all those African '"nationalist fighters" who have turned "collaborator"' (El-Nouty 1983: 232).

This remark is quite fair. But what also comes out in the case of Penda is that his transformation is more the result of misguided assumptions than of selfishness or greedy calculations, as is the case with the *diarafs*. He *genuinely* came to see the wider interests of the kingdom as inseparable from the specific destiny of the House of Ndiaye. This belief, which is sincere but flawed, is exploited by men like the *diaraf* of Thingue, whose real reason for not wishing to go into exile is totally different from Penda's. Penda wishes to stay on to fight. The *diaraf* of Thingue, on the other hand, wants to stay on to be able to take part in the negotiations with the French for which he has been arguing and which he hopes, as he admits in a moment of inattention, will guarantee him his 'lands', 'granaries' and 'farms' (p. 55).

The idea, therefore, of a self-seeking Penda pitted against a selfless Albouri, which a cursorily Manichaean reading of the play might suggest, is simply not tenable. This contrast is perhaps what the dramatist intended to depict. It is certainly not what he achieved. Albouri, as has been shown, is not straightforward heroism, any more than his brother is crass selfishness. In the behaviour of both men there are ambiguities and these give the characters a depth that is all too often absent in dramatised historical figures.

A notable feature of *L'Exil d'Albouri* resides in the way in which the main characters are differentiated through language. The examples of two characters will illustrate this point. First, Samba the *griot* uses a variety of styles depending on his situation. They range from the supplicatory through the eulogistic to the poetic. The incidence of supplicatory language comes in his prayers to his Sun-God:

O Soleil, Souffle du Buffle sur les savanes! Délivre les femmes en gésine dans les ténèbres des cases. Que nos enfants poussent drus et droits, comme des épis au coeur de l'hivernage. (p. 17)

(Oh Sun! Breath of the buffalo in the savannah! Grant safe delivery to women lying in child-bed, in the darkness of huts. Grant that our children grow strong and sturdy like sheaves of corn in mid-Harmattan.)

When he is addressing the king during formal occasions, Samba's language becomes eulogistic. He uses praise names and allusive and figurative language in the tradition of panegyric poetry to describe him:

Tison Ardent vomi par les flancs du Lion en plein midi. Le voilà l'éléphant, l'astre du zénith, le Lion de Guilé. (p. 21)

(Flaming Firebrand thrown up from the flanks of the Lion at full noon. There he stands, the elephant, the star at its zenith, the Lion of Guilé.)

In the seventh tableau, where the *griot* exhorts Albouri and the exile party to show courage and determination in the face of the difficulties ahead, and sketches out his vision of the future, his language becomes poetic:

Peuple! Du futur nos femmes feront des boucles d'or suspendus à leurs oreilles. Ah! écloront les bourgeons de leurs seins comme fleurs de flamboyant. (p. 77)

(People! Our women will make golden earrings of the future that will dangle from their ears. And the buds of their breasts will blossom like the flowers of the flame tree.)

Samba's language can also be straightforwardly factual, as when he narrates in the sixth tableau the following events to Albouri:

Le Diaraf des Esclaves a été tué par les courtisans de Laobé Penda. En vérité, le Prince voulait combattre les spahis quand il s'est rendu à Coki. Mais l'Emissaire du Gouverneur lui a dit que son intention n'était pas de se battre avec le peuple du Djoloff. (p. 73)

(The *Diaraf* of the Slaves has been killed by Laobé Penda's courtiers. The truth is that the Prince wanted to fight the spahis when he arrived in Coki. But an emissary from the governor explained that the latter's intention was not to wage war against the Woloff.)

Secondly, perhaps the character that stands out most clearly through language is Seb. She is not only a Racinian figure (a kind of Senegalese Bérénice, as I have described her) by her lustful passion for the king but by the depth of her frustration at what she sees as her unrequited love. These twin emotions find expression in accents that are distinctly Racinian in their elegant simplicity, their brutal formulation of irreconcilable dilemmas and in their liberal use of words like 'hélas', 'solitude', 'destin cruel', 'providence' and so on. It would be tedious to give all the examples of this style. However, a few will suffice. In her *tête-à-tête* with her husband, Seb exclaims:

La présence d'un fils m'aurait tenu compagnie. Hélas la Providence ne l'a pas voulu. Que vais-je devenir? (p. 68)

(The presence of a son would have kept me company. Alas, Providence didn't wish it thus. What is going to become of me?)

She describes the impact of her husband's preoccupation with the affairs of state and her position caught between her mother- and sister-in-law in these terms:

O Albouri! Quelle solitude pendant ces années... Quelle solitude pendant tes nombreuses absences. J'étais entre ta sœur qui me donne des ordres et la Reine Mère qui défend à tes enfants de me parler. (p. 68)

(Oh Albouri, how lonely I've been all these years ... How lonely during your numerous absences, stuck between your sister who gives me orders and the Queen Mother who forbids your children to speak to me.)

She expresses her helplessness in the face of an implacable destiny that is working to destroy her happiness in the simple question: 'Qu'avons-nous fait au Destin? Qu'avons-nous fait' (p. 64).

Ndao's ability to pitch the language of his characters at the right level, to conceive them as more than mere stereotypes and to make their conflicting passions the basis of dramatic action is what justifies the position of *L Exil d'Albouri* as one of the most successful of French-African historical plays.

CHAPTER 7

Jean Pliya: 'Kondo le requin'

Like Césaire and Dadié, the Beninois writer Jean Pliya has had a
varied career as teacher, civil servant and politician. Born in July
1931 in the north-west region of Dahomey (now Benin), he received
his early education in his country before proceeding first to the
University of Dakar and then to that of Toulouse in France, where he
graduated in 1957 with a degree and professional teaching qualifications in history and geography. On his return home in 1959, he
taught in various secondary schools – the Lycée Béhanzin in Porto-
Novo, the Lycée Technique in Cotonou – before joining the staff of
the University in Lome, Togo and thereafter that of his home country
where he subsequently rose to become rector. In between his teaching
positions Jean Pliya held, successively, the posts of Permanent
Secretary in the Ministry of Education and Culture and Minister of
Information and Tourism (Edebiri 1975; Ricard 1973; Zell *et al.*
1983: 468–70).

But like Césaire and Dadié, it is as a writer that he is best known
abroad and is most likely to be remembered. He has not only written
an important history book (Pliya 1975) on his country that is used
widely in educational institutions there, but also short stories (Pliya
1971; 1977) and above all two very successful plays, *Kondo le requin*
and *La Secrétaire particulière*. The first won the Grand Prix Littéraire
d'Afrique Noire in 1967 and has enjoyed many production successes,
playing to packed audiences in Benin, naturally, but also in the Ivory
Coast, Togo and Nigeria. It has since been translated into Fon, the
language of its central character and author, and one of Benin's most
important.

Writing about what he calls its 'ideological importance' (Ricard
1973: 5), Alain Ricard states: 'it will not be an exaggeration to say
that modern Dahomean theatre was born with *Kondo le requin*'
(1974a; see also Huannou 1984: 201–4; Koudjo 1983).

As is perhaps appropriate for the founding play of Dahomey's national theatre, *Kondo le requin* is centred on the man who has come to symbolise that country's Independence; the last of its sacred kings, the one who used arms and diplomacy to preserve its integrity but who, after four years of bitter fighting, was finally defeated in 1893 by the French: Gbéhanzin. This play differs from the history plays studied so far in two important aspects: first in its purely celebratory approach to the past, and secondly in its attitude to the facts of history, which is one of strict fidelity. For Dadié, as we have seen, historical drama is not about some slavish subservience to historical fact, but about the understanding of contemporary political issues through an exploration of the past. This led him in his plays to suppress matters irrelevant to their dramatic purpose, to invert the order of events and to telescope lifetimes into a few scenes.

No such metaphorical conception of history is present in *Kondo le requin*. What remarks of contemporary relevance it might contain are incidental to its purpose, which is first and foremost to chronicle as faithfully as possible the last years of a great ruler, and through him, to celebrate a culture and its people. This impulse to historical fidelity, which can be explained not only by Pliya's training as a historian but also by his closeness to his material (his great-grandfather was Gbéhanzin's 'Migan', or prime minister, and his mother-in-law Gbéhanzin's granddaughter) is in evidence in a number of ways. One of these is the exactitude with which he recounts the military strategies adopted by the armies in conflict and the various campaigns they conducted. Thus in the case of the French we learn of their military successes, in their chronological order, first at the battles of Dogba and Kpokissa, then through the capture of the holy city of Kanan, and finally to the fall of the capital, Abomey (Act III, scene 2). Also, almost all the characters in the real-life story, with their titles and functions, are represented in the play, which gives it the quality of a huge fresco, of an entire historical period brought alive. Even minor details such as the names of localities like the one to which Gbéhanzin fled after the fall of Abomey, Atchérigbé; the insults which in a fit of anger he directed at the then French president Carnot (Act I, scene 1: 17); his doubt as to whether the latter was in fact king or president; all are faithfully reproduced. Finally, to create the proper atmosphere of the period and to give the play an authentic national character, the dramatist devotes two entire scenes to the court of Gbéhanzin: one (Act I, scene 1) to the enthronement rituals and social customs that accompany it and another (Act I, scene 3) to the king-in-council, as it were, conducting the affairs of state.

What emerges from all this is that *Kondo le requin* is not so much a play that uses historical elements as a historical chronicle that takes the form of a play.

Divided into three acts, *Kondo le requin* covers a period of five years (1889–94). Act I, which sets the tone of the play, contains the central events of the illness and death of Glélé; of Gbéhanzin's succession to the throne and of the impending threat to his country represented mainly by the Frenchman Bayol, but also, to an extent, by his rival kingsmen Kinvo and Vichégan, who are both plotting with the French to overthrow him. The dominant mood of this act, and the one which pervades the entire play, is of confusion and crisis. This is conveyed by Etchiomi who, in a fit of exasperation at the bad news pouring in from all directions, wonders whether her husband will be able to do anything more than mourn his dead father:

Will the panther's son have only enough time to carry out the ceremonies to lay his father's soul to rest? (p. 36)

Her anxieties and intuition turn out to be tragically prophetic in so far as Glélé's death not only marks the end of a great man but also the beginning of the end of the Kingdom of Dahomey. And this latter fact gives a cruelly ironic twist to the otherwise consecrated forms of lament used by the mourning Gbéhanzin: 'We are in darkness, brothers! We are lost, brothers. Father has left us to join the ancestors' (p. 19) and even more so by the public crier: 'Our sun has gone into decline and the kingdom of Dahomey is sinking into darkness' (p. 20).

But apart from the last episode in the act in which Gbéhanzin mobilises his troops and decides to confront the French in battle for the first time, Act I is basically lacking in action. Nothing in it seriously thwarts the hero's plans. It contains two moments of tension: the heated exchange between the King and Bayol and the announcement of Glélé's death. But these are quickly dissipated with the shift to the coronation in scene 2. What action there is in the play does not really come until the third act. It is in this that all-out war with France is declared and fought. The third scene of Act III is particularly dramatic and would be effective in production.

Although the military encounters the play describes are not shown on stage, the playwright uses a number of techniques to make their impact on the spectators no less real. First, there is the vivid account of epic battles by one of Gbéhanzin's generals:

Exhausted by thirst and hunger, our men are panicking; however, they maintain relentless attacks against the French, whose fire-spitting guns roar in unison like thunder. Shells are exploding into fireballs everywhere and clods of blood-stained mud are splattering on the living. (p. 82)

This is immediately followed by the eruption on stage of a messenger whose hysterical report of the fall of various strongholds brings the war much closer to the palace.

THE MESSENGER: Father and King, the French have crossed the Hlan and are approaching Zogbodemé. Chackabloukou himself is advancing with his unit to protect you.

GBÉHANZIN: The Kingdom of Dahomey is about to fall into enemy hands and you're concerned about me?... And where is Kokodo Kakada's division?

THE MESSENGER: Crushed! Its commmander killed and two assault units routed.

GBÉHANZIN: And how about the right wing of the Amazons?

THE MESSENGER: Completely decimated. (p. 83)

The messenger's entrance is given more theatrical impact by his physical appearance which, the stage direction indicates, should depict a man panting and in a state of panic (p. 83). He has hardly ended his report when Captain Chackabloukou, whom he had just announced as rushing from the battlefield to come protect the king, emerges 'covered in blood and dust' to announce more defeats. Before Gbéhanzin has had time to hear him, gunshots ring out, signifying the fall of the capital and the imminent capture of his palace. It is at this point that Gbéhanzin decides to flee in the midst of more gunshot, fire and the hysterical wailing of a terrified population. The emergence of a French soldier on to the stage once occupied by Gbéhanzin is a visual sign of the latter's total defeat and of the subjugation of his country.

In spite of the episodic nature of *Kondo le requin* and the frequent change of scenes between palace and battlefield, the play's events are firmly enclosed within an Aristotelian-type linear structure with a definite beginning and end. And it is between these two poles that the action unfolds, describing a progression that has the inevitability of tragedy. The play describes a trajectory from prosperity to misery, with its opening coinciding with the beginning of a reign and its close coinciding with the end of a rule. Coronation and preparation for war in Act I, outbreak of hostilities in Act II, defeat and surrender in Act III, such then are the main phases of the play.

But it is not so much in the organisation of these events for the purposes of creating suspense and excitement that Pliya is interested. It is rather in the opportunity it affords him to reassess the image of the main characters involved in the drama. He challenges the prevalent image of a bloodthirsty, fiercely despotic and belligerent ruler (Campion-Vincent 1967: 25–58; Ross 1978: 114–19) first dramatised in 1936 by the Dahomean students at the Ecole William Ponty in *L'Entrevue de Béhanzin et Bayol*. This sketch, it will be remembered from the review quoted in chapter 2 above, also contained a discussion between a Frenchman who, we are told,

defends his rights and wants to establish respect for contracts and a ruler who feels his authority threatened and still continues to fight. (Cornevin 1971: 56)

The idea of a Hegelian conflict of equal rights between an honourable Frenchman defending his rights and an African ruler also defending his power, implied in the William Ponty production and echoed in the review, is precisely what is rejected in *Kondo le requin*. This rejection is conveyed in the hero's thunderous question to Bayol:

In whose name and in the name of what dare a stranger talk of rights over Dahomey to the descendants of Houégbadja? (pp. 17–18)

If anything, it is Bayol who is made to look dishonorable in this play for it is he who, in his country's name, is trying to convert mere trading concessions with Dahomey into territorial rights. 'Under cover of trade, you harbour evil intentions for our country' (p. 18), Gbéhanzin accuses him. It is also he who is made to look like an intruder by Gbéhanzin, who dismisses his case for French rights over Porto-Novo with the reminder that the Abomey-Porto-Novo conflict is a family affair which does not concern France:

White stranger, as far as our brothers in Hogbonou, which you call Porto-Novo, are concerned, be reassured! Sooner or later, we're going to settle our differences, for the umbilical cords of our ancestors are buried in the same corner of Adja-Tado. (p. 16)

The use of the word 'stranger' here and previously, the recourse to the original African names for towns like Porto-Novo and the reference to Huégbadja, with all the responses of awe and respect which the name of this founder of the Dahomean kingdom will produce in a Dahomean spectator, are meant to underscore Bayol's position as that of nothing but an impertinent intruder in search of trouble.

Indeed, it is with Bayol cast in the role of villain that the play opens. Unlike his interpreter Béraud, who tries to understand various Dahomean customary practices without necessarily approving them – 'I'm trying to understand them' (p. 13) – Bayol adopts an aggressive and dismissive attitude which, from the outset, removes the basis for any future dialogue between himself and his hosts, and undermines whatever positive role he could have played in their society. He interprets Béraud's matter-of-fact approach to the signs of violence around him as evidence of esteem for his hosts: 'You seem to hold them in high esteem' (p. 13). In the royal enclosure, he rails at having been kept waiting for forty days to see the monarch. When he discovers, again from Béraud, that this was due to the latter's illness, he asks in a manner indicative of his contempt:

Won't they accuse me of having caused the illness of their old decrepit king through the use of sorcery? They who are usually so noisy, see how quiet they are and the way they're eyeing me. They need to be civilised. (p. 14)

What the last two sentences reveal, in their glaring logical incoherence, is that Bayol's endless complaints against Dahomean society are not born of genuine moral revulsion. They are a pretext for war. His visit is clearly meant to extract a surrender and not to negotiate, and he himself admits that much when he asks about his hosts:

Who do they think they are? I'll not treat as equals bloodthirsty barbarians. I'll outline in strong terms the goal of my visit and I'll not stay a day longer in Abomey. (p. 14)

And this is exactly what he does. Misconstruing, as he was bound to do, the traditional royal Dahomean practice of not shaking hands with strangers as a personal insult, he immediately lashes out at Gbéhanzin. He accuses him of pillage and orders him, under the threat of war, to stop interfering in the affairs of Porto-Novo (p. 16). In the face of the warmongering Bayol, Gbéhanzin is portrayed as committed to the defence of his country's independence and its right to settle matters of internal concern without outside interference:

However difficult the struggle against the French, were I to perform extraordinary feats, I'll save this country. (p. 48)

The central image of Gbéhanzin's fierce determination and nobility
that emerges in the course of the play is reinforced by his language.
His proverbs and imagery, vocabulary and syntax, his constant use of
either the first or third persons singular to refer to himself match his
status as an absolute monarch. Thus he proclaims after his enthronement:

I'll accomplish great things, I'll at last conquer Abeokuta. Like those fierce
sharks, I'll sow terror on the Dahomean coasts and God help those sea
animals who dare come close. (p. 24)

Elsewhere, pursuing the animal imagery, he tells a courtier:

Vilon, I can see what you're getting at; but it's obvious that the panther's
son whose father was as feared as a lion can fear no animal on Dahomean
soil. (p. 41)

Gbéhanzin's imperious and threatening language, coupled with the
stylised patterns of address directed at him by his subjects – 'Our
rising sun', 'Master of the dawn', 'Master of the world' – confirm his
position as the dominant figure in Dahomean society. This status is
thrown into sharp visual focus by a number of elements. First, there
is the richness of his ceremonial dress, 'velvet cloth, white gown' and
'a blue pearl necklace, made of pure coral stone' (pp. 22, 23). Then
there is the setting in which he evolves – if he is not sitting on his
throne in his palace, he is surrounded by courtiers, assistants, women.
Finally there is the proxemic 'language' of his subjects who can talk
to him only kneeling, crouching or genuflecting.

However, as Gbéhanzin increasingly faces the prospect of defeat,
and is deserted by all but a few trusted friends, the dominant
metaphor of the fearless panther, lion or shark gives way to that of the
tracked hare. The royal costume gives way to a 'simple dress' and the
traditional upright sitting position on a throne to a half-lying one on
a sofa. Imperiousness has been replaced by submissiveness; heroism
by pathos:

I, who was born to live in a palace big enough for ten royal families, am
today in the wild tracked like a hare on the land of my forefathers. (p. 99)

To better bring out Gbéhanzin's qualities, Pliya contrasts him with
those characters who, in spite of the crisis, are more concerned with
private gain than with the public good. Agada the peasant, for
example, not only prides himself for successfully avoiding all

contributions to the war efforts, but openly states that in the king's place, he would have remained in the comfort of his palace and left others to do the fighting:

Oh! if I were king, I'd remain in the quiet of my palace and send my soldiers to fight. (p. 73)

When Dahomey finally falls, all he is concerned with is rescuing his house and treasures. But Agada's attitude is not a characteristic of the poor and powerless alone. Prince Gbégnon, in a scene that can either be performed simultaneously with that of the peasants or separately, is portrayed as a war profiteer. He finds the sacrifices required of individual Dahomeans far too great, and secretly nurses the hope of a snap French victory which he intends to hasten by defecting to their side. While waiting for this to happen, however, he dreams of taking a new wife. This he finally does. But not surprisingly she turns out to be the newly widowed wife of a warrior killed in battle. Sétondji's sarcastic remarks to him: 'Happy marriage! I pity Dahomey' (p. 76) are meant to underline an incompatibility between private interest and the collective good.

This incompatibility is, of course, not limited to *Kondo le requin*. It is one of the constants of French-African drama and reflects the traditional communalistic ethos of African societies, and their emphasis on collective over individual interests; an emphasis which found expression, in modern times, in, among other institutions, the now contested and discredited one-party, dictatorial, political regimes. Although powerful moral, political and economic arguments also exist in defence of an ethic of individualism, these are never explored by the dramatists. What they often present, instead, is a caricature of the position, with the characters used to embody that position – Gbégnon and Agada here, Général Cotou in *Iles de tempête*, the merchant in *Sikasso*, Malangana and Dingana in *La Mort de Chaka*, Mokutu in *Une Saison du Congo*, Laobé Penda in *L'Exil d'Albouri* and so on – depicted either as irresponsible pleasure-seekers or power-hungry and selfish individuals. The collectivist ideal is rarely presented in its negative possibilities. It is unproblematically posited as a superior moral position.

But Pliya is not concerned uniquely with Gbéhanzin and the threat to his kingdom, but also with the portrayal of the cultural values and beliefs of his society. He uses these last-mentioned to give a composite picture of traditional life in ancient Dahomey but also to develop the theatrical resources and drama in the play. Thus the recreation in Act I, scene 2 of the highly ceremonial coronation ritual lends a dimension of spectacle to the play. A theatrical performance in itself, the ceremonial is directed by a master of ceremonies, the Agassounon, with Gbéhanzin cast in the principal role. Striking elements of this spectacle include the procession, in their hierarchical order, of traditional notables like the *migan* or prime minister, the *mehou* or preceptor to the royal family and minister of foreign affairs, the *adjaho* or minister of justice, to pledge allegiance to their colourfully attired new king. Then there is the display of symbolic traditional items representing power and authority, like the 'sacred amulette' (p. 23), the 'blue pearl necklace' (p. 23), the 'royal staff' (p. 23). The formal praise names and ritualised gestures by which the king is addressed, the music and dancing which close the coronation scene, the farewell ceremony before the king's surrender and the various *Ifa* divination sessions, all contribute to this sense of spectacle.

Like the other traditional practices evoked in the play, the *Ifa* divination sessions are not mere exotica for the benefit of foreign audiences. They are integral to the author's dramatic conception of character and situation. Thus the advice given in Act I, scene 3 by Guédégbé, the *Ifa* priest, that the oracle is against war with the French is dramatically important since it divides the court between those in favour or those against war with France, and leaves the kingdom weakened through lack of unity. Unlike men like Akplogan, the minister of religious affairs, Agada or Gbégnon, who represent a blind and uncritical submission to tradition and whose fatalism virtually leads them to abdicate to French might, Gbéhanzin embodies will-power and the spirit of resistance. In the crucial moments of his life – when, for example, he actually declares war on the French or decides to set the palace on fire – he relies on his will rather than oracles. He tells his senior commander:

Leave others to lean on oracles as on crutches. Will the army which embodies my will-to-resist collapse? (p. 82)

Other instances of his flouting of traditional practices include his insistence on talking to strangers directly and not through inter-mediaries (p. 16), on even touching them if necessary, on forgoing pre-war propitiatory rites and on eating and drinking in public (p. 94). While he does not always reject tradition, he insists that it should serve man, rather than reduce him to inaction and slavery:

Isn't it nobler to remain faithful to the land and people who elaborate the customs than to submit blindly to passing and fanciful customs? (p. 95)

Towards the end of his career, Gbéhanzin loses all faith in divination. He tells Guédégbé, who still insists on consulting the Ifa oracle: 'Don't waste time any longer consulting ancestors and voodoo oracles, for what is happening is beyond them' (p. 102).

Of course, he is defeated by the French, as was prophesied. But his stature is not more diminished for his having disobeyed the oracle. If anything it is enhanced by his determination not to be cowed into submission by the superiority of the adversary's army or the prophecy. The final picture that he leaves in the minds of the audience is one of tragic nobility and courage.

CHAPTER 8

Tchicaya U'Tamsi: 'Le Zulu'

With Tchicaya U'Tamsi, we turn to a Francophone dramatist who, like Aimé Césaire, is above all a poet. Born in 1931 in the then French Congo, now the Republic of Congo, U'Tamsi was taken to France in 1946 by his father, who was then serving his country as its first member of Parliament in the French National Assembly. After his secondary school education at the Lycée Janson-de-Sailly in Paris, he embarked on a literary career with the publication in 1955 of his first volume of poetry, *Le Mauvais sang*. He subsequently published another six volumes of poetry. In 1977, U'Tamsi turned to drama, publishing his first play *Le Zulu*, which had received its première the year before at the Avignon Theatre Festival. In addition to a short dramatic monologue, *Vivène le fondateur*, which is published in the same volume as *Le Zulu*, U'Tamsi also wrote a hugely satirical play on political dictatorship in Africa, *Le Maréchal Nnikou Nnikon Prince qu'on sort*, and a dance drama, *Le Bal de N'Dinga* (still unpublished), which ran very successfully in French theatres for about two years from 1988. U'Tamsi, who died in April 1988, was also the author of five novels (see Dalembert 1990: 110–11; Moore 1980: 146; Zell *et al.* 1983: 503–5).

As its title suggests, *Le Zulu* is based on the dramatic career of the Zulu empire-builder and military strategist, Chaka. Born around 1787, he propelled himself to power in 1816 through force of arms, and from a life of vagrancy spent in the armies of various overlords. For eleven years, Chaka waged implacable wars against neighbouring peoples, conquering and absorbing them into a new and powerful Zulu nation which, at its height, extended over an area of 100,000 square miles (Ritter 1978). He built the modest army which he had inherited into one of pre-colonial Africa's most disciplined fighting forces; one which, decades after his death, it took to conquer, in Ritter's words, a British army of 20,000 Imperial footsoldiers and cavalry armed with breech-loading rifles, cannon and rocket batteries, in addition to colonial mounted troops and thousands of native levies, many armed with rifles. (Ritter 1978: 80)

In 1827, grief-stricken by his mother's death, Chaka lapsed into one of his reign's most abominable phases of homicidal excesses. The atrocities he committed during this period, coupled with a certain war-weariness on the part of his people, led to his assassination in 1828.

Le Zulu is not the only Francophone or even African play to have been devoted to Chaka (see Agyeman 1983; Blair 1974: 113–41; Burness 1976; Obumselu 1976; Ridehalgh 1991; Scholz 1970; Spronk 1984; 1992; Swanepoel 1990; Tschikumambila 1974). By 1956, as we saw earlier, Senghor based a dramatic poem, *Chaka*, on him. This was followed in 1961 by Badian's *La Mort de Chaka* and then in 1970 by Condetto Nénékhaly-Camara's *Amazoulou*. In 1971, Djibril Niane also published a Chaka play. This was followed a year later by Abdou Anta Ka's *Les Amazoulous*. More recently two dramatic works, *On joue la comédie* by the Togolese playwright Senouvo Zinsou and *Chaka ou le roi visionnaire* by the Senegalese Marouba Fall, have been written with Chaka as subject. And this short list does not include creative works by Anglophone writers like, *Ogun Abibiman* by Soyinka or Mulikita's *Shaka Zulu* (see Sévry 1992).

Le Zulu, then, is part of a significant African literary tradition. But it also stands apart in a singular way from the works that constitute that tradition, at least in the Francophone world. To most Francophone writers, Chaka is just a convenient symbol for personal and political myth-making. Senghor, for example, sees him as a nationalist who is driven by only the purest of political motives: that of liberating his people – famished and enslaved, expropriated of their lands and alienated from their labour – from colonial rule. His Chaka justifies his involvement in politics in these terms:

I saw one morning, emerging from the mist of the dawn, a forest of woolly-haired heads. Arms drooping, bellies hollow, immense eyes and lips calling to an impossible God. Could I stay deaf to such suffering? (Senghor 1956: 123–4)

He suffers from none of the megalomania of the hero of Thomas Mofolo's historical romance. If anything, his recourse to the politics of destruction (which Senghor does not deny but instead defends with rare lyrical brilliance) involves great personal loss and sacrifice in so far as it goes against the fundamental poetic and contemplative impulse of his nature.

Badian for his part depicts a man who is pure heroism in thought and action. He exhibits none of the conflict between private values and the public interest that threatens to engulf Senghor's protagonist with self-pity and reduces him to ineffectual sentimentalism. His play is not a lament on the evil necessity of self-sacrifice but a vibrant hymn to it. To Abdou Anta Ka, Chaka is above all a 'man of the people' whose principal merit is to have liberated his country from the grip of obscurantist beliefs and the tyranny of petty chiefs, while in Zinsou's play (to be discussed in chapter 10) he becomes a theatre activist and anti-apartheid agitator. But even when he is shown to have been very destructive, as is the case in Nénékhaly-Camara's work, it is his advisers Ndélébé and Malonga who are held responsible for that. Malonga, for example, boasts:

We've injected into his poor, deprived brain of a shepherd the poison of ambition and hate. (Nénékhaly-Camara 1970: 73)

On the whole, then, Francophone dramatists have been united in their exaltation of the Zulu ruler. And it is in the context of this general chorus of praise that U'Tamsi's play erupts like a discordant note. His hero is neither Badian's patriot nor Senghor's martyr but rather Mofolo's protagonist: a great man possessed by the desire for power and personal glory and in the end ravaged by it. But unlike Mofolo or the Francophone writers who were attracted to him for moral and political reasons, U'Tamsi's interest is primarily artistic. He seems to have been drawn to the Chaka theme by the possibility it offered him for a *Macbeth*-type tragic play, one based on the subtle exploration of character, on the study of a destructive passion. And, indeed, it is in terms of the birth, development and decline of such a passion, ambition, that the play is conceived (see Chemain 1977: 33–41; Chemain and Chemain-Degrange 1979 on *Le Zulu* and Congolese theatre).

Le Zulu is divided into three acts preceded by a prologue. When the play starts, it is very early in the morning and the setting is an eerie, deserted place, possibly a field. Chaka, who has spent the entire night there is standing motionless on one leg, completely absorbed in his thoughts. Although he says nothing throughout the prologue and gives the impression of being in contact with some invisible, supernatural entity, the spectator is able to penetrate his mind largely through the exchanges of two wizards, Ndlébé and Malounga. The wizards sniff out his presence on the heath and, in response to his calls ('I feel we are getting closer to the man who's calling us with all his heart' (p. 1)), are moving towards him. From them, we learn that Chaka is infected by the virus of ambition and that he dreams of exercising complete domination over the earth:

He is cursed ... He has the virus. He wants to entrap in the web of his dreams all the fierce tribes including those living on the confines of the earth. (p. 18)

The function of the prologue is to capture the imagination and awaken the curiosity of the spectator. And with its two wizards and mysterious voice divining Chaka's intentions even before meeting him, talking puzzlingly of being the genie of the earth and skies and boasting that they will have their fair share of human cries, tears and blood, it could be very effective in performance.

But in spite of the atmosphere of magic and the supernatural in which the play's opening scene is bathed, it is clear that the dramatist is not inviting us to see his hero as the helpless victim of supernatural forces. Ndlébé and Malounga might have magical powers, but they do not cause Chaka's downfall. Their role, as they explain themselves, is supportive, rather like Bacoulou's in Dadié's *Voix dans le vent*. It consists mainly in helping the hero realise his dreams: 'We shall lead him to the height of his dream' (p. 17). They feel attracted to him and succeed in influencing him only because his innate ambition, of which he is only dimly aware and which the wizards coax to the surface, predisposes him to such influence. Indeed, as they say, Chaka is their brother in evil: 'He is in truth our man' (p. 17).

The playwright underlines this point by a number of stage devices. Ndlébé and Malounga listen to Chaka more than they talk with him. Thus in the prologue Ndlébé, hearing human sounds on the heath, 'cocks his ear' (p. 19). And what does he hear? Chaka swearing an oath to some invisible being: 'On my blood, I swear that I'll be master of this world' (p. 19). In Act I, scene 1, we are again shown Ndlébé 'listening attentively' (p. 23) to Chaka as the latter attempts to give meaning to a dream he has had.

In psychological terms Ndlébé and Malounga can be seen as the objectivisation of the hero's unconscious desires. Their transformation at the end of the prologue into human beings, that is into solid shapes, marks in symbolic and visual terms their full emergence into the hero's consciousness. And the fact that Chaka *immediately* recognises them when they move from their initial state of immateriality to assume human form (p. 20), shows that he is dealing not with strangers but with embodiments of his subconscious desires. The playwright further highlights this transformation in theatrical terms by making Ndlébé and his friend move from the penumbra (Chaka's unconscious) to light (p. 19).

But Chaka does not understand the tricks that his mind has played upon him at this point. He sees in his various experiences – the dream during which a warrior, who turns out to be Chaka himself, emerges triumphant over the powerful chieftain Zwidé; the discovery of blood-stained weapons by his doorstep, the weapons he used against Zwidé in the dream; the rainbow which is supposed to signify enthronement – invitations from above, 'supernatural soliciting' as Macbeth would have put it, to conquer absolute power. This belief is greatly reinforced when in Act I, scene 3, Chaka is repeatedly addressed by a mysterious Voice as 'A man unlike all others. One from above, descended on a united world' (p. 27). The shock he experiences at being so addressed is reminiscent of Macbeth's at being hailed as Thane of Cawdor and the future king by the three witches. And, like Macbeth too, rather than see this as the devil's ploy, his 'honest trifles' to better betray and destroy, Chaka interprets it as evidence of his pre-ordained destiny: 'Umzikulu is great for making me his servant' (p. 35).

Chaka's initial doubts as to the truthfulness of the pronouncements of the Voice are dispelled when one of the latter's enigmatic predictions, 'The gateway to Nobama is open. The Master can move across' (p. 29) is fulfilled. The meaning becomes clear when shortly after the prediction has been made, news is brought to Chaka of his father's death and of his people's desire to see him become their king.

Up to this point, that is Act I, scene 5, Chaka has been groping towards an articulate awareness of his own desires. In this process he has been helped by Malounga, Ndlébé and the Voice, who miss no opportunity to insist that they are only his servants and that he is in fact the architect of his own designs:

THE VOICE: You're the master. I'm your servant. Command and I'll rush out to go wherever you so desire. (p. 27)

From now on, Chaka is going to set about realising his dreams, and this despite the warnings by the Voice that the price of success will be his life:

CHAKA: What shall be your wages?
THE VOICE: They are inscribed on this shield with the tip of the spear.
CHAKA: Is this blood mine?
THE VOICE: Yes, it's the blood of your ambitions, of your designs. The unity of the heavens is that of the earth. (p. 28)

Chaka's first move a year after settling down as King of Nobamba is to betray his protector and overlord Ding'Iswayo, the conquest of whose throne he sees as a necessary step in the march to success. Inevitably, this incident again brings to mind Macbeth's betrayal of Duncan, his king and host. But unlike the Shakespearian hero, Chaka does not take part directly in the murder. He enters instead into a pact with Ding'Iswayo's enemy Zwidé, whom he encourages to go on the attack on the understanding that he would stay neutral in the ensuing hostilities. To cover up his treachery from his mother Nandi and allay the fears of a suspicious Ding'Iswayo, he dispatches the former to the latter with gifts, and a request on his behalf for the hand of Noliwé, Ding'Iswayo's sister. But the message has hardly been transmitted and the marriage concluded when Ding'Iswayo is attacked by Zwidé and killed. Thinking that Chaka is unaware of what has happened, Nandi and Noliwé hurriedly return to Nobama to inform him and press for revenge. They discover him conferring with an envoy from Zwidé. Convinced, however, that he would never have received the envoy had he been aware of the true picture, they promptly denounce the envoy as one of the culprits and demand immediate action against him:

NANDI: This is one of his men; his master carries the weight of a crime in his heart; his hands are soiled with Ding'Iswayo's blood...
CHAKA: Could Ding'Iswayo be dead?
NANDI: ... Ding'Iswayo is no more! Say something, do something. Chaka, move.

This incident is one of the high points of the play, and sets in motion a series of dramatic actions that lead to the hero's destruction. In the immediate moment it brings him a dilemma: to let the envoy go free and in so doing arouse the suspicions of his mother and wife, or have the envoy severely punished as the women demand and run the risk of seeing the extent of his complicity divulged. Chaka tries to satisfy both parties by ordering the envoy's arrest while at the same time instructing that he be treated gently. But this delicate and tension-laden balancing act collapses when Epervier, one of Ding'-Iswayo's generals and stout defender of Chaka against charges of betrayal, walks in unexpectedly only to surprise the latter and his adviser Ndlébé making preparations for a visit by Zwidé:

NDLÉBÉ: Here I am.
CHAKA: Is everything in place for Zwidé's arrival? Oh, there you are, Epervier!
EPERVIER: What is it that I hear? You, receiving Zwidé? (p. 73)

Embarrassed, Chaka tries to lie about the planned visit by suggesting that it was only a ploy to lure Zwidé into Nobamba to have him punished for killing Ding'Iswayo. But this explanation runs into considerable difficulty when the detained envoy intervenes to ask Chaka innocently: 'But how about your pact with Zwidé?' (p. 73). With this question threatening to bring his machinations and intrigue into the open, Chaka has no choice, if he is to maintain his credibility, but to carry out his threat against Zwidé. And this is exactly what he does. Shortly after the latter's arrival to the sounds of trumpets and drums and in full confidence of visiting a friend, Chaka has him brutally murdered. Zwidé dies cursing him: 'You betray and condemn. I'm laying a curse on you. Your own blood will stifle you' (p. 87).

This second act of betrayal on Chaka's part in just over a year marks a watershed in his life. With it, the blood which has been so much part of the language of the play (both in the various predictions and in Chaka's dreams) is made manifest on stage. But Chaka views such destruction with equanimity. To him, it is necessary if he is to attain the goal of 'sovereign sway and masterdom' promised him by the Zulu god Umzikulu.

What he fails to grasp, however, or deliberately ignores, is the interconnectedness, stressed by his supernatural assistants, between absolute power and destructiveness, both of others and ultimately of oneself. For, as in the case of Zwidé, having killed him to conceal his own role in Ding'Iswayo's death, Chaka now discovers that he has to keep destroying people, especially those with his blood, to prevent Zwidé's curse from coming true – rather like Macbeth fighting to prevent the kingship from falling to Banquo's descendants as prophesied by the witches. But instead of constituting the first step on the path to greatness, murder, he finds out, leads him on to the slippery slope of self-destruction.

The first relation to fall victim to Chaka's brutality is Noliwé. Mentally unhinged by Ding'Iswayo's, her brother's, death, but intuitively convinced that her husband Chaka is behind it all, Noliwé remains unimpressed by the latter's action against Zwidé, knowing it to be fraudulent, and taunts him into further action: What will you do to avenge my brother's death?' (p. 94); 'My brother's assassin isn't dead' (p. 93). In themselves these remarks might not have led to her death had she not revealed also that she was expecting Chaka's baby. Mindful of Zwidé's dying words, which ring out hauntingly in his ears at the very moment as Noliwé is making her revelation, Chaka gets into a state of mortal fear

What have you said … In your womb … No, never, never will my blood leave your body. (p. 94)

and stabs her.

The murder of Noliwé, first invented by Mofolo (the historical Chaka was actually outlived by his wife, Pampata), to signify his total heartlessness, and used since by most French-speaking African dramatists as the symbol of Chaka's willingness to sacrifice his love for the salvation of his people, is restored to its original Mofoloesque significance. But by making Noliwé both wife and mother-to-be, U'Tamsi not only intensifies the grimness of the crime against her, but he invests it with added significance. Chaka has murdered love but also emptied his future – symbolised by the unborn baby – of all hope.

From now on, the only driving force in Chaka's life is fear. Fear of his mother, half-brothers and friends; fear of the ordinary sounds of birds which his guilty imagination converts into ominous signs, and, above all, fear of sleep. Even when he manages a few moments of sleep, he feels the need to be securely guarded. But guards do not prevent nightmares and he gets many of them. One such is of Noliwé holding a broom, no doubt in a symbolic act of cleansing, and threatening revenge by her son:

My son will be like the mashilashila tree that can't be touched without immediate death ensuing. His father won't see him because he is coming as an avenger. (p. 108)

Frightened by this dream, Chaka intensifies his resolve to get rid of all his blood relations. And acting on a tip-off from Ndlébé that his mother and friend Epervier are plotting to kill him, he moves first and murders them.

Although this latest instalment in violence looks like the fault of Ndlébé, who leaks out the victims' plans, it has in reality been very much part of Chaka's designs. For even before the idea of a plot had taken root in Nandi's heart, Chaka was determined to destroy her. He says this openly after Noliwé's death: 'Next is my mother, for my mother is also my blood' (p. 101). So what looks like a grim act of self-defence is in fact the result of a long-thought-out plan.

But this crime, like the previous ones, solves nothing. For he has hardly removed his mother's body from the stage than he is now obsessed with his half-brothers in the south, Dingana and Malangana, and by another aspect of the wizards' prophecy he had ignored until now – the need to fear anything white coming from the south – 'Pray that nothing white appears in the south ... ' (p. 28). It is in an attempt to forestall this double threat by waging a military campaign on his southern flank against his brothers that he meets his end. With their troops vastly strengthened by hired white soldiers (and this is the meaning of the prophecy), Dingana and Malangana are able to rout Chaka's army. Deserted by his loyal generals and totally demoralised, Chaka commits suicide before he is captured.

In Badian's *La Mort de Chaka*, the hero's death (he is murdered by his half-brothers) is portrayed as an act of betrayal. In *Le Zulu*, on the other hand, it is depicted as the reassertion of an order that has been upset. But in spite of his evil, U'Tamsi's protagonist does not fail to evoke in the spectator emotions of pity. And this is because, on occasion, Chaka himself is aware of the destructiveness of his passion, wishes to free himself from its stranglehold, and yet is unable to do so:

If only I could despise my ambition ... It's as if I wasn't free ... This dream enslaves me. (p. 30)

To some critics, he is all the more pitiable because it is in pursuit of greatness for his people that he gets into difficulty (Moore 1980: 168–89). For does he not declare,

I gave them reasons to dream and they haven't dared dream! To whom can I bequest a dream that has turned to a nightmare ... I told the tribes: 'Be Zulu' but they were tired out by impatience; just a little bit more effort and they would have become Zulu ... I weep, I the Zulu, because I dreamt too much. (p. 130)

Although attractive, this point is not convincing. Chaka's reference at the end of the play to an ideal of greatness for his people sounds very much like a rationalisation for his dastardly atrocities. At no point throughout the play do we see him actually fighting for such a goal. Indeed, he had no time to do that even if he had wished it, for the very first step he took (the betrayal of Ding'Iswayo) was what led him inexorably to his death. *Le Zulu* is indeed a story of a dream that became a nightmare. But it is a dream of self-aggrandisement rather than of national greatness.

CHAPTER 9

Guillaume Oyono-Mbia: ' Trois prétendants ... un mari'

Although he has published only four plays to date, the bilingual Cameroonian writer Guillaume Oyono-Mbia nevertheless remains one of Francophone Africa's foremost comic dramatists. His plays have not only been widely produced to great acclaim in his native Cameroon, but also in England and France, where two of them, *Until Further Notice* and *Notre fille ne se mariera pas*, have won radio drama competitions.

Unlike many Francophone writers whose plays have a large dose of didacticism, Oyono-Mbia's are constructed principally as dramatic entertainment (see Banham and Wake 1976: 68–73; Bédé 1975; Bjornson 1991: 238–61; Eyoh 1981; Jeyifo 1985: 64–77; Okeh 1982; Ongom 1985). In other words, their serious and pressing social themes are as much a source of concern to Oyono-Mbia as they are a pretext for the development of comic situations. He writes:

my aim is not to moralise but to entertain.... It is only through entertainment that the writer can really hope to create an awareness in the public's mind of certain aspects of our cultural and social life. (Preface to *Trois prétendants* [Most references are from the English edition. Those from the French edition are indicated by FE.], pp. 6–7).

Nowhere is this double objective – indeed an ancient and commonplace objective of all comic drama – better fulfilled than in his earliest play, *Trois prétendants ... un mari*. First published in 1964, although written five years earlier during the author's school years, the play dramatises the troubles and near disaster that befall a village community determined to marry off its city-educated daughter to the highest-paying suitor. Set in the village of Mvoutessi, the author gives in his opening set a visual image of a locality absorbed in its time-honoured activities, traditions and pastimes:

Atangana is making a basket ... Abessolo is busy sculpting an ebony figurine ... Ondua and Oyono are playing a game of 'songho'. (p. 11)

But the village's isolation and immunity from foreign influences is illusory, for just outside its protective hedge lies (the English edition of the play indicates) a road. Marginal as this road might be, it is of symbolic importance. Not only does it shatter the stillness of the community with the noise from the odd vehicle, or create intense drama with its not infrequent cargo of unwanted visitors (venal tax-collectors and policemen), it brings in 'dangerous' city ideas.

One such idea, recently imbibed in the neighbouring school by one of its children Juliette, is the right of women to choose their husbands regardless of their parents' wishes. 'I am a free person' (p. 31), she asserts defiantly and questions her father:

What? Am I for sale? Are you trying to give me to the highest bidder? Why can't you ask me my opinion about my own marriage? (p. 20)

It is Juliette's unflagging determination to defend her right to choose, her refusal to be reduced to 'a goat' that can be disposed of at will by its owners that plunges her into headlong conflict with her parents and creates the drama in the village.

Such a conflict, in essence one between 'traditional' and 'modern' values and a constant of African literature, can be treated in either the melodramatic or the tragic mode. In the hands of the indifferent writer, it might even be the occasion for ponderous didacticism. Not so with Oyono-Mbia. He treats the conflict lightheartedly and with great humour. A talented craftsman of the drama, with the satirist's eye for the incongruous and the extravagant in human behaviour, the reality behind the appearances, he exploits to the full – even at the risk of some 'longueurs' – the sheer comic and dramatic potential of the subject. Many sequences in the play, like the viper and witch-doctor scenes (Acts III and IV) or one in which Engulu, Mbia's chauffeur-valet, trips over his baggy trousers while transporting drinks, or, indeed, the many dancing interludes have an essentially dramatic or circus entertainment value.

In this sense, *Trois prétendants* can be compared to Soyinka's *The Lion and the Jewel*. Both are satirical comedies with music, song and dance. Both deal with the theme of love from the conflicting perspectives of 'tradition' and 'progress'. Where they differ significantly, of course, is in the portrayal of the parties to the conflict. In the Soyinka play, the 'progressive' outlook as embodied by the village schoolmaster Lakunlé loses the contest. He is portrayed as a pathetic figure: confused, superficial and more in love with a warped idea of progress than truly progressive himself. In *Trois prétendants*, on the other hand, it is the 'traditionalist' outlook that is roundly defeated.

Its principal representatives, a gallery of conventional comic types, cut an unedifying spectacle. They show none of the elemental vitality of a Baroka, have nothing of his wisdom or at least craftiness. They are systematically presented instead as figures of fun and ridicule – avaricious, gerontocratic and stiflingly communalistic with no redeeming flashes of tradition intelligently understood *à la* Baroka. But Oyono's satirical portrayal is gentle and not as cutting as Soyinka's sometimes is of Lankulé, which makes them appear more like harmless fools and entertainers than dangerous men.

Take Abessolo, for example, Juliette's grandfather, clan patriarch and keeper of its traditions. We observe him as an old man – toothless perhaps – stuck in the past and constantly uttering imprecations against the present. But what does he really object to? Some degenerate new practices? A disfigurement of tradition? Nothing of the sort. His anger is directed instead at the abandonment of those aspects with which tradition can most easily dispense – rather like Lankulé's advocacy is of things that are of no value to the modernity of which he so much wants to be a part: breakable plates! Abessolo laments:

You let your wives wear clothes! You let them eat all sorts of taboo animals! You even ask them their opinion on this and that!... (He pauses to catch his breath.) Well, what else could you expect? (Firmly) I tell you, you must beat your wives! Yes, beat them! (p. 15)

But there is no danger that Abessolo will ever be able to impose his views on his community for he also emerges as ineffectual. All his attempts to get his way end in failure. Juliette openly defies him. Worse still (in a reversal of the *Lion and Jewel* denouement), she tricks him and the other elders, with all their proclaimed wisdom, into accepting her choice of husband.

Also, Ndi, the peasant suitor, whom he tries to bully into both losing Juliette and his 'bride price' gets him shivering with fear the moment he threatens to call the local police, while Mbarga, the village chief, overrules his objections to Mbia's marriage to Juliette.

This last episode also brings out the comic dimension in Abessolo's character, for while he is quick to evoke traditional kinship laws, to proclaim his credentials as keeper of the tradition, he is equally quick to abandon this tradition when the material advantages in so doing are suggestively conjured to him. 'We'll forget about your being related to our daughter' (p. 39) are his final words to Mbia on the matter of the latter's marriage to Juliette.

Another of Oyono-Mbia's memorable figures of fun is the already mentioned village chief Mbarga. Finding himself upstaged by Abessolo during the 'great Civil Servant's' visit and in danger of losing out on his gifts, he gets his own back when his community, in despair, appeals to him to appease an Mbia enraged by Abessolo's objections. Here we discover a man adept at flattery and a keen observer of the nature of the likes of Mbia. First he advertises what he sees as the latter's considerable powers: the power to free the people of Mvoutessi from police harassment, to obtain satisfactory prices for their produce and to get them gun permits. Although these powers are more a reflection of what the villagers would like to see him achieve than what he actually does or can do, Mbia is sufficiently flattered by them to reward Mbarga with gifts. It is a show of fatuousness which convinces Mbarga that all he needs do to get more rewards is to be more fulsome in his praises. And this he does effectively – predicting a future for the 'great Civil Servant' that involves his promotion to mayor, member of parliament and finally minister. This gets Mbia so excited that he showers drinks and gifts on Mbarga. The episode ends in great farce when Engulu, unable to keep pace with his master's growing demands for more drinks for Mbarga, trips over his trousers – in a scene reminiscent of the gags of a circus clown – and falls down.

It is obvious from this episode that Oyono-Mbia does not only direct his satirical barbs at the villagers, but also at the men of the city, here represented by Mbia. In addition to his vanity, he is also portrayed as pompous and empty. His physical appearance – bemedalled and bespectacled, with a servant holding his briefcase to boot – depicts a figure of fun, imbued with a sense of self-importance vastly incommensurate with his achievements. For what does Mbia really have to his name? Nothing but the fact that he 'occupies a large office' (p. 20) and has been working for twenty-five years, knows the minister (p. 20) and has some police officers in his pay. In him, Oyono-Mbia ridicules a certain African bureaucrat more interested in political influence-peddling than in the actual charges of his office, in exploiting poor and ignorant villages than in enhancing their well-being.

The villagers of Mvoutessi – in a subtle exploration of the rural/urban imbalance in Africa – are shown to be at the mercy of the 'city-boys' of Sangmélima for whom they are a source of cheap agricultural produce (Mbarga's oblique complaint) village belles (on offer to the richest of them preferably) and illegal levies for corrupt policemen and other such officials.

But of all the characters in *Trois prétendants*, Sanga Titi the witch-doctor is perhaps the most ridiculed. A figure respected and even feared in traditional societies for his presumed supernatural powers, the witch-doctor in this play is on the contrary exposed, in the tradition of Molière's doctors, as a charlatan, rather like Dr Purgon is exposed by Toinette in *Le Malade Imaginaire*. He is shown as incapable of sniffing out the person who made away with Atangana's money and as relying instead for a solution on bits of information unwittingly provided for him by the villagers. In a divination ritual performance that is presented as nothing short of traditional theatre with costumed actors on a performance space, props, an audience and so on (see the elaborate stage descriptions for it, p. 51, FE, p. 83), the lead actor, Sanga Titi, plays on his audience/clients' desperation to extract the maximum number of gifts without offering anything in return. His Purgon-like techniques are a mixture of threats, half or obvious truths, latinesque mumbo-jumbo, inspired guesses or plain lies. This is how he explains the frequent deaths in Mvoutessi:

Listen to me, all of you! Do you want to know why people die in this village? ... Great people like your ancestors were couldn't die without a cause!... Why aren't your ancestors still alive? Because they're dead, and the proof is that they're no longer alive! (p. 54)

But Sanga Titi's success does not last long. Emboldened by the villagers' gullibility and increasing confidence in him, he commits the fatal error of being more precise, giving dates and figures.

SANGA TITI (*consulting his mirrors*): Didn't you go to Sangmélima two days
    ago to sell your cocoa?
ANTANGANA: It's almost a week now!!
SANGA TITI: Two days ago! How dare you contradict me? (p. 56)

After this series of factual errors which make even the credulous villagers grow suspicious, he is finally challenged by the young schoolboy Kouma on a point of geography, exposed and chased out to the jeers of the public.

The unmasking of Sanga Titi can be said to signal in his clients the disappointing realisation that his 'ritual' was nothing but entertainment; that they were an audience in a play and not clients in a ceremony. The dramatist, in other words, lets ritual in this scene undermine its claim to instrumental efficacy, expose itself as mere theatre – which is the only role most Francophone dramatists see and make for it.

The dramatist's decision to let Kouma expose Sanga Titi, like his decision to make Juliette triumph over the traditionalists, reflects his view that in the context of the play their position is more defensible. Juliette, the more individualised of these school-going characters, emerges as a respectful but determined young woman who does not bow down to either pressure or cajoling. Although her arguments in favour of personal choice, of love unrestricted by considerations of clan interests are due to her Western education, they never sound borrowed as in Soyinka's Lakunlé who sounds artificial in his attempts to practise against his nature those things he has dangerously misunderstood about Western marriage. Juliette, on the other hand, is natural, asking her grandmother disarmingly 'Does money prove love?' and her father furiously:

What? Settled? Do you really mean to ignore me when you make decisions affecting me? Couldn't you have consulted me? At least this once? (p. 45)

She can be sarcastic, but is never insulting. She makes no grand statements on the need to overturn the old order in the name of 'progress'. She does not, in other words, affect a pretentious city contempt for ancient, rural traditions. She concentrates on her happiness, wielding arguments that are irrefutable in their simplicity and that carry the force of an inner conviction.

Oyono uses several techniques to enliven his play. Apart from his caricatured portraits among which, incidentally, must be included Ondua, the village drunk, and Matalina the empty-headed country girl dreaming of a city gent who will buy her 'tergal skirts' and 'blonde wigs', he shows skill in constructing comic situations. And the play is full of them.

One such is Mbia's first encounter in Act II with his prospective in-laws. The comedy in this scene derives from the endless mixed list of demands – for cola-nuts, bicycles, cattle and 'serious' radios that speak only Bulu from time to time – in exchange for Juliette; their outrageous sense of calculation, and undignified jostling for attention; their anguish when it looked as though alcohol was going to be omitted from the list and their explosion of joy when this fatal error is rectified. Mbarga's decision to pay 'the great man' a visit alone to introduce a supplementary and no doubt very personal list all make for great comedy.

Another situation whose comic potential is fully exploited is that in which Oko, Juliette's schoolboy fiancé, is being introduced to her family. The scene is doubly comic. First because of the reversal of roles it describes. The young man who earlier had been condescendingly dismissed as penniless and therefore worthless is now shown to hold the trump card, with the older people at his mercy. What gives added piquancy to the scene is the fact that to the end, Abessolo does not realise this reversal. He continues to curse at the 'little schoolboy from Abam' at the same time as he is trembling before him in his disguise as the great man from Yaoundé, and gratefully handing over his granddaughter to him in marriage. The sight of a manipulator manipulated, of authoritarianism deflated is one that gives delight to the audience.

The situation is also hilarious because of the manner in which Oko is introduced. Conscious of the villagers' obsession with age and appearances, he has himself dressed up in sumptuous if borrowed African robes and Western titles. In a particularly comic episode, he is described as having doctorates in mathematics and 'white languages' – qualifications which are interpreted respectively to the villagers to mean the ability to 'count all the leaves of a palm tree' and to speak 'French, English, German, Spanish, German, English French [*sic*]' (FE, p. 65).

But perhaps the most comic situation of all is the viper incident in Act III where Mbarga and Abessolo bemoan the eating of a viper by the young without permission. By making their lament coincide with another by Atangana over the stealing of the money so far paid by rival suitors, Oyono creates a situation in which the different concerns of various characters merge to produce a dialogue at cross-purposes.

Verbal humour, in the sense of the use of language not to express the comic but as its source, is a device that is widely used in *Trois prétendants*. Most of the examples of this type of humour are provided either by the villagers' attempts to understand European languages (especially French) and the concepts they express, or by the mispronunciation of some of their words. Thus the word 'mister' becomes 'massa', 'tergal' 'tregar', while 'German' is systematically rendered in the French edition as 'jaman', and its native equivalent as 'doiche'. Sometimes all three words are strung together as if to denote three different languages. Thus Atangana, boasting of Juliette's many qualities to Tchétgen, one of her suitors, concludes proudly:

She also speaks English, German, doiche, jaman (FE: p. 107)

To which Tchétgen the practical trader replies, unimpressed:

But what do you expect me to do with all these languages? I only need pidgin English for my trade! (p. 107)

The literal interpretation of words, like the confusion that can result from an insensitivity to their various shades of meaning, are also a source of humour exploited by Oyono-Mbia. Thus, taking the adjective 'High' in 'Mr High commissioner' (p. 65) to signify the physical sense, the villagers immediately give a non-existent antonym 'Low commissioners' (p. 65). And Matalina's understanding of the word 'valuable' in a strictly material sense leads her into the error of thinking she is in agreement with Juliette:

JULIETTE: Mais je suis un être humain! J'ai de la valeur.
MATALINA: Bien sûr que tu as de la valeur, Juliette… Ndi… a versé 100,000 francs pour t'épouser. (FE: p. 24)

Sometimes, Oyono-Mbia creates fun from the sheer piling up of high-sounding but meaningless words. Oko, the reader is told, is a 'Doctor in Doctorate' and a 'Baccalaureate Doctor' (FE, p. 115).

In addition to these comic effects provided by character, situation and language, there are also those derived from facial expressions, gestures and slapstick. In point of fact, *Trois prétendants'* material is not so much built upon the elaborate literary elements of 'high comedy', as in a properly integrated plot, but more upon the comic personality of the stock characters. Its action is a juxtaposition of a series of tableaux, mostly describing encounters between rich rival suitors and Juliette's family, which enable these characters (like the narrator-actor in *kotéba* or *sougounougou* theatre) to perform typical comic responses that rely heavily on elements of theatre's physical language, like mime and slapstick.

There are numerous examples of such stock farce numbers. Apart from the one already mentioned with Engulu tripping over his trousers, the most obvious is in Act III, pp. 48–9, where Mbia accompanies his accusations of the villagers of insolence and brewing illicit gin with screams, voice modulations and elaborate gestures (faithfully reproduced in mime by his valet) emphasising his importance and wounded dignity.

In Act I, p. 19, Atangana's excitement at the arrival of the alleged 'rich civil servant' Mbia, is conveyed by his stammer; Ondua's approval of Mbarga's speech in support of Mbia by broad gestures while Abessolo's shock over Juliette's refusal to be coerced into marriage is conveyed by his fall. Finally, to translate the villagers' greed, Oyono has them rushing at the first opportunity to take possession of drinks that are meant for them anyway.

The physical act is everywhere in evidence in the play and it is this that gives the work its eminently theatrical quality. This quality is further reinforced towards the end of Act II, when, in a bid to break the impasse between himself and her parents, Juliette and her schoolfriends resort to the stratagem of the stolen bride price, presented (like the Dance of the Lost Traveller in the *Lion and the Jewel*) in terms of play production:

JULIETTE: We want to play a good joke on all these people...
KOUMA: We're going to stage something simply great for them! (To the audience) See you in the fifth act! (p. 36)

The portrayal of these characters not only as actors within a play, but as producers of and actors in a sketch entitled 'The Wealthiest Man in the World' (p. 36) within this play clearly reveals the status of *Trois prétendants* as pure theatre. It is a measure of Oyono-Mbia's talent that his primary aim of creating drama is successfully combined with that of social critic.

CHAPTER 10

Senouvo Zinsou: 'On joue la comédie'

Senouvo Agbota Zinsou is one of the most exciting dramatists currently writing for the stage in Francophone Africa. Born in 1946 in Togo and educated in schools and university in that country, he showed an early interest in the theatre, producing his first play 'L'Amour d'un sauvage', when he was still in school. He also played an important role during his school days in the formation of an inter-secondary school dramatic society, the 'Entente scolaire pour le théâtre et le folklore'. In 1969, while at university, where he became leader of the university dramatic society Les Etoiles Noires, he wrote his second play, 'La Fiancée du vaudou.' This was followed in 1972 (his final year at university) by his most popular play to date and his first published, *On joue la comédie*.

First issued in 1972, and revised in 1975, *On joue la comédie* won Zinsou both the first prize in the 1972 Inter-African Radio Drama Competition, organised by Radio France Internationale, and a scholarship to Paris. In Paris, he did graduate work in theatre studies at the Institut des Etudes Théâtrales of the University of Paris and wrote a dissertation 'Eléments pour un théâtre national Togolais' under the supervision of Jean Schérer.

On his return to Togo, he was appointed to the Ministry of Culture where he founded the National Company for the Performing Arts, which he headed until 1992 (Gbéasor 1975: ix–xxv; Ricard 1986a: 100–3). Zinsou's other published plays (some ten are still in manuscript form) include *Le Club* (1983), *La Tortue qui chante*, *La Femme du blanchisseur* and *Les Aventures de Yévi au pays des monstres* (1987).

On joue la comédie, which was successfully performed in 1977 in Lagos during the second Pan-African Cultural Arts Festival, has since been produced in many African countries including Togo, Zaire and Burundi. It revealed Zinsou as an original and innovative dramatist, and one anxious to give a popular dimension to modern theatre. Eschewing the declamatory tones, epic characters and sermonising of the dominant Francophone drama of the time – a drama which it in fact humorously parodies – *On joue la comédie* defines the search for a new theatre. This search is based on a skilful exploitation of the resources of modern Togolese popular theatrical traditions, especially the concert party, and to a lesser extent the kantata. He writes:

In *On joue la comédie*, I've sought to adapt to the written theatre the techniques of popular forms which derive from an oral and improvised theatre. I've wanted, in so doing, to render a personal tribute to the popular actors of the concert party. (quoted in de Saivre 1982: 74–5)

The play displays a welcome formal consciousness that is absent from the earlier literary theatre of debate and, mostly, of words only, of Francophone Africa. This consciousness is manifested in the play's manipulation of truth and illusion, the face and the mask, the actor and the spectator and its pervasive use of the play-within-a-play technique. The work emphasises the nature of drama as an art that should give a total theatrical experience through the integrative and functional use of mime, song, dance and gesture, and not an evening school where edifying lessons in heroism or civic responsibility are offered.

It is a process and not a product; a 'game' (the word recurs often in *On joue* – pp. 7, 13, 17, 61 etc.) with no pre-defined rules, but one whose rules must be collaboratively worked out between actors and audience. It is the failure of one of the spectators in the play to grasp this fact – reared no doubt as he is on more Western-inspired heroic and textual African drama – that leads to his enraged reaction:

THE SMALL GENTLEMAN: I want to watch a play or take my money back … This is not what I call a play. Plays have to be educative. (p. 16)

To which the Presenter replies:

In that case you'll be better off attending night-school. (pp. 16–17)

To Zinsou, then, theatre should stimulate the audience into a critical judgement and appraisal both of the action represented and its mode of representation. He comments:

The public should not follow blindly without being personally involved or aware. If the public has to follow, it must do so in full knowledge. (quoted in de Saivre 1982: 75)

The audience, in other words, should not be reduced to the level of the passive consumer of a finished art-product. Rather, it should be encouraged in terms reminiscent of Augusto Boal's concept of 'forum theatre' to become an active partner in its production. But how exactly does Zinsou achieve this aim in his play? Before discussing this issue, it is necessary to give a fairly full account of the play to convey an impression both of its dramatic style and themes.

Divided into four acts and a prologue, the play opens in the streets of Johannesburg where a group of street actors decide to perform a play on apartheid. After a preliminary sketch in which they parody various aspects of apartheid, their leader Xuma announces the play:

Now our main play's going to start. I assure you it's the world's greatest play! (pp. 5–6)

But just when it is about to begin, two policemen climb onto the stage. Suspicious that the so-called actors could be the urban terrorists they have been looking for, they interrupt the performance, allowing it to continue only after an elaborate identity check.

But the action has hardly taken off again when it is interrupted a second time; this time, however, not by the police, but by an old spectator who wishes to avail himself of the opportunity given to the audience to contribute – 'I'm told this is a theatre where everyone's free to take the floor' (p. 10). Calling himself a preacher, he delivers a stirring sermon in which he announces the advent of a Messiah called Chaka, who will deliver the suffering blacks of South Africa from their plight.

While the impatient actors gently try to persuade him to leave the stage, an argument breaks out between two spectators. One sees the sermon's message as an appropriate theme for a play, while the other – a younger spectator – vigorously disagrees, arguing that what is needed now is not another escapist or anti-colonial history play, but one that addresses post-colonial issues of politics and society. His protests notwithstanding, it is decided towards the end of the prologue that a play entitled 'Chaka le Messie' will indeed be improvised on the preacher's sermon. Roles are distributed, a general outline of the action is worked out and the actors prepare to enter on to a hastily erected stage.

In a sustained exploitation of the play-within-a-play device, Act I of *On joue la comédie* coincides with the opening of the play to be improvised, 'Chaka le Messie'. But, as in the prologue, the latter play will not be produced, for just when Xuma the presenter finally agrees to play the title role in it, there is a double interruption. First by a group of the original street actors who, absent when the decision to improvise a new play was taken, are now astonished to see their leader in a different play; then again by policemen who arrest Chaka and his men, convinced this time that they are indeed the terrorists on their list.

SECOND POLICEMAN: That's him, the agitator and rebel leader. That's enough Darkie (talking to Chaka). Your game's up. Follow us. (p. 25)

But the arrest proves to be shortlived as Chaka in turn disarms and incarcerates the police, promising to release them only if they accept to help him storm a prison and free African revolutionaries condemned to hard labour.

By this time, of course, the actors have abandoned all attempts to stage a play – either the one announced in the Prologue or 'Chaka le Messie'. And now openly admitting to being terrorists, they attack the prison in Act II with the help of one of the policemen and set several prisoners free. But just as Chaka and his men are savouring their victory, Chaka is betrayed and re-arrested.

Act III finds him in gaol, where he learns of his death sentence over the radio, 'after,' the announcement adds, 'he was arrested trying to throw a bomb at a hospital' (p. 47). Asked in Act IV to express his last wishes before execution, Chaka requests that he be allowed to perform a one-man skit called 'The President of Repression' and to give a press conference. But these are mere delaying tactics meant to give his friends time to finish plotting his escape.

With only a few minutes to go before he is hanged, his friends storm the prison and free him. The play ends with Chaka high on their shoulders reminding the audience that all that they have seen is theatre, but theatre meant to drive them into real action against oppression.

On joue la comédie then can be characterised as a play on the impossibility of producing an anti-apartheid play in South Africa. But while in one sense the spectator feels cheated of the pleasure of watching one play 'Chaka le Messie', he has in another sense been closely involved in the creation of another, *On joue la comédie*.

From the résumé above, it is quite easy to infer strong Brechtian and Pirandellian influences on Zinsou. The way in which his play constantly exhibits its fictionality, shows itself in the process of being made, destroys the realist illusion by the continuous interruption of 'planted' actors (as spectators or policemen) will all be given in support of this claim. The plot of *On joue la comédie*, in which the production of one play is abandoned in favour of another to be improvised on material suggested by someone external to the cast, is strongly suggestive of Pirandello's *Six Characters in Search of an Author.* Other points to buttress these influences will include the production techniques and style of acting the play requires. Under the former, the play's action is constantly commented upon or announced in advance; roles are distributed on stage in full view of the audience and characters are called upon to play several parts each. Thus Xuma the Presenter doubles up as Chaka and, in Act IV, as president of an imaginary country, while an unnamed male actor puts on a disguise to play Noliwé, Chaka's female companion.

For the style of acting, the actor is encouraged not to give himself up completely to his part. Thus, to keep the necessary distance between himself and the character he portrays, Xuma (as Presenter for example) is made now to speak out the part, now to read it out as haltingly as possible because of what he alleges to be the bad handwriting of the script writer: 'I didn't write this speech, so I have some difficulty understanding it' (p. 6). Also, as Chaka in 'Chaka le Messie', he maintains a self-conscious attitude throughout, having to be constantly reminded to recite his lines.

N'KOULOU N'KOULOU: Listen Xuma, do you want to act Chaka or not?
   (p. 24)

Sometimes another character quite simply resorts to reminding the spectator of Chaka's true identity.

A THIRD ACTOR: But...it's our ringleader. It's Xuma who's performing
   there right in the middle of the spectators.
A FOURTH ACTOR: That isn't possible.
THE ACTOR PLAYING
   N'KOULOU N'KOULOU: Don't you know he's acting Chaka? (p. 25)

While all these techniques do indeed point to a clear European inspiration, another source of influence nearer home and freely admitted to by Zinsou is that of the concert party. Replying to an interviewer who detects the twin influences of Brecht and the *commedia dell'arte* in *On joue* he states:

I don't deny that I've read a lot of Brecht and that I borrowed some techniques from him ... Concerning the *Commedia dell'arte*, if you're referring to the play within a play or improvisation techniques ... I'll say to you that it's not necessary to go so far away. Our *commedia dell'arte* is right there ... it's the concert party. (quoted in de Saivre 1982: 75)

The links between the concert party (see above: pp. 77–9) and *On joue* are many. One of these is the nature of their plots. The action in *On joue*, like that in a concert party piece, is improvised. No sequence of events has been planned in advance. Although the staging of a play is announced in the prologue ('our revolutionary comedy is soon going to start' (p. 2)), it is quickly abandoned in the face of continuous interruption and heckling. Opinion for an alternative play is canvassed and some sort of consensus laboriously emerges, only for the play to be abandoned once again. In the end, what one has is not a plot that progresses logically in the tradition of the well-made play, but an open-ended structure where a series of disconnected episodes, mostly concerned with staging plays, revolve around a central character and his fellow actors.

Although the danger of anarchy haunts all such improvised theatre recommended in *On joue* (especially if the actors are new to one another), it is reduced in the case of this play by the directing work of the Presenter, Xuma. Like his concert party counterpart, *le meneur de jeu* – a kind of ringleader, an internal producer who is also an actor – he controls both action and performers. Thus after a long discussion as to which play to stage, he authoritatively tells the spectators:

We've laughed enough, Ladies and Gentlemen. Now let's think of our game. The subject of our improvision will be Chaka the Messiah. (p. 17)

His various announcements – 'now we're going to start our main play' (p. 5), 'he is an actor', p. 11 (about the old man); 'don't fear them, they're not real policemen' p. 10 – are all meant to give direction to the events and help the spectator out of the inevitable confusion that might otherwise occur as a result of the constant conflation of reality and theatrical illusion.

The actors also take their cue from the Presenter, breaking into dance or a session of grimacing or parody when he so directs. If he feels a particular performer has not had the opportunity to act, he invites him to do just that. 'Look at this old man', he says about one such and calls on him 'He's going to tell you his life. Aren't you M'Kizé?' (p. 33). In Act II, the Presenter similarly invites the ex-detainees N'dula and Mpala to come forward to be seen and heard.

In addition to all this the Presenter, like the concert party *meneur de jeu* that he really is, distributes roles according to his actors' individual talents. Thus after choosing the role of Chaka for himself towards the end of the Prologue, he gives two fellow actors the following instructions:

You'll act N'koulou N'koulou; you'll send me to earth to free men. And you'll disguise yourself to play Noliwé, Chaka's wife. (p. 19)

The various roles distributed, he counsels his cast:

Well to each one his preferred role, as long as the outline is respected. (p. 20)

Another area in which *On joue* derives much from the concert party is in characterisation. All the characters are types: the warder, the policeman, the prisoner and so on. But more than this, the play has two of the conventional types in concert party drama – the houseboy, or 'massa boy' as he is called in that tradition, and the old man. The former is represented by the Presenter who, as Chaka, has the distinctive costume of the 'massa boy': a pair of modern trousers over which is worn a torn pair of shorts, in this case a raffia mini-skirt, and the latter by the actor playing N'koulou N'koulou who wears the equally significant white hair and beard. Also, the female parts in *On joue* – Noliwé, Chaka's wife and the female spectator who betrays Chaka – are all played in concert party tradition by men disguised as women.

Of humble origin – miners, village heads, members of the unemployed urban youth – again like their concert party counterparts, the characters in *On joue* are the complete antithesis of the earnest, exalted and humourless princely figures of traditional Francophone drama. Expert at self-deprecation and conscious of only playing a part, they are more like jesters or clowns acting out circus numbers. And for this they do not rely on words alone, of course, but very significantly on mime, music and dance. Entire sequences, like the prison-storming episode (pp. 42–3) are acted in mime.

Also like concert party performers, the style of their acting is constantly satirical or parodic. They ridicule just about everything. Apartheid of course, but also foreign aid (p. 18), religion, dictators (Act IV) and not least a certain form of Francophone African dramatic literature. Apartheid is criticised in many ways, notably in the scene that parodies a public lecture in its defence by one of apartheid's leading intellectual exponents. In this scene, the master–

servant relationship along racial lines characteristic of the apartheid doctrine is depicted in the spectacle of the white speaker pulling along his black servant on a rope. Sarcastically introduced by the servant as Professor Têtepleine (literally 'Full Head'), he is anything but a scholar. His lecture, an attempt to derive apartheid from a divine order, is a cocktail of prejudice, illogicality and empty rhetoric. All he achieves in the end is confirmation, in the spectator, of an earlier description of him by his servant as a 'célèbre con...conf... conférencier' (p. 3) – the humour is contained in the word-play on the first syllable of 'Conférencier' which signifies 'a fool'.

Parody is also used to great effect in the playlet 'Chaka le Messie' against Francophone African historical drama with its debates and visionary heroes. In it, the traditional drift towards solemnity and grandiloquence – embodied in N'koulou N'koulou's tirades – is simultaneously subverted either by his comic tics and appearance or by his envoy Chaka. Always acting drunk and constantly refusing the heroism that goes with his part, the latter reduces the entire playlet to comic proportions. Thus, whenever N'koulou N'koulou waxes poetic, he is ready in counterpoise with some unheroic response in colloquial language:

N'KOULOU N'KOULOU: Son of the Zulus, be happy because you've been rejected and held in contempt by men ... I've made you know suffering, misery and humiliation so you can understand the unhappiness of all those who thirst and hunger for justice.

CHAKA (to himself): Hmm! I'm not drunk. I've only had some fire-water. (pp. 21–2)

N'KOULOU N'KOULOU: You'll also be called the Saviour, the Redeemer, the Messiah, the Giver of Freedom...

CHAKA: You know my name is Xuma for short. I've got no surname... In fact mum tells me daddy was an ass who died in gaol after failing to escape with an ordinary bag with some money that he tried to nick from a Johannesburg industrial tycoon. (p. 23)

But present in this playlet is not just concert party influence, but also that of another popular theatrical Togolese genre, the Kantata (see above, p. 79).

The link between this genre and Zinsou's playlet in *On joue* lies in the very story the former proposes for dramatisation. It is a secularised version of the Bible story of 'Moses sent to deliver Israel' (Exodus, chapter 3), in which Chaka as Moses is called upon by N'koulou N'koulou (God), to deliver his oppressed black people (the children of Israel) from bondage in South Africa (Egypt). Even the description of the Promised Land for the South African blacks, one in which

water from our rivers and mountains will be milk and honey and fruit juices will flow in abundance. (p. 22)

is not without recalling that of the Promised Land of the Israelis.

Another original feature of *On joue* is its use of stage space. The 'planted' actors used during the play – a device borrowed straight from the concert party – the full use of various areas of the auditorium for the action, the singing and dancing in which the audience is invited to join are all attempts to establish a rapport between the audience and actors, to abolish the constraints of the proscenium arch and the rigid separation of stage and auditorium.

Zinsou's aesthetic of total participation of actors and audience in the construction of a play has clear ideological implications. Just as artistic creation should be the product of a collective endeavour and not the work of the Great Writer with the ready-made message, so democracy, social and political change (in the play, the fight against oppression) can be brought about only through an understanding of the issues by the wider public, and its active involvement in the search for solutions. Zinsou's theatrical practice is liberating and empowering, and one in which the subject is not prescribed but *negotiated* between stage and audience. Both as an aesthetic and an ideology, it is a radical departure from, and in fact, a challenge to, the more élitist post-colonial aesthetics and politics in Africa. And it is in this sense that *On joue la comédie* was a truly 'revolutionary play' (p. 2) for the mid-1970s, embodying in the sphere of dramatic creation an aspiration for greater popular participation which, in the realm of political life, only found expression some fifteen years later in the popular, social and political protest movements for democratic governance.

CHAPTER 11

Zadi Zaourou: 'L'Œil'

University teacher, poet and playwright, Bottey (formerly Bernard) Zadi Zaourou was born in 1938 in the Ivory Coast. He received his early education in that country before proceeding in 1965 to the University of Strasbourg in France. On completion of his MA degree in 1970 (he subsequently obtained and published his doctorate on the poetry of Aimé Césaire) he returned to his country where he took up a teaching appointment at the University of Abidjan.

Zaourou is a controversial figure. In the 1960s, while still at school, he had a spell in prison for extreme left-wing activities. He is no less controversial in the field of drama where, with the other Ivorian or Ivory Coast-based playwrights and theatre practitioners referred to in chapter 1 above – Niangoran Porquet, Souleymane Koly and Sidiki Bakaba – he has been involved in efforts, and sometimes embroiled in spirited polemics, to renew Francophone theatre (on the polemics, see *Fraternité Matin* February to May 1980 and Hourantier 1984: 35–47). He founded the *didiga* theatre company in 1980. Borrowed from his native Bété language, the word *didiga* signifies a hunter's narrative told to music (Bonneau 1972: 2–11; Kotchy 1984: 232–53; Zagboto 1987: 77–9). It is considered the highest and most accomplished art form in that society. The hunter in Bété culture (the hero of the narrative) is endowed with a special status. As an individual who confronts the mystery of the forest, of wild animals and of the elements in the interests of man, he is seen as defending human society against the forces of destruction. He lives dangerously and mysteriously and it is this element that constitutes the subject of his narrative. Generous and fearless, the hero of a *didiga* narrative is imbued with an ideal of love which pushes him to risk and sometimes to sacrifice his life.

It is this ideal that Zaourou wishes to pursue through his *didiga* theatre company. Today's jungle, he contends, is human. It is peopled not by wild animals but by human predators and dictators of every hue. The duty of the modern *didiga* hero or play is, like that of his counterpart in Bété tradition, to identify these dangers to human society and fight against them. In order to do this successfully in the context of theatrical creation, Zaourou sees the first task at hand as being that of freeing Francophone theatre in general and that of his country in particular from the dominant Ecole William Ponty aesthetic of dramatic art as this is embodied in the historical and social dramas of Bernard Dadié especially, but also of Amon d'Aby and Koffi Gadeau.

The new form of theatre, which Zaourou sought to create with his fellow theatre practitioners, does not so much concern itself with exhuming the historical past, even if it is to criticise it, as with reflecting the present. The social and political problems of the Ivory Coast, the insensitivity of the ruling élites to the plight of the ordinary mass of people, the injustices of which these are the victim should, in Zaourou's view, be the proper concern of the dramatist. He asks:

Why should ancient acts of prowess be exhumed at all cost? What Africa needs today are other songs... It suffices that from year to year, the sorcerer's third eye is able to reveal the nature of the new winds and advise on how best to pacify them. (*L'Œil*, p. 67)

To Zaourou, as to his colleagues, the duty of the dramatist is to use his power of vision to unravel (as the shaman allegedly does with his mystical third eye) invisible connections; connections in this case between the socio-economic plight of the poor – the bewitched, so to speak – and the political system put in place by the élites, the malevolent spirits.

There is nothing new, of course, in this advocacy of a political theatre neither for Francophone Africa in general nor for the Ivory Coast in particular, where theatre is nothing if not political, even when it is draped in the garb of myth, history or legend. What is new, however, apart from the thematic emphasis on the ills of the post-colonial as opposed to the colonial state, is its openly political nature and, more significantly, the agitprop function attributed to it.

Drama inspired by the William Ponty tradition is sedate. It mostly teaches, now denounces or satirises but almost always entertains. Its audience is made up of the Western-educated members of society. Plays in the mould advocated by Zaourou and his colleagues, on the other hand, are angry. They are intended for and directed at a mass audience whose problems they reflect, whose language they use abundantly and whose representative characters they put on stage. They seek to raise the consciousness of the people by leading them from understanding through anger to agitation; from a resigned acceptance of their fate to revolutionary action.

But if this type of literary theatre is popular, it is so not only in the sense that it serves the interest of the ordinary people, but because, like Zinsou's *On joue la comédie*, it derives from conventions and forms, mainly of the traditional performing arts, that are valued by their mass audience, and actually uses and not merely suggests the use of language forms that are comprehensible to them. Thus, unlike plays in the William Ponty tradition, which are invariably in French (using African languages only in the songs), works like *L'Œil, C'est quoi même* by Sidiki Bakaba or *Adama Champion* by Souleymane Koly employ in the dialogue a variety of languages spoken in the Ivory Coast – from the various types of French (standard, 'tough-guy' slang, pidgin) to African languages like Malinké and Bambara. But more than this, they also use the language of symbol, of song, of music, mime and body movement as an integral part of the action. Referring to the relationship between these arts, the Ivorian theatre director Abou-bacar Touré observes:

Even if a play starts off with a dance, the dancer knows that the theme developed has to be related to that of the texts, that his theme must be inscribed in the song, the music, the text. (quoted in Kotchy 1984: 242)

A significant scripted play in this new tradition is Zaourou's *L'Œil*. First staged in 1974 but banned in 1975 after three performances – on the grounds of incitement to class hatred and violence – *L'Œil* is a grim work. It treats the theme of the exploitation of a poor and underprivileged group of people by a rich and corrupt ruling élite.

Embodying this élite is the district governor Sogoma Sangui. Anxious to buy his wife's silence after she discovers an extra-marital relationship, he promises to replace one of her eyes, damaged in a car accident, with one obtained from a healthy donor. He gives the contract for an eye to a colourful character of the underworld, the gangster Django. He in turn approaches a vulnerable man – the impecunious and debt-ridden petty functionary Djédjé. Shocked at first by Django's suggestion that he persuade and if necessary force his wife Amani to sell off one of her eyes, Djédjé finally succumbs, albeit agonisingly, to the attractive offer.

News of this sordid transaction and the restlessness it has provoked among the ordinary people reaches the President, Tiéffimba. To head off social unrest, he has Sogoma Sangui arrested and imprisoned. But in a dramatic *coup de théâtre* he is rehabilitated shortly after and promoted to regional governor, while Djédjé is rewarded with the post of managing director of a state company.

During cocktails in the presidential mansion to celebrate this event an angry crowd, enraged by a rumour that Amani did not survive the operation to remove her eye, rushes towards the mansion and provokes a showdown with the rulers.

The élite as depicted in this play emerges as callous and greedy. Sogoma Sangui, its chief representative, is totally insensitive to the plight of his junior workers, whom he dismisses at will for crimes they have not committed, transfers arbitrarily and insults constantly:

SOGOMA SANGUI (to Koffi Kan): Insolent wretch, you seem to forget don't you, that I'm the District Governor. Your Lord and Master. I'll destroy you Koffi Kan if you dare stand up to me. I'll break you like a match stick. Now get out of my office. (*L'Œil*, p. 71)

and to Gonougo who pleads against a transfer on the grounds of his family:

Shut up and out of my office. Out I say you idler ... idler I say. Whimper as much as you like, but you'll go. (p. 70)

Sangui's callousness and immorality reach despicable depths when he takes advantage of his superior economic power and position in society to engage in a trade (which has a metaphorical dimension in the play) in human organs. Unmindful of the leadership role expected of a man in his position, he puts his office in the service of his private interests. Constantly on the phone to either friend, mistress or business partner, he is unable to do the simplest of office jobs, much to the annoyance of his assistants. The only office meeting he attempts to chair is so often interrupted that it does not go beyond the preliminary opening remarks. And yet with characteristic dishonesty he asks that the minutes of the said meeting be prepared. All Sogoma Sangui wants, as he tells the Marabout, is 'power, power, money and domestic bliss' (p. 113). Moral considerations count for nothing in his life and it is precisely because Djédjé too shows a willingness to forgo them that he is so readily coopted into the ranks of the Sogoma Sanguis.

Pitted against the ruling class in *L'Œil* is the ordinary mass of
people. This is composed of office messengers, drivers, the urban
unemployed and militant students. When we first meet them, they
display no group consciousness. In Django and Gringo, they seek
solutions in gangsterism and crime. In Gonougo, Koffi Kan and
especially in the Deuxième Homme, they are in their colourful
French submissive and resigned to their fate:

Comment on va fait? C'est pas leur soleil qui brille? Comment on va fait?
Tu gagnes pas rien. Kissikia tu pé? (p. 79)

But this initial fatalism soon gives way to the first stirrings of
awakening when, in their crowded drinking-houses, the workers
actually start discussing Sogoma Sangui and the regime in spite of the
obvious risks:

FIRST MAN: C'est moi qui te dis. Le jour que ça va chauffer ici, Congo même
    n'est rien à côté. (p. 79)

The discussion, conducted at first in hushed tones for fear of
informants, and oscillating between resigned acceptance and outrage
at his evil power, becomes more daring. Emboldened by militant
students who have now joined the conversation, the workers
increasingly see Sangui not as a god, but as an ordinary, corrupt
individual who can and must be challenged. Criticism of him
becomes fierce and denunciatory:

FIRST MAN: Sogoma Sangui c'est pas Dieu ka même
SECOND MAN: ... i vient, i baise ton femme, i baise ton fille, i baise ton bonne
    amie et pi i veut baiser toi même encore. (pp. 82–3)

The workers' growing understanding of their situation leads to still
greater anger which finally erupts, after their leader's speech, into the
violence of the last scene.

One of the shortest, this scene is nonetheless perhaps the most
powerful. In accents reminiscent of the inflammatory rhetoric of an
Etienne Lantier in Zola's *Germinal* (incidentally also a work on the
growth of a revolutionary consciousness) the Premier Etudiant whips
up the collective emotions of the workers to fever-pitch and galvanises
them into action. In a three-part speech, he first dilates on their lot:

Cette fois, il faut que ça craque c'est nous les mains du labeur, la sueur des
trésors interdits à notre soif... c'est nous! Pour la paix des autres, pour la joie
des autres, pour leur sommeil de rêves dorés...

(This time, something has to give. For ours are the hands of labour, ours the sweat of treasures denied to our thirst. It is us, the peace of others, the joy of others, the guardians of their sleep of golden dreams.)

then emphasises, in a highly metaphorical expression, their fruitless efforts at self-improvement:

vous voici, travailleurs matinaux, gravissant de vos mains qui saignent, chaque maillon de la chaîne, pour vaincre l'espace et mordre aux racines du soleil. Et à peine y êtes-vous parvenus qu'il vous faut redescendre, à nouveau dans le tourbillon des éléments déchaînés...

(Here you stand workers of the dawn, clambering, with your bleeding hands, each link of the chain in order to conquer space and bite at the roots of the sun. But you have hardly reached the top than you're forced down again to the whirlpool of the elements in fury.)

before finally summoning them, in a skilful conflation of the issue of Amani's eye and their fate, to rise up and fight:

Non! Nous ne mourrons pas de cécité. Et c'est dès demain qu'il nous le faudra crier à la face du soleil! Fermement. Fermement! Fer-me-ment. (p. 121)

(No, we shan't die of blindness. And its as from tomorrow that we must shout this message out at the face of the sun! With determination. Determination. De-ter-mi-na-tion.)

It is hardly surprising that this tableau was censored by the Ivorian authorities. But in a play like *L'Œil*, which relies as much on verbal as on non-verbal language to communicate, the scissors of the censor, excising various speeches, does little to mutilate its impact. If anything, the recourse by directors to the greater use of space, silence and body language to get round the problem of the incriminated speech can only give the play a greater dramatic intensity. And this is precisely what happened in the case of a notable production of the play by the Ivorian director Sidiky Bakaba that has been described in detail by the critic Barthélémy Kotchy.

Unable to produce the last tableau as a written text, Bakaba, Kotchy tells us, composed 'a scene based on the use of space and mime' (1984: 249). In his production, the young student agitator expresses his anger on the news of Amani's death not in words, but by smashing glasses and bottles which he then pretends to hurl all around him. He then mounts the podium as if to harangue the crowd. But, instead of words, he offers only silence. The puzzled and angry workers follow him around the stage as if hypnotised, waiting for an outburst that never comes. This stifling silence is then suddenly shattered by the throbbing of the '*attoungblan* drum', whose sounds are a call to action.

The ensuing confrontation with the ruling class which ends the play is also executed in the non-verbal language of sounds, gesture and looks. Here, the arrival of the angry crowd is first suggested by echoes of their cries and thumping feet which become more insistent as they approach the presidential mansion (p. 121). Transfixed with horror, the bourgeois stand motionless with their glasses in their hands. Suddenly a menacing crowd appears, surges forward as if to attack them. But then a barrier suddenly drops from the ceiling, stopping them in their tracks. However, determined not to be stopped even by the physical obstacle of a wall, the crowd dashes forward to smash it. The wall at this point is suddenly winched up, leaving the conflicting forces face to face.

If *L'Œil* is striking by its limited and yet effective use of mime, silence, drum and body language, it is no less so by its use of verbal language. The entire linguistic spectrum in the Ivory Coast is reflected in the play – standard French, French slang, pidgin French and to an extent African languages. And language variety is used not only to reflect cultural diversity in the Ivory Coast, but also as an instrument of class and character differentiation. As Louise Jefferson has observed about the play, the 'theatrical rendering of linguistic differences... is indicative of the basic political, economic and ideological conflict' dramatised (1982: 832).

Thus standard French, the language of the bureaucracy and of power and privilege is used mostly by members of the Westernised ruling élite. The standard variety ranges from informal styles and colloquialisms to more conventional modes of expression. Examples of informal French, in the case of Sogoma Sangui, come at moments when he is either relaxed and talking to a friend on the phone or exploding with rage at Koffi Kan:

Tu connaîs Dieu toi? Pauvre diable c'est toi qui as fait le coup et tu veux mentir comme un pauvre diable. Toi! c'est fini. Je te raie de mes listes. Définitivement. Encore que j'aurais dû te foutre en tôle. (p. 70)

(Do you know God, you? Poor devil, you mounted it all up and now are lying like a devil. I'm finished with you. I cross you off my list. Forever. I really ought to have flung you in jail.)

At the other end of the continuum is the elevated and formal French of the governor general rehabilitating Sogoma Sangui:

Mes chers Amis j'ai tenu à présider moi-même à cette cérémonie de retour. Au nom de Fama et en mon nom personnel, qu'il me soit permis de placer cette fête de famille sous le signe de la réconciliation. (p. 116)

(My dear friends, I have made it a duty to chair this ceremony myself. On behalf of Fama and on my personal behalf, I pray that our gathering be informed by a spirit of family reconciliation.)

In between these types of French is the tough-guy slang – an influence no doubt of French gangster movies – of Django and Gringo. Here is an extract of their conversation:

DJANGO: Gringo, blague à part. Y'a du grabuge dans l'air. On va traiter. Y'a cinq cents gaillards à toucher ... Ou rien.
GRINGO: Tu t'amuses ou quoi? Il faut zigouiller quelqu'un ou quoi?
(DJANGO: Gringo, jokes aside, there's bread in the air. We go fix up everything. There's half a million quid for the taking.
GRINGO: You're kidding, or what? Do we need to bump off someone?)

Next to these varieties of metropolitan French, the dominant and most widely used language in *L'Œil* is pidgin French, known in the Ivory Coast as 'le francais de Moussa'. The language of inter-ethnic communication among the urban illiterate or semi-literate, it symbolises in the play the language of the powerless, the victims. Here is an example of such sub-standard French:

Joutement! Auzrodi même Koffi Kan il est là souffri son maison là-bas. Dis nans il a travaillé avec type là et pi matin seulement, à cause de Sogoma Sangui lui-même son connerie il a fait, i chassi lui son travail comme ça. (p. 83)

This French is marked by distinctive traits – defective pronunciation ('auzrodi' for 'aujourd'hui'), various tense and syntactical modifications ('i chasse lui son travail comme ça' for 'il l'a chassé de son travail sans avertissement'), an indifference to gender relations ('son maison' for 'sa maison') and a liberal sprinkling of various African expressions.

Although African languages are not used in the dialogue of the printed work, apart from some exclamations or the odd word in Mandingo, the dramatist, anxious to reach his target audience, suggests their possible use in future productions in at least two scenes. One of these relates to the encounter between Sogoma and the Islamic diviner, the *marabout*, in the cemetery. The dialogue in the playtext itself is in pidgin French, but Zaourou adds in his stage directions that the 'tableau would benefit from being played in Bambara' (p. 112). The other sequence where the use of an African language is suggested is the last one in which the angry crowd is hurling menaces and threatening violence against their rulers.

Although *L'Œil* is a political play with an interest more in social groups than in individuals, it does contain tableaux of intense psychological realism. One such is the domestic scene between Djédjé and his wife. Here the ravaging effects of unemployment on a family are depicted – the futile rounds at job centres, the debtors, the children whose basic needs cannot be met, the landlords who threaten expulsion, and, finally, the loss of self-esteem and the consequent domestic tensions and fights.

It is precisely after one such fight between Djédjé and Amani that Django appears on the scene. The way in which he exploits the husband's vulnerability – now sympathising with him, now brandishing the prospect of wealth – is also done with fine psychological realism.

L'Œil is a notable attempt to create a literary yet popular, revolutionary theatre in the Ivory Coast. It is not only directed at the ordinary people, it also stimulates them to a critical awareness of their condition.

CHAPTER 12

Werewere Liking: 'La Puissance d'Um'

Whereas Francophone Africa can boast important female writers in the novelists Mariama Bâ, Aminata Sow-Fall (Senegal) and Calixthe Béyala (Cameroon) and in the Ivorian poets Véronique Tadjo and Yanella Boni, it has produced only one female dramatist of stature, the Cameroonian Werewere Liking. The other two women who have occasionally written for the stage in Francophone Africa are Josephine Bongo, author of *Obali*, and the Cameroonian Rabiatou Njoya, author of *La Dernière Aimée*, *Toute la rente y passe* and *Ange Noir*, *Ange Blanc*.

Born in May 1950 in the village of Makak in the Bassa region of Cameroon, Werewere Liking, née Eddy Njock, had very little formal education. At a time when many Cameroonian girls of her age were being initiated into the mysteries of Western culture through formal schooling, she was instead being initiated into those of the many secret cults of her Bassa people. It was much later, rather like the Senegalese novelist Sembène Ousmane, that she taught herself to read and write in French – skills which she subsequently used to explore for the stage those myths and ritual ceremonies that were such a vital part of her early experience.

But Werewere Liking did not come directly to writing for the stage. She started her creative career at age sixteen as a singer, which is hardly surprising for the daughter of traditional musicians. She then moved into painting before producing her first literary work in 1977; a collection of poems entitled *On ne raisonne pas le venin*. It was also around this time that she left her native Cameroon for the Ivory Coast. This step was to prove particularly decisive in her creative career, for in Abidjan, where she worked as a researcher in the university, she not only discovered artistic freedom, but also 'a real effervescence' as she describes it (in Tagne 1989: 195) of ideas and intellectual stimulation.

She was able to take part in and benefit from the then on-going debates and research into African theatre led by Zadi Zaourou (see chapter 11 above), Niangoran Porquet and Souleymane Koly. A piece of collaborative endeavour in Abidjan that was to prove especially fruitful was undertaken with Marie-José Hourantier (see chapter 1 above). From the latter's intellectual interest in African traditional culture and especially ritual, and Werewere Liking's insider knowledge of it, was born the Cameroonian's career as a dramatist and the French researcher's as a theoretician of 'ritual theatre', the label by which Werewere Liking's plays are known (Bjornson 1991: 430–53; Digome 1990: 318–19; Hawkins 1991: 207–22; Magnier 1985: 17–21).

Werewere Liking published her first play, *La Queue du diable* (known in Cameroon as *Ngonga* after one of its main characters and to Radio France Internationale listeners as *Les Bâtards*) in 1979. This was followed in rapid succession by *La Puissance d'Um* (1979), *Une Nouvelle terre* and *Du Sommeil d'injuste* (1980), *Les Mains veulent dire* and *La Rougeole arc-en-ciel* (1987). More recently she has written a second prose work, *Elle sera de jaspe et de corail*, subtitled *Journal d'un misovire*, that is 'journal of a man-hater', 'misovire' being a neologism coined on the analogy of 'misogyne' (misogynist) from 'miso' and the Latin 'vires'. Her first prose narrative *Orphée-Dafric* was dramatised in 1981 by Hourantier, alias Manuna Ma Njock, as *Orphée d'Afrique*.

Werewere Liking's theatre, as has been observed in chapter 1 above, constitutes a radical departure from anything yet produced in Francophone Africa. It has variously been described as 'provocative', 'impertinent' (Borgomano 1987: 68) and 'obscure' (Magnier 1985: 19). Anne-Claire Jaccard observes:

Werewere Liking's researches are too complex and rooted in the Bassa cultural universe to appeal to a public of non-initiates. (1989: 161)

This lack of a wide appeal can be attributed to her work's extensive use of an esoteric and highly ritualised language; of dream, trance and spirit-possession techniques, of an intricate symbolism of gestures, colours, costumes and sounds and of the repetition of songs, dances and movements.

Also, unlike the theatre of her predecessors and contemporaries, hers is resolutely non-realistic. Neither the revelation of character nor the construction of realistic plots or indeed the presentation, in clear communicative language, of social, historical or political subjects is the concern of her drama.

Her plays are religious in essence, rooted in Bassa healing, initiation or death rituals of which they are in fact the dramatic recreation, both in content and structure. They deal invariably with the eruption of disorder in the life of a rural community – death, illness, crime – and their object is not to entertain, to inflame or to educate. It is rather to lead the audience and participants to overcome their traumatic experience, as successful ritual ceremonies allegedly do: to 'heal' and restore them. This is how Hourantier summarises their psychotherapeutic functions:

to create a healthier and stronger body, more stable and refined emotions; to define a clearer and more creative love of thinking, a firmer and better directed will; to assert oneself with a more open consciousness. (1984: 63)

Nowhere, perhaps, are these characteristics of African ritual better illustrated than in Werewere Liking's *La Puissance d'Um*.

The play deals with the pre-inhumation ritual ceremonies of a freshly deceased Bassa village elder, Ntep Iliga. Since according to this community's beliefs, death is never natural, but always someone else's responsibility, the question that arises and which the ritual ceremony is supposed to resolve (in the interests of the community's health) is that of the guilty person(s).

After a period of bitter recrimination, of confessions, of accusation and counter-accusation hurled by various people at one another, peace and harmony are finally restored to the community.

Que vienne la paix qui annihile la haine
Que la paix descende sur nos coeurs

Que la force envahisse nos mains
Que sur nous descende la puissance d'Um. (*La Puissance d'Um*, p. 52)

are the words intoned by the entire audience at the end of the play.

The death of a community elder, in other words, has become the opportunity for an exercise in collective stock-taking and critical self-examination; for the release of frustrations and pent-up energies – a release from which the community emerges revitalised and strengthened.

But *La Puissance d'Um* is not only ritualistic in content but also, as we noted in connection with Werewere Liking's plays, in structure. In its movement, it describes the phases of Bassa healing and

initiation rituals as these have been outlined by Hourantier (see
pages 12–13 above). Opening with a 'preamble' during which the
reason for the ceremony is given, the play moves into a 'warming-up'
sequence, the aim of which is to create the proper mood and
atmosphere between the various participants in the ceremony. This
in turn is followed by the 'search-for-the-guilty phase'. The third
movement issues into a 'poetic interval' and then culminates with a
'sequence of trance and psychodramas' before ebbing out into the
'dénouement'.

When *La Puissance d' Um* opens, Ngond Libii is engaged in a kind of
dialogue with a calabash that she is fondly caressing. Her husband
has just died and she is busy preparing the stage on which his body is
lying for the ritual ceremony that will follow her public announcement of his death. A striking feature of this preamble (pp. 9–12) or
introductory sequence is its mood. Although freshly widowed, Ngond
Libii does not so much display grief as deep frustration and bitterness
at what she sees as her own unfulfilled life:

C'est ici que je vis ma vie. Statique mais lovée, prête à déborder du vase
comme toi, vin de palme bouillant de rage, dans une outre trop petite,
enfermé. (p. 10)

(This is where I lived my life. Motionless but bottled up, ready to overflow
from the vase like you, palm wine, locked up in a tight goat-skin bottle and
boiling with rage.)

Her anger continues into the warming-up phase (pp. 13–23),
where her recollections of the late Ntep Iliga – solicited from her and
others in keeping with tradition by the Old Man (the ritual priest)
– sharply contrast with those of another participant, the Third Man.
Whereas he remembers in the deceased only 'a lion of a man', the
scion of 'a great family and of a race of noblemen' (p. 16), she
astonishingly remembers him as 'a piece of filth [which] does not
merit a funeral' (p. 12); a faithful member of the village's 'league of
idlers, gossips and drunks' (p. 17). She then shocks the assembly
further by claiming responsibility for his death:

Yes, I killed my husband and no one else's; I killed my husband! And if he
had nine lives similar to the one he lived, I'd kill him nine times over. Bury
him quickly as he's already making the place stink. (p. 14)

Naturally, this outburst shocks the assembly, which demands that
Ntep's murderer be punished:

THE THIRD MAN: Ntep's murderer owes the entire tribe an explanation.
His death won't go unpunished. (p. 23)

But just when the eyes of the entire community are focussed on her,
Ngond Libii causes more consternation – this time by shifting the
responsibility for her husband's death on to the community itself. She
screams out at her assembled clansmen:

Start punishing yourselves by burying him. You killed him. Aren't you all
Ntep's assassins? (pp. 23–4)

This accusation and the frantic search for Ntep's murderer to
which it gives rise (pp. 23–8) is followed by an interlude (pp. 28–34)
characterised by emotional laments in densely poetic language and
made mostly by the deceased's children. Wails Ntep's First Son:

Les larmes, mes pères, les larmes, mes frères, ont souvent un goût de papayes
pourries, leur jus abondant dégoulinant des chairs écrasées et des pépins
s'égrénant comme les secondes et les minutes lors des mauvais jours. (p. 30)

(Tears, my fathers, tears, my brothers, often have the taste of rotten pawpaw
fruits, their abundant juice dripping down their crushed flesh and then seeds
dropping away like seconds and minutes during a bad day!)

In the trance and spirit-possession sequence that follows this
interlude, the dead Ntep Iliga is ritually resurrected. Endowed by
new powers of vision, as it were, he is now able to see the true motives
and character of his clansmen, to see through what he now knows to
be their mask. Thus he discovers beneath his eldest son's studied
indifference to anything political, to any public cause, intense
ambition and a will to dominate others, while all the fulsome praises
heaped on him by the Third Man conceal a violent desire to succeed
him as clan elder. 'They all say the opposite of what they think' (p.
35) is his great discovery.

But also in this sequence (pp. 34–47) various characters under the
intoxicating influence of drum music, lower their guard, so to speak,
and admit to themselves or quite simply become aware of their
hitherto unconscious motives and desires. In other words, they
achieve greater self-knowledge and inner freedom. The play ends
(pp. 47–52) on a note of general reconciliation between Ntep Iliga
and his wife and his community.

It is easy to conclude from *La Puissance d'Um*'s intense preoccupation with Bassa magic and mysticism, from its undeniable and
near-pervasive obscurity that it is a theatrical experiment of little or

no interest to modern African audiences. Ivorian critic Barthélémy Kotchy has said as much (1984: 235). But such a conclusion can only be the result of a partial or impatient reading of the play. For beneath its apparent and, to me, deliberate and unnecessarily mystifying esotericism issues of great social significance are explored. What Werewere Liking has cleverly done, in fact, is to use a traditional African form to prosecute a vigorous campaign against certain traditional values. As Jeanne Dingome has rightly observed about the playwright's use of Bassa myths and rituals,

they serve as symbolic representations of all manner of social conflicts, providing as it were, the backdrop against which higher issues of topical relevance are focussed. (1990: 322)

One such issue in *La Puissance d'Um* is that of female subjugation in traditional Africa. The play enacts the quest for women's emancipation and creativity. If Ngond Libii in whom this quest is embodied is in such a rage, it is because of the realisation – which she can no longer ignore after her husband's death – that her life with him has been a waste. It has been a life unfulfilled, reduced (as tradition prescribes) to working on the farm while her husband idles away his time, and to bearing his children. To the Third Man who, in his recollections, contemptuously dismisses her as a slave girl (the meaning of the words Ngond Libii) lucky to have been married to the noble Ntep, she angrily points out:

Tous ici, vous m'avez vue monter sur le palmier à l'huile. Tous ici, vous m'avez vue défricher mon champ et tous ici vous avez passé du, moins une journée avec Ntep à la ligue des bavards, des fainéants et des soulards. Il n'aurait plus manqué qu'il ne me fasse d'enfants. (p. 17)

(All of you here can remember seeing me up the palm tree. All of you here can remember seeing me farm my fields. All of you here have at least spent a day with Ntep in the league of gossips, idlers and drunks. What else could he do but make me constantly pregnant.)

Elsewhere she complains of her ruined health and dissipated wealth, of the language of force which he used on her, when she was speaking that of love:

Ntep gave away all my livestock and broke my furniture. He exploited my health and I didn't realise it. I preached love while he convinced me that force was more appropriate. (p. 21)

Further, she was meant to be always understanding and forgiving while he made no such reciprocal efforts:

Yes, I had to understand that my husband, like all men, was weak ... and to forgive him for having sex in my bed with my friends. (p. 42)

In short, she concludes to the Old Woman, who eggs her on during her trance to make a clean breast of her frustrations:

The man that I love most is the negation of all the efforts that I've made for him and for our love. Now I want to be respected, to reap what I've sown: dignity. (p. 41)

But Ngond Libii does not revolt only in the name of women. For the very ancestral traditions whose shackles have kept her a prisoner are also responsible, in her view, for ruining many a man, including her husband. Alive, he thought he was a great and respected member of his community; one chosen, as the Third Man recollects, 'by the finger of destiny ... before his birth ... to be the flag-carrier of [their] traditions' (p. 21). But in reality, he was a victim. Ngond Libii is convinced that in his efforts to conform to the traditional image of a man which his community had created for him for their selfish motives, he destroyed his own creative potential and brought misery on himself and his family:

It isn't possible that a man with such potential could have gone through an entire life uncreative in the name of I don't know which tradition. (p. 43)

It is for this reason – which she is also trying to let the 'resurrected' Ntep understand – that she holds them responsible for his death. She gives a long explanation:

Vous commencez par mettre dans la tête d'un pauvre enfant qu'il est l'élu des Dieux. Vous l'engagez au service de votre vanité. Vous l'acculez à l'image de votre propre création ... c'est vous qui l'avez tué. Vous l'avez condamné dans une carcasse qu'il a traînée toute sa vie pour vous protéger, vous et *votre satanée tribu, vos fichues traditions, vos monstrueuses conventions.* (pp. 24–5, emphasis mine)

(You begin by putting into a poor child's head that he is God's chosen one. You then conscript him in the service of your vanity. You force him to conform to your image ... Yes you killed him [i.e., her husband]. You condemned him to a straitjacket that he wore all his life *to protect you, your satanic tribe, your damned traditions, your monstrous practices.*)

By couching the community's responsibility in these terms, Ngond forces it to cast a critical look at itself, to come to a better understanding of the limitations of some of its values. In the terminology of ritual theatre, the community is being 'initiated' into a higher truth. Ntep Iliga's death has become the opportunity for individual and collective stock-taking. It is this revelatory function of hidden or repressed truths performed by the healing rituals of her community that Werewere Liking wishes to see transferred to modern Francophone drama.

Ritual theatre, as Ola Rotimi has observed, 'effervesces with movement, rhythm and spectacle beyond the ordinary' (1981: 77), and Werewere Liking, who is sensitive to this quality of spectacle in Bassa rituals, tries to maintain it in her play. For its total meaning and effect, *La Puissance d'Um* combines both language and a variety of non-linguistic elements. The latter are all meaning-laden, constituting a code by which she communicates. Chief among these elements is song. Although there are many types of song in the play (healing songs, dirges, laments) the kind that particularly stands out is the ritual or sacred song.

A good example of this is 'Me Ngond Ntep Iliga me nol inloo wem Ntep' intoned throughout the play (pp. 15, 23, 29 etc.). A traditional Bassa song about a mythical woman who kills her husband and then unrepentantly defies her community, it constitutes *La Puissance d'Um's* theme song (see Hourantier 1984: 143 on this song). It accompanies important moments of the action, such as when Ngond Libii denounces female subjugation and pleads for a society of creative and not tradition-enslaved individuals.

Another important element in *La Puissance d'Um* is costume. The *lappas* ('pagnes') and their colours which the various participants carry, have great significance. They give information on their wearer's state of mind and on the relations between them. White signifies purity and tradition and it is the colour of the cloth worn by those arch-representatives of tradition the Old Man and the Old Woman. Black, the *Hilun's* (a *griot*-like character), *lappa* represents self-knowledge and it suggests his role in the ritual, which is to coax the participants into an articulate awareness of their repressed desires or ambitions. Red, finally, is the colour of life, of the present. On Ngond Libii and Ntep's children, it indicates self-affirmation and the quest for identity respectively, and in the three men it signifies that ambition for power which, until their trance, remained locked up in their subconscious (on the Bassa symbolism of colours and their role in the play, see Hourantier 1984: 170–5 and her production notes on the play appended to the published play, pp. 54–7).

Equally important to the play is drum music and its accompanying dances. The dances are not meant merely to entertain but to suggest or induce (rather like the music in Soyinka's *Death and the King's Horseman*) the passage by various participants into a state of trance, of 'higher consciousness' as Werewere Liking would prefer it. The music and dance act on their minds, freeing them from inhibition and making it possible for the release of repressed emotions (Hourantier 1984: 175–9).

But vital as these non-linguistic signs are, they are complementary to language, which, of course, remains the principal mode to convey meaning. But language in *La Puissance d'Um* is not, as we already observed, of the transitive type. It is not, in other words, a vehicle for the communication of everyday, factual information. There is, in fact, no dialogue as such between characters in this play. It is the ritualised, poetic language of invocation in

Que Vienne l'amour qui enfante le beau
Que l'Amour investisse nos bouches. (p. 52)

(May the love that giveth birth to the beautiful become reality. May Love taketh over our mouths.)

Of cathartic release, in Ngond Libii's

Laisse couler les eaux de mon angoisse … Oui il me faut comprendre que l'homme est faible, admettre qu'il est méchant avec les autres et sincère avec moi, et lui pardonner de coucher mes amies dans mon lit … Non! Le pardon a des consonances de prison et la compréhension des attitudes de réddition. Malheur a qui perd la tête! Le pardon a un gout de cendres froides et pas de cavités où déposer le pollen, non! … Je ne veux plus rien comprendre, le froid, la solitude, non! Je ne veux plus comprendre personne, O mère! (p. 42)

(Let the waters of my anguish flow … Yes, I had to understand that my husband, like all men, was weak … to admit that he was wicked with others but sincere with me, to forgive him for having sex in my bed with my friends … No! Forgiveness smacks of imprisonment, and understanding of surrender. Woe betide she who loses her head! Forgiveness has the taste of cold ashes and not cavities in which to put pollen, no! I don't want to understand anything – the cold, the loneliness, nothing. I no longer want to understand anyone, O mother.)

of fantasy in the Old Man's

Nous sommes des cieux bleus aux yeux étales et bridés comme les eaux sous la brise.

(We are the blue skies, with eyes large and wrinkled like rippling water under the caress of the wind.)

and finally of celebration in

c'était au pays de la jouissance, c'était au pays de la mort. Il y avait des cieux, il y avait des lieux … Des visages jaunes et des visages couleur de fer … Et ils entonnaient un hymne victorieux, un hymne à la gloire de l'existence. (p. 51)

(It was in the country of pleasure, it was in the country of death. There were skies, there were places … Young faces and iron-coloured faces … And they all intoned a victorious hymn to the glory of existence.)

The emphasis in *La Puissance d'Um* is on the materiality of language, its euphonic, rhythmic and metaphoric, as distinct from its signifying, qualities. By acting on or giving shape to troubled emotions, it soothes and heals. And herein lies its principal function in the play.

Conclusion

In concluding this book, I wish to bring into focus some of the issues studied in the previous chapters. As its title indicates, I have concentrated not only on modern scripted plays, even if most of the book is devoted to them. I have included, both in the interests of presenting a fuller picture of theatrical activity in Francophone Africa and of providing the framework for a better understanding of the literate version of this activity, traditional (ritual and secular) as well as popular forms of performance. In other words, I discuss Francophone drama and theatre as well as theatre *in* Francophone Africa.

The book attempts to go beyond the usual acknowledgement of a relationship between modern drama in French and the traditional theatrical heritage, to probe, in more precise terms, the nature of this relationship. We discovered in the process that if the link (between ritual and modern drama for example) does indeed exist in the area of performance idiom and, occasionally, in that of structure and function (especially in the works of Werewere Liking), it is virtually non-existent in that of vision. On the other hand, we saw a much greater affinity between modern Francophone and traditional drama. Characters, situations, subjects and formal procedures are extensively borrowed from traditional dramatic performances by African playwrights using French in a manner that often makes their plays a mere literate extension or stage adaptation of their source material.

Another topic discussed is the rise, with the advent of Western (French) education, of a African drama in French. From its fairly modest origins at the Ecole William Ponty, this drama developed, in the immediate pre- and post-Independence period, into a major cultural force in the struggle for national self-determination. Its predilection for events and heroes of Africa's past was explained as part of a strategy to reconnect with a glorious heritage and to present as irrelevant the colonial interlude. But Francophone drama, we saw, was soon to move away from its anti-colonial stance. With the problems of Independence emerged a drama that increasingly focussed attention, from the late 1970s onward, on the ills of the new nation-states. In addition to the heroes of yesterday's plays now appeared the rogues and dictators. Parallel to this thematic shift was also one in theatrical style. From being predominantly text-based and highly rhetorical, Francophone drama shifted significantly to being performance-based. The need to be relevant not just to a minority, but to be accessible to the majority of the non-French speaking public led some dramatists to integrate more systematically in their plays hitherto marginalised modes of acting and play-construction characteristic of traditional and modern popular performances. While such an evolution holds promise for the creation of a truly popular modern drama, it will remain only a promise as long as the crucial problem of the language of drama is not resolved.

The French government, which has been the single most important promoter of Francophone drama, from its origins to the present day, is adamant that only dramatists using French will receive its support. The Francophone governments, on the other hand, suspicious of a form which has the potential to reach a mass audience and which has recently become increasingly critical of them, are far from eager to promote it – be it in French or worse still in African languages – except in its government-supervised 'Developmental Theatre' aspect. That the continued development of so vital an art form as the modern theatre should depend on the good will of an external benefactor does not bode well for its long-term sustained growth.

References

LIST OF ABBREVIATIONS

ALA	*Afrique Littéraire et Artistique*
ALT	*African Literature Today*
AUA	*Annales de l'Université d'Abidjan*
BIFAN	*Bulletin de l'Institut Français d'Afrique Noire*
CJAS	*Canadian Journal of African Studies*
CLA	*College Literature Association*
CLE	*Centre du Livre Evangélique*
KRQ	*Kentucky Romance Quarterly*
NEA	*Nouvelles Editions Africaines*
PA	*Présence Africaine*
PNPA	*Peuples noirs, Peuples d'Afrique*
RAL	*Research in African Literatures*
RHLF	*Revue d'Histoire Littéraire de France*
RLC	*Revue de Littérature Comparée*
RLENA	*Revue de Littérature et d'Esthétique négro-africaines*
RPC	*Recherche, Pédagogie, Culture*
RSH	*Revue des Sciences Humaines*
TRI	*Theatre Research International*
WLT	*World Literature Today*

Actes du Colloque sur le Théâtre Négro-Africain, 1971, Paris: PA.

Adé-Ajo, S. 1983, 'L'écrivain africain et ses publics: le cas de Bernard Dadié', *PNPA* 32: 64–99.

Adédéji, J. 1975, 'Le Concert-party au Nigeria et les débuts d'Ogundé', *RHLF* 1: 21–5.

1981, '"Alarinjo": The Traditional Yoruba Travelling Theatre', in Ogunbiyi (ed.), pp. 221–48.

Afrique en créations, 1990, Paris: Ministère de la Coopération et du Développement.

Agyeman, O. K. 1983, 'The Image of Chaka in the Neo-Negritude Drama of Francophone West Africa', *Africana Marburgensia* 16: 36–56.

Akam, N. and Ricard, A. 1981, *Mister Taméklor suivi de Francis le Parisien par le Happy Stars Concert de Lomé*, Paris: SELAF.

Antoine, R. 1984, *La Tragédie du roi Christophe d'Aimé Césaire*, Paris: Bordas.

Apedo-Amah, T. 1985, 'Le Concert-Party: Une pédagogie pour les opprimés', *PNPA* 44: 61–72.

Apter, D. 1968, *Some Conceptual Approaches to the Study of Modernization*, New Jersey: Prentice Hall.

Armah, A. K. 1975, 'Chaka', *Black World* 24: 51–2; 84–90.

Arnold, A.-J. 1986, 'D'Haiti à l'Afrique: La Tragédie du roi Christophe', *RLC* 2: 133–48.

Arnold, M.-J. 1977, *Bamana and Bozo Puppetry of the Segou Region Youth Societies*, Lafayette: Purdue University.

Artaud, A. 1958, *The Theatre and Its Double*, New York: Grove Press.

Atta-Koffi, R. 1969, *Le Trône d'Or*, Paris: ORTF.

Auclaire, E. 1986, *Jean-Marie Serreau, découvreur de théâtre*, Paris: L'Arbre Verdoyant.

Bâ, A.-H. 1981, 'The Living Tradition' in Ki-Zerbo (ed.), pp. 166–203.

Bâ, T. 1980, *Bilbassy*, Dakar-Abidjan: NEA.

Bablet, D. (ed.) 1970, *Les Voies de la création théâtrale II*, Paris: CNRS.

Badian, S. 1962, *La Mort de Chaka*, Paris: PA.

Bailey, M. 1987, 'Césaire: père du théâtre africain' in Leiner (ed.) pp. 239–50.

Bailey, M. W. 1992, *The Ritual Theatre of Aimé Césaire: Mythic Structures and Dramatic Imagination*, Tübingen: Gunter Narr Verlag.

Bakhtin, M. 1970, *L'Œuvre de Francois Rabelais et la Culture populaire au Moyen-âge et sous la Renaissance*, Paris: Gallimard.

Balandier, G. 1955, *Sociologie Actuelle de l'Afrique Noire*, Paris: Presses Universitaires de France.

1968, *Daily Life in the Kingdom of the Kongo*, London: Allen and Unwin.

1970, *Political Anthropology*, New York: Vintage Books.

Bame, K. N. 1975, 'Des origines et du développement du concert-party au Ghana', *RHLF* 1: 10–20.

Banham, M. (ed.) 1988, *Cambridge Guide to World Theatre*, Cambridge University Press.

Banham, M. and Wake, C. 1976, *African Theatre Today*, London: Pitman.

Baños-Rõbles, B. 1990, '8 années de coopération au Congo', *Notre Librairie* 102: 134–9.

Barber, K. 1987, 'Popular Arts in Africa', *African Studies Review* 30, 3: 1–78.

Bédé, J. 1975, 'Le théâtre de Guillaume Oyono-Mbia', *CJAS* 9, 3: 531–6.

Beik, J. 1987, *The Hausa Theatre in Niger*, New York and London: Garland Publishing.

Bemba, S. 1972, *L'Homme qui tua le crocodile*, Yaoundé: CLE.

Bénamou, M. 1975, 'Demiurgic Imagery in Césaire's Theatre', *PA* 93: 165–7.

Benon, B. 1990, 'Deux Experiences Théâtrales: Jean-Pierre Guingané et le

Théâtre de la Fraternité et Prosper Kompaoré et l'Atelier Théâtre Burkinabé', *Notre Librairie* 101: 76–81.

Benston, K. 1984, 'The Topos of (Un) Naming' in Gates (ed.), pp. 150–63.

Biddle, B. and Thomas, E. (eds.) 1966, *Role Theory: Concepts and Research*, New York: John Wiley.

Biebuyck, D. 1971, *The Mwindo Epic from the Banyanga*, Berkeley: UCLA Press.

Bjornson, R. 1990, 'Writing and Popular Culture in Cameroon' in Granquist R. (ed.), pp. 19–34.

  1991, *The African Quest for Freedom and Identity*, Bloomington: Indiana University Press.

Blachère, J.-C. and Sow-Fall, A. 1977, *Les Genres littéraires par les textes*, Abidjan-Dakar: NEA.

Blair, D. 1974, 'The Shaka Theme in Dramatic Literature in French from West Africa', *African Studies* 33: 113–41.

  1976, *African Literature in French*, Cambridge University Press.

Boal, A. 1979, *Theatre of the Oppressed*, New York: Urizen.

Bonneau, R. 1972, 'Panorama du théâtre ivoirien', *ALA* 23: 2–11.

  1973, *Ecrivains, Cinéastes et Artistes Ivoriens: Aperçu bibliographique*, Abidjan-Dakar: NEA.

Borgomano, M. 1987, 'Des femmes écrivent', *Notre Librairie* 2, 87 (Apr.–Jun.): 65–9.

Bouelet, R. S. 1987, *Espaces et dialectiques du héroes césairiens*, Paris: L'Harmattan.

Bradby, D. 1984, *Modern French Drama 1940–1980*, Cambridge University Press.

Brink, J. 1977, 'Bamana Kote-tlon Theatre', *African Arts* 10, 4: 36, 61–5.

  1978, 'Communicating Ideology in Bamana Rural Theatre Performance', *RAL*: 382–94.

Brunschwig, L. 1962, 'Histoire, passé et frustration en Afrique', *Annales Economies, Sociétés, Civilisations* 17, 5: 873–4.

Burness, D. 1976, *Shaka, King of the Zulus in African Literature*, Washington: Three Continents Press.

Burns, E. 1972, *Theatricality: A study of Convention in the Theatre and in Social Life*, London: Longman.

Champion-Vincent, V. 1967, 'L'image du Dahomey dans la presse française', *Cahier d'Etudes Africaines* 7, 25: 25–58.

Case, F. I. 1975a, 'Le théâtre d'Aimé Césaire', *Revue Romane* 10, 1: 10–16.

  1975b, 'Sango Oba Ko So: Le vodoun dans La Tragédie du roi Christophe', *Cahiers Césairiens* 2: 9–24.

Césaire, A. 1956, *Cahier d'un retour au pays natal*, Paris: PA.

  1962, *Toussaint Louverture: La Révolution Française et le problème colonial*, Paris: Présence Africaine.

  1970, *La Tragédie du roi Christophe*, Paris: PA.

  1973, *Une Saison au Congo*, Paris: Seuil.

Chemain, R. 1977, 'A propos de Le Zoulou: Entrevue avec Tchicaya U'Tamsi', *Notre Librairie* 38: 33–41.

Chemain, R. and Chemain-Dégrange, A. 1979, *Panorama critique de la littérature congolaise contemporaine*, Paris: PA.

Chévrier, Jacques 1984, *Littérature nègre*, Paris: Nathan.

Clark-Bekederemo, J. P. *The Song of a Goat* and *Ozidi* in Irele, A. (ed.), 1991, *J. P. Clark-Békédéremo, Collected Plays 1964–1988*, Washington: Howard University Press.

Condé, M. 1978, 'Naissance du théâtre en l'Afrique de l'Ouest', *Notre Librairie* 41: 29–35.

Conteh-Morgan, J. 1980, 'Politics as Tragedy: Aimé Césaire's *La Tragédie du roi Christophe* in the Light of Albert Camus' *L'Homme révolté*', *Ba Shiru* 11, 2: 98–105.

1983, 'A Note on the Image of the Builder in Aimé Césaire's *La Tragédie du roi Christophe*', *The French Review* 52, 2: 224–30.

1984, 'Albert Camus, Aimé Césaire and the Tragedy of Revolution', *ALT* 14: 49–59.

1985, 'History or Literature: A Critical Study of Bernard Dadié's *Beatrice du Congo*' *CJAS* 19, 2: 387–97.

1992, 'French-Language African Drama and the Oral Tradition: Trends and Issues', *ALT* 18: 115–32.

1994, 'Francophone African Drama' in M. Banham *et al.* (eds.) *Cambridge Handbook to African and Caribbean Drama*, Cambridge University Press.

forthcoming, 'Tragic Drama or Morality Play: A Study of Bernard Dadié's *Les Voix dans le vent*' in Janis Mayes *et al.* (ed.), *Essays in Honour of Bernard Dadié*, Washington: Three Continents Press.

Cornevin, R. 1970, *Le Théâtre en Afrique noire et à Madagascar*, Paris: Le Livre Africain.

1979–80, 'Théâtre et traditions africaines, le mythe historique africain dans la tradition orale: son passage au théâtre, à la radio et à la television', *ALA* 54–5: 49–52.

1982–3, 'Le théâtre de langue française en Afrique noire', *Culture Française* 31–2: 18–32.

1984, 'Littérature et théâtre en Afrique', *Artes Populares*, pp. 531–50.

Coulon, V. 1984, 'Francophone Literature' in Lindfors (ed.), pp. 123–44.

Crow, B. 1983, *Studying Drama*, London: Longman.

Crowder, M. (ed.) 1989, *West African Resistance*, London: Hutchinson.

Cuche, F. X. 1970, 'L'Utilisation des techniques du théâtre traditional africain dans le théâtre négro-africain moderne' in *Actes du Colloque d'Abidjan*, pp. 137–42.

D'Aby, F. D. 1988, *Le Théâtre en Côte d'Ivoire*, Abidjan: CEDA.

D'Alméida, L. P. 1976, 'Le bestiaire symbolique dans *Une Saison au Congo*', *Présence Francophone* 13: 93–105.

Dadié, B. 1966, *Légendes et Poèmes*, Paris: Seghers.

1970a, *Béatrice du Congo*, Paris: PA.

1970b, *Monsieur Thogo-Gnini*, Paris: PA.

1970c, *Les Voix dans le Vent*, Paris: PA.

1973, *Iles de Tempête*, Paris: PA.

1979, *Assémien Déhylé: Roi du Sanwi*, Abidjan: CEDA.

Dahl, M. 1987, *Political Violence in Drama: Classical Models, Contemporary Variations*, Ann Arbor: UMI Research Institute.

Dailly, C. 1970, 'L'Histoire' in *Actes du Colloque sur le Théâtre Négro Africain*, pp. 87–93.

Dalembert, F.-J. 1990, 'Afrique le bal raté', *Notre Librairie* 102: 110–13.

Deberre, C. 1984, *La Tragédie du roi Christophe d'Aimé Césaire étude critique*, Paris, Abidjan: NEA.

Deffontaines, T.-M. 1990, 'Théâtre-Forum au Burkina Faso et au Mali', *Notre Librairie* 102: 90–3.

Delafosse, M. 1916, 'Contribution à l'étude du théâtre chez les noirs', *Bulletin du Comité d'Etudes Historiques et Scientifiques de l'AOF*: 352–5.

Derrida, J. 1978, *Writing and Difference*, trans. Alan Bass, Chicago: University of Chicago Press.

Dervain, E. 1968, *La Reine scélérate suivi de la Langue et le Scorpion*, Yaoundé: CLE.

1969, *Abra Pokou*, Yaoundé: CLE-Théâtre.

Dia, A.-C., 1947, 1966, *Les Derniers jours de Lat Dior suivi de La Mort du Damel*, Paris: PA.

Diabaté, M. M. 1972, *Une Si belle leçon de patience*, Paris: ORTF.

Diawara, G. 1981, *Panorama critique du théâtre malien dans son évolution*, Senegal: Sankoré.

1990a, 'Tendé et Takouba, Théâtres tamasheq et bellah' *Notre Librairie*, 102: 28–30.

1990b, 'Le Théâtre rituel malien en tant qu'acte social' in *Théâtres Africains*, Paris: Silex, pp. 51–8.

Digome, J. 1990, 'Ritual and Modern Dramatic Expression in Cameroon: The Plays of Werewere Liking', in Janos Riesz and Alain Ricard (eds.), pp. 317–26.

Diop, B. 1958, *Les Contes d'Amadou Coumba*, Paris: PA.

1977, *L'Os de Mor Lam*, Dakar/Abidjan: Nouvelles Editions Africaines.

Doho, G. 1989, 'Les Funérailles Bamiléké: Elements de Théâtralité', *Notre Librairie*, 99: 78–82.

Domenach, J.-M. 1967, *Le Retour du tragique*, Paris: Seuil.

Dunton, C. 1992, *Make Man Talk True: Nigerian Drama in English since 1970*, London: Hans Zell.

Dutoit, F. 1967, 'Quand le Congo ne sera qu'une saison que le sang assaisonne', *PA*: 64: 138–45.

Duvignaud, J. 1965, *Sociologie du théâtre: Essai sur les ombres collectives*, Paris: PUF.

1973, 'La Révolution, théâtre tragique' in Jacquot (ed.), pp. 82–7.

Echeruo, M. 1981, 'The Dramatic Limits of Igbo Ritual', in Ogunbiyi (ed.), pp. 136–48.

Edebiri, U. 1975, 'L'espérance tacite de Jean Pliya, écrivain dahoméen', *ALA* 37: 9–13.

1984a, 'Le pidgin dans le théâtre francophone', *PNPA* 40: 97–114.

1984b, 'The Development of the Theatre in French-Speaking West Africa', *TRI* 9, 3: 168–80.

El-Nouty, H. 1983, 'L'Exil d'Albouri' in Ambroise Kom (ed.), p. 232.

Etherton, M. 1979, 'Trends in African Theatre', *ALT* 10: 57–85.

1982, *The Development of African Drama*, London: Hutchinson.

Eyoh, H. N. 1981, 'Contemporary Cameroonian Drama 1959–1979', *Annales de la Faculté des Lettres et Sciences Humaines de l'Université de Yaoundé* 10: 5–17.

Fage, J. D. (ed.) 1971, *Africa Discovers Her Past*, Oxford University Press.

Fall, M. 1984, *Chaka ou le Roi visionnaire*, Abidgan-Dakar: NEA.

Fanon, F. 1970, *Les Damnés de la terre*, Paris: Maspéro.

Finnegan, R. 1970, *Oral Literature in Africa*, Oxford University Press.

Foté, H. M. *et al.* 1979, 'Conscience et Histoire en Afrique', *Godo Godo* 4–5: 9–30.

Fuyet, H. and N. and Levilain, G. and M. 1973, 'Décolonisation et classes sociales dans *La Tragédie du roi Christophe*', *French Review* 46, 6: 1106–16.

Gates, L. (ed.) 1984, *Black Literature and Literary Theory*, London: Methuen.

Gatémbo, Nu-Kate, 1984, 'Essai de périodisation du théâtre négro-africain francophone', *Ecriture Française* 15–16: 34–43.

Gbéasor, T. 1975, rpt 1984, 'Introduction' to Zinsou, pp. ix–xxv.

Gellner, E. 1961, 'The Struggle for Morocco's Past', *The Middle East Journal* 15, 1: 79–90.

Gérard, A. 1971, *Four African Literatures*. Berkeley: California University Press.

(ed.) 1986, *English Language Writing in Sub-Saharan Africa*, vol. 1, Budapest: Akadémiai Kiado.

Glissant, E. 1961, *Monsieur Toussaint*, Paris: Seuil.

Godry, S. 1977, 'Littérature noire d'expression française et émancipation des peuples: le cas de *L'Exil d'Albouri* de Cheik A. Ndao', *AUA* Série D, 10: 207–29.

Goffman, E. 1959, *The Presentation of Self in Everyday Life*, New York: Anchor Books.

Gooch, G. P. 1928, *History and Historians in the Nineteenth Century*, London: Longmans Green.

Gordon, D. 1971, *Self-Determination and History in the Third World*, Princeton University Press.

Gorer, G. 1949, *Africa Dances*, London: John Lehmann.

Götrick, K. 1984, *Apidan Theatre and Modern Drama*, Göteborg: Almqvist and Wiksell.

Graff, G. 1980, *Poetic Statement and Critical Dogma*, Chicago and London: The University of Chicago Press.

Graham-White, A. 1970, 'Ritual and drama in Africa', *Educational Theatre Journal*, 22: 339–49.

1974, *The Drama of Black Africa*, New York: Samuel French.

Granderson, C. 1978, 'The Image of the Chief in Francophone drama' in Oyin Ogunba and Abiola Irele (eds.) pp. 73–90.

Granquist, R. (ed.) 1990, *Signs and Signals: Popular Culture in Africa*, Stockholm: Umeå University.

Gugelberger, G. M. (ed.) 1985, *Marxism and African Literature*, Trenton: Africa World Press.

Guingané, J. P. 1990, 'Du Manuscript à la scène', *Notre Librairie*, 101: 67–72.

Hale, T. 1987, 'Dramaturgie et public: La nature interactive du théâtre d'Aimé Césaire' in Leiner (ed.), pp. 195–200.

Hama, B. and Ki-Zerbo, J. 1981, 'The Place of History in African Society' in Ki-Zerbo (ed.), pp. 43–52.

Harris, J. 1981, 'Toward a New Senegalese Theatre,' *The Drama Review* 25, 4: 13–18.

Harris, R. 1973, *L'Humanisme dans le théâtre d'Aimé Césaire*, Sherbrooke: Naaman.

Hawkins, H. 1986, 'Césaire's Lesson about Decolonisation in *La Tragédie du roi Christophe*', *CLA* 30: 144–53.

Hawkins, P. 1991, 'Werewere Liking at the Villa Ki-Yi', *African Affairs* 90: 207–22.

1992–3, 'Un "neo-primitivisme" Africain? L'Exemple de Werewere Liking', *RSH* 227: 233–41.

Heusch, L. 1958, *Essai sur le symbolisme de l'inceste royal en Afrique*, Brussels: Institut de Sociologie.

Heuvel, V. 1991, *Performance Drama/Dramatizing Performance*, Ann Arbor: University of Michigan.

Heywood, C. (ed.) 1976, *Papers on African Literature*, London: Africa Educational Trust.

Hilton, A. 1985, *The Kingdom of Kongo*, Oxford: Clarendon Press.

Horn, A. 1981, 'Ritual Drama and the Theatrical: The Case of Bori Spirit Mediumship' in Ogunbiya (ed.), pp. 181–202.

Hourantier, M.-J. 1984, *Du Rituel au Théâtre-Rituel*, Paris: L'Harmattan.

1990, 'Portrait: Francoise Kourilsky et L'Ubu Theater de New York', *Théâtre Sud* 2: 131–9.

and Liking, W. 1981, 'Les vestiges d'un Kotéba', *RLENA* 3: 35–50.

and Liking, W., and Schérer, Jacques 1979 *Du rituel à la scène chez les Bassa du Cameroun*, Paris: Nizet.

Huannou, A. 1984, *La Littérature Béninoise de langue française*, Paris: Karthala, ACCT.

Huguet, D. and Diawara, G. 1984, 'Bibliographie (Littérature)' *Notre Librairie*, 75/76: 241–2.

Hunt, G. 1985, 'Two African Aesthetics: Wole Soyinka vs. Amilcar Cabral' in Gugelberger (ed.), pp. 64–93.

Hussein, I. 1970, *Kinjeketile*, Oxford University Press.

Hyokaa, T. 1982-3, 'History as Drama: The African Playwright' *Kuka* 82-3: 18-26.

Idowu, B. E. 1966, *Olodumare, God in Yoruba Belief*, London: Longman.

Imperato, P. J. 1970, 'The Dance of Tyi Wara' *African Arts / Arts d'Afrique* 4: 13, 71.

Innes, C. 1981, *Holy Theatre*, Cambridge University Press.

Irele, A. 1973, 'Negritude Revisited' in Paul F. Nursey-Bray (ed.) pp. 22-43.

1990, 'Orality, Literacy and African Literature' in Janos Riesz and Alian Ricard (eds.), pp. 251-63.

Jaccard, A.-C. 1989, 'Des Textes novateurs, la littérature feminine', *Notre Librairie*, 99 (Oct.-Dec.): 151-61.

Jacquot, J. (ed.) 1973, *Le Théâtre moderne II*, Paris: CNRS.

James, C. L. R. 1938, 1984, *The Black Jacobins*, London: Allison and Busby.

Jefferson, L. 1982, 'A Clash of Codes: *L'Œil* by Bernard Zadi Zaourou', *The French Review*, 55(6): 824-34.

Jeyifo, B. 1984, *The Yoruba Travelling Theatre*, Lagos: Federal Ministry of Social Development.

1985a, 'Tragedy, History and Ideology' in Georg Gugelberger (ed.) pp. 94-109.

1985b, *The Truthful Lie*, London: Beacon.

(ed.), 1988, *Wole Soyinka: Art, Dialogue and Outrage*, Ibadan: New Horn Press.

Johnson, A. 1983, 'Two Historical Plays from West Africa', *Komparatistische Hefte* 8: 39-54.

Johnson, J. 1986, *The Epic of Son-Jara*, Bloomington: Indiana University Press.

Joulia, D. 1984, 'Le grand escargot bambara', *Notre Librairie*, 75-6: 135-9.

Jukpor, B. 1982, 'Le rôle de l'Ecole William Ponty dans le développement du théâtre ouest-africain francophone', *Présence Francophone* 24: 47-64.

Kampaoré, P. 1990, 'Le Théâtre d'Intervention Sociale en Afrique: Expérience de la Troupe "Atelier-Théâtre Burkinabé" au Burkina Faso', in Richard and Mauzauric (eds.), pp. 147-60.

Kane, C.-H. 1961, *L'Aventure ambiguë*, Paris: Julliard.

Kane, M. 1971, 'L'actualité de la littérature africaine d'expression française', *PA* (Numéro special): 227-8.

Kasoma, K. *Black Mamba Two* in Etherton, M. (ed.) 1975, *African Plays for Playing*, vol. II, London: Heinemann.

Kesteloot, L. 1964, '*La Tragédie du roi Christophe* ou les indépendances africaines au miroir d'Haiti', *PA* 51: 131-45.

1971a, 'Les formes théâtrales dans la vie africaine traditionnelle' in *Actes du Colloque sur le Théâtre Négro-Africain*, pp. 21-24.

1971b, 'Les thèmes principaux du théâtre africain moderne' in *Actes du Colloque sur le Théâtre Négro-Africain*, pp. 51-4.

and Barthélémy Kotchy 1973, *Aimé Césaire, l'homme et l'œuvre*, Paris: PA.

et al. (eds.) 1972, *Da Monzon de Ségou, épopée Bambara*, vol. IV, Paris: F. Nathan.

Ki-Zerbo, J. (ed.) 1981, *UNESCO General History of Africa I*, London: Heinemann; Paris: UNESCO.

Kirby, E. T. (ed.) 1969, *Total Theatre*, New York: Dutton.

Klaffe, G. 1982–3, 'Le théâtre de Césaire: L'exploitation du fait historique dans le théâtre', *Culture Française* 31–2: 114–22.

Knight, V. 1972, 'The West Indian Attitude to Tragedy: The Example of Aimé Césaire', *African Studies Association of the West Indian Bulletin* 5: 60–9.

Kodjo, L. 1981, 'Les personnages de Ponty', *RLENA* 3: 51–70.

Kom, A. (ed.) 1983, *Dictionnaire des œuvres littéraires négro Africaines de langue française*, Sherbrooke: Naaman, ACCT.

Konaké, S. 1973, *Le Grand Destin de Soundjata*, Paris: ORTF.

Konaté, M. 1985, *L'Or du Diable suivi de le Cercle au Féminin*, Paris: Harmattan.

Kotchy, B. 1979, 'Les sources du théâtre négro-Africain', *RLENA* 2: 91–103.

1984, 'New Trends in the Theatre of the Ivory Coast 1972–1983', *TRI* 9, 3: 232–53.

1989, 'Le jeu dramatique africain moderne entre l'oralité et le textuel', *Theatre Sud* 1: 105–12.

Kotchy-Nguéssan, B. 1976, 'Sémiologie du temps et de l'espace dans le théâtre de Bernard Dadié', *AUA* Série D4: 269–82.

1984, *La Critique sociale dans l'œuvre théâtrale de Dadié*, Paris: L'Harmattan.

Koudjo, B. 1983, 'Kondo le requin de Jean Pliya, nouvelle version', *Notre Librairie* 69: 109–10.

Koudou, A. 1981, '*Iles de Tempête*: Schéma idéologique', *AUA* Série D14: 187–93.

Kunene, M. 1979, *Emperor Shaka the Great: A Zulu Epic*, London: Heinemann.

Kuper, L. 1975, *Race, Class and Power: Ideology and Revolutionary Change in Plural Societies*, Chicago: Aldine.

Labouret, H., Travélé, M. 1928, 'Le Theatre Mandingue', *Africa* 1: 73–97.

Laroche, M. 1973, '*La Tragédie du roi Christophe* du point de vue de l'histoire d'Haiti', *Etudes Littéraires* 6, 1: 35–47.

Laye, C. 1971, *The Dark Child*, trans. James Kirkup and Ernest Jones, New York: Farrar, Strauss and Giroux.

Leclerc, G. 1971, *Anthropologie et Colonialisme*, Paris: Fayard.

Legum, C. 1962, 'Forward', Lumumba, pp. vii–xxix.

Leiner, J. (ed.) 1987, *Aimé Césaire ou l'athanor d'un alchémiste*, Paris: Caribbéennes.

1993, *Aimé Césaire, le terreau primordial*, Tübingen: Gunter Narr Verlag.

Leloup, J. 1973, *Guédio*, Yaoundé: CLE.

1982, 'La Naissance du théâtre en Afrique: Théâtre traditionnel ou préthéâtre', *RPC* 61: 89–99.

1990, 'Tradition et modernité dans le théâtre africain: la résolution d'une antinomie', in Richard and Mauzauric (eds.), pp. 39–50.

Lierde, Jan 1975, 'Patrice Lumumba, Leader and Friend' *PA* 93: 60–8.

Ligier, F. 1982, 'La politique de la stimulation. Théâtre et radio: une collaboration positive', *RPC* 61: 30–44.

1989, 'Le Kotéba traditionnel', *Théâtre Sud* 1: 149–53.

Liking, W. 1979a, *La Puissance d'Um*, Abidjan: CEDA.

1979b, *La Queue du diable* in Marie-José Hourantier, Werewere Liking, Jacques Schérer.

1979c, 'Le rituel du "Mbak" de Nsondo Sagbégué' in Marie-José Hourantier, Werewere-Liking, Jacques Schérer, pp. 85–98.

1980, *Du Sommeil d'Injuste* in *Une Nouvelle Terre*, Dakar: Nouvelles Editions Africaines.

Lindenberger, H. 1975, *Historical Drama – The Relation of Literature and Reality*, Chicago University Press.

Lindfors, B. (ed.) 1984, *Research Priorities in African Literatures*, Munich–New York–London–Paris: Zell.

Little, R. 1990, 'Césaire's Hammarskjöld and an Unattributed Quotation in *Une Saison au Congo*, *French Studies Bulletin* 35: 13–17.

1992, 'A Further Unacknowledged Quotation in Césaire: Echoes of Ourika', *French Studies Bulletin* 43: 131–15.

Lombard, J. 1965, *Structures de type féodale en Afrique Noire*, Paris: Mouton.

Lubin, M. 1984, 'L'histoire d'Haiti dans la dramaturgie africaine: *Iles de Tempête*', *Conjonction* 160: 17–22.

Lukács, G. 1962, *The Historical Novel*, London: Penguin.

Lumumba, P. 1962, *Congo my Country*, London: Pall Mall.

Magnier, B. 1976, 'Bio-bibliographie de Dadié, *Présence Francophone* 13: 49–62.

1985, 'A la rencontre de Werewere-Liking', *Notre Librairie*: 5 ans de littératures africaines 1979–1984 79 (Apr.–Jun.): 17–21.

Maiga, Moussa, 1984, 'Le Kotéba', *Notre Librairie* 75–6: 131–4.

Malanda, A. 1980, 'Le mythe et l'histoire dans le théâtre africain d'expression française', *Le Mois en Afrique* 247–8: 116–26.

Maupoil, B. 1937, 'Le théâtre Dahoméen: les auteurs-acteurs de l'Ecole William Ponty', *Outre-Mer* 4: 301–18.

Mbom, C. 1979, *Le Théâtre d'Aimé Césaire*, Paris: Nathan.

1987, 'La femme dans le théâtre Aimé Césaire' in Leiner (ed.) pp. 223–37.

Meillassoux, C. 1964, 'The "Kotéba" of Bamako', *PA* (English edition) 52: 28–61.

Melone, T. 1971, 'La vie africaine et le langage théâtral' in *Actes du Colloque sur le Théâtre Négro-Africain*, pp. 143–54.

Memel-Fote, H. 1971, 'Anthropologie du théâtre négro-africain traditionnel' in *Actes du Colloque sur le Théâtre Négro-Africain*, pp. 25–30.

Memmi, A. 1957, rpt 1973, *Portrait du Colonisé*, Paris: Payot.

Menga, G. 1969a, *La Marmite de Koka Mbala*, Paris: ORTF.

1969b, *L'Oracle*, Paris: ORTF.

1980, 'Le théâtre moderne au Congo', *Ethnopsychologie* 35: 81–6.

Mercier, R., Battestini, S. and M. 1964, *Bernard Dadié*, Paris: Fernand Nathan.

Midiohouan G. 1983, 'Le théâtre négro-africain d'expression française' *PNPA* 31: 54–78.

Miller, C. 1985, *Blank Darkness: Africanist Discourse*, University of Chicago Press.

Monteil, V. 1966, 'Le Dyolof et Albouri Ndyaye', *BIFAN* 3–4: 615–30.

Moore, G. 1980, *Twelve African Writers*, London: Hutchinson.

Morawski, K. 1962, *Le Théâtre historique moderne en France*, Warsaw: Panstwowe Wydawnicto Naukowe.

Moreau, A. 1987, 'Le bouc émissaire dans le théâtre de Césaire' in Leiner (ed.), pp. 269–82.

Morris, R. 1966, 'A Typology of Norms', in Biddle and Thomas (eds.), pp. 110–12.

Morrison, J. 1991, 'Forum Theatre in West Africa: An Alternative Medium of Information Exchange', *RAL* 22, 3: 29–40.

Mouralis, B. 1974, 'L'image de l'indépendence haitienne dans la littérature négro-africaine', *RLC* 3–4: 504–35.

1981, *Littérature et Développement*, Lille University Press.

1986, 'William Ponty Drama' in Albert Gérard (ed.) pp. 130–41.

Mu-daba, Yoka Lye 1967, 'Le griot dans le théâtre africain', *Présence Francophone* 13: 63–71.

Mudimbe, Y.-V. 1988, *The Invention of Africa*, Bloomington: University of Indiana Press.

Mudimbe-Boyi, M. 1976, '*Béatrice du Congo* de Bernard Dadié: signe du temps ou piéce à clé', *ALA* 35: 19–36.

Mudunku, M. 1984, 'Les procédés dramatiques dans *La Tragédie du roi Christophe*, *Ecriture française dans le monde*', 15–16: 28–34.

Mulikita, F. 1967, *Shaka Zulu*, London: Longman.

Naville, P. 'Aimé Césaire et Jean-Marie Serreau, un acte politique et poétique: *La Tragédie du roi Christophe et Une saison au Congo*' in Denis Bablet (ed.), pp. 239–96.

Ndao, C. 1967, *L'Exil d'Albouri suivi de la Décision*, Paris: P. J. Oswald.

1973, *Le Fils de l'Almamy suivi de La Case de l'Homme*, Paris: P. J. Oswald.

Ndébéka, M., 1973, *Le Président*, Paris: P. J. Oswald.

1987, *Equatorium*, Paris: PA.

Ndédi-Penda, P. 1971, *Le Fusil*, Paris: ORTF.

N'Diayé, B. 1970, *Les Castes au Mali*, Bamako: Editions Populaires.

Ndiaye, R. 1985, 'Bibliographie de la littérature sénégalaise écrite', *Notre Librairie* 81 (1985), pp. 173–4.

N'dumbé III, K. A. 1973, *Kafra-Biatanga*, Paris: P. J Oswald.

1976, *Lisa, la Putain de*, Paris: P. J. Oswald.

Ndzie, P. 1985a, 'Le théâtre politique, en Afrique noire et son expression dans la langue française' in *Quel Théâtre pour le Développement en Afrique*, pp. 93–116.

1985b, 'Psychiatrie et théâtrothérapie dans la médecine en Afrique noire' in *Quel Théâtre pour le Développement in Afrique*, pp. 60–74.

Neale, C. 1985, *Writing 'Independent History'*, New York: Greenwood Press.

Nénékhaly-Camara, C. 1970, *Continent d'Afrique suivi d'Amazoulou*, Paris: P. J. Oswald.

Ngal, M. à M. 1970, 'Le théâtre d'Aimé Césaire: une dramaturgie de la décolonisation', *RSH* 35: 613–36.

1975, *Aimé Césaire, un homme à recherche d'une patrie*, Dakar-Abidjan: NEA.

1985, 'Aimé Césaire devant le grand public africain francophone' in M. à M. Ngal and M. Steins (eds.), pp. 163–202.

Ngugi, Wa Thiongo 1972, *Homecoming: Essays on African and Caribbean Literature, Culture and Politics*, London: Heinemann.

Ngugi, Wa Thiongo, Mugo, M. 1977, *The Trial of Dedan Kimathi*, London: Heinemann.

Ngugi, Wa Thiongo 1986, *Decolonising the Mind: The Politics of Language in African Literature*, London: Heinemann.

Niane, D.-T. 1960, 1971, *Soundjata ou l'epopée mandingue*, Paris: PA.

1971, *Sikasso ou La Dernière Citadelle, suivi de Chaka*, Paris: P. J. Oswald.

Nicholls, D. 1979, *From Dessalines to Duvalier: Race, Colour and National Independence in Haiti*, Cambridge University Press.

Nietzsche, F. 1967, *The Birth of Tragedy*, New York: Alfred Knopf, Inc. and Random House.

Njoya, N. 1973, *Dairou IV*, Yaoundé: CLE.

Nkashama, N. 1979, *La Littérature africaine écrite*, Paris: Saint Paul.

Nokan, C. 1970, *Abraha Pokou ou Une Grande Africaine suivi de La Voix grave d'Ophimoi*, Paris: P. J. Oswald.

Nursey-Bray, P. F. (ed.) 1973, *Aspects of Africa's Identity: Five Essays*. Makerere Institute of Social Research.

Obumselu, B. 1976, 'Mofolo's *Chaka* and the Folk Tradition' in Christopher Heywood (ed.) pp. 33–44.

Oddon, M. 1973, 'Le théâtre de la décolonisation' in Jean Jacquot (ed.), pp. 85–101.

Ogunba, O. and Irele, A. (eds.) 1978, *Theatre in Africa*, Ibadan University Press.

Ogunbiyi, Y. (ed.) 1981, *Drama and Theatre in Nigeria: A Critical Source Book*, Lagos: Nigeria Magazine.

Ojo-Adé, F. 1974, 'Le théâtre engagé de Bernard Dadié, *ALA* 31: 67–75.

Okeh, P. 1982, 'Du sens au tragique: une vue sémiotique de Jusqu' *à nouvel avis*, comédie de Guillaume Oyono-Mbia', *Sémiotica* 42, 2/4: 215–33.

Okpewho, I. 1979, *The Epic in Africa*, New York: Columbia University Press.

1992, *African Oral Literature: Background, Character and Continuities*, Bloomington: Indiana University Press.

Ongom, M. 1985, *Comprendre Trois prétendants ... un mari de Guillaume Oyono-Mbia*, Paris: Saint Paul.

Ormond, J. 1967, 'Héros de l'impossible et de l'absolu', *Les Temps Modernes* 23, 259: 1049–73.

Osofisan, F. 1977, *The Chattering and the Song*, Ibadan: Ibadan University Press.

1982, *No More the Wasted Breed* in *Morountodun and Other Plays*, Ikeja: Longman Nigeria Ltd.

Owusu-Sarpong, A. 1987, *Le Temps historique dans l'œuvre théâtrale d'Aimé Césaire*, Sherbrooke: Naaman.

Oyono-Mbia, G. 1964, *Trois prétendants ... un mari*, Yaoundé: CLE.

1971, *Notre Fille ne se mariera pas*, Paris: ORTF.

1973, *Jusqu'à nouvel avis*, Yaoundé: CLE.

Pageaux, D.-H. 1984, *Images et Mythes d'Haiti: Alejo Carpentier, Aimé Césaire, Bernard Dadié*, Paris: L'Harmattan.

1987, '*La Tragédie du roi Christophe*: De la tragédie au mythe', in Leiner (ed.), pp. 269–82.

Pairault, C. 1971, 'Où trouver le théâtre' in *Actes du Colloque sur le Théâtre Négro-Africain*, pp. 15–20.

Patterson, O. 1971, 'Rethinking Black History' *Harvard Educational Review* 41, 3: 297–335.

Pliya, J. 1971, *L'Arbre fétiche*, Yaoundé: CLE.

1973, *La Sécretaire particulière*, Yaoundé: CLE.

1975, *Manuel d'Histoire du Dahomey*, Issy-les-Moulineaux: Saint Paul.

1977, *Le Chimpanzé amoureux, Le Rendez-vous, La Palabre de la dernière chance*, Issy-les-Moulineaux: Saint Paul.

1981, *Kondo le requin*, Yaoundé: CLE.

Pont-Hubert, C. 1990, 'Bakary Sangaré, Comédien malien à Paris' *Notre Librairie* 102: 114–19.

1990, 'Gabriel Garran et le Théâtre International de Langue Française', *Notre Librairie* 102: 102–9.

Premduth, B. 1980, '*Une Saison au Congo*: Problématique de la décolonisation' *Indian Cultural Review*: 33–46.

Prouteaux, M. 1929, 'Premiers essais de théâtre chez les indigènes de Côte d'Ivoire', *Bulletin du Comité d'Etudes Historiques et Scientifiques de l'Afrique Occidentale Française*, pp. 448–75.

Quel Théâtre pour le développement en Afrique 1985, Dakar, Abidjan: NEA.

Quénum, O.-B. 1946, *Légendes Africaines*, Rochefort: Thoyom Thèze.

Quillateau, C. 1967, *Bernard Binlin Dadié: L'Homme et l'Œuvre*, Paris: Présence Africaine.

Rattunde, E. 1970, 'Die Gestalt des Chaka in der littérature africaine d'expression française', *Romanische Forschungen* 82: 320–44.

Ricard, A. 1973, 'Jean Pliya, écrivain dahoméen', *ALA* 27: 2–9.

1974a, 'Francophonie et théâtre en Afrique de l'Ouest: Situations et perspectives', *Etudes Littéraires* 7, 3: 453–58.

1974b, 'The Concert-Party as a Genre: The Happy Stars of Lome', *RAL* 2, 5: 165–79.

1975, 'Théâtre scolaire et théâtre populaire au Togo', *RHLF*, 1: 44–86.

1982, 'Réflexions sur le théâtre à Lomé, la dramaturgie du concert-party', *RPC* 57: 63–70.

1986a, 'Au pays des tortues qui chantent' in *Mélanges Schérer*, Paris: Nizet, pp. 100–3.

1986b, *L'Invention du théâtre*, Lausanne: L'Age d'Homme.

Richard, C. and Mazauric, C. 1990, 'Autour du Théâtre au Mali' *Notre Librairie* 102: 38–43.

(eds.), *Théâtres Africains*, Paris: Silex.

Ridehalgh, A. 1991, 'Some Recent Francophone Versions of the Shaka Story', *RAL* 22, 2: 135–52.

Riesz, J. and Ricard, A. (eds.) 1990, *Semper Aliquid Novi: Mélanges Offerts à Albert Gérard*, Tübingen: Gunter Narr Verlag.

Ritter, E. A. 1978, *Shaka Zulu*, London: Penguin.

Ross, D. 1978, 'Dahomey' in Michael Crowder (ed.), pp. 114–19.

Rotimi, O. 1971a, *The Gods are Not to Blame*, Oxford University Press.

1971b, *Kurunmi: An Historical Tragedy*, Oxford University Press.

1981, 'The Drama of African Ritual Display' in Ogunbiyi, pp. 77–80.

Sahlien, F. 1983, *Panorama du théâtre africain d'expression française*, Zaire: CEEBA.

Sahlien, J.-M. 1982, 'Négritude et luttes de classes dans *La Tragédie du roi Christophe* d'Aimé Césaire: essai de socio-critique' *Présence Francophone* 24: 147–55.

Saivre, de, D. 1980, 'De Madagascar, un théâtre populaire: L'Hira-Gasy', *RPC* 49: 68–71.

Saivre, de, D. 1982, 'Entretien avec Senouvo Agbota Zinsou', *RPC* 57 (Apr.–Jun.): 74–5.

Sandier, G. 1970, *Regards sur le Théâtre Actuel*, Paris: Stock.

Sartre, J.-P. 1964, *Situations V*, Paris: Gallimard.

Sautreau, S. and Velter, A. 1965, 'Aimé Césaire à l'échancrure du poème', *Les Temps Modernes* 21, 231: 367–70.

Schechner, R. 1977, *Essays on Performance Theory*, New York: Drama Book Specialists.

Schérer, J. 1973, 'Le Théâtre en Afrique noire francophone' in Jean Jacquot (ed.) pp. 103–16.

and Hourantier, M.-J. 1979, *Les Pagnes* in Hourantier, M., Liking, W., Schérer, J., *Du Rituel à la scène Chez les Bassa du Cameroun*, Paris: Nizet.

Schérer, R. 1992, *Le Théâtre en Afrique noire francophone*, Paris: PUF.

Schipper, M. 1984a, 'Traditional African themes and techniques in African Theatre and "Francophonie"', *TRI* 9, 3: 215–32.

1984b, *Théâtre et Société en Afrique*, Abidjan-Dakar, NEA.

Scholz, H.-J. 1970, 'Shaka: an African Conqueror in Historical Perspective', *Africana Marburgensia* 3, 1: 3–23.

Semidei, M. 1966, 'De l'Empire à la décolonisation à travers les manuels scolaires', *Revue Française de Science Politique* 16, 1: 56–86.

Senghor, L., 1956, 'Chaka', in *Ethiopiques*, Paris: Seuil.

Senghor, S. 1985, 'Le théâtre Sénégalais' in *Quel Théâtre pour le Développement*, pp. 25–34.

Sévry, J. 1991, *Chaka Empéreur des Zoulous: Histoire, Mythes et Legendes*, Paris: L'Harmattan.

Séydou, C. (trans.) 1972, *Silâmaka et Poullôri*, Paris: Colin.

Sileniecks, J. 1968, 'Deux pièces antillaises: du témoignage local vers une tragédie moderne', *KRQ* 15: 245–54.

Smith, R. 1982, 'History and Tragedy in Bernard Dadié's Béatrice du Congo', *The French Review* 55, 6: 818–23.

Smith, S. 1985, *Masks in Modern Drama*, Berkeley and Los Angeles: University of California Press.

Sonfo, A. 1970, 'Les sources d'inspiration du théâtre négro- africain' in *Actes du Colloque sur le Théâtre Négro-Africain*: 67–82.

Songolo, A. 1985, *Aimé Césaire: une poétique de la découverte*, Paris: L'Harmattan.

Soyinka, W. 1966, 'After the Narcissist', *Africa Forum* 1, 4: 53–64.

1968, 'The Writer in a Modern African State' in Per Wastberg (ed.), p. 19.

1973, *A Dance of the Forest, The Lion and the Jewel* and *The Strong Breed*, in *Collected Plays I*, Oxford University Press.

1975, *Death and the King's Horseman*, London: Methuen.

1976a, *Myth, Literature and the African World*, Cambridge University Press.

1976b, *Ogun Abibiman*, London: Rex Collings.

1988, 'From a Common Backcloth' in Jeyifo (ed.), pp. 7–14.

Spackey, G. 1968, 'Aimé Césaire: *Une Saison au Congo*', *ALT* 1: 48–51.

Spronk, J. 1982, 'History and the Development of the French Theatre of Black Africa', *Selecta* 3: 52–7.

1984, 'Chaka and the Problem of Power in the French Theatre of Black Africa' *The French Review* 52, 5: 634–40.

1992, 'Imagery and Symbolism in *Le Zulu*', *Selecta* 13: 15–20.

Steins, Martin, and Ngal, M. à M. (eds.) 1985, *Césaire 70*, Paris: Silex.

Swanepoel, C. 1990, 'Thomas Mofolo's *Chaka* and the Oral Legacy' in Janos Riesz and Alain Ricard (eds.), pp. 287–96.

Tagne, D. N. 1989, 'Werewere Liking créatrice, prolifique et novatrice', *Notre Librairie* 1 99 (Oct.–Dec.): 195.

Tansi, S. L. 1981, *La Parenthèse de sang suivi de Je, soussigné, cardiaque*, Paris: Hatier.

1984, *Qui a mangé Madame d'Avoine Bergotha*, Brussels: Promotion-Théâtre.

Thomas, L.-V. 1964, 'De quelques attitudes africaines en matière d'histoire locale' in Jan Vansina, Raymond Mauny and Louis-Vincent Thomas (eds.), pp. 358–74.

Tidjani-Serpos, N. 1974, 'L'image de la femme africaine dans le théâtre ivoirien: le cas de Bernard Dadié et de Charles Nokan', *RLC* 3 & 4: 455–61.

Touré, J. M. 1987, 'Mobiliser, informer, éduquer un instrument efficace: le théâtre', *Notre Librairie* 88/89: 86–96.

Traoré, B. 1958, *Le Théâtre Négro-Africain et ses fonctions sociales*, Paris: PA.

1970, 'Les tendances actuelles dans le théâtre négro-africain', *PA* 75: 34–48.

1971, 'Le théâtre africain de l'Ecole William Ponty' in *Actes du Colloque sur le Théâtre Négro-Africain*, pp. 37–44.

Tschikumambila, N. 1974, 'Le personnage de Chaka: du portrait épique de Mofolo au mythe poétique de L. S. Senghor', *Zaire-Afrique* 87: 405–20.

Turner, V. 1967, *The Forest of Symbols: Aspects of Ndembu Ritual*, Ithaca: Cornell University Press.

1982, *From Ritual to Theatre*, New York: Performing Arts Journal Publication.

1986, *Anthropology of Performance*, New York: PAJ Publication.

U'Tamsi, T. 1977, *Le Zulu suivi de Vwène le Fondateur*, Paris: Nubia.

1979, *Le Destin Glorieux du Maréchal Nnikon Nniku Prince qu' on sort*, Paris: PA.

1987, *Le Bal de Ndinga*, Paris: L'Atelier Imaginaire.

Vansina, J. 1971, 'Once Upon a Time: Oral Traditions as History in Africa', *Dedalus* 100: 442–68.

'Oral Tradition and its Methodology' in Ki-Zerbo (ed.), pp. 142–65.

and Mauny, R. and Thomas, L.-V. (eds.) 1964, *The Historian in Tropical Africa*, Oxford University Press.

Vinciléoni, N. 1986, *L'Œuvre de Bernard Dadié*, Issy-les-Moulineaux: Les Classiques Africaines.

Warner, G. 1975, 'L'histoire dans le théâtre africain francophone', *Présence Francophone* 11: 37–48.

1976, 'Education coloniale et genèse du théâtre néo-africain d'expression française', *PA* 97: 93–116.

1981, 'Le dilemme esthétique de l'écrivain francophone', *Présence Francophone* 23: 119–30.

1983, 'Technique dramatique et affirmation culturelle dans le théâtre de Bernard Dadié', *Ethiopiques* 1, 1: 53–70.

1984, 'The Use of Historical Sources in Francophone African Theatre' *TRI* 9, 3: 180–94.

Wastberg, Per (ed.) 1968, *The Writer in Modern Africa*, Uppsala: The Scandinavian Institute of African Studies.

Waters, H. 1978, *Black Theatre in French: A Guide*, Sherbrooke: Naaman.

1981, 'Black French Theatre: The Latest Plays', *WLT* 55, 3: 410–12.

1983, 'Black French Theatre Update', *WLT* 57, 1: 43–8.

1984, 'Black French Theatre of the Eighties', *TRI* 9, 3: 195–215.

1988, *Théâtre noir: Encyclopédie des pièces écrites en français par les auteurs noirs*, Washington, DC: Three Continents Press.

Wellek, R. 1956, *Theory of Literature*, New York: Harcourt, Brace.

Wilks, I. 1971, 'African Historiographcial Traditions: Old and New' in J. D. Fage (ed.), pp. 7–17.

Williams, E. 1970, *From Columbus to Castro: The History of the Caribbean*, London: André Deutsch.

Wolitz, S. 1969, 'The Hero of Negritude in the Theatre of Aimé Césaire', *KRQ* 16: 195–208.

Wright, G. 1993, *Soyinka Revisited*, New York: Twayne.

Zagboto, L. K. 1987, 'Les Tendances actuelles des représentations dramatiques', *Notre Librairie* 87: 74–80.

Zaourou, B. Z. 1975, *Les Sofas suivi de L'Œil*, Paris: P. J. Oswald.

Zell, H. *et al.* 1983, *A New Reader's Guide to African Literature*, London: Heinemann.

Zinsou, S. A. 1984, *On joue la comédie*, Lomé-Haarlem: Haho de Knipscheer.

　1987, *La Tortue qui chante suivi de La Femme du blanchisseur et les Aventures de Yévi au pays des monstres*, Paris: Hatier.

Index of plays, playwrights and selected critics

For all critics consulted and referred to in the text, see the list of references.

Index of theatres, theatre companies, groups and festivals

Lightning Source UK Ltd.
Milton Keynes UK
UKOW04f1814060815

256523UK00001B/75/P